The Blood

The Blood

E. S. Thomson

CONSTABLE • LONDON

CONSTABLE

First published in Great Britain in 2018 by Constable

Copyright © E. S. Thomson, 2018

The moral right of the author has been asserted.

A CIP catalogue record for this book is
available from the British Library.

ISBN: 978-1-47212-657-3 (hardback)
ISBN: 978-1-47212-656-6 (trade paperback)

Typeset in ITC New Baskerville by SX Composing DTP, Rayleigh, Essex
Printed and bound in Great Britain by Clays Ltd, St Ives plc

Papers used by Constable are from well-managed forests
and other responsible sources.

MIX
Paper from
responsible sources
FSC® C104740

Constable
An imprint of
Little, Brown Book Group
Carmelite House
50 Victoria Embankment
London EC4Y 0DZ

An Hachette UK Company
www.hachette.co.uk

www.littlebrown.co.uk

For Guy and Carlo

They say that life on the river depends on the direction of the wind. Every day those who live by the waterside turn their faces, bright with hope, towards the sunrise, nostrils flaring, hoping to catch the briny scent of money. If the wind blows from the east it will bring with it the riches of seven continents. Ships – hundreds of them – sent into the heart of the city by a single sigh.

The poor thrive along the river, amongst the wealth-filled warehouses. Brown as rats they sift through its mud for treasures of their own – a lump of coal, a bone, an old shoe. They paddle back and forth across its pestilent waters, and breathe its vapours. They crowd the streets that run down to its shores, toiling amongst the ever-changing city of sails and decks that lines its banks, the dark water present only in the heave and swell beneath their feet.

Anything is for sale here: spices, tea, cotton, labour – men's and women's, bodies, or souls, for a shilling. Anyone might hide here, in the cheap lodging houses, the damp cellars, the dark spaces between buildings. In these streets no one stands out. No one is noticed.

What wickedness might walk amongst us here, hidden in plain sight, concealed by the urgent press of bodies, the scramble for money, for life?

I will tell you.

Chapter One

━━◇━━

The first time I saw the waterfront I was eight years old. My father took me. He had been in a good humour that day – one of the many reasons why I remember it so clearly. He was taking me to the Seaman's Dispensary, which occupied cramped premises on the shore not far from the Seaman's Floating Hospital. Before us, on the riverside, a crowd had gathered – sailors, dock workers, stokers, fishwives.

'What is it?' I said, peeping between their legs and catching a glimpse of wet, silvery flesh. I thought immediately of the booths and penny shows I had seen at the fair, at Cremorne and Vauxhall Gardens. 'It's a mermaid, isn't it? A real one, pulled from the Thames!' My father tried to turn me away, but I would not be persuaded, and I broke from him to push through legs and skirts.

The smell should have told me what to expect. Soon to be an apprentice apothecary, I had accompanied my father about St Saviour's Infirmary on countless occasions and I knew the smell of death well enough. But here the sweetness of decay was tainted with something else, something new and different. It was a curious, moist smell, damp and dark; a smell that spoke of the ooze and slap of water, of gurgling wet spaces and the sticky, yielding mud of low-tide.

I saw straight away that I would find no silvered scales here, no long glittering fish-tail or slender, webbed fingers. Her flesh was pale and mottled, as white and grey as the belly of an eel, but bloated from long immersion. It was streaked with mud, and blotched with bruises, her hair dark and plastered to her skull like a layer of brown weed. The side of her head had been crushed, and a ragged blue-lipped gash against her cheek told where a clumsy boathook had gouged.

I remember Dr Graves, St Saviour's most revered anatomist, appearing from a shadowy thoroughfare between two soot-smothered buildings, as black as a crow in his flapping frock coat and tall hat, a half dozen students in his wake.

How had he known to come here? But Mrs Speedicut, the matron, always said that the man could smell a cadaver from a mile away. Perhaps she was right. I looked back at the corpse he had come for – the mouth a slack, gaping tear; the eyes two dark, wet holes – and the ground beneath me seemed to rise and fall like the deck of a ship.

When I came to I was lying in a place scarcely less fearful than the one I had just left, for my father had carried me to the mortuary which was just beside the quay. The day was warm, and he had laid me out on one of the cold marble slabs until I regained consciousness. I opened my eyes to see the body of a dead sailor on the slab next to

4

mine; the tattoos upon his forearm proclaiming his occupation. His head and neck were tanned and leathery, his legs and body as white and soft-looking as curds. A doctor from another medical school was standing guard over him jealously.

I heard footsteps outside, and the sound of gasping and retching. The door burst open and in marched four men with their neckerchiefs over their noses, the mermaid wrapped in an old tarpaulin slung between them. Dr Graves followed, grumbling.

'These river cases are the worst,' he said. 'But we must do what we can, gentlemen, and there is much to learn about the miracle of decay.' His students followed, their faces pale and appalled.

My father bundled me onto my feet and dragged me outside. 'What happened to her?' I asked, trying to look back over my shoulder as the canvas shroud was peeled back. 'Was it an accident?'

'The corpses of men find their way into the river by accident,' he answered. 'Women's arrive there by design.'

He was correct, as he so often was, and I heard later that the dead girl had been beaten to death by her husband, a vicious man who was known to abuse her and had set her to work on the streets. He had thrown her battered, half-clothed body into the water, bricks and stones in the pockets of her dress to weigh her down. But the river is a capricious ally for murderers, and he had not reckoned on the flimsiness of her clothing, and buoyancy afforded by the gas of putrefaction.

Hers was the first body I saw that had been in the river; the first body I saw that had been murdered. It was not to be my last of either – nor was it the first time that I would wonder at the cheapness of a woman's life, and the violence they endured at the hands of men.

❧

Over the following years I had little reason to return to the waterfront. My work at St Saviour's Infirmary had meant that I was confined largely to the hospital's precincts and its neighbouring streets, though I became acquainted with the apothecary who worked at the Floating Hospital – a man named John Aberlady, with whom I had taken my licentiate examination at Apothecaries' Hall. He and I paid each other visits occasionally, though as my commitments were greater than his it was more usual for him to appear at our door.

'Nothing but syphilis and the ague, Jem,' he used to say, dropping into the chair before the apothecary stove and closing his eyes. I knew there was more to his work at the Floating Hospital than he admitted, though he often seemed glad to be away from the place – given the cramped conditions on board I was not surprised. Despite the tribulations that I had endured in recent years, however – incarceration in Newgate, my father's execution, the murders at Angel Meadow Asylum – I had heard nothing from him for a long time, and I had been too busy and too preoccupied to seek him out myself.

I had not thought about the river, nor about John Aberlady, for quite some time, when two occurrences brought both to the front of my mind. The first of these was a letter from Aberlady himself, asking me to come to the Floating Hospital as a matter of urgency. The second was my friend Will's return from the offices of Prentice and Hall, the firm of architects he worked for, bearing news of his next commission.

'It's on the river,' he said. 'A new warehouse. The site is currently occupied by an old villa, and a stretch of water called Tulip's Basin. D'you know it?'

'Yes,' I said.

'Is it a pleasant situation?'

'Pleasant?' I smiled as I pulled on my coat.

Will was my dearest friend, a man to whom I owed my life, and upon whom I would depend for anything, and yet sometimes his naivety – and his optimism – amazed me. He had been in London for more than two years, long enough to be accustomed to its dirt and squalor, but not long enough, so it appeared, to have lost the hope that nature and beauty might still find a home here. He would be thinking of a field of crimson goblet-shaped flowers, nodding in the breeze as the river flowed by, I was sure.

'I'm afraid the place is a notorious slum, Will. The "old villa" you speak of is boarded up to keep out the whores and beggars; Tulip was an old rogue who ran a boatyard and drank himself to death, and Tulip's Basin – his "stretch of water" – is a foul ditch filled with effluent, known more colloquially as "Deadman's Basin" on account of the fact that no one found Dick Tulip dead in his bed for nigh on two weeks.'

'Oh.' Will's face had fallen. 'I should have guessed.'

'It was a long time ago now, though I can't imagine the place has improved much. Didn't they tell you?'

'No.'

'Perhaps we should go and see it,' I said. Then, taking pity on him, added, 'It might not be quite so bad after all.'

'I'm sure it's considerably worse.'

'I'll come with you. I'm going that way anyway.' I passed him his hat.

He nodded to the workbench, where a batch of poke-root ointment was half-made, and three score milk thistle pills were awaiting their sugar coats. 'Can you spare the time? Perhaps I might help you with those pills instead?'

My apprentice, Gabriel Locke, was working the pump, filling the sink with water so that he might wash the retorts I had used that morning to create a tincture of clove for the toothache. He looked over his shoulder at me, his expression revealing his alarm at my evident preparations for departure. 'What about those prescriptions,' he said. 'Mr Jem, you can't just leave me—'

I turned away. I had lots to do, it was true, and yet, as much as I loved my apothecary, I had to admit that I did not find serving cough drops and rose water to chattering customers quite as satisfying as I'd thought I would when I first opened the place. I had once been the apothecary at one of the city's busiest hospitals. I did not regret that St Saviour's had been pulled down, but there were times when my new life as the owner of a small apothecary shop seemed very dull in comparison to my old life on the wards. Besides, there was also Aberlady's note, which had arrived only minutes before Will came home, and was still clutched in my fingers.

Come quickly, it said. *God help me, Jem, for if you cannot then only He can. Come quickly, or all is lost.*

It was a ragged, anxious scrawl, not the neat measured hand I was familiar with, though there was enough in the slope of the 't' and the length of the 's' to convince me that it was written by my friend. It had been sent to St Saviour's Infirmary, which had long since moved south of the river, so that by the time it had found its way to my premises on Fishbait Lane almost a week had passed. The urgent matter John Aberlady had written of would either be resolved, I thought, or irredeemable.

'Three bottles of iron tonic, one tincture of cleavers and burdock, and a plantain and calendula salve,' I said, snatching up my hat. 'You can manage that easily enough, Gabriel.' The bell danced on its spring as the door slammed behind us.

We walked east along Fishbait Lane, before plunging south between two rows of tall soot-covered houses. We passed down ever-narrowing thoroughfares, through seedy courts, and past lodging houses festooned with grubby washing. There were people everywhere, though as we drew closer to the water the costers and cabmen, shop-keepers and street sellers gave way to more unusual people and faces. To our left I saw a Chinaman, a thick white scar across his forehead; to our right a Lascar with one eye, and beside him a tall black man with a Dutch sailor's cap on his head and a cage of small green birds in his arms. A group of blue-faced men passed by, their skin stained with the indigo they unloaded all day; the hands and faces of others glowed yellow from hours spent amongst saffron and spices.

'You fit in perfectly,' said Will.

I grinned. I knew he was referring to the port-wine birthmark that covered my eyes and nose. As a child I had hated it. I had not grown to love it – I could never do that – though I had, in time, grown used to it. Always it had set me apart – that and the fact that I hid my woman's body beneath a man's apparel. But it had made me what I was. It had given me the confidence to accept the stares of strangers, and its ugly mask had helped to conceal my identity, allowing me to achieve freedoms and liberties beyond the compass of most women's lives. I was grateful to it for that, at least. And yet now that we had neared the Thames, now that we were surrounded by all manner of different coloured skins, the birthmark that always marked me out had grown less singular. Will was right; no one looked at me here.

'So, who is this Aberlady fellow?' he said. 'You've never mentioned him before.'

'We sat our examinations together, though he is a few years older than I. I've not seen him for some time. There was no address to the note he sent so I can only assume he's still working on the *Blood*.'

'The *Blood*?'

'The Seaman's Floating Hospital. It's named the *Golden Fleece*, though it's known more colloquially as the *Blood and Fleas*. The place has certainly seen plenty of both.'

'Is there an infirmary in this city that is *not* both bloody and pestilent?' Will took the note from me. '"*Come quickly or all is lost.*" You don't know what worries him?'

'No,' I said. 'And as I know him to be a confirmed atheist I'm troubled all the more by his choice of words.'

'The paper is of the cheapest kind,' said Will, rubbing the letter distastefully between his finger and thumb. 'It has no watermark or distinguishing features. And what's this stuff here?' There was a scattering of dry specks, yellow and rust-brown in colour, caught in the letter's folds. Will tipped them carefully into his hand. 'Sawdust?'

I nodded. 'I think he wrote this in the operating theatre. I presume on board the *Blood*.'

'Why not write it at his desk?'

'Precisely. Even worse, the force of his handwriting and the angle of the pen suggests—' I plucked the letter from Will's fingers and held it close to my eye, '—suggests to me that he was kneeling on the floor.'

'You think he was ill? Or wounded?'

'He makes no mention of it—'

'Drunk, perhaps?'

'He only ever drank tea.'

'Then what?'

I shrugged. 'Crouched out of sight? Hiding? I'm hoping we'll soon find out.' I said no more. Those desperate words, that fearful hand, the bloody sawdust clinging to the rough nap of such cheap paper – all troubled me. But most unsettling of all was the final sentence, scrawled across the page above a signature I hardly recognised as the mark of a rational and lucid man: '*Come now, Jem, but come ready to face the Devil.*'

⚜

We emerged onto the waterfront from a narrow stinking thoroughfare known as Cat's Hole. To the west were the London Docks, warehouses and wharves, and Tulip's Basin. To the east not one hundred yards away were the Seaman's Dispensary and the waterfront mortuary. On the river opposite, at the edge of the stretch of water known as the Pool of London, was the Seaman's Floating Hospital. She lay out on the Thames, at the very heart of the city of ships that crowded the riverside from London

Bridge to Limehouse Reach, her smoking chimneys just visible through the thicket of masts and rigging. I had always been of the opinion that there was not a more dilapidated hospital than St Saviour's Infirmary in the whole city – with the exception of the *Blood and Fleas*. As a former naval frigate her decks had once been loaded with cannons. Thirty years ago these had been replaced by hospital beds, so that she rode high in the water, her sides black and sticky-looking, bellying out like the bloated carcass of a great drowned beast. Here and there bits of her tarry paint had fallen away, allowing the rank weeds of the riverside to colonise the softening timbers. Her gun-ports had been transformed into windows – the apertures of which might be closed off with wooden shutters, though many of these were propped open, revealing the murky glass beneath. Some of the windows were standing ajar, though nothing but blackness was visible within. We looked up as a trap door opened in the bow and a stream of lumpy brown liquid was discharged into the river.

A narrow jetty led out to her mooring, a spindly stair-case zigzagging up the ship's scrofulous flanks to the quarterdeck. Makeshift sheds clustered about the sawn-off masts like toadstools sprouting about the base of a severed tree. Between these, a series of washing lines had been strung, hanging with limp, grey bed linen. Her hull had been modified over the years, with hutch-like struc-tures, balconies and staircases crudely fixed to her greasy wooden sides. In stark contrast, new, freshly painted frigates bobbed in the water fore and aft, their hulls gleaming, their sails neatly furled. Rotten and swollen, blotched with patches of mould and scabrous with rude repairs, the *Blood* loomed between them in a grim *memento mori.*

'Do we have to shout "ahoy there"?' said Will.

I shaded my eyes and looked up. For a moment, up there on the deck, a figure was silhouetted against the sky – a man, tall and thin, but stooped, his black top coat loose on rounded shoulders. His hands gripped the rail like claws.

Behind us, on the yard-arm of one of the new frigates, a magpie croaked and hopped.

'One for sorrow,' muttered Will.

When we looked back the man had gone.

We climbed the flimsy steps that clung to the ship's starboard side, the rope banister as brown and sticky as if it had been fashioned from chewed tobacco. I found myself wondering how many diseased hands had gripped it, and I resolved to wash my hands as soon as I was able to. There was no one about, though from a hatch in the deck of the ship I could hear the familiar sounds of sickness – coughing, hawking, moaning. St Saviour's Infirmary had sounded the same. I missed the old place, though I had to admit that there were some things – coughing, hawking and moaning amongst them – I would have been happy never to see or hear again.

The hatch, and thus the bowels of the ship and the hospital proper, were accessed by a steep wooden ladder-staircase. 'Down there?' Will looked at the hatch, his expression appalled. 'The place stinks like a latrine, even from up here.' Downstairs, I knew from experience, was far worse than Will could ever imagine. I was glad not to be destined for the 'tween decks that day.

I pointed to the quarterdeck. 'Aberlady's apothecary is

in the former captain's cabin, up there at the back – cramped, compared to St Saviour's, but spacious enough. Below it are his living quarters.'

Will started forward, his relief evident. 'Then perhaps we should go up there directly—'

'You!' cried a voice. 'You there! Where do you think you're going?'

The deck towards the front of the ship – an area of the vessel Aberlady had always referred to as 'the fo'c'sle' – had been roofed over to create a committee room, and a library cum consultants' sitting room. It was from the latter that two men had appeared. Behind them, through the open door, I could see walls covered with books and a cluster of brocade-covered armchairs. A breath of warm fragrant air billowed out, heated by the fire that danced behind the door of a large round-bellied stove.

The first man was old, tall and gaunt, and recognisable as the fellow I had seen looking out at us before we boarded. His eyes were pale, greenish and watery, like sputum, his greyish-coloured skin covered with a powdery sort of eczema, so that he looked as though he had been fashioned from ash, and might crumble away to nothing if the wind blew. The other was much younger, small and red-faced above a cleric's collar. Tiny oval spectacles sat crookedly on his nose, obscuring his gaze.

'Who are you?' It was the old man who spoke this time, his voice harsh as a crow's.

I knew who he was, for I had met him before, though he had never deigned to speak to me.

'Dr Sackville,' I said. 'My name is Flockhart, and this is my friend Mr Quartermain.' I held out my hand. His grip was firmer than I had expected. The parson's was moist,

14

as if he had been licking his palms. I explained that we were 'just passing by' and hoped to see Mr Aberlady. 'I assume he's still your apothecary?'

'Aberlady?' said Dr Sackville. He glanced at his companion. 'We were just speaking of him. He *is* our apothecary, sir, but for how much longer I cannot say.'

'How so?'

'He is, at best, indolent and, at worst, a danger to us all – when the fellow bothers to appear,' said the man who had introduced himself as 'the Reverend Dr Ambrose Birdwhistle'.

'A danger?' I said. 'In what way, sir?'

Dr Sackville shook his head. 'Where might one begin—?'

'Perhaps with the snakes?' butted in the parson. 'Or the scorpions? Not to mention the matter of his infidel's views. He reads Ruskin, you know. To the patients!'

'Ah, the snakes,' Dr Sackville chuckled. 'Yes, the fellow's certainly very fond of them. I'm surprised he's abandoned them – that big one especially. He often brings it on deck when the sun's out. Oils its skin with linseed and a cloth. The men enjoy it too – they all want a go.'

I smiled. I remembered Aberlady's fondness for his snakes – a nasty-looking stripy viper and a brown, muscular python. 'That big one' had always been his favourite. It was hard to like the smaller, striped creature, with its fangs and its vicious ways with the pigeons.

'Is he here?' I said.

'He is not,' said Dr Birdwhistle. 'We have not seen him for a week. We have sent ashore to look for him more than once, but he's nowhere to be found.' He turned to his companion. 'I fear we may need to replace him altogether,

Dr Sackville, no matter how long he's held the post. The ship has descended into complete misrule. There's gambling below decks, sir, and worse, since Aberlady vanished. I'm afraid I really *must* take the matter before the Governors. "For what shall it profit a man, if he shall gain the whole world and lose his own soul?" Mark, chapter eight, verse thirty-six—'

'Gentlemen, you find us perplexed and inconvenienced in equal measure by our apothecary's disappearance,' said Dr Sackville. 'I have been away for a number of days or the matter would have been addressed before now, but I believe he has quite disappeared.' He turned to his companion. 'I fear I cannot stop you, Dr Birdwhistle. If you wish to bring the matter of Mr Aberlady's "infidel's views", as you call them, to the governors then bring it you must, though perhaps it might be wise to *find* the fellow first. Perhaps if a matron might be engaged too? She might at least be prevailed upon to stop our nursing staff from running away.' He frowned at me. 'Do we know one another, sir? Flockhart, you say? And Quartermain?' His lips twitched into the beginnings of a gleeful smile. 'I remember now. Your father, Flockhart—'

'Was murdered,' I said, irritated by his insinuating tone. 'By the hangman at Newgate. I think you'll find it was a member of your own profession who was responsible for what happened at St Saviour's, and to my father.'

'You do me an injustice, sir. I was about to say that your father was a good man – from what I knew of him. We are rather out of the way of things here on the river, and my private practice never took me near to St Saviour's, but I knew of his reputation. I was sorry to hear of what happened.'

'Thank you,' I said. I felt myself blush to the roots of my hair. And yet, I could not help but feel that this was not what Dr Sackville had intended to say at all, but that he had quickly changed his sentiments purely for the pleasure of seeing me discomfited. He was watching my embarrassment with something like relish. I cleared my throat. 'But we are here about Aberlady—'

'Ah, yes,' he said mildly. 'Aberlady. Has he taken anything, Birdwhistle? Anything that might tell us where he's gone or for how long?'

'His quarters are as they usually are, and the apothecary is so untidy it's hard to tell.'

'Might we see?' I asked.

Dr Birdwhistle frowned. 'I'm not sure it's appropriate—'

'Come now, Birdwhistle,' said Dr Sackville. 'What harm can it do? Besides, should Aberlady fail to return, or – assuming you get your way – be turned out altogether, we may well need the assistance of men such as Mr Flockhart. You carry on, sir. I'll show these gentlemen around.'

The apothecary was low-ceilinged, tall enough for a man to stand up in but not tall enough to hang herbs up to dry, though the air on the river was too damp for such practices, and Aberlady generally bought what he needed from a wholesaler, or from the herb woman who came round with her cart. The stove was lit and the room warm, and the place smelled strongly of rosemary and lavender – we were all of us sorely troubled with moths – along with the sweet, distinctive smell of liquorice root. Beneath this I recognised the earthy scent of chickweed and cleavers, both excellent against the itch – another perennial problem in the close confines of ill-ventilated wards. There was a strong aroma of citrus too, from a crate of oranges and limes that stood beside the table – contraband, no doubt, for the docks were all around us.

It was a bright room, with astragalled windows looking out on three sides – at the ships that were moored alongside, at the shore, and out to the river – their ledges lined with a familiar array of bottles glinting with coloured liquids. Beneath them were ranked rows of labelled drawers. I had the same in my own premises on Fishbait Lane. I tried to keep my shop tidy, as my father had always taught me. Here, however, the paraphernalia of the apothecary was spread out in such disorder and confusion that even Gabriel, a boy of the most slovenly habits, would have been appalled.

I glanced around me. Aberlady was a knowledgeable and capable man. Despite his protestation that he was faced daily with the most banal of complaints, he was also keen, and dedicated to his work. I was surprised to see how disordered his remedies were, and how run down his stock of herbs and tinctures. What distractions had caused him to neglect his duties so badly?

'I'm afraid Mr Aberlady left the place in a terrible muddle, though I'm sure it's nothing that can't be set straight in no time by a man of your capabilities,' said Dr Sackville. 'We're currently reliant on his apprentice, a girl from Siren House. The League for Female Redemption,' he added, by way of explanation. 'Aberlady took her on as a grinding boy – I mean girl.' He tut-tutted. 'You know I can't for the life of me get into the habit of describing her as a *girl*. She has no place here, not really, no place at all amongst the *materia medica* of physic. I saw her earlier – Pestle Jenny, Aberlady calls her – though where she has got to now I have no idea.'

'A *girl?*' I said.

'Good Lord!' cried Will.

'Quite so,' said Dr Sackville. 'Can't imagine what he was thinking! Another experiment, no doubt. A girl could never be an apothecary, I told him, but he wouldn't listen.'

A cushion on the floor bore the imprint of a pair of bony buttocks, beside which a pestle and mortar had been set. There was no sign of Pestle Jenny, though she had clearly been there only moments earlier, for the cardamom she had been grinding hung fresh on the air, and the chewed end of the liquorice root she had left on the table was still moist. But Dr Sackville was still talking.

'Of course, the physic we use here is no different to what you might find elsewhere, though we are sorely troubled by the ague, as so many men have spent time in the tropics.'

'You prescribe cinchona?' I said absently, looking about. I noted the desk in the corner, the writing slope with sheaves of cheap paper upon it, the pen missing from the inkstand.

Dr Sackville shrugged. 'Certainly. We all prescribe it.'

'How many of you are there on board, sir?' asked Will.

'Of patients, some two hundred or more. We have – or had – Mr Aberlady, and of course a number of students. Of doctors, we have five – I include myself, though I am here rarely these days. My health—' He held a hand over his heart. 'I'm an old man now, and we do not last forever. But there are others here, young men, keen and ambitious, as I once was.' He smiled indulgently. 'I have high hopes for two of them, at least – Dr Cole and Dr Antrobus. Do you know of them?'

I admitted that I did not. I saw Will looking at the

signatures in the prescription ledger that lay on the table beside a carboy of witch hazel and a large jar glistening with leeches. 'Dr Septimus Cole. Dr David Antrobus. How long have they worked here?'

'Cole and Antrobus have been with us some five years. Dr Cole is assistant physician, Dr Antrobus assistant surgeon.'

'And Dr Rennie,' said Will, his finger still poised upon the prescription ledger. 'Dr James Rennie. What are your hopes for him?'

James Rennie. I had not heard the name for a long time, though as a child I had thought of him often. For James Rennie was the stuff of nightmares. I had first met him when my father had sent me to the Seaman's Dispensary. His face was scarred from small pox, wrinkled from the sun, and bore the yellowish tinge of the malaria sufferer. Most macabre of all was his eye patch. Having spent much of his working life as a naval surgeon, Dr Rennie had seen numerous engagements, during one of which his right eye had been skewered by a flying splinter, and his cheek torn away by a musket ball. To cover the wound, and replace his missing feature, he had fashioned a metal plate painted in flesh-coloured enamel. It was decorated with an eye, blue and flawless, a perfect copy of the one that was lost. The whole thing was held in position by a ribbon tied about his head. When he was a younger man the eye must have been ingenious – precise and lifelike. But time works upon flesh and metal in different ways, and the former was now weathered and sagging, the living eye as pale and moist as an oyster. Beside it, the painted eye shone as bright and unblinking as ever, as though the young James Rennie still peeped out from

20

inside the old. I could hardly believe the man was still alive, for he must have been over eighty years of age.

'Well, well,' I said. 'Dr Rennie is still with you, sir?'

'In a manner of speaking,' said Dr Sackville.

'You know him, Jem?' said Will.

'A little,' I said. I told him what I knew. 'Dr Rennie lives on the *Blood* – has been aboard since she was first rigged. Cape St Vincent, the Nile, Trafalgar – the *Blood* was a ship of the line at all three battles and James Rennie was her surgeon. Am I right, Dr Sackville?'

'Indeed.'

'He stayed with the *Blood* while she was on active service, and chose to remain when she became a hospital. "Older than the ship, with a past as murky as the Thames", that's how my father used to describe him.'

'I'm afraid he is not what he was,' said Dr Sackville. 'His mind, you know.'

'Poor fellow,' said Will. 'And yet he still treats patients?'

'Oh yes. The ague, the pox, remedies for boils and sores – he can manage those well enough. He's been treating them all his life, and the routine of sameness seems to comfort him. But these days there is little Dr Rennie remembers. I am sorry for it, though it comes to many who live so long.'

We did not stay. With Dr Sackville standing beside me there was little in the apothecary I could examine closely. I had the feeling he was watching me, waiting to see whether I might notice something he himself had missed, and I was unwilling to give him the satisfaction. The grinding girl might be worth talking to, I thought, should I be able to get her alone, but I would not do so in front of Dr Sackville. I sensed that the girl was hiding in a cupboard, but if she had reason to conceal herself from strangers, or from Dr Sackville, now was not the time to find out why. Will was anxious to leave, I could tell, though as I knew what awaited us at Deadman's Basin I was in no hurry. I had not been to the *Blood* for a long time, and was intrigued by the picture of misrule that Dr Birdwhistle had painted, so when Dr Sackville asked if we would like to see the place I agreed.

We went down the hatch amidships that we had seen earlier. The steps were steep and slippery, the rope handrail moist and gummy to the touch, like a great length of twisted intestines. Descending without taking hold of it was quite impossible, and I saw Will wipe his hand on his handkerchief in disgust as soon as he was able to let go.

The place had changed little since my last visit, some fifteen years ago, with what had once been the gun decks now known as the top ward, mid ward and lower ward. To left and right, narrow beds mounded with grubby blankets were set out side by side in neat ranks running down the ship from stern to bow. The light that filtered through the thick glass of the gun-port windows – those that were not closed and shuttered – gave the place a dark, fish-tank air. A beam of sunlight entering on the starboard side illuminated dust particles floating like flecks of plankton. A hunched figure moved towards the privy with the slow, heavy steps of a man underwater, so that the whole effect was as if we were caught in a wreck at the bottom of the deep. There were no attendants visible, though beyond the beds I could make out the dim glow of a lantern and the dark bulk of human shadows. The place echoed with coughing and talking, and here and there small huddles of men in grey nightshirts were gathered. Beneath their muttering came the rattle of dice and the slap of cards. The smoky, gamey stink of frying bloaters was thick about us, and I could hear the spit and crackle of hot fat, and the cough and cackle of nurses. The silhouette of a woman, tall and angular, moved amongst the beds, bending towards each occupant, one after the other. I heard the *chink* of the spoon against a bottle – laudanum, perhaps, or the tincture of cinchona I had seen in the prescription ledger. The air was wreathed with blue-grey smoke, and as my eyes became accustomed to the darkness, I could make out pale smudges – men's faces, each garnished with a pipe, the bowls of which trickled more of the stuff into the thick atmosphere.

'They smoke in their beds?' said Will.

'They probably hide their pipes in their bedclothes if anyone tries to stop them,' I said in a low voice, for a dozen faces had turned towards us. 'It was the same at St Saviour's. Besides, it probably deters the parasites, though I imagine the place is pestilent in the extreme no matter what.'

Will coughed, and stifled a retch with his handkerchief. 'How could this fellow Aberlady bear it here,' he muttered. 'It makes St Saviour's look luxurious. Had he no ambition to go elsewhere?'

But John Aberlady had never wanted to run an institution like St Saviour's; indeed, he had laughed at me for working amongst what he considered to be the most tedious and pedestrian of cases.

'Syphilis, childbirth, constipation, tumours, kidney stones? Oh no, Jem,' he used to say. 'That's not for me. I'll take what limited resources the *Blood* has to offer over your handsome salary and luxurious accommodation any day of the week. D'you know what I came across yesterday? D'you know what a fellow brought me? He'd just arrived on a clipper from West Africa and after two days in the most excruciating pain pulled *this* out of the privy.' He'd held up a jar of spirits containing a gigantic worm – pale and segmented, and as thin as a shoe lace. 'It's six yards long,' he'd said. 'Straight out of the fellow's guts. What do you make of that? Have you ever seen anything like it?'

I'd had to admit that indeed I had not – and that I hoped never to again.

Dr Sackville led us forward, beneath dark beams of seasoned oak burnished with the patina of a half-century of pipe smoke, cooking fumes, and gunpowder, the touch of hands and the bump of oily heads.

'The operating theatre is down there,' he said. He gestured to the back of the ship, where a door stood open on a dark room illuminated by a glazed hole cut in the deck above. I saw an operating table of pale scrubbed deal, the dark familiar shape of the blood box at its foot, but the rest of the room was in shadow.

'It was once the ward room, for the officers, of course,' said Dr Sackville. 'The cabins for the officers were on either side here, and are now occupied by our physicians and surgeons.'

'They stay on board?' said Will, clearly appalled that anyone would choose to reside in such a place.

'Only occasionally. But they each have a space down here in which to work – to write, to keep their books and papers. To sleep in, if needs be.'

'Including Aberlady?'

'Mr Aberlady has his apothecary in the poop cabin, as

24

you saw. His living quarters are below that, and in addition
to that he kept lodgings ashore, though he never seemed
to go there. As he is – or *should* be – here all the time, we
could not expect him to be accommodated in what is
little more than a hutch. But for those who are *not* here all
the time—'

'Dr Cole? Dr Antrobus?'

'Precisely.'

'And what about Dr Rennie? Jem – Mr Flockhart – said
he lived on board.'

'Dr Rennie is a different matter,' said Dr Sackville. 'Dr
Rennie lives down below.'

'Below what?'

'Below everything, sir. This is the top ward, below us
are the middle and lower wards, and below *those* is where
Dr Rennie makes his home.'

To our right, where Dr Sackville had pointed, another
set of steep stairs led down to the middle and lower wards.
A dim flickering light was visible below, and the sounds of
sickness drifted up to us. That there might be somewhere
lower still in which a man lived clearly horrified Will.

'Such a place would be below the waterline, would it
not?' he whispered. 'And therefore quite blind?'

'Indeed,' replied Dr Sackville.

We passed between the beds, the men hiding their dice
and cards, pretending to be asleep. They had done much
the same at St Saviour's, though that place had been
better lit, and such misdemeanours far easier to see and
prevent. I saw a rat scamper across a man's bedding – Will
saw it too and he blanched. Dr Sackville was talking to me
about his cases – a docker who'd had his leg amputated
after an accident at the warehouses on Pennington Street,

two sailors who had arrived suffering from yellow fever, a man who had started his journey in Tobago, and whose condition defied diagnosis.

'It looks like yaws, but the sores are rather different, the suppuration almost gangrenous. He is in the lower deck. Will you take a look?'

I glanced at Will. Even in the dim light I could see that he was looking queasy. 'I think we should be on our way, sir,' I said.

Dr Sackville smirked. 'Not what you're used to, eh? I suppose you're all cough drops and lavender water these days.'

'Yes,' I said. 'I suppose I am.'

'A prettier view of the world than the one we have here, sir. Perhaps you should be grateful, and leave places like this to those who have the stomach for them.'

Look out at the city on a clear day. The number of spires that prick the heavens would make even an infidel think that London is a city of God. And yet there are more brothels here than any other type of business, some of them cheek by jowl with the grandest addresses in the land. These are fine places, where rich and powerful gentlemen wait in warm drawing rooms, their hats and coats kept safe by liveried footmen, and where whatever might be needed by way of an aphrodisiac – oysters, champagne, truffles – is brought forth on silver plates by girls, bare breasted and as beautiful as Salomé herself. There are no signs of the pox here – those girls are kept hidden until their symptoms pass. Or they are sent away to make a living in less select houses, ones that lie further east and closer to the river, houses where the lamps stink of whale grease, and the air inside is hot and damp with panted breath and hired sighs. In these places the light is kept dim – to save on oil, of course, but so that the lank hair of the girls might

27

be mistaken for a healthful sheen, and the bruises and sores beneath their face paint cannot be seen. The smell here is as rich and briny as the Thames, for there is no musk and rose water to smother it.

Still closer to the water, the girls work alone. Outside, braced against a wall, torn stockings slipping down over thighs mottled with smoke smuts and bruises. I meet Mary down there, on the waterfront. I watch what she does, how she goes with others because of their money and their promises. But they don't mean it. They never will.

I am different, though.

Chapter Two

I steered Will westwards, towards Deadman's Basin. The buildings that faced the water reared over us, the sun vanishing behind a bank of brownish cloud and turning the light as muddy as a glass of Thames water. The tide was on the turn, and we could hear the suck and slap as it left the foreshore. Mud larks would be out before long – already I could see a group of them gathered at the riverside, their clothes and limbs as brown as the sludge they raked through.

'Is it possible that there's a perfectly innocent explanation for Aberlady's absence?' said Will. 'Perhaps he's simply been called away to his family—'

'He has no family.'

'Perhaps he couldn't bear it on board any longer. I'd not blame anyone for that. Could he have lost interest in the work altogether? Certainly his apothecary looked neglected. What are his interests? Does he have a physic garden?'

'No,' I said. In fact, Aberlady had always shown less interest in medicinal plants than I. There were a number of occasions when he had come up to the physic garden at St Saviour's – he had admired it, especially the poison beds – though how I had managed to grow so much in the dirty London climate was of no interest to him. 'Aberlady is more interested in the exotic,' I said. 'Venoms, toxic parasites, tropical diseases. He's well-known among the sailors and dock workers – he's treated many of them himself on board the *Blood*, or at the Seaman's Dispensary. They bring him things – for a fee, of course.'

'What things?' said Will.

'For his "collection". Insects and parasites, mostly. Sometimes bottled, sometimes live. Snakes and spiders too, as well as frogs and beetles.'

Aberlady had brought a number of his creatures up to St Saviour's – a small, brown spider, all the way from Australia, a box of tiny harlequin-coloured Amazonian frogs or a pair of gleaming, jet-black scorpions from Chile. He had brought snakes too – including the two he still possessed, and which were now housed in his room on board the *Blood*. Although we often tried poisons on ourselves, the venom of spiders and snakes was a different matter, and we were cautious, as well as respectful, of the power our fellow creatures exerted over life and death. There was every chance that a herb might cure in small quantities and kill in large ones, but the potential for physic offered by venom was far more subtle and elusive. Dogs, of course, provided the best subjects for our inquiries. I had never liked the practice, but how else might we understand the workings of the poisons we tested? And so

I had joined John Aberlady in his experiments, and I had watched dogs die from the bites of snakes, spiders and scorpions. Whether they lived or not, we had observed the dogs as they suffered. Afterwards we dissected them, and noted the state of their internal organs.

'Aberlady is a man of infinite curiosity,' I said now. 'He is drawn to the macabre, and the exotic. He sees physic, in its current form, as medieval in its limitations and vision. The standard practices of medical men – bleeding, sedating and purging – he sees as worthless. There are a growing number, myself included, who agree with him. As for traditional physic, "nothing but leaves, leeches and toadstools, Jem," he used to say. "Has nothing changed since Culpeper?"'

'And was he right?'

I shrugged. 'Most physic these days relies on mercury and opium and ignores Culpeper altogether. Hardly an improvement—'

'What about cleanliness?' muttered Will, looking about him at the dark sooty walls and sticky, refuse-strewn pavement. 'All this filth can't possibly be good for us.' He wiped his hands on his handkerchief again. 'So what does Aberlady suggest? Where does he hope to make his contribution?'

'Where? Throughout the world!'

'A man of modest ambitions, clearly.'

'He said that trade across the globe, the opening up of the colonies, had given us access to new poisons, new parasites and diseases – but perhaps new cures too. The people of India, Australia, South America have the same right to life and health as anyone—'

'Admirable sentiments,' said Will.

31

'—and as the most progressive, rational and scientific nation in the world it behoves us to help them.'

'And yet he chose not to work amongst the people whose lives and health you say meant so much to him, but elected to remain in London.'

'All the world passes through London.'

'And if he should make any discoveries, then who would benefit?'

'Everyone,' I said. 'From London it would reach the world in no time.'

'Eventually, perhaps,' Will replied. 'But surely the first person to benefit would be John Aberlady, and the whole world would also know about that.'

There was something else, too, something I had suspected about John Aberlady for a long time, and which I feared might now be affecting his mind and behaviour. I had never been able to prove it, not for sure, for men with Aberlady's penchant were notoriously devious individuals. And yet I was certain, almost certain, that he was an opium eater. I had not seen him for a while. He had either got the better of his addiction, or it had got the better of him. Reading his letter, and hearing of his disappearance, I was inclined to fear the worst. But I said nothing of this, and Will was still talking.

'Men change, Jem. Time and experience make all of us different to what we were, or to what we once hoped to be. What's he been doing these last few years? Where has it led him?'

'I don't know—'

'Perhaps you don't know what he's been doing because you don't know *him*. Not any more.'

'But I *do* know him. He is kind, generous, hard working.

His work matters more to him than anything in the world. Of *course* I know him—'

'Do you?' He didn't look at me as he spoke. 'We all have our secrets, Jem. You of all people know that.'

We turned up a narrow passage, Tulip's Entry, which lay between two tall buildings, opposite a flight of slippery stairs leading down to the water's edge. Underfoot the crooked flagstones were green with age and damp, the sky overhead visible between black sooty walls in a ribbon of dirty grey. Despite its decayed appearance it was clear that the passage was in constant use as a thoroughfare, for I could see a dark smear on the wall from the rub of greasy shoulders. A criss-cross of black scratches on the brickwork at the corner told where men had stood out of the wind to strike a match for their pipes. Tulip's Basin was on the left. A narrow canal, crossed by a wooden bridge and filled with sluggish water, oozed from the Basin into the Thames.

I held out my arms. 'Your commission, Will. Drink it in.'

The basin itself was some forty feet long and sixty feet wide, lined with dark stones and filled to the brim with black water. Low buildings of crumbling stone and ancient wood clustered at the sides like mushrooms. Parts of the place reminded me of St Saviour's Infirmary – the stone was the same, as was the sodden, decayed look of the place – and I found the comparison unsettling. Had we really treated the sick in buildings not much more salubrious than these? At the time, I had been used to it. Now, the similarity appalled me. Most of the buildings here, however, were in far worse condition. A group of low sheds, now green with moss and slime, had been built out onto the water. The lock gates that led out into the canal were huge and black, colonised by weeds and patched with moist, brightly coloured excrescences. At the head of the basin a conduit dribbled a thin stream of dark liquid into the pool. Behind it, crouched before the warehouse that towered at its back, an ancient boarded-up villa peered sightlessly – I had no idea what purpose it had once served, though it was far older than the surrounding buildings.

Little went to waste in London, and if there had ever been anything of value dumped in Tulip's Basin it would have been culled from those dirty waters long ago. What remained was a stinking mush of effluent, rubble and dead things – from where we stood I could see the matted flanks of a dog and the pale, curved ribs of another, smaller animal. The stink of the place was abominable. I turned up my collar, and thrust my hands into my pockets as a thin rain began to fall.

Will stared out, his expression stony. The sounds from the main thoroughfare, and from the river, were muted, the air curiously still and quiet for all that we were stand-ing in the very heart of the city's most unquiet streets.

'How long since the place was used? Ten, twelve years?'

'At least.'

'Dear God, Jem,' he said, suddenly vehement, 'is there a fouler and more pestilent place in all of London? Where did the fellow die?'

'Over there.' I pointed to a sagging hovel, little more than a pile of stones, with a crooked black chimney. The door was missing, and inside we could see only fallen

34

masonry. 'The boatyard was owned by his father, and grandfather. I came with a prescription once. It looked little different here even when Dick Tulip was alive.'

'Why didn't they live in that old villa?'

'Dick owned the cottages and the yard. I don't know who owned the villa. Didn't your master tell you?'

Will pulled out a sheaf of paper from this pocket and flicked through it. 'Yes,' he said. 'The place has been tied up in chancery for years as Dick Tulip died intestate. The villa was sold to the East India Company by—' he squinted at the paper. 'Callard estates. Plantation owners.' He shrugged, and stuffed the papers back out of sight. 'It seems nothing could happen until Tulip's property had passed through the courts. Now that's happened the Company have possession of the whole basin. They're keen for a new warehouse as soon as possible, and I am the lucky man who has the job of surveying the area and demolishing the whole lot. I have designed a warehouse already. It can easily be modified to fit what space we have.'

He sighed as he opened his bag and pulled out his notebook and pencil. 'I wish I didn't always get the demolition jobs,' he said. 'They are unutterably nasty – there's always something horrible underground. You recall my work at St Saviour's?'

I did. Will had been tasked with emptying the infirmary's ancient and overflowing graveyard – the memory of it still haunted us both.

'Still,' he said. 'Now that we're here I might as well take a proper look at the place.'

I stood against the wall and took out my pipe while Will skirted the edge of the basin. I watched him peering up at the buildings and scribbling down his observations. He rummaged for his theodolite, set it down on a rotten post embedded into the stones at the waterside, and squinted into it. He dug at the stonework of Dick's hovel with his knife.

'I'm surprised it's still standing,' he said. His voice echoed strangely, as if he were standing at the bottom of a well. 'This stonework is as soft as pastry.'

'What about that dribble of water?' I said, pointing to the trickling pipe. 'It looks persistent.'

'It can easily be culverted.' He sat on a capstan beneath one of the old sheds and began to sketch.

The sun came out, shining a brief beam of gold against the dark, forgotten walls. The day was cloudy. Rain threatened, and the light had taken on a peculiar colour, tarnished and brassy as it glanced off the water. Without the sun it had looked almost solid, like a slab of wet tar, but its oily surface was now iridescent with colour, the light illuminating whatever debris lay beneath.

Had the sun not come out I would not have noticed anything. Weeks might have passed, the waters lying undisturbed until the building work proper was scheduled to start. But the sun did come out. And as I stood there with my gaze fixed upon those dark and murky waters I saw something that turned my skin cold.

'How deep is this basin?' My voice was sharp, urgent.

Will looked up. 'How should I know?'

'Shall we find out?' I sprang over to the lock gates. A windlass, coated with thick black grease, glinted with the first drops of rain. I tugged at the handle. I had not expected it to move, and yet move it did, with a deep groan, and the scream of ancient gears.

I could open the gates no more than a few inches. The water sprayed out in a filthy arc, splattering against the muddy floor of the canal and racing down towards the Thames.

'What is it?' said Will. 'What did you see?'

The sun had gone in again now, and the rain was falling in earnest. I was scanning the water, searching for what I had seen, and yet hoping that I had been wrong, that it had been a trick of the light—

'Jem!'

'A face,' I said. 'I saw a face. In the water, I'm sure of it.' At least, I *had* been sure, just for a moment, as the sun shone down and Deadman's Basin turned from jet to translucent bronze. A face as pale as marble, the mouth open, the hair tangled, the eyes – oh God, the eyes – and yet perhaps I was wrong. Perhaps it was a mistake, for there was no sign of it now. And yet I had been so certain.

I thought at once of Eliza. She was the daughter of one of St Saviour's most infamous medical men. She had been my friend, and my lover, though her life had been more cruel and unhappy than anyone had realised. Broken by all that had happened to her, she had vanished into the city's crowded streets. No one knew where. I had looked for her – I always looked for her, and I could not walk anywhere without scanning the faces that came towards me, hoping one of them might be hers, for I loved her still. I knew I would find her again one day. And yet I dreaded it too, for life on the streets was brutal, for women and children especially. As I stared out at the vile waters of Deadman's Basin my father's words, uttered so long ago, whispered in my head: *The corpses of men find their way into the river by accident. Women's arrive there by design—*

All at once Will was beside me. He seized the handle of the windlass. 'Together,' he said. 'One, two . . .' The spout of water became a thick, swirling mass, thundering against the aged brickwork.

I stared out over the basin. 'How long will this take to empty?'

'It depends how deep it is.' Will tugged at the windlass. The gates shifted another inch and the contents poured into the canal. There was no perceptible decrease in the water level, though currents beneath swirled darkly, releasing bubbles of gas that bobbed to the surface, like frogs' eyes. A half-submerged barge shifted where it lay, and a horrible, wet, sucking sound echoed from the walls. The dead dog circled lazily, and began drifting towards the gates.

In the end, it was the rain that guided us, for it washed her face free of the dirt and slime in which she had lain. Her skin glimmered against the substance of her grave, emerging from the cold and dark like a ghost from the shadows. I recognised the pallid fish-belly flesh of the recent dead, her mouth gaping in a black and silent scream, the jaw set wide as the waters slipped away.

Chapter Three

～～

Her skin was white-grey, the veins at her temples visible in a bluish tracery. She wore only a chemise, a poor ragged garment that had absorbed the foul matter of her grave and now cleaved to her body, dark and muddy, as though it were fashioned from the essence of London itself. From out of these filthy underclothes her legs protruded, as pale as tallow beneath streaks of brown and black.

'Who is she?' said Will, his face white in the lamplight.

The mortuary attendant, crouched at his side like some curious bunch-backed familiar, sniffed, and wiped a droplet of moisture from his nose with his sleeve.

'Girl,' he said, shaking his head. 'Drowned.'

'Recently too, by the looks of things,' said Will. He fumbled in his pocket for his salts.

'Drowned?' I said. 'What was she doing out there in her chemise?'

'My God,' muttered Will. 'What a place to die.' I put my hand upon his shoulder. 'Had we not gone there today

Lord knows when she might have been found,' he said. 'Weeks, perhaps. I suppose we must assume the person who put her there didn't know the place was to be drained and built upon.'

'Perhaps,' I said. 'Unless they didn't care, unless haste, or convenience, were more pressing concerns than finding the perfect grave.'

The police inspector appeared, brought by the mortuary assistant's boy. He took one look at the dead girl and shook his head.

'That thoroughfare past Deadman's Basin, you say, sir? Well, they will insist on using it. Whores mostly. That's what this girl is, sir, there's no respectable women round these streets. Any evidence of violence?'

'Not demonstrably,' I said.

'Was she weighted down, sir? Stones and such?'

'No,' I said.

'There you are then, sir. I wouldn't worry about it unduly. One less girl on the streets isn't much to fret about. Fell in drunk, probably. Death by misadventure.'

'"Isn't much to fret about?"' said Will. '"Death by misadventure?" Is that the only conclusion you're prepared to consider?'

'It is till the doctor or the magistrate tells me otherwise.' He shrugged. 'Dead girls is always a shock, sir. 'Specially young 'uns. But them stones on the passage are slippery. Easy to fall in and drown on a dark and foggy night, an' we've had some thick 'uns these last few weeks, what with the warm weather coming to an end and the cold setting in proper. Most unfortunate, I agree, sir. Still, the anatomy school will be most grateful. I've already sent for Dr Graves – from new St Saviour's, sir. D'you know him?'

'Yes,' I said. I closed my eyes. Dr Graves with his long knives and his yellow teeth. He was fast, and skilful, there was no doubt. And yet his gusto in the face of death had always perturbed me.

'He'll be along soon enough. And I've sent for the superintendent from Siren House. That's the League for Female Redemption, sir—'

'I know what it is,' said Will.

'Then you'll know the superintendent is familiar with all the girls, sir. All the girls around here, at any rate.' He lowered his voice. 'Pointless, if you ask me, sir, having such a place at all, never mind around here. "Once a whore, always a whore," as my old dad used to say. Still, it's Christian to make the effort, I suppose.'

A shadow appeared in the doorway. It was the constable, a short burly fellow, his belly straining against the buttons of his blue swallow-tail coat. He carried his hat in his hands, which was more than the Inspector had done. Behind him was a woman. I could not see her properly because she was in the shadows, but she was tall, taller than the man who accompanied her. She was wearing a long cloak, the hood drawn up over her hair, her head bowed as if in mourning.

'From Siren House, sir, like you asked,' said the constable. He led the woman forward.

'Well, miss?' said the Inspector. 'D'you recognise this girl?'

She stood tall and straight, her back to Will and me as if we did not exist. She looked at the girl on the slab for a long time. For a moment, I thought she might faint, for she swayed where she stood. I put my hand upon her arm, but she shook it off. When she spoke her voice was low and calm.

'Her name is Mary Mercer.'

'Street girl.' The Inspector sounded unconcerned. 'I suspected as much. Next of kin?'

'None,' said the woman. 'At least, none that knew where she was or cared anything about her.' She put out a gloved hand, and took hold of the dead girl's fingers.

'Righty-ho, miss.' He turned to Will and me. 'Of course, it's not the dead what worries me, sirs, so much as the living. There's thieves up at Drake's Warehouse – again. If you'll excuse me, gentlemen. Miss.' He tugged the edge of his hat. Even with the thing on he was hardly taller than the woman before him.

'Of course, Inspector,' she said. 'Don't let *me* keep you. Protecting the property of the wealthy is evidently far more important than bringing to book the murderer of a young woman.'

'Murdered?' I said. 'You think so? Miss – Miss—'

'I do, sir.' She did not turn to look at me as she spoke, and did not care to give me her name. It was as if she disdained me, disdained all men.

'Misadventure in all likelihood, miss,' said the Inspector. 'Don't you go upsetting yourself with words like murder. Mr Flockhart here agrees, don't you, sir?'

'Of course,' I said.

Should I have told him that as the waters receded we had found a thick fold of black oilskin, slimy and blotched, plastered against the lock gates like a great flap of wet flesh? It was my belief that this had lain over the body, concealing it in a shroud that mirrored the waters in which it had lain. Some movement of the refuse in the basin had caused it to shift, so that her face was revealed, and then once the waters had started to move, draining away into the Thames, the current had dragged the covering aside completely. I could think of no more obviously contrived concealment – far more cunningly thought out than crude measures such as stones in pockets. Had we not opened the gates and fished her out of the water the girl would have rotted away to nothing where she lay, concealed and yet in plain sight, her decomposition masked by the stinking environment. But I said nothing. I had no faith in the police and their methods. Twice now I had seen them arrest the wrong person – condemning one to be hanged and consigning the other to a mad house until her mind was all but gone. Death by misadventure would suit the magistrate for now. But it did not suit the woman before me, and as I spoke, her head snapped up. I thought she was going to speak, but she didn't even look at me. She drew her hood closer, pulling it tight against the mortuary's chill. I saw her breath, white and furious in the freezing air, and then she was gone.

❦

We did not have long to ourselves. Already Dr Graves would be racing across town in the wagon he had built especially for conveying bodies from the gallows or the mortuary to his dissecting rooms at St Saviour's.

'You there,' I said, turning to the mortuary attendant's boy. 'Run up to the *Blood* and bring any of the doctors that happen to be about. A body found not a hundred yards from the Seaman's Hospital?' I said to Will as the boy scampered out. 'I'm sure any medical man with his wits about him would be sorry to see Dr Graves make off with a corpse found on his own doorstep. Students will pay handsomely to see one anatomised, no matter where, and no matter who's doing it. Besides,' I added, 'it's probably the only chance we'll have of making sure the body stays here when it is dissected.'

'There'll be trouble,' said Will. 'Dr Graves will claim her for his own.'

'Very likely,' I replied. 'Quick, let's see what we can find before anyone comes. You there. What's your name? Bring another lantern, will you?'

'M'name's Toad, sir. And that there young 'un's known as Young Toad. There's been Toads on the waterfront since as long as there's been a river. But 'old on, sir!' He stepped forward, his face alarmed. 'You sure you know what you're doin'? Ain't you better wait for Dr Graves?'

I was bending over the girl, my magnifying glass in my hand. The afternoon was dark now, the skies outside heavy and grey, and the light that filtered through the mortuary's windows – thick green squares of glass set high in the wall – turned the place sepulchral. I took the man's lantern and held it up, peering down at the corpse. 'I don't take orders from Dr Graves, Toad,' I said. 'Bring another lamp. I need light. Quickly now!'

I could see that my first impression was correct: she had clearly not been in the water for long – the skin was a pale blue-grey in colour, but lacked the bloated, flabby appearance of long immersion. She was thin, small and dark-haired, and beautiful.

There were bruises on her arms and legs that I could see, but this was a girl from the streets: her bitten-down nails and hollow cheeks betrayed her troubled life, and bruising was only to be expected. There were small round marks on her upper arm – perhaps from the rough grasp of an assailant, perhaps from any number of altercations she might have got into, though there was no sign of bondage at wrist or ankle. I laid my hand on her body. Even through her chemise I could count her ribs, feel the deep concave between her hips.

There was a bucket of water on the cold stone flags beside the slab, a slimy hank of chamois leather draped over the side. I rinsed the leather and wiped the girl's arms and legs. Her skin was icy to the touch, softish and pliant, like a lump of raw meat. Here and there small thread veins were visible, where the blood had started to seep through the delicate walls of the smaller vessels, though I was sure that the freezing cold waters of Deadman's Basin had done something to slow down this process. There was no discolouration of the body's underside, so she had not lain still in one place after death but had been moved quickly – before she was hidden in the water. I would not have put her death any more than seven days earlier, 20th October. In my pocket was Aberlady's crumpled note bearing that very date. *Come now, Jem, but come ready to face the Devil . . .*

I examined the fingers of her right hand, looking for the calluses of the seamstress, or the ingrained coal dust of the parlour maid. Had she once had an occupation? Many girls turned to prostitution when times were hard, dipping in and out of that desperate profession as the need arose. I looked down at her. How little there was to show us how she had met her end – no trauma to the head, no marks about the neck, no stab wounds.

And yet there was one thing that gave me pause: on her collar bone, on each side, was a fine neat cut, hardly visible in the gloom, but deep, slicing through the skin and flesh right through to the clavicle. There were similar incisions on the tops of her feet. They were done with precision, the skin around them swollen due to the ingress of water, and they had opened very slightly, like pursed lips.

'What do you see?' said Will.

'Incisions,' I said.

'Perhaps she cut herself when falling in.'

'Perhaps.'

It *was* possible. But not probable.

There was no time to say more for at that moment there was a clattering of boots on the stair. The door burst open and two men strode into the mortuary. Ten excited students followed in their wake.

'Where are they, Toad?' called the first man, a blond, curly-haired fellow, tall and handsome, with bright, eager blue eyes and rosy cheeks. Even in the yellow light of Toad's grubby oil lamps he looked healthy. It was unusual for London – most of us looked terrible. 'Young Toad said there was a girl. Dead and fresh! "Like a drowned angel" I believe were his words, though I admit he was even more garbled than usual—'

He stopped short when he saw me. I held up my lantern, and I knew that he was looking at my birthmark, lurid and disfiguring in the lamplight.

'Who might you be?' said the fellow behind him. He was an inch taller than the first, red haired, with dark eyes and a serious expression.

'Where's Aberlady?' I said. 'Still not back?'

'Obviously not,' said the first man. 'And he's not here either, though just about everyone else seems to be. And you are?'

46

I made our introductions. He grinned, and held out his hand. 'Dr Cole,' he said. 'Septimus Cole, assistant physician on board the *Blood*. And this surly fellow here is Antrobus. Come along, Antrobus, shake hands, can't you? Dr Antrobus is assistant surgeon on the *Blood*.' He gestured to the group of young men who were now clustered about the corpse. 'And these merry men are our students.'

'When did you last see him?'

'Aberlady? About a week ago. I'm sure he'll come back eventually. He usually does. You were up at the *Blood* earlier, weren't you? I'm sure Dr Sackville has already told you all this.'

'I was hoping you might tell me something else.'

He shrugged. 'You might try asking down on Spyglass Lane. He often takes a pipe there.' He saw my surprise, and raised his eyebrows. 'Didn't you know? Look, I hope I've not broken a confidence. Everyone knows – well, Antrobus and I do, at least. It's nothing he can't manage, though I'd not let on to Sackville about it. Nor Birdwhistle. *Especially* not to Birdwhistle. He's convinced Aberlady's the root of all evil, even *without* knowing he's a regular at the Golden Swan down on Spyglass—'

'Yes,' I said, my heart heavy. 'Yes, I did know.' And yet I had not realised my old friend had sunk so low. Laudanum was one thing, and the black drop might be got in any strength he chose – he might make the stuff up himself, for the recipe was simple enough: two ounces of opium dissolved in a pint of port wine and fortified with cloves and cinnamon. But an opium den? Such places were dangerous, filthy caverns frequented by wretched, lost souls.

'Oh, never mind all that,' said Dr Antrobus. 'Let's get started. Aberlady can look after himself.' He turned to the door at the sound of more footsteps and clicked his tongue. 'Who is it now?'

'Oh, come along, Antrobus,' cried Dr Cole. He slapped his companion on the back. 'The more the merrier, what? Dr Graves!' He sprang forward, his hands outstretched. 'What a great pleasure, sir, a great pleasure indeed. Will you not come in, sir? It seems we have a treat in store, and something of a welcoming party too!'

'I came for the body,' said Dr Graves, who had arrived in his gallows wagon with two henchmen, both of whom loomed behind him in the shadows. 'She's mine now.' He glowered at Will and me, his disappointment evident at finding the mortuary filled with the living as well as the dead. He stood back from the crowd of students, his arms swinging, his posture, as usual, slightly crouched, as if he were about to spring onto the slab beside the dead girl like an orang-utan.

Dr Antrobus, who had clearly hoped to take the lead amongst his students, tried to hide his annoyance. 'But no, sir,' he said. 'This is *our* body. It is for the *Blood*, and her students, and we cannot permit you to take it away, not before we have done our duty as medical men.'

'She's mine,' repeated Dr Graves. 'I was sent for,' and he made as if to lift the corpse there and then, and carry her off over his shoulder.

Dr Antrobus sprang forward to stop him, and a brief tussle ensued. 'Good God, gentlemen,' cried Will, as the girl's head knocked against the slab. 'Have you no respect?'

'I must protest, sir,' said Dr Cole, stepping forward. 'Dr Antrobus is quite right. Dr Graves, this corpse belongs to the *Blood* and her students and we cannot let you take it away. However, we would be honoured to work with you.

48

If you might be kind enough to share your expertise and experience?'

Dr Graves eyed the naked feet of the girl hungrily. 'Well. Well,' he said. 'As long as I have a corpse before me and a knife in my hand, I don't much care where I do it or who looks on. But it will be two guineas each. Two guineas from each one of these students.'

'And you will divide the fee between us equally?' said Dr Cole.

'I take half,' replied Dr Graves. 'I have come all the way from St Saviour's, after all, and there is the matter of my reputation and experience. I take half, and the other half you share between the two of you.'

The girl lay pale and still, the water from Deadman's Basin pooling around her cold dead limbs. The mortuary echoed with the sound of men's voices, and the rattle of coins exchanging hands, and I wondered whether her body had been worth so much to anyone when she was alive. His pockets full at last, Dr Graves produced his box of knives, and the students gathered round.

Confession of Mary Mercer on arriving at Siren House

❧

My name is Mary Mercer. I am twenty years old. I don't have much to tell you about my life, sir. I am not sure that I should tell you anything for it's a shameful story, I do know that much. The other girls here – some of them – they don't know anything else but being on the streets. I don't know whether that's better or worse, that I have known a life that is not miserable and degraded, or that they are unaware that goodness and kindness exist and so hold out no expectation of it.

I came to my current state by sorry means, through my own weakness. I can read and write, sir, and could write down my own confession if you'd prefer it, though I would rather not see it set out on the page. My father and mother worked at a big house outside London. I'll not say where it is, for I'll not bring further disgrace upon them. They believe me to be dead, and so I am to them. I will not tell you their names, only that they are good people, my father a gamekeeper and my mother a cook. The master had a son and a daughter, and I was well known to the daughter of the house for we were of the same age, born on the same day, and liked to consider ourselves twins, though we looked nothing at all alike.

We were good friends as children, as far as it's possible for such a friendship to be encouraged when one comes from below stairs and the other is the jewel of her father's eye. But friends we were, and I was permitted to attend her lessons with her for it was a lonely business in the schoolroom with only the governess, for her brother was older and away from home and her mother dead. It was a solitary life and her father was happy enough for me to be her companion. Those summers we had together, I can hardly describe for they seem to me like heaven itself. But they lasted no time at all, for childhood is gone in an instant, and she was to be a lady as I was to be her maid. She was my darling, sir, nothing much to look at, being pale and wan, and not like her mother, so I was told, who had been a great beauty.

But my girl was sick. She had a cough – we all knew what it meant, and we pretended she would get well again soon enough, though she never did. In time I became her nurse. I wheeled her about the park; I read to her; I warmed her limbs with my own during the night. I loved her, sir, and I did all I could to keep her alive and safe. The doctor knew I was careful and he entrusted me with her medicines. I grew adept at changing her sheets in the night when she woke sweating, and I was careful with her laudanum for I knew how stupid it made her feel. I hid the blood in her handkerchief, as the sight of it made her afraid.

51

The doctors came all the time. The bleedings they inflicted upon that poor girl, sir. I could hardly bear it – carrying away bowls full of her precious blood, watching her grow paler and paler, though there was nothing that would get rid of those fierce red spots of colour on her cheeks. The glitter of her eye and the red on her hand-kerchief were all the more startling and fierce for she was so thin and white.

And then one day they took her away. The summer had ended and the doctor thought she would not be able to bear another English winter, so she was bundled up and sent abroad. I begged that I might go with her. She begged that I might come too, but no one listened to either of us. The doctor said she wanted a proper nurse, though she needed no such thing, for no one knew her as well as I did, no one cared for her as I did, and the woman they employed was cold and hard and pinch-faced, and would have the rings from her fingers before she was even in her grave.

I learned later that she had died before they even got to Switzerland. That was four years ago now, though it still grieves me every day. And then my darling's brother came home. How like her he was to look at, for he was slim and golden haired, as she had been. I know now that he hardly knew his sister, no matter that he pretended that he did, and that he understood my grief. Rather, he did not know her at all, and cared nothing for her. He was so much older and had rarely been home when she was growing up. He had been trained by his father in the ways of men. Selfishness, indifference, arrogance and guile were in his blood, and he believed, like his father, that women were put onto God's earth for two reasons only – for

52

breeding, and for sport. And if one used women of one's own class for the first of these, one used all others for the second. And yet I could not see it. Not then. He was so like her to look at, I could not believe that he would not also be like her in his heart. But he was not. He took what he wanted, and then he left me with his child growing inside me. A girl, I hoped. I would call her Marianna, after my darling, for I liked to think of my baby as hers, not his.

Well, sir, I knew they would take her away from me if they knew, and so I concealed my condition. My mother called the doctor, who looked at me and asked whether I was pregnant and I said 'no, sir', but it was just that I had got fatter, and was feeling unwell, and it was nothing that some castor oil wouldn't solve. My mother asked me the same question and I said 'no' to her, though I knew I was, and I still did not know what I would do when my time came. But come it did, one afternoon in August when everyone was about their business as the harvest was being brought in. I felt the pains and I crept away to my tiny room at the top of the house. It was in the middle of the day when the maids' rooms were empty, and I bit down on a leather strap I had taken from the tack room to stifle my cries.

I hardly knew what I should do when the baby came. I thought I could manage it alone, but I could not. The pain all but drove me mad, and I ripped the cord with my bare hands. The baby – a boy – was not moving. There was blood everywhere. I tried to clear it up, but I was weak and in pain and I could hardly move, and more of the stuff was pouring out of me. The baby was dead, I could see that, and so I put it in the coal scuttle and closed the lid. And then I lay down again.

Oh, sir, I can hardly say what happened next. My mother came looking for me and found me where I was. The doctor came and a bloody trail showed where my baby was hidden. After that I went quite mad. Puerperal insanity, they say, and I was taken to an asylum and kept there for days until I was quiet. I almost died, sir, and I wished I had for what awaited me now but the assizes?

Because I had hidden my condition from everyone, and had put the dead child in the coal scuttle, I was charged with concealment of pregnancy. They told me I would be convicted, but that I should be glad I was not charged with murder, for so I would have been had the doctor not agreed that my baby was already dead when I put it in the coal scuttle, for murder is a capital offence and I should surely have hanged for it.

I was sentenced to a year's imprisonment. My mother and father refused to see me again, so disgraced were they by my actions. I had told the magistrate who the father was and my master was furious to have his family shamed in so public a place as a criminal court. Worse still, I had confessed all – how I had shared my beloved's bed, how I had cared for her in the most intimate of ways. How vile and unnatural I seemed, to love a woman and seduce her brother and hide his dead baby in the coal. That I was young and grieving for my mistress was no one's concern.

And so I came to prison. I saw your pamphlet, sir. And yet I didn't take it. Not at first, for I was not ready for redemption. Instead, I was filled with pain and sorrow. My love for Marianna had been held up to ridicule and scrutiny as a vile and corrupt thing that had likely sent the poor girl into an early grave. I walked for miles,

though I could not escape my thoughts. I stayed in cheap
lodging houses, though I had little money and pawned
what clothes and possessions I had. And then one night
when a man approached me in the street I went with him.
I bought some laudanum with the money he gave me.
The taste of it reminded me of her lips, and after that it
was much easier.

Chapter Four

By the time we left the evening had drawn in. The setting sun was no more than a bloody smear against the western sky and the lanes we now walked down were dark and filled with shadows. On either side of us the walls were stained and streaked with damp. One moment the air was heavy with the stink of wet leather and boiled bones, the next it was fragrant with spices and coffee, the sharp salty tang of fried fish followed by the damp earthiness of spilled beer. I had not realised how many public houses there were when we had walked down the same streets earlier that day, but now every other door seemed to lead into a drinking den – cave-like places, dimly lit and full of lurching shadows and rough voices. On all sides of us men flowed up from the waterfront. One step away from prison or the workhouse, the docks were the only place in London where a man's character, or his past, was of concern to no one. All that mattered was whether he could lift and haul, whether he could tramp the tread wheels that worked the lifting gear in the dockside warehouses, or carry burdens on his shoulders all day.

As the night crept up from the east, so did the fog, the air about us taking on a familiar gritty feel. Overhead, crooked chimneys poked the sky from sagging roofs, each of them trailing a ribbon of black smoke. Lanterns hanging outside public houses, chandlers and pawn shops glowed. We walked in silence, Will and I, shoulder to shoulder, the streets too clamorous for conversation.

At length the thoroughfare broadened out and grew less crowded. We turned left, and then right. The lamps had been lit along Barnaby Street, a dingy thoroughfare by anyone's estimation but which seemed a vision of air and brightness compared to the lanes and courts we had passed through that day. Our strides lengthened now, heading, though neither of us mentioned it, to Sorley's chop house.

Sorley's was crowded. The cold weather, the darkness and the rising fog had driven men inside, and the whole supper room was filled with a warm smoky fug. The smell of hot chops and pork fat made my mouth water. I asked Sorley to send a pheasant pie and two bottles of porter down to the apothecary. I hoped the food would do something to mollify Gabriel before we got back. I ordered two plates of cutlets and some oysters to have with our beer, and we pushed our way through to a booth near the fireplace.

We drank our ale in silence while we waited for our food. 'You think the Inspector is wrong?' said Will.

'Undoubtedly. Don't you?'

'His seems the most likely explanation.'

'But one which hardly fits with the facts we have before us: a girl in her underclothes—'

'A prostitute—'

'*Former* prostitute,' I said.

'Former? And therefore unlikely to be with a man?'

'*Less* likely. If she was no longer on the streets, then what was she doing on the streets?'

'She must have come from nearby. And a girl in her underclothes would surely attract attention.'

'Unless it was dark, which it would surely have to be if he were to get her into the water.'

'He?' said Will.

'You're quite right. To get her into the water, to hide her, I think strength would be necessary, but it would be wrong to assume a man. One man, or two men, or a man and a woman, two or more women – there are a number of possibilities. And yet men are more likely to commit crimes of violence. The girl would have come from the nearby streets, certainly, or the nearby houses. Perhaps she came from Siren House itself. And anyone – any man – might stagger along the footpath through Tulip's Basin with their arms around a dead girl. To any passers-by she would simply appear drunk – especially in these streets. Drunk women are ten a penny on the riverside.'

'And the oilskin?'

'Quite possibly the oilskin was already there,' I said. 'A new tarpaulin would have been dragged out by scavengers, though it can hardly have been an accident that she was covered.'

'Though it might have been an accident that she drowned. Water was found in her lungs, Jem, we both heard Dr Graves say so.'

We had stayed for the post-mortem, though as I had refused to hand Dr Graves two guineas for the privilege I had been obliged to stand at the back. I had seen the girl's lungs for myself, for they had been put into a bowl and set to one side and I had sneaked round to take a look. They had definitely been full of water. And yet—

'What about the marks? The cuts upon her collar bones, her feet, the bruises on her arms?' I said.

'She lived a dangerous life. Cuts, punctures, bruises, all might easily have been sustained hours, perhaps even days, before she drowned. Perhaps as she fell into the water.'

'And you think they are merely the marks of a brutal life?'

'It is quite plausible.'

I said nothing. It *was* possible. Equally, it might be evidence of something else entirely. Something far more sinister. And those cuts were too regular to be anything but incisions – clean, deliberate, precise.

'What about your missing friend?' Will tossed a picked-clean bone to Sorley's dog, which lay panting beneath the table.

'Aberlady? What about him?'

'Is it like him to disappear for a week without saying anything to anyone?'

'No,' I said. Then added rather sulkily, 'Though you were determined earlier to imply that I hardly know the man. As such his habits are quite mysterious to me.'

Will grinned. 'So I did. Did you notice that those on board the *Blood* seemed rather disinclined to speak well of him?'

I had noticed and I did not know what to make of it.

Aberlady had always commanded the respect of his colleagues, or so I had thought. I took a deep draught of beer.

'And their remarks about his opium habit,' continued Will. 'You knew he was a slave to the stuff?'

'I . . . I knew he depended on laudanum for . . . for his own peace of mind,' I said. 'It did not affect his work.' I shrugged. 'There's barely a man in the land who has not used laudanum.'

'Though not everyone progresses to the opium houses of the waterfront.'

'Indeed,' I said. 'That I had *not* realised.'

'And that ship!' continued Will. 'I've never seen anything quite like it. Why on earth did he choose to work there?'

'I've told you. Where else might he make study of the diseases that afflict the world? The *Blood* is a hospital like no other.'

'That's certainly true.' Will wiped his lips, and tossed his napkin onto his empty plate. But I had not eaten, for as soon as our food had been brought over, I had found I was not hungry. I pushed my plate to the side. 'You think there's some connection between the note from Aberlady and that dead girl?' he said.

'We have no evidence of a connection,' I replied. 'I'm reluctant to jump to conclusions.'

Will pulled open his bag and drew out a map of London. Every street and court, every lane and alley was marked, though as the city was growing and changing with every month that passed it would not be long before a good many of the thoroughfares we looked at now would no longer exist, the map before us becoming nothing more than a ghostly reminder of what had once been. Tulip's Basin was one such place. Soon to vanish from the face of the earth altogether, and yet there it was, marked on the map as a cramped square adjacent to the river.

Will laid a finger on it. 'Tulip's Basin – colloquially know as Deadman's Basin.' He moved his hand towards the river. 'Here's where the *Blood* is moored,' and back towards where we were, north of the basin on the road to Prior's Rents. 'Here's Siren House. They are not far from each other, and all on an easy route – Deadman's Passage, Cat's Hole, Bishop's Entry, Cuttlefish Lane—'

Will put his map away and produced his sketch book. He flipped the pages until he came to the drawing he had made of Deadman's Basin. He had captured the place well – the lock gates, the boarded-up villa, the warehouses looming behind, their thickly barred windows as black as scabs against the damp walls. He had drawn the waters of the basin with an ominous oily sheen, and the tumbled buildings that surrounded the place seemed lonelier and more derelict than ever – the hovel in which Dick Tulip had lived and died, the crooked pier on its rotten timber legs, the half-submerged barge. Against the skyline a tenement reared, smoke trickling from crooked chimney pots. A crow sat hunched on the finial of a rotten gable-end, and a face peered out from the gloom of a top floor window. Beside the water he had drawn a tall, slim figure in a stovepipe hat. Even in so simple a drawing Will had captured the slight swagger to the fellow's stance: the pose was confident, head back as if he were looking down his nose at the scene before him, hands in pockets and hat slightly to one side. It was me. And in the corner, where the greasy flagstones vanished into a dark gash between the walls known as Bishop's Entry, was another figure.

'Who's this?' I said.

Will peered at the drawing. 'I don't know. There was someone standing there the whole time – I'd quite forgotten about it. I didn't think much of it at the time, the place is a thoroughfare after all—'

'How long was he there?'

'Long enough for me to draw him. Most of the time, I think.'

'What was he doing?'

'Just watching.'

'Can you describe him?'

'No. I mean, no more than what you can see here.'

'Medium height, half-respectable clothing, dark coat and a hat not unlike yours. What of his face?'

'It was in the shadows. Besides, he was too far away.'

I stared at that figure. The way his shoulders sloped, his height and slenderness, the angle of his hat, the sharp lines of the face. After all, Will had captured me perfectly in only a few strokes, why might he not do the same with a stranger?

'What is it?' said Will. 'Who is it?'

'I don't know,' I said. 'Though I'm almost certain that it's John Aberlady.'

Chapter Five

⁓⧟⁓

It was almost seven o'clock by the time we got back to the apothecary. Gabriel was not alone, and he and his companion were reclining in front of the stove with their feet on a footstool. The air was filled with pipe smoke. I had cautioned him against tobacco at so young an age, but he was convinced it would give him a more manly voice. The October fogs had settled on his chest and he hoped the tobacco would aid in the warding off of winter chills and the production of sputum. As if to demonstrate the efficacy of the stuff, his fellow smoker gave a great hawking cough, and jettisoned a bolus of brown phlegm through the open door of the stove. It bubbled like toffee on the hot coals.

'Ah, Mrs Speedicut, what a pleasure,' said Will. 'I see you're not at Angel Meadow this evening.'

'Nah!' Mrs Speedicut clamped her teeth – the few she had left – about the stem of her pipe. The smoke curled upwards from it in an ochre-coloured plume. More of the stuff trickled from her nostrils. 'I've left.'

'Left?' I said. 'But why, madam? And when?'

'Just now.' She shook her head. 'That Angel Meadow ain't no hospital! That ain't a place for them what's sick. Sick means sores and coughs and broken limbs. It's worms and scratchin's and the pox – there's none o' that sort o' thing hardly at all at Angel Meadow!'

'It's an asylum, madam,' I said. 'A place where we might offer care and sanctuary to the mad. It is their minds that are troubled, not their bodies. You knew that when you went there.'

'Ain't the same,' she muttered. 'Them up there, they ain't proper sick.'

'What will you do?'

She sat up and put her pipe on the hearth. 'Well, sir—'

Sir, I thought. *That's not a good sign.* 'No,' I said.

Her face sagged. 'But you don't know what I were about to suggest!'

'You were about to suggest coming here to work.'

'No,' said Will. 'Definitely no.'

Mrs Speedicut sank back. 'I will die in the streets,' she said. 'You're all I got! What would your dear father say if he were to hear you treating me with such cruelty?' Tears filled her beady eyes and she covered her face with her apron. The sight would have been quite affecting had it not been for the fact that I could see her peeping craftily out at me from around the edge of it.

I surveyed the apothecary. I had expected turmoil, but the place was surprisingly neat. The pills I had left unfinished had been cut, rolled, silvered and left to dry; the lozenges too had been cut and dried and put into boxes; the condenser had been cleaned and a fresh batch of St John's Wort gleamed red-orange in a flask at its side. The workbench was scrubbed, the floor swept, the jars gleaming, the windows cleaned. Mrs Speedicut had made a lot of effort in her attempt to persuade me of her value.

In fact, I was fully aware of her worth, for I had known her all my life. She had worked at St Saviour's for as long as I could remember – had known my father and my mother. I knew her for a drunken, lazy slattern, and yet she was loyal, and she could keep a secret when she had to – she had kept mine all her life. Moreover she could clean – or at least, she could effectively coerce others to do it – and knew how to deal with people who were even lazier than herself. She had picked up plenty of knowledge about physic over the years too.

'I have a job for you,' I said. 'Though it's not here.'

She looked up at me, her expression wary. 'Oh?'

'We were up at the *Blood* today.'

'That floating flea pit?'

'The very one. They need a matron.'

'The *Blood*,' whispered Gabriel. 'I've heard such things about that place. Such things as you wouldn't believe.'

'What things?' said Will.

'About the doctors. They cut a man's leg off for the fun of it.'

'That Virginian shag of Mrs Speedicut's must be affecting your brain,' I said. I reached for the coffee pot. It was still hot, the brew within dark and bitter as wormwood. It had been there since the morning – since before I had received Aberlady's letter, before we had walked down to the *Blood*, before we had pulled a corpse from the city's most poisonous waters. I poured two cups, and took mine to the workbench, ready to set out everything I needed for the next day.

I had hardy put my cup down when the door burst open. The bell danced on its spring so that we all jumped as if the Devil himself had stabbed us with his toasting fork. A girl stood before us. Her face, streaked with tears, was pale beneath a layer of dirt. Her skirt hung in damp rags against her thin ankles, her boots huge and loose upon her feet.

'Do come in,' said Will calmly.

She backed away from him, looking from Will to Gabriel to Mrs Speedicut, her eyes wide beneath a tangle of yellow hair, a look of fear and confusion on her small pinched face. And then she saw me, my blemished face rendered all the more fearful by the light from the open stove. She raised her hand and pointed. 'The mask,' she said. 'The red mask!'

❧

The girl stood gaping at me. 'What is it?' I said. 'What's happened?'

'Who is she?' said Will.

'She's Pestle Jenny, of course.' The front of the girl's skirt was shiny from where she held the mortar against it; her right hand calloused at the root of her thumb from gripping the pestle – I remembered the blisters that had to be endured before the skin grew hard and the job became easier. I took the girl by the shoulders. An aura of liquorice and burdock clung to her still, despite her race through the darkling streets.

'Jenny,' I said gently. 'I'm Mr Jem – Jem Flockhart. I'm Mr Aberlady's friend. Did he send you? What's happened?'

Pestle Jenny opened her mouth, and then closed it

again without saying anything. She began to shake, her eyes wide.

'Shock, ain't it?' said Mrs Speedicut. 'The girl can't speak.'

'I can see that,' I replied.

'Where's she come from anyway?'

'From the *Blood*.'

'And you want *me* to go there? To be matron at a place what scares the wits out of hardened street children—'

'Yes, Mrs Speedicut, I do,' I said. 'I would like you to present yourself at the *Blood* at six o'clock tomorrow morning offering yourself on my recommendation for the position of matron. I'm sure they'll be delighted to accept you.' I was pulling on my boots as I spoke. The night would be a long one, I was certain. 'This evening you can stay here. Give the girl broth, tea, whatever you think fit.' I wrinkled my nose. 'Perhaps you might give her a bath too.' I put my hand on the girl's shoulder and gestured to Gabriel to come closer. 'Gabriel, can you spare some clothes, a warm blanket, some kindness?'

'*Boys'* clothes, Mr Jem?'

I hesitated. Then, 'Why not? We have nothing else.'

'But—'

'Never mind "but", just do as I say. And then tomorrow, whilst Mrs Speedicut is out and whether I am back or not, you will employ her about the apothecary. She is to assist you in any way she can.'

I looked down at Pestle Jenny. I had seen it once before, that shivering silence. It was years ago now, a child from Prior's Rents who had watched his father beat his mother to death with a flat iron. Neighbours had heard the screams, and when they broke the door down they found the walls splattered with the woman's brains. The man, half-insensible with drink, was crouched beside her body trying to force a gin bottle between her lips. On the bed two babies lolled in filth, and in the corner stood a six-year-old boy. His eyes were staring but unfocused, his mouth open, as if he were watching the scene play over and over in his head.

They had brought him to St Saviour's but there was little we could do for him, for apart from lice and worms and hunger there was nothing physically wrong. He had stayed on the women's ward at first, but the sight of them seemed to remind him of his mother and made him cry. He was sent by Dr Graves to the men's ward instead, but that reminded him of his father and made him scream. In the end he was sent to Angel Meadow Asylum, and from there to the Hospital for Destitute Children. For ten days he said not a word. I went to see him some time later and was told that he had disappeared. One morning he had woken up, asked where his baby brother and sister were, and then run away. London is not a place for friendless children and I had often wondered what had become of him. And now here was Pestle Jenny – silent, shaking, gaping at the unknown horror that was etched upon her mind.

Gabriel put his arm around the girl's shoulders, and steered her towards the warmth of the stove. Mrs Speedicut jammed the poker in and levered the coals into life. She turned to Gabriel. 'Bring the poor little thing over 'ere,' she said, the poker gripped in her fist. 'I'll make 'er some tea.' She pointed it at the table. 'And there's some o' that pie left—'

Pestle Jenny gazed at the poker's smoking metal tip,

her face frozen in terror. She made a curious, high-pitched screaming sound, and dropped to the floor in a faint.

❈

Outside a thick fog had crept up from the river. We both had a lantern, though they made little difference, for the fog absorbed the light like blotting paper. How Pestle Jenny had found her way to us I could not imagine. I hoped for the best as I took Will's arm and plunged forward.

'Perhaps the fog will lift,' I said. 'I think it seems to be thinning out.'

'It's a harvest moon tonight,' muttered Will, pulling his scarf over his mouth. 'Would you believe it? I might as well have a sack over my head, as I can't see a thing!'

We turned left, and then right. Dim lights here and there told where a street lamp glowed, or a lantern shone outside a public house. Underfoot the ground felt soft and wet – the usual mush of ordure and refuse – and on either side of us were walls, dark and hardly visible through the fog, though we could touch their cold stones with our fingertips. And then there were those smells again – spices, coffee and Madeira from the warehouses, stale beer, sweat and rancid tallow from the lodging houses and the people crammed inside. Beneath this, always present, was the stink of the river: damp, rotting weed, effluent. We could hear the sound of voices – singing, and shouting from inside a public house. From up ahead came the gentle creak of timbers and ropes, the suck and slap of water and the rhythmic *clang* of a loose rope striking a bell. Bowsprits and sterns reared before us, rope and rigging glistening with moisture, ghostly in the dark. The moon appeared, visible in a dim, veiled light as the fog thinned and billowed. I had sensed that it was drawing out – did I not know the city's vaporous moods as well as I knew my own? – and in that instant the *Blood* loomed into view. We were closer to her than I had imagined, and our lanterns shone dully onto the wet timbers of her great black belly.

The windows were shuttered, the body of the ship quite dark. At the stern, however, we could see lights moving, and as we drew closer we heard the splash of oars and the sound of activity upon the river. Beneath the apothecary windows, on the Thames itself, small crafts moved back and forth, men with boathooks raking and jabbing at the waters. An orderly was on his knees on the jetty at the water's edge – I recognised him from the *Blood* earlier that day, a bulky, blank-faced man with roughly tattooed forearms and what looked like a bite out of his left ear. Beside him stood a sailor, a rope in his hands. Both were in their shirt sleeves, despite the cold of the night. Dr Sackville was standing beside them. His shoulders were more bowed than ever, as if he were weighted down with sorrow.

As we approached he turned towards us. 'Gentlemen,' he said. 'How fortuitous.'

'Pestle Jenny came for us,' I said. 'I assume on your orders, sir—'

'Mine? Not at all. But it is just as well you're here.' He shook his head. 'I should have expected it. I am not without experience of such things—'

'Expected what?' I said. 'What's happened? Is it

Aberlady?' I looked up at the apothecary windows. Behind the veil of fog and darkness I could see that there was a lamp aglow inside. I saw too that the window gaped wide.

'He jumped,' said Dr Sackville. 'Jumped from the apothecary window into the Thames.'

The orderly with the clipped ear cried out. 'They have him! Dr Sackville, sir, they have him.' The man plunged off the jetty and into a boat, bending to help another man – a lighterman or bargeman, I could not say – drag something cumbersome out of the water. I heard their breathing grow heavy, grunting with effort as they hauled the thing aboard.

'Stand back!' someone shouted as the boat came to the waterside. Out of the shadows came other lumpen forms – more orderlies from the *Blood*, and sailors from nearby ships and drinking dens. They started forward as the burden pulled from the filthy water was manhandled onto the jetty. A body, fully clothed and soaking wet, is a difficult burden to manage, and my poor friend's head banged horribly against the edge of the boat. They dragged him onto a tarpaulin, and stood back, those who had come from nearby ships to offer help, or lanterns, melting away into the night once they saw what had become of him.

At any other time it would have been possible to leap from the apothecary window onto the gunwale of the neighbouring vessel, a square rigged Indiaman that had recently been unloaded and was awaiting repairs. Perhaps that had been Aberlady's intention, though how he thought he might have made such a leap on that particular night was a mystery, for the ebbing tide had swung the ships apart, and there was a gap of some twenty-five feet between the two. The *Blood* rode high in the water, her ancient ballast hardly enough to keep her upright, and the distance between the apothecary window and the waters below was considerable. The body of John Aberlady, rimmed with crimson from a gash that seeped at his temple, lay like refuse beside the ship's hull, his limbs awry, his neck twisted and his mouth slack. There is no dignity in death, no matter what anyone says.

I bent down and touched my fingers to his head. I felt something hard – the shards of his skull – and beneath this something pulpy and wet. The angle of his head made it clear that his neck had broken. His face was pale, his eyes, now closed, were ringed with dark skin. He had always been slim, but I could see clearly that he was now quite wasted, his flesh fallen away to almost nothing, his cheekbones sharp as blades in his face. If only his letter had not been delayed, might things have turned out differently? Will put his hand on my shoulder.

'What drove him to do such a thing?' I whispered.

I was looking down at Aberlady as I spoke. He was without a coat, his right sleeve undone and loose at the wrist. It bore a crimson taint, I could see that much even in the feeble glow from my lantern, though the Thames had washed most of it away, leaching the red stain pink. The wet cotton clung to his flesh like a second skin. I peeled it back. On the outside of his upper arm was a terrible wound, red and suppurating. I felt someone standing beside us and I looked up. Dr Sackville's face betrayed nothing as he stared down at the apothecary's corpse.

'Did anyone see him jump?' I said.

Dr Sackville nodded. 'I saw him,' he said. 'He must have struck his head on something as he entered the water for he was alive when he leaped. That barge, perhaps? I cannot think what.' For a moment he closed his eyes as if in prayer. Then, 'The fellow had not been himself for some time, Mr Flockhart. I was quite aware of that. But to take his own life?'

'Perhaps he did not intend such a thing at all,' said Will.

'You think he thought to swim ashore?' said Dr Sackville, his voice rising angrily. 'Or that he expected to leap such a distance? Or perhaps you think he fell whilst taking the air?'

'I have no idea, sir,' said Will.

'How was it that you came to see him jump?' I said.

'He returned from wherever he had been this past week a couple of hours ago. I had to rebuke the fellow for his unauthorised absence – Dr Birdwhistle was determined to tell the governors. They would not stand for it, you know, and we had been thrown onto our resources to manage without him—'

'And how did he seem?'

'Agitated. Almost wild.'

'How did he respond to your reprimand?'

'He told me to go to Hell. Then he laughed, and said "But what am I thinking? For I am already there and you are the Devil come to gloat upon my sins."'

'And then?'

'Then he slammed the apothecary door in my face, and locked it.'

'And he was alone in there?'

'Well that's the thing of it. I *thought* he was alone when he went in there – apart from Pestle Jenny, of course – and yet he was not, he couldn't have been, for a few moments later I heard two voices. Raised voices. I heard them quite distinctly.'

'It was not Aberlady and Pestle Jenny?'

'Aberlady was one of them, the other . . . I have no idea who it was. But it certainly wasn't his grinding boy.'

'Might this other person have already been in there?'

'It's quite possible.'

'Is there another way in to the apothecary?'

'No.'

'What were they saying?'

'They were arguing. There was no doubt about it, for I could hear quite clearly. "It's no use. You *must* do it," said the other person.'

'What type of voice was it?' I said.

'A low whining voice, tearful and cringing.'

'It was a man's voice?'

'Oh yes. I can say that for certain.'

'Then what happened?'

'Then I heard the sound of footsteps pacing back and forth. I heard a second voice. It was Aberlady—'

'Are you certain?'

'Quite certain. "I must get rid of it," he said. There was a pause, and more footsteps, and then the first wretched voice said, "I cannot". There was some muttering, and the sound of glass jars being moved. I heard Aberlady cry out, "Do it! Do it now!" There was a whimpering sound, and then a scream—'

Dr Sackville dabbed at his lips with his handkerchief. 'I shouted his name and battered on the door, but it seemed to make him more agitated, and I heard him shout "They're here! Oh God!" And then there was the other wretched voice crying out, "It's too late! Too late!" I heard the Pestle girl scream, and the sound of scuffling, and breaking glass, and then all at once the key rattled in the lock, and the girl flung open the door and burst out of the apothecary like a rabbit out of a trap. She slipped between my legs and vanished up the stairs onto the deck. I rushed inside and was just in time to see John Aberlady spring out of the window.'

'And when you entered the apothecary was anyone else in there?'

'No one. I have no idea who the other person was, or where he went. I assume he has jumped into the river, too. Perhaps Aberlady hoped to save him. There's no sign of the body, though as it's so dark it may not be found until daylight. Besides, there are currents amongst the ships, especially when the tide is on the ebb, and there is every chance that the poor fellow's corpse has been sucked downriver. But he *will* surface. Everyone does, in the end.'

He turned slowly, his face lost in shadow, to watch two orderlies carry the tarpaulin-shrouded body of John Aberlady towards the mortuary. 'Mr Flockhart,' he said. 'It seems the *Blood* has a vacancy.'

Confession of Jenny Quickly
on arriving at Siren House

❦

My name is Jenny Quickly. I don't know how old I am though I believe my age to be twelve years. I've never had a birthday, but I was told the Queen got married as I was born and the excitement of it brought me into the world. My mother worked on Spyglass Lane, in one of the houses there. One of the better houses, so I were told, though I don't know what makes for better or for worse as I've not seen any but the one I worked in and it never seemed any good to me. My mother was one of the girls. I don't know which for they all looked after me – which is to say all of them kicked me up and down the stairs and clipped my ear for me when I didn't answer them fast enough. I got no name but Jenny, though they called me Quickly on account of the fact that they was always shouting it at me when they wanted me to do something.

I got no memory of being a baby, or even of being a child, though Mr Aberlady says I still am a child, so I *should* know what it's like. If that's the truth then I don't think much of being a child, neither.

I've always done the same things for as long as I can remember – changing beds and kindling fires and pulling corset strings tight. I heard what went on in those rooms and I knew it was coming to me, though I didn't see why it should.

They used to send me up to the Seaman's Dispensary for raspberry leaf and pennyroyal, or valerian for the cramps. Or sometimes for mercury when things was bad. Mr Aberlady used to give me liquorice root to chew. Like a twig it was and you chewed it and chewed it. It lasted for ages and I kept it in my apron pocket. I used to ask about the medicines – all those jars and bottles and drawers, and powders and coloured liquids. Mr Aberlady told me what they were for. He used to let me measure stuff on the scales when Dr Proudlove was out, for Dr Proudlove liked things done proper, and he wouldn't have a street urchin touching his precious things. Sometimes Mr Aberlady let me grind the powders with his pestle and mortar. I remember those times when I went to the dispensary as the best days of my life. The others used to chase me away, but not Mr Aberlady.

Back at the house it was mostly scolding and slapping and cleaning. Then one day a gentleman asks if he might have me. He offered me a silver sixpence and said I might have it for my very own if I would just do as he asked. And one of my mothers said he might certainly have me, if the price was high enough, and that I might have the sixpence but that she'd keep the rest. She told him it was no more than what I'd been expecting all my life and that I was most excited to have such a fine gentleman as my first and it was high time I earned my keep.

But I wasn't excited at all and I didn't want one single bit of it. I knew what those gentlemen did in those rooms upstairs and I'd dabbed enough of my mothers' bruises with witch hazel and put powder over their pox sores to know what sort of a life I would be getting into if I stayed. And so I ran away. I ran to the apothecary on board the *Blood* where I knew I would find Mr Aberlady. Mr Aberlady said I should go to Siren House first, and so here I am.

Note on Jenny Quickly on leaving Siren House.

I have decided to take on Jenny Quickly as a grinding boy – to help in the apothecary on board the *Blood*. Should she prove to be adept, and biddable, I will train her as my apprentice, with a view to her sitting the licentiate examinations at Apothecaries' Hall. Might a woman manage the training required to practise medicine? Proudlove and I think so. Antrobus and Cole think not. Three guineas rest upon the outcome.

Chapter Six

On board, the apothecary was in disarray. On the floor beside the open window was a set of keys. I snatched them up and put them into my pocket. The night air that drifted in was damp and sulphurous, and I shivered as it tickled my neck like the trace of a ghostly finger. Instinctively, I moved closer to the stove. Its door was open, though the coals were dying, and their glow was pitiful. On the hearth was a teapot – the white, round-bellied style Aberlady favoured. He avoided spirits, I knew, preferring instead to get tea directly from one of the warehouses near the East London docks. Beside the teapot lay the poker and a bloody rag, a splash of red matter streaking the boards beside it.

'D'you notice the smell?' I whispered.

Will wrinkled his nose. 'Something horrible. Something scorched. But not the stove; not coal or wood or paper.'

'Skin,' I said. 'Burning flesh. That's what it is.' I picked up the poker from the hearth and wiped its tip on my handkerchief. It came away red. 'Blood,' I said. I looked around the apothecary. On the table, a single lantern burned dimly. About it broken glass glittered in angry shards. There was more of the stuff on the floor.

'Was he looking for something?' said Will. 'What's this all over the bench and the floor—?'

I crouched down, and touched the mixture of black powder and crushed dried leaves with my fingertips. 'Coconut shell charcoal,' I said. I picked up a broken jar. 'Bayberry. And this other one here's black mustard seed.'

'And their uses? Is there some logic to this—?'

'In controlled quantities, the mustard seeds are used as a liniment, for chest infections, headache, cholera or typhus,' I said. 'In larger amounts – say three drachms mixed with warm water – it serves as an emetic.'

'The bayberry?'

'Also an emetic. Or a throat gargle—'

'Chest infections or cholera?' said Will. 'Throat gargling? It hardly seems likely, does it? What of the charcoal? What does that signify?'

'These remedies are all used against poisoning – the first to encourage vomiting, the charcoal to absorb the toxin before it enters the blood. Given what I know of his interests it's not impossible that Aberlady poisoned himself by mistake. Dr Bain at St Saviour's regularly tested poisons on himself – many doctors do.'

'But to undertake such experiments on his own?'

I shook my head. 'It's unlikely. What's *more* likely is that John Aberlady became convinced that he'd been poisoned, and was endeavouring to purge himself of it before it was too late.'

'Can you identify what it was?'

'Something that made his fears become bigger and more terrifying. Ergot, perhaps, or henbane. Possibly belladonna. Or even lily of the valley. He clearly had moments of lucidity – thus the herbs to make him vomit the poison up, the charcoal to absorb it. We might also ask how the stuff entered his system. The teapot seems the most likely source.'

Will put his hand to the belly of the pot. 'Stone cold,' he said. He peered inside. 'The dregs. Does anyone drink the dregs from a pot of cold tea?'

'No,' I said, perplexed.

'Are you *sure* he was poisoned?'

'He must have been. There's no other explanation.'

'Might it have been the effects of opium, Jem?'

'But opium induces languor, sleepiness. It does not turn men into maniacs.'

'And yet are not the cravings for the stuff a torture of a particularly violent kind?'

'Yes.' I sighed. 'The body as well as the mind are quite torn apart. There's every chance that opium consumption added to his sense of distraction, his derangement. But mania, of any kind, is not what one expects from an opium eater, even when they are in the depths of their suffering. Muscle cramps, shivering, self-pity, waking nightmares, yes. But this? I don't think so. Besides,' I pointed to the bottle of laudanum on the shelf. 'There's plenty of the stuff up there if he wanted it.'

'Perhaps *that's* poisoned, and he did take some.'

'And he put it back on the top shelf afterwards? I doubt it. Besides, laudanum is used by physicians for everything from toothache to cholera. If you took the stuff away they would have very little else in their bag. If the poisoner put his lethal drops into the *Blood*'s own laudanum bottle he would risk killing the entire ship. No, Will, this is something else entirely.'

I turned about, imagining my friend entering the apothecary, struggling to hold onto his final unclouded thoughts as the poison gripped his mind and body. Hallucinations would have assailed him, strange fancies and distorted notions of what was real and what was not. And yet there would be physical symptoms too: dizziness, cramping, pain in the abdomen. 'And so, in his agony and confusion he dropped the remedies he thought he needed,' I said. 'He became overwhelmed. And then when Dr Sackville battered on the door his disordered mind convinced him that his persecutors had arrived, and in his panic, he leaped from the window.'

'Who were his persecutors?'

'That we must find out.'

'And why did the poker have a bloody tip?'

'Think, Will! The smell of burning flesh, the fresh wound on the arm of the corpse—'

'What!' Will's face was ashen, his eyes wide with horror. 'Who amongst us would deliberately brand himself, or cauterise his own flesh?'

'Anyone, if they were out of their mind with fear and delirium. It is *why* that is the more pertinent question.'

'What of the man Aberlady was with? I suppose we must ask Pestle Jenny—'

I clicked my tongue. 'He wasn't *with* anyone,' I said. 'He was talking to himself. I'm surprised Dr Sackville did not realise – especially when it turned out that there was no one here but Aberlady.' I stared out of the window for a moment, and then with a shiver pulled it closed. The shadows seemed to rear and jump around me, my own head buzzing with the horror at what we had stumbled upon, so that I was half-tempted to open the window again, despite the damp stink of the river. 'I must see Aberlady's rooms – he has quarters downstairs. We must find out what happened. He was murdered, Will—'

'Murdered!' The voice came from behind us. 'But why, and by whom?'

Neither of us had heard anyone enter, and when we turned around the door was still closed.

'Forgive me, gentlemen—' A man stepped forward out of the shadows. I could only conclude that he had been there, listening in silence, since we first came in. The reason we had not seen him was because he was dressed in a long black travelling cape, buttoned to the neck, with the collar turned up against the cold and foggy night. His face, too, was as black as the shadows from which he had emerged. 'My name is Erasmus Proudlove – I am one of the surgeons here.'

I felt my cheeks colour at our carelessness. We should have checked we were alone before we said anything to one another. 'Really, sir?' I said sharply. 'No one here mentioned you.'

His lip curled. 'No doubt they forgot. They are adept at forgetting me – when it suits them, of course. And yet I've been away for ten days so perhaps there lies their excuse on this occasion. And yet, it is *you*, I think, who are the real mystery. *I* am a man with every right to be here, but who are you, and why are you creeping about Aberlady's apothecary in the night time?'

I made our introductions. 'I was a friend of John Aberlady's,' I added. 'And I have just been hired by Dr Sackville to be acting apothecary.'

'A friend, you say? Aberlady made no mention of you.'

'Dr Proudlove,' said Will, with some impatience. 'If you

are on this ship then how can it be that you didn't know that Aberlady is dead? The place has been in uproar—'

'I came on board not five minutes ago via the larboard steps – men use them who are coming aboard from clippers and merchantmen out on the water. I came straight through to the apothecary. A moment later you and your companion entered. I waited to see what you were about. I heard your conversation – eavesdropping is often the only way I am included in the goings on aboard this ship. And now here we are. Are you satisfied?'

For a moment there was a silence between us. I could see that his coat was moist from the fog and the river, and he had a travelling bag at his feet. 'What made you come to the apothecary?'

'I wanted to show Aberlady what I'd found.' He held up a small glass bottle. Inside were a pair of houseflies, five mosquitoes and a bluebottle. 'They're all from a single room at Mill Pond Lane over in Rotherhithe,' he said. 'There's an outbreak of the ague over there, a number of cases all in the same dwelling. I am unconvinced by the prevailing notion that the ague is caused by bad air.' He shrugged. 'Wouldn't London be crippled by malaria if that was the case? And yet it isn't. Instead we find the disease only in low places – marshy stagnant waters. During the summer mostly, though it's been unseasonably warm throughout the autumn and as a result the ague hasn't abated. Stagnant waters breathe vapours, it's true, but they also breed insects such as these.'

'I've always doubted the capacity of bad air to cause the diseases men blame upon it,' I said. 'The same applies to miasma. The microscope—'

'Precisely,' said Dr Proudlove. 'You've compared air

and water?'

'I have,' I said.

'Gentlemen,' said Will. 'A man has just died—'

'A man who would be fascinated to hear my conclusions,' said Dr Proudlove.

'Indeed,' I said. 'To the naked eye air and water both appear colourless – or almost so. Yet under the microscope water contains all manner of tiny creatures and putrescent matter whilst air contains nothing perceivably alive.'

'Air is one part carbonic acid, seventy-eight parts nitrogen and twenty-one parts oxygen,' said Dr Proudlove. 'No part of it is made up of anything that might conceivably cause malaria, cholera, typhus, or any of the diseases generally attributed to it.'

'My thoughts exactly,' I said. Dr Proudlove and I smiled at one another.

'And the murder?' said Will. 'What of that?'

'What microscope do you have?' said Dr Proudlove.

'Lintz and Munn,' I replied.

'A beauty!' he said. 'I have a von Krause. All the way from Vienna.'

'So what *does* cause the ague,' interrupted Will. 'If we *must* continue this fascinating discussion before we can return to the subject of a man's death.' He looked at Dr Proudlove's bottle. 'Flies?'

'I believe it's a plausible theory,' he said. 'Mosquitoes are the most likely as they live in all areas where the ague is found – even Gibraltar, a place not known for its pestilent vapours. Their anatomy is designed to pierce flesh quickly and with precision, to draw blood. And if they might suck blood *out*, might they not also inject some sort of matter *in*? Aberlady was convinced too. This last week I've been in

Liverpool. There's a fellow there, recently returned from Panama, who thinks the same way.'

'And you have just returned to London?' said Will.

'I journeyed to Rotherhithe directly. It's notoriously damp and marshy, especially in the region bounded by the Halfpenny Hatch and Mill Pond Lane, and I'd left some malarial patients there – there seemed little point in bringing them aboard as I had left medicine enough where they were. While I was away I charged them to catch all pests, whether crawling or airborne, that inhabited the room where they lived. They gave me these.' He held up the bottle. 'Mosquitoes, amongst other things. The colder weather makes the creatures sluggish and they were able to trap them quite easily.' He put the bottle back into his pocket. 'And that's why I came to the apothecary – to discuss the matter with Aberlady, whom you now tell me is dead.'

'He jumped from the window,' I said, 'whilst in the grip of some delirium. Poisoned – as you heard. Did you see him before you left for Liverpool?'

'Yes,' said Dr Proudlove.

'How did he seem?'

Dr Proudlove shrugged. His eyes darted to the mess on the table, the open door of the stove and the bloody rag in the hearth. 'Well enough,' he said.

'Soon after you left, John Aberlady disappeared. Perhaps you have some idea where he went?'

'No,' said Dr Proudlove.

'And he was not with you?'

'He was not.'

'Dr Cole seemed to think he might have been in an opium den,' I said. 'I knew he was fatally drawn to the laudanum bottle. Was he in the habit of smoking the stuff too?'

'I don't know.'

'And yet you say you *did* know him?' said Will.

'Of course! But opium eating is not a habit one always admits to one's friends.'

I nodded. It was true. The opium fiend was a notoriously devious and shame-filled individual. Many of them conducted their lives perfectly normally, and yet the truth was that they could not remain themselves without daily recourse to the black drop.

'Then how did Dr Cole and Dr Antrobus know of it?' said Will. 'Were *they* his friends?'

'Not especially.'

'Did Aberlady have a tattoo on his arm?' I said.

'A tattoo?' Dr Proudlove looked taken aback. And then, to my surprise, his face seemed to close. It was as though he had stepped back within himself, withdrawing from us, and from the scene before him.

'You think such things are the preserve of those on the edges of society?' said Will.

'Of convicts, sailors and soldiers, yes,' he said. 'And we see plenty of them here, I can assure you. But not on us, Mr Quartermain.'

'*Us?*'

'I meant not on medical men.'

'A moment ago you implied that you were a man disdained by the doctors on board the *Blood*,' said Will. 'And yet now you are happy to claim their brotherhood? I can't help but wonder what lengths a man might go to in order to feel truly a part of this ship.'

'He would not poison his friend, sir, that I *can* tell you,' replied Dr Proudlove. 'Your Mr Quartermain here has a most suspicious mind, Mr Flockhart. One might think that his acquaintance with *you* would have taught him not to judge a man by the colour of his skin.'

'A man is dead, Dr Proudlove,' I said softly. 'I'm afraid all of those on board are to be regarded with suspicion.' I leaned towards him. 'Something is going on here,' I whispered. 'And we will find out what it is, whether you help us or not.'

We looked at one another, he staring at my red face, and me staring at his dark one, both of us wondering what truths might lie beneath. He licked his lips. 'I cannot help you,' he said. 'Aberlady was my friend, though I can't say what misguided ways he had strayed into recently.'

'Misguided ways?' I said.

Dr Proudlove picked up his travelling bag. 'I can say no more. Not here. Not now.'

'Then when?' I said.

'Tomorrow. You will undertake Aberlady's post-mortem?'

'I will. First thing in the morning.'

'Then I shall see you in the mortuary at six bells.'

'What time is that?' said Will.

'Seven o'clock,' said Dr Proudlove.

'Very well,' I said, though it was earlier than I had intended and I feared a long day was in store for us. 'Six bells it is.'

'You think you can trust him?' said Will, as Dr Proudlove vanished from the apothecary. 'A man shows you a bottle of flies, admires your choice of microscope, and you're ready to believe what he tells you?'

'He's an outsider, Will. On this ship, that makes him our ally.'

'Does it? I'm not so sure. We must be vigilant, Jem. This

place isn't like St Saviour's – or even Angel Meadow, where we could at least be certain who our friends were, even if we were not sure of our enemy. On the *Blood* we are amongst strangers. And one of them, at least, is a murderer.'

He was right, I knew, and yet there was something about Dr Proudlove that I liked, something that made me warm to the man, and I was not ready to lump him with the others just yet.

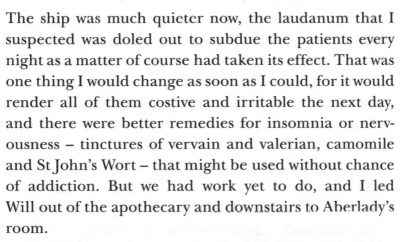

The ship was much quieter now, the laudanum that I suspected was doled out to subdue the patients every night as a matter of course had taken its effect. That was one thing I would change as soon as I could, for it would render all of them costive and irritable the next day, and there were better remedies for insomnia or nervousness – tinctures of vervain and valerian, camomile and St John's Wort – that might be used without chance of addiction. But we had work yet to do, and I led Will out of the apothecary and downstairs to Aberlady's room.

The door was open, as if Aberlady himself had just burst out. I held up my lantern as we went inside. The place was a similar size to the apothecary – spacious enough, but rendered oppressive by the low ceiling, which was little higher than our heads. There was a desk, more books, and in the corner an iron bedstead. Those were the only unremarkable things in a bedroom that was quite unlike any I had ever seen, for John Aberlady slept in what might only be described as an anatomy museum. Every available surface was covered with jars and bottles, their glass faces glittering in the lantern light, the pale remains within floating white and soft-looking, as if fashioned from bits of uncooked dough. I was used to anatomy museums; any medical man of any calibre would have a collection of his own – tumours he had excised, or grotesquely diseased organs, curiosities he had found, such as a mouse with no eyes, or a lizard with two tails. What was distinctive about John Aberlady's collection was the number of creatures he had collected that lived in or on the human body. Lice, worms, leeches, ticks – all of them pickled and bottled and labelled. Alongside were jars containing those parts of the body that might be affected: a liver blighted by flukes, a section of intestine containing a tangle of tapeworm, a head whose grey water-logged skin bore the moist sores of the yaws sufferer.

Beside them stood a row of glass tanks: one whirred and chafed with locusts, another contained a plant with large rubbery leaves dotted with tiny jewel-like frogs, a third contained Aberlady's red, black and yellow striped snake. It was a poisonous snake, a viper of some kind, though smaller than one with similar markings that I had seen in Aberlady's possession some years earlier. Perhaps that first one had died and he had obtained another. I heard Will groan.

'Oh God,' he said, looking at the anatomy collection. 'Not more of these bottled *things*. And what's *that*?'

He pointed to the corner of the room, where another glass tank, some four feet high and five feet long, stood on a low table against the wall. Inside it was the branch of a tree, and looped around that the smooth muscular coils of a gigantic snake. It was a python, the one Dr Sackville had mentioned as being Aberlady's favourite, the one whose coils he had oiled lovingly, on deck beneath the rare London sun. Maximus, Aberlady had named it, and the smaller one was Minimus. I wondered whether it was dead. After all, Aberlady had been missing for over a week and there was every chance the thing had not been fed. Perhaps pythons were used to fasting. I had no idea. Perhaps the first thing Aberlady had done on his return was come to see his beloved snake. I saw a slight movement as the light from my lantern disturbed the creature – the gleam and flutter of a reptilian eye, and the shining flick of a black tongue.

Beside the snake's home was another tank, inside which was a mass of fur. Rats. Dead by the looks of things, though I could see one or two of them moving sluggishly. Breakfast, lunch and dinner for the snake, no doubt. I raised my lantern. The place looked ordered, rational, the way I might expect from a man of science like John Aberlady. But something was wrong.

'Why are the rats dead?' I said.

'Have they starved, without Aberlady here to look after them?'

'They would have turned on each other long before they starved to death,' I said.

'So?'

The room was warm – the stove lit and belching out a deal of heat, though most of it had escaped into the night air through the open door. 'And who lit the stove?'

Will shrugged. 'Aberlady? Pestle Jenny?'

I went over to the stove. It was rounded, with a flat top upon which Aberlady was in the habit of standing a kettle so that he might have water for tea at all times. His teapot stood on a trivet in the hearth. I bent to touch it, to see whether it was warm, but like the one in the apothecary it was stone cold. As I crouched down, my face drew near to the stove top, and I caught a whiff of something. It was a familiar smell, acrid and astringent, but not unpleasant. I felt my head grow light, my lips start to tingle. I cried out and lurched away, my hand over my mouth. 'Cover your mouth and nose,' I snapped. 'Quickly.'

'What is it?'

I held my breath as I snatched up the hearth brush and shovel, and swept up the scattering of crushed seeds that were smouldering on the stove. 'Henbane,' I said from behind my handkerchief. 'Most of it has gone, drifting out of the open door, but not before it killed the rats and turned Aberlady's wits—'

'But if he breathed the poison in, taking an emetic would be useless,' said Will.

'Perhaps he didn't realise *how* he'd been poisoned, but was only aware that he *had* been. If we'd been much later all the evidence would have burned away and these seeds would look like nothing more than coal dust. Had the poison been administered via the teapot – which was my first assumption, then even the stupidest of policemen would surely have worked it out before long.'

I tipped the cooled seeds onto a sheet of paper torn from my notebook, folded them up, and slipped them into my satchel. The discovery had shocked me. Not only was there no doubt at all that Aberlady had been murdered, but it was clear that his murderer was a singular opponent.

Chapter Seven

⁂

When I came downstairs in the morning Gabriel was already up. Pestle Jenny was still asleep, curled in a nest of blankets in front of the hearth. I told Gabriel to look after the girl – give her work and food – the two of them would run the place alone that day, and perhaps for the next week, though what I would do with her in the long term I had no idea.

Gabriel looked pleased. 'Shall I get her to talk?'

'If she wants to talk she will,' I said. 'Just be kind. Give her tasks to distract her. Make her feel welcome – and let her grind.'

Will and I ate a hasty breakfast – bread and butter with some cured ham I had bought back from Sorley's the night before, washed down with a cup of coffee. I didn't want to linger about the apothecary – Mrs Speedicut had already gone, and I was sure that news of last night's tragedy would already have reached the ears of Dr Graves. Dr Proudlove had promised to meet me at the mortuary at seven, and I wanted to be sure that he and I were not troubled by anyone else from the *Blood*.

'Did you sleep?' said Will, as we walked towards the river. The sun was not yet up, though the sky to the east bore a savage gash of scarlet. Last night's fog had vanished, and the dilapidated thoroughfare was lit by a bloody first light. Already there were people everywhere.

'Yes,' I lied. He knew better than to ask me more, and so we walked together in silence, neither of us looking forward to what awaited us that morning. 'You don't have to come,' I said after a while. 'If you wished to go up to Tulip's Basin—'

'I'll go there later,' he replied. He put his arm through mine.

The mortuary was illuminated by a panel of windows set high in the wall. The place was in a damp and chilly basement and the window looked out at ground level onto the yard at the back of the building. It was too early for good light – not that anyone could rely on such a thing in London, for even at midday the city might be as dark as evening – and against the walls lamps burned. The wicks of two of them needed trimming, and sooty wraiths of smouldering whale oil trailed from them like narrow strips of black crêpe. The place stank of the sewers, of stale water and putrefaction. I would stink of it too before the morning was done. I had spent enough time at St Saviour's dissecting rooms to know.

The mortuary attendant, Toad, greeted us at the door. The body of the girl had been taken away. Her organs had been carried off by the students to be preserved in spirits and added to their collections; what remained had been loaded onto Dr Graves's corpse wagon and trundled off to St Saviour's across the river. Now, there was only Aberlady down there, alone upon the slab.

'Thank gawd you've arrived, sir,' said Toad. 'The other doctor's already here—'

'Dr Proudlove?' I said, peeling off my top coat. 'Good—'

'Oh no, sir,' said Toad. 'Not *'im*.'

I suppose I had half-expected it. After all, the man was as omnipresent as a blowfly when it came to a dead body, and I had a feeling he had an arrangement with Toad to make sure he was informed before anyone else when a body found its way onto the slab. Dr Graves grinned at me as I entered, and lifted his boning knife by way of a greeting.

'I didn't see your corpse wagon, sir,' I said.

'I came straight from home,' he replied. 'But I have sent for the wagon, you may be sure of that.' He had evidently just breakfasted, as the smell of fried whitebait hung on the air. 'Well, Flockhart,' he said, wiping his salty lips and fingers on Aberlady's winding sheet. 'Here we are again, eh? And Mr Quartermain too. Well, well. Let us hope we're not disturbed by that rabble from the *Blood* this morning.' He flourished his knife as if he were about to carve the Sunday roast. 'Shall we?'

'I was expecting Dr Proudlove,' I said. It was already seven o'clock – 'six bells', in the nautical parlance used on board the *Blood* – he should have been there. 'Perhaps we might wait a moment?'

'Proudlove?' Dr Graves frowned, and lowered his knife. 'I'll not work with *him*.'

'Why ever not, sir?' I said.

'He has no place in this profession,' said Dr Graves. 'A negro? Good God, sir! We will be training up women next. I can't imagine what university allowed him in.'

'I believe it was Glasgow University, sir,' said Will. 'I saw his medical certificate upon the apothecary wall at the *Blood*—'

'Oh, well, there you are then,' scoffed Dr Graves. 'That's the Scots for you! They'll take anyone!'

'And yet I believe they offer the best medical training in the world,' said Will. 'And I understand Dr Proudlove received the class medal. So, he will surely be more than adequately equipped to anatomise the corpse of his friend, whether you like the colour of his skin or not.'

'I can hardly believe he was granted a place,' muttered Dr Graves. He was speaking to me, not to Will, as if by addressing a fellow medical man he was addressing a sympathiser. 'And then they give him a position on board the *Blood*! Mind you, the place is not what it was, anyone can see that. No doubt they were sore pressed to find a man willing to work there for nothing. It is an honorarium, of course. And yet the city is full of medical men. Any one of them would give his right hand for a hospital position—'

'Has the place changed that much, sir?' I said. 'I remember it when I was a child. Its reputation was no worse than ours at St Saviour's, and it is admirably placed for those who arrive in the city afflicted with the diseases of the tropics. Dr Sackville and Dr Rennie must surely have a great deal of expertise between them—'

'Oh, *those* two, certainly,' said Dr Graves. 'Though no one quite understands why they are still there. Rennie is too old to be of use to anyone, and Sackville, well, surely he hardly needs the place. His private practice is very lucrative indeed. But they were instrumental in setting up the *Blood* in the first place, and are perhaps loyal to it for sentimental reasons. It has trained a good many men in its time. Those who plan to work in the colonies often walk the wards there. But it is not what it was. And taking on a black man – I can only say how glad I am that such experiments have not found their way up to St Saviour's.'

'You think it an experiment, sir?' said Will.

'What else can it be?'

'Perhaps it is an example of the best man for the job actually getting the job.'

I felt my irritation rising. 'Perhaps one day it will be the best woman who gets the job,' I said.

'A woman?' Dr Graves laughed. 'Ha ha! Ah, Flockhart, you are funny. And yet, might I remind you that we are a serious profession, sir! Nine times out of ten who "gets the job" is the person who knows the surgeon, or who has married his daughter, or who has enough money to pay for the acquaintanceship.' He shook his head. 'It is the same everywhere. Mostly it is a perfectly sound arrangement, though occasionally, I admit, there are mishaps. Look at that idiot Monro they appointed to teach anatomy at Edinburgh!' He shook his head. 'His father and grandfather were geniuses. But he was a buffoon.'

'And those without money or connections?' said Will. 'What do they do?'

'They must go abroad. Otherwise there's only the special hospitals – eyes, ears, diseases of women or children – and none of those allow a man to make a name for himself. If a man has no money, it is only patronage that will get him on. Or an exceptional discovery and I'm afraid that since Harvey published his work on the circulation of the blood there's not much left of great significance to be found.'

97

'Surely not, sir,' I said. 'There is everything left to discover. The workings of the body are still shrouded in mystery.'

'And yet its general *mechanics* are not—'

Will pulled out his watch. 'I wonder where he is?'

'You see?' said Dr Graves. 'The fellow cannot even observe the necessary punctuality. They are a notoriously lazy and indolent race.'

I pulled on an old overcoat. It was common for anatomists to cover their clothes when in the mortuary, though Dr Graves never bothered with such niceties, and the mortuary's reek of death and drains followed him everywhere. I had nothing for Will to wear, though I knew he would spend most of his time standing in the door like a wraith, unsure whether to faint, or to lurch up the steps onto the riverside.

'I suppose he can join us when he comes,' I said. I saw Will staring at Aberlady's corpse; his face was as white as wax and we had not even made the first incision. 'Perhaps you might step outside, Will. To see whether Dr Proudlove is coming,' I said.

'Before we start, Flockhart,' said Dr Graves as Will vanished up the steps to the dockside. 'The mortuary attendant has brought something to my attention. Swears he knows nothing about it, of course, and I must say I see no reason to doubt the fellow. Says he was in here all night – he and his son—'

'Young Toad, sir,' supplied the attendant.

'You sleep in the mortuary?' I said.

'Ain't got no place else.' The man jerked a thumb towards the partly open door at the back of the room. I could dimly make out a blanket against the wall, beside it a brimming chamber pot and a cracked stone sink covered in green slime. Water dripped from a pump alongside.

'And Young Toad?'

'Young Toad sleeps there too, sir.'

I eyed the filthy child who stood at his father's side. I had seen him out on the mud of the Thames at low tide, I was certain.

'It seems that Aberlady's body has been violated,' continued Dr Graves in a low voice. 'A most singular and grotesque occurrence.'

I looked down at the body. The orderlies had left him as they found him, fully clothed, though when Dr Graves flung back the shroud it was immediately apparent that the body was not quite as I had last seen it. Aberlady's pockets had been turned out, the linings exposed, the contents – a metal stirring rod, a pipette, a pencil stub and a matchstick – scattered on the slab beside him.

'Did you do this?' I said to the attendant.

'No, sir,' said Toad.

'This man has been here all his life, Flockhart,' said Dr Graves. 'He knows better than to tamper with a body.'

'He knows precisely how to tamper with a body,' I replied. 'Especially if there might be a shilling in it. Empty your pockets, man.'

'It were only a shillin', sir,' the man whined. 'This dead feller ain't got much use for it.'

'It's stealing.'

'Oh, no, sir! It's no more than my due. They got to pay the wherry man, ain't they? Perk o' the job, rootin' in the pockets o' the dead.' He leered up at me, his cracked teeth as streaked and brown as the tiles on a privy floor.

'So you lied when I asked you whether you had done this?' said Dr Graves, indicating the strewn pocket contents.

'No, sir.'

I put a hand to my head. 'You *did* look in this dead man's pockets, but you *did not* leave the contents spread out like this?'

'That's right, sir. When *I* does it you can't tell.' He looked sulky. 'No use doin' it and makin' a mess so you get accused o' stealin'. *Someone else* looked in 'is pockets after I done put it all away again, nice an' tidy like.'

'And did you find anything, apart from a shilling?'

'Not much, sir.'

'Come along, man. I'll give you half a crown for it, whatever it was, and then that will be an end to it.' I held out a coin.

The fellow stared at it for a moment, then thrust a filthy hand into the inside pocket of his overcoat. He opened his fist, to reveal a small circular object. It was a silver sixpence, new and shining like a star. And yet it was like no sixpence I had ever seen. On one side was the wreath and crown, and the date, 1850. On the other the Queen's head had been smoothed away, and in its place another picture had been drawn, hammered into the metal with the point of a sharp instrument. I held it close to my eye. What was it? I could make out the four rounded petals of the forget-me-not – a typical motif for a love token – and behind it a spray of fine, delicate leaves.

'This belonged to Aberlady?' I murmured.

'It didn't belong to no *lady*,' said the man. 'That *lady* didn't 'ave no pockets.'

'She did 'ave a pocket,' piped up Young Toad. His eyes,

100

fixed upon his father's half crown, gleamed like little black beetles. '*I* found 'er pocket, though no one else did. *I* found a thing in it too. Jus' like that!'

'The dead girl?' I said. I cursed myself for not checking the girl's clothes when we found her. And yet she had been wearing only a chemise. How was I to know that women's underclothes contained pockets? 'What thing?' I held out another half crown. 'Show me.'

The boy rummaged amongst his rags, and brought out a silver sixpence, wreath and crown on one side, forget-me-not and leaves on the other. Both tokens had a small hole punched in the top so that a chain might be threaded through.

'You took this from the girl that was here yesterday?'

'Yessir.'

'She must o' been a thief,' muttered Toad senior. 'Only thief-women 'ave pockets in their petticoats.'

'Never mind that,' said Dr Graves. 'There's a more pressing matter at hand – far more pressing and far *worse* than shillings and trinkets. Look there, sir!' He pointed to Aberlady's shirt sleeve. The fabric was ripped, or rather, when I looked more closely I could see it had been slit, cleanly, so that it could be flapped up to reveal the flesh of his upper arm.

The dead don't bleed, not like the living, and what I saw beneath made me catch my breath, for in the centre of the corpse's upper arm a disk of flesh, some four inches in diameter, had been cleanly excised: cut out and peeled away. The red musculature below the skin was exposed, a wet crimson circle against the surrounding white flesh. It was the arm that I had looked at when Aberlady had been dragged from the water. The part that had been sliced away was the same area of skin that Aberlady himself had sought to burn off with the tip of a red-hot poker.

'You haven't been out of here since this body was brought in last night, Toad?' I said.

'No, sir.'

'Did you sleep? Were you drunk?' I leaned forward and sniffed at the man. He stank of sweat and urine, of dirt and mildew and drains, but he did not smell of beer – at least, not much.

'Only a ha'penny bottle, sir. Small beer, from the White Anchor up on Spyglass Lane. Young Toad 'ere went for it.'

'So you could have fallen asleep?'

'I 'as to sleep, sir. But I weren't drunk.'

'And you heard and saw nothing?'

'No, sir.'

'And what about you?' I was speaking to Young Toad now. The lad was silent, turning his half-crown around and around between his fingers, his gaze fixed upon its glittering surface. His face was pinched and crafty, his beady eyes shifting. He glanced first at the door, then at the slab; from Dr Graves, to me, and then back to Aberlady, lying dead and cold between us. I saw how afraid he was, and I crouched down and put my hand on his, stopping their restless distracted motion.

'Well, boy?' I said. 'Did you hear anything? Did you see anything?' From somewhere far away came the slow *plop . . . plop . . . plop . . .* of water.

'Oh, I heard 'im, all right, sir.' Young Toad's face was green and sickly, his voice a whisper, as if he feared the dead might rise up there and then to gainsay him. 'Saw 'im too, though I pretended I were asleep.'

'Who?' I said. 'Who did you see?'

'A man.'

'Did you know him? What did he look like?'

'A tall man. Tall and black as night. All of 'im black, like the Devil—'

At that moment Dr Proudlove entered with Will. 'Am I late?' he said. He pulled out his pocket watch. 'I'm sorry, gentlemen, I had what might have been an urgent case to attend up on Spyglass. Fortunately, it turned out to be nothing. And yet it is only two minutes past seven—'

Behind him, young Toad had shrunk back into the shadows, his gaze fixed on the tall dark figure of Dr Proudlove. His face beneath the streaks of dirt was pale with fear. Before I could put out a hand to stop him he had scampered up the mortuary steps, and disappeared into the noise and bustle of the wakening riverside.

❧❦❧

I thought at first that Dr Graves was going to refuse to work with Dr Proudlove. But it appeared that his love of dissection outweighed his prejudice. He forgot the 'violation' to the flesh of the corpse, and set to work unpacking Aberlady's body with the brisk efficiency for which he was famous.

Dr Proudlove talked about the case that had made him late, a dock worker who had been bitten by a spider that had crawled from a bunch of bananas. The spider had been large and furry, and he had taken it home in his tobacco pouch to show his children. The bite the man sustained had turned red and angry-looking, the skin that surrounded it darkening in colour. Deciding that the creature was murderous rather than a plaything, he had killed it with his shoe.

'I have the creature in my pocket,' said Dr Proudlove. 'And a remarkably large specimen it is too, gentlemen, if a little squashed. Would you like to see it?'

'I would indeed,' I said. I looked at Dr Graves, but he was peeling back Aberlady's scalp and did not answer.

'The fellow sent his wife up to the Seaman's Dispensary, and finding it closed she almost broke the door down with battering upon it, she and her children screaming and crying beneath my windows that their father was at death's door,' Dr Proudlove continued. 'Meanwhile, back at home, the dying man had drunk a bottle of gin to "chase out the poison" as he had heard that whisky had a good effect against snake bites, and so why might not gin serve as a remedy for spiders?

'In fact, these large hairy spiders, tarantulas, as they are called, are less frightening than they look. They might be able to kill a small animal, but aside from some localised pain they are no threat to a fully grown human being. Still, I had to go, as there have been far worse cases – usually with far smaller spiders. The brown recluse, for instance, or the black widow. Both small, both deadly. Fortunately, they only arrive on these shores by accident. We have had a number of them on board the *Blood*, brought to us by seamen or dockers.'

'A fascinating story, sir,' I said.

But Dr Proudlove had clearly hoped to impress Dr Graves with his morning's adventure, for he continually looked in the older man's direction as he talked. But Dr Graves made no response at all. Dr Proudlove sighed. 'Aberlady would have enjoyed the tale,' he said looking down at his friend's corpse. 'He had a large collection of spiders.'

But Dr Graves was not interested in spiders or, indeed, in any conversation at all, and the only remarks he made were with regard to the procedures of anatomy or the state of the cadaver. It did not take three people to conduct a post-mortem, but as Dr Proudlove and I had agreed to do it, and Dr Graves was not a man to turn his back on a corpse, we all stayed, and in fact the job was done in no time at all. We worked together in silence, opening the body, examining the organs one by one, noting down our observations in Dr Graves's post-mortem ledger. I was preoccupied with my thoughts, wondering what I might say to Dr Proudlove afterwards, as he was sure to deny it if I accused him of stealing a circle of tattooed flesh from John Aberlady's corpse. I had seen him perceive the red patch of flayed flesh on his friend's arm as we had removed the shirt. His knuckles had turned white as his grip tightened on the handle of his scalpel, but he had not remarked on it. I wished he had not come. Not because of the colour of his skin, but because I did not want him to be privy to whatever evidence I might find about the body. Will was right, we could trust no one, and if Dr Proudlove had also rummaged through Aberlady's pockets then he was evidently looking for something. And so, I too worked in purse-lipped silence. I felt Dr Proudlove looking at me, at my stony face and downcast eyes, and I was sorry for the conclusion that he was sure to be reaching: that my hostility was caused by the same prejudice about his abilities that he met with every day of his life.

As for Aberlady, how thin and white he looked when he was stripped bare and lying on the mortuary slab. I was looking for something – anything – that might tell us what his body had endured in his final hours, though his corpse, at first, yielded no surprises. There was evidence of opium use in the smell of the lungs and the costive nature of the bowels.

'Dr Cole and Dr Antrobus tell me he was a habitual opium eater,' I said.

'Is this your understanding, Dr Proudlove?' said Dr Graves. 'As the dead man's colleague I assume you knew him better than most people did, in the end.'

'I'm afraid it is more than likely,' said Dr Proudlove. 'The unfortunate consequence of an experimental turn of mind and a ready supply of the drug on Spyglass Lane. And yet there are many who are addicted, and few who behave wildly when under the influence. It tends to stupefy, rather than excite, and I never saw Aberlady in either state. His habit was a private affliction, and one he managed well. It never impinged upon his work.'

'Indeed,' said Dr Graves. 'Though his irrational behaviour might be an aspect of the mania that results from abstinence after a prolonged bout, rather than as a consequence of the drug *per se*.' He shrugged. 'Such a conclusion would be enough to convince any magistrate.'

And yet it did not convince me. Besides, did I not have the charred seeds of henbane in my pocket? And so, I looked for other clues that might tell me *why* he had died, and *who* had killed him.

'Excoriations to the oesophagus,' said Dr Graves, who was bent over the head and neck. 'Rather unusual to find scratches in the throat like this – unless he sought to induce vomiting by violent means. The stomach might tell us more.'

'And the heart?' I said.

'Haemorrhage in the epicardium, and throughout the endocardium,' said Dr Graves, shouldering Dr Proudlove aside so that his face might hover intimately close to the corpse's gaping viscera.

'What does that mean, sir?' said Will. He was still standing by the door. I had expected him to faint at the noise of the saw, at the cracking sound of the rib cage being pulled open, or the moist squelch of our hands moving amongst the internal organs, but so far he had remained upright.

'It means his heart is congested,' said Dr Proudlove. 'The chambers are full of a thick, dark blood.'

Dr Graves jabbed at the delicate tracery of the lungs with the handle of his knife. 'Severe hyperaemia and oedema here too.'

Henbane, I thought. It left no trace in the lungs, but its effects – hyperaemia and oedema – were quite evident. Of course, opium smoke would have a similar result.

'Again, we're seeing the effects of opium,' said Dr Graves, as I knew he would. 'And the stomach contents, Mr Flockhart?' He grinned.

I had always hated stomach contents, and Dr Graves knew it. The smell of them was, to me, even worse than the smell of the bowels, and for a moment I was tempted to tell Dr Graves to examine them himself. I glanced at Will, who had chosen that moment to look over at us, and was watching me as I lifted the stomach clear of the body and slithered it into a bowl. The corpse twitched, and let out a belch of air. Will's face drained of colour completely and his bottle of salts clattered from his fingers. But he was familiar now with the clammy skin, the tingling limbs

107

and tunnel vision of an imminent swoon, and he sank to his knees and slid to the floor in one graceful movement.

'He's not getting any less lily-livered, is he?' remarked Dr Graves without looking up. 'I'd have thought he'd have toughened up by now, what with all the time he spends with you.'

'*I* thought he'd 'it the ground much 'arder,' said Toad senior, his tone conversational. 'Bein' so tall an' all. But some men don't. Some men just sorts o' melts away, like. I seen it before.'

'He knows what to expect,' I said. 'He's fainted often enough. Put my coat under his head will you, Toad? And use his salts.' I pointed with the blade of my scalpel. 'They're on the floor over there.'

Dr Proudlove clicked his tongue. 'You cannot just leave him there!' he said. 'Is this the way you treat your friends?' He put down his knife and went to crouch down at Will's side. 'Mr Quartermain?' he said, slapping at Will's face and reaching for the salts. 'Mr Quartermain?'

'He'll be quite well in a moment,' I said. My voice sounded high-pitched and cross, like a jealous girl's. I did not want to leave my task and see to Will, and yet I did not want anyone else to touch him either. I knew him better than anyone, and I knew he would revive in a moment or two. He was always fainting, always being fussed over by others; he didn't need Dr Proudlove mollycoddling him.

I swallowed my irritation, my possessiveness, and bent to my task, slitting open the tough silken bag of the stomach. It contained no charcoal – Aberlady had evidently failed to ingest any of the stuff, despite his intentions. There was no sign of the other emetics he had pulled from the apothecary shelf either. Instead, I found the usual mixture of half-digested food – though there was little enough of it, as though he had had no interest in eating during his final hours. I felt something hard, like a bone of some kind as I sifted through the slime, and I caught it up between finger and thumb. I rinsed it in the bucket of water at my feet, and examined it beneath the light of the lantern. Its shape was familiar, though I could not for the life of me imagine why it should be. I squinted down at it in disbelief, for it was not a bone at all, but a tiny key, little more than half an inch long. Was this what Erasmus Proudlove had been looking for when he rifled through the dead man's pockets?

On the mortuary floor, Will was stirring. Dr Proudlove helped him to sit with his back to the wall, his head between his knees. Beside me, Dr Graves had turned his attention to the brain and was quite oblivious to anything else. I slid the key into my pocket.

Chapter Eight

It did not take long to finish our examination, and there were no other conclusions to be drawn from John Aberlady's body. Dr Graves said he would be informing the magistrate that he had leaped from the window whilst under the influence of a mania related to opium addiction. I did not gainsay him, neither did Dr Proudlove, and we helped to load our friend's remains onto Dr Graves's corpse wagon in silence. The night before it had been clear that Dr Proudlove had wanted to talk. Today, apart from his initial keenness to discuss the tarantula found in the bananas, it appeared he wanted to say as little as possible. He seemed agitated and restless, as if the sight of Aberlady's flayed arm had made him nervous – afraid almost – and he made his excuses and walked hastily over to the *Blood* as soon as Dr Graves's wagon had disappeared from view.

'I'm sorry I fainted,' said Will. He was looking pale still. 'I keep thinking I will get used to it, but I never do.'

'You're much better though,' I remarked. 'You always have your salts, and you seem to lie down almost before you actually pass out. Today you even had time to take your hat off and put it to one side. Besides,' I took from my pocket the tiny key, 'whilst you were swooning in front of Dr Proudlove, I found this in John Aberlady's stomach.'

Will took it up. 'This would most likely fit an item of furniture,' he said. 'A drawer, perhaps, or a cabinet? Possibly a desk – an escritoire – or a box? It might even be the key to a book. Or a jewel case.'

'All manner of possibilities,' I remarked. 'We must keep our eyes open for locked books, boxcs, escritoires, desks, cabinets, jewel cases and drawers – amongst other things. But whatever it unlocks it is obviously of some importance or else why would he have swallowed it?'

'He was hallucinating,' said Will. 'Hallucinating so much that he also tried to burn off his tattoo with a poker. Who knows what was going through his mind?'

'And, while we are looking out for tiny locks that are missing their key, we also have these. One from Aberlady's pocket, the other from Mary Mercer.' I held out the two identical love tokens. 'The flower is the forget-me-not, which is a common enough motif and speaks for itself.'

'And the other?' He held up the sixpence, peering at the fine lines that marked out the shape of a pointed leafy bract, as fine as gossamer, hammered into the silver.

'The other motif is the maidenhair fern.'

'And it means?'

'It means "a secret bond of love" – as far as I understand these things.'

'A secret bond of love between the dead girl and John Aberlady?'

'It would seem that way. Perhaps we should go up to the League for Female Redemption and see what else we can find out about the girl.' I put the tokens back into my pocket. 'For what wouldn't one do for love?'

Siren House, the premises of the League for Female Redemption, was not far from the waterfront at the end of Cuttlefish Lane, a dingy thoroughfare adjacent to the Seaman's Dispensary. The door was opened by a girl with a bored expression. Her lank hair was parted in the centre and looped under her ears. From behind her we could hear the discordant sounds of women singing, thunderously accompanied by a badly tuned piano. At the sight of us the girl beamed. 'Hello, sirs! You're up early!'

I blinked. 'Annie,' I said. 'This isn't . . . I mean . . . you're not at Mrs Roseplucker's now?'

'Ain't no one at Mrs Roseplucker's now,' replied Annie. 'Since St Saviour's moved south of the river there's no one to come a-callin'.'

'And so you decided to come here?'

'May as well,' said Annie.

'What's happened to your hair?' said Will. 'And your dress?'

I remembered the girl's coy ringlets, her yellow flounced dress. The dress she wore now was a simple high-necked garment of dark green cotton. The last time I had seen her – some two years ago now – she had been lounging on a sofa in the front parlour of Mrs Roseplucker's Home for Young Ladies of an Energetic Disposition wearing a garment that threatened to slip from her shoulders altogether. She had been introduced to me as 'a virgin, sir. But keen to learn.'

'I look an absolute mess,' she said. She scowled and touched a hand to her hair. 'But Dr Birdwhistle says if I stick it out I'll get a new life. In Australia if I wants to.'

'Dr Birdwhistle?' said Will.

'He's one the "founding fathers" of the League for Female Redemption.' She gestured behind her. 'That's what this place is, and that's what he calls himself.' I noticed she was doing her best to speak properly – re-affixing aitches and other consonants she had formerly disregarded.

'D'you want a new life in Australia?' I said. I thought of what I had learned of the place during my adventures up at Angel Meadow Asylum. 'From what I hear it won't offer you an easy life.'

'Some of the girls from here get work in London. Some go to Australia. Some run away. Some goes back to their old life.' She grinned. 'Suppose I ain't decided yet which of those suits me best.'

'Anne?' A voice called out from inside. 'Anne, who is it? And at such a time too! We have not even finished our morning hymns.' The piano had fallen silent. I heard a great rustling of silk skirts and starched petticoats and a gigantic woman appeared on the doorstep. She wore an expression of delighted welcome, until she saw who we were – two strange men, talking in a familiar fashion to an ex-prostitute – at which point she glowered at us as though we had horns and forked tails.

'There can be no men on these premises,' she said. 'Didn't Anne tell you? Do you not know *who* and *what* we are here?'

'Why, yes, madam—' I began.

'Oh, these gentlemen ain't like *that*,' said Annie. 'Why, I knowed them both at Mrs Roseplucker's—'

'We do not mention our shameful pasts here,' cried the woman, holding her hands over her ears. 'Only our hopeful futures.'

'Not like *that*, ma'am. Mr Jem here's the apothecary from St Saviour's. Used to help us out – against the pox, and such like.'

The woman's face turned purple. 'And the other one?'

'I'm Mr Flockhart's assistant against the pox, ma'am,' said Will. He swept off his hat. 'A pleasure to find such a worthy cause here on the riverside.'

Annie winked at him broadly. 'Mr Quartermain, that's who *he* is. Still a virgin, sir? Lord, I hope not!'

'And you, madam?' said Will hastily.

'I am Mrs Birdwhistle.'

'We are here to see the superintendent,' I said realising that I had no idea what the name was of the woman who had identified the dead girl.

'No gentlemen may cross this threshold,' cried Mrs Birdwhistle. 'Aside from the Reverend Dr Ambrose Birdwhistle.'

'And the real doctors,' said Annie.

'The Reverend Dr Birdwhistle *is* a real doctor,' cried the woman. 'A doctor of divinity.'

'I meant the medical doctors.'

'Dr Sackville, Dr Antrobus and Dr Cole come here in a purely professional and philanthropic capacity.'

'And Mr Aberlady.'

'I believe he is dead, the poor fellow—'

'And, of course, there was the constable that time.' Annie's eyes twinkled as she slid the fat woman an arch look. 'Remember *him*, ma'am? He crossed the threshold, and more besides!'

'That constable had no business in here. He was asked to ensure that none of you received stolen spirits from over the wall.' She turned to us confidentially. 'Drake's Bonded Warehouse is at the end of the garden. The constable was *supposed* to be making sure nothing came over.' Her cheeks trembled. 'We found him in the front parlour with one of the girls.'

'Big white arse,' cackled Annie.

'Get inside!' thundered Mrs Birdwhistle. 'You'll be fined for that.'

'Fined?' I said. 'Please, ma'am, don't punish the girl on our account.'

'I will do nothing at all on *your* account. The fine refers to Captain McConnochie's Mark System. Marks awarded for good behaviour, marks deducted for ill-temper, disrespect, bad language, that sort of thing. What's good enough for Norfolk Island is good enough for us.'

'Norfolk Island is an Australian penal colony, is it not?' said Will.

'If we might speak to the superintendent,' I repeated before she could answer him. I did not want a lecture on methods of penal control. 'There was an unfortunate incident. A drowning. I believe the . . . the girl involved was known to her.'

'I shall let you in just this once,' said the woman. She pulled the door wide. 'I am secretary to the ladies' committee. Today is our committee day, and you are in luck, for you would not be permitted inside otherwise. We were enjoying some music. We have hymns every morning from nine to half past. You are just in time, sirs, to hear our final song, *There is a Land of Pure Delight*. Our girls do

115

not play, of course, that's an accomplishment for a lady. But sing everyone can. Everyone *must*.'

'The superintendent,' I said. 'Is she here?'

'She has not yet arrived, sir.' She stared at me crossly. 'You are rather *early*. It is fortunate for you that here at Siren House an early start is considered a virtue. Formerly our girls were "of the night", and we do all we can to counter so wretched and perverse an inclination.'

'And when might the superintendent arrive?'

'She will be in at any moment. In the meantime, perhaps you would lend your voices to our morning choir?'

'Your work here,' said Will as we were ushered into a wide hall tiled in black and white. 'It seems most . . . beneficial, and . . . and—' He groped for a word that would be acceptable, 'humane,' he said. 'No beatings, I trust?'

'No,' Mrs Birdwhistle sounded uncertain. Then, deciding she was being mocked, she drew herself up. 'We are a philanthropic concern devoted to helping the fallen women of the waterfront and beyond. We are *not* a penitentiary, gentlemen, we are a refuge.'

She led us through to a drawing room with high ceilings and elegant cornices depicting sea shells and waves. It was simply furnished, with drugget on the floors and uncomfortable straight-backed chairs positioned about the walls. The tall sash windows were partly obscured by blinds, the glass behind them textured and stippled, so as to prevent those inside from seeing out, and those outside from seeing in.

The girls were seated on the chairs, in a ring before the piano. Their dresses were all of the same cut and fabric, with a high neck and close bodice above wide skirts. They were corseted stiffly, and sat poker-straight, their hair, like Annie's, in imitation of the Queen, whose likeness hung on the wall – rosy cheeked and bulging eyed, with a slightly pained expression, as if she were suffering from indigestion after a heavy meal. The girls looked at us as we entered, their gazes, for a moment, eager and hopeful. They saw me, tall and thin, stony-faced, with my mask of red across my eyes, and Will wide-eyed and worried-looking, anxiously squeezing the rim of his tall hat between his hands, and they looked away, disappointed.

There were a number of pinched-faced women occupying more comfortable chairs – ladies, judging by the opulence of their dress and the smooth complexity of their hair styles – and we were introduced to them one by one, 'Mrs' this and 'Mrs' that, each of them giving their title with an air of relish and superiority. At the piano sat the Reverend Dr Ambrose Birdwhistle.

'You find me at my charitable work,' he said, rising to his feet and coming foward to shake our hands. 'I can be found here, at the *Blood* and at the Seaman's Mission. "And now abideth faith, hope and charity, these three; but the greatest of these is charity". First Corinthians, chapter thirteen, verse thirteen.'

'The pastoral and the spiritual are of equal importance,' I remarked, for want of anything more interesting to say.

'The teaching of the Lord forms the backbone of our work here at Siren House,' he said. 'Though we do not force them into His arms.'

'Dr Birdwhistle leads the women in prayer every day and joins us in singing whenever we have a committee meeting,' said Mrs Birdwhistle. 'The piano, at which he excels, is a rare treat for us all. The morning hymns are usually sung without any accompaniment – it does the girls the power of good to depend on one another for harmony.'

'How many girls are resident here?' I said.

'We can take no more than twelve,' Dr Birdwhistle shook his head. 'Would it were more, gentlemen. There are so many of them. The Irish, you know—'

'Indeed, sir,' I said. Prior's Rents, the rookeries close by my apothecary, were full of the Irish. They had come in droves in the '40s, driven from their own country by famine, but had found nothing in London but a different type of miserable poverty, one steeped in crime and vice. 'We wanted to speak to you about Mary. Mary Mercer—'

'The house was owned by a naval captain – before the area fell into disrepute for the neighbourhood is not what it once was,' said Mrs Birdwhistle, her voice loud.

'Indeed,' said her husband. 'But with help from our numerous contributors we have been able to turn it into a home to help those who wish to help themselves.'

'There is a similar institution out at Shepherds Bush,' said Mrs Birdwhistle. 'Patronised by Mr Dickens, you know.'

'Ah, but Mr Dickens disapproves of us, my dear.' Dr Birdwhistle smiled, his small spectacles glinting. 'We are *insalubrious.*' He laughed. 'And so we are, for the river stinks to high heaven! But the rent is far cheaper.'

'And how do these fortunate girls find their way to you, sir?' said Will.

'Mrs Birdwhistle and I tour the penitentiaries of the city,' said the reverend doctor. He reached into his pocket and pulled out a fold of paper. 'I have penned a short pamphlet, "The Horrors of the Degraded Life". Girls read it and if it speaks to them they seek us out when their sentences are done. Please.' He handed it over. 'Do take one.'

'And Mary Mercer came here? Where was she before?'

'I cannot say,' replied Dr Birdwhistle.

'But you did know her?'

'She was here, yes.'

'What can you tell us about her? About her past?'

'Nothing,' said Dr Birdwhistle. His face had turned pink, his smile fixed. 'Nothing at all.' He lowered his voice to a whisper and leaned towards me. '"Judge nothing before the time, until the Lord come, who will bring to light the hidden things of darkness, and will make manifest the counsels of the heart".' His breath in my face was stale and metallic-smelling.

'Corinthians!' cried Mrs Birdwhistle. 'There is no need to whisper your insights, my dear.'

'And yet you are here every day, sir?' I said.

'I am.'

'And do you not know the girls under your care?'

'They are under the care of the superintendent.'

There was something he was not telling me. He knew about Mary Mercer, I was certain. And yet he chose to say nothing? 'And who – and where – is the superintendent?' I said.

'I would prefer it, sir, if you spoke *to* me rather than *about* me.'

I had not heard the door open, had not seen her standing behind me. She was taller than I remembered, narrow at the waist, but with unfashionably square shoulders and long lean arms. Her dress was a dark blue, the white edging at her collar and cuffs bright against the dark fabric of her dress and the ebony skin of her hands and throat. Her complexion was flawless, her eyes narrow above high, sharp cheekbones, her head finely shaped, her hair dull against the burnished sheen of her skin, pulled tight into unnatural straightness by pins and clips and forced into a tight bun at the back of her long slender neck.

'Ah, Miss Proudlove,' said Dr Birdwhistle. He sounded relieved. 'There you are at last. These gentlemen would like to speak to you.'

∽

She led us out of the drawing room, down a dingy corridor and into a small parlour situated at the back of the house. The window looked out onto a long, narrow garden imprisoned by high walls – one side bounded by Cat's Hole, the other by Cuttlefish Lane. The opposite end of the garden looked out onto the back of Drake's Bonded Warehouse. She did not sit, and she did not ask us to sit. Instead she stood beside the fireplace, her profile silhouetted by the light of the window.

'You're related to Dr Proudlove?' I said.

'I don't define myself by what my brother does for a living.'

'Of course not—'

'Then why ask?'

'I just thought—'

'I see what you *think*, sir. You think it easier to judge a woman's worth by the profession of her male relations.'

'I—'

'I am Gethsemane Proudlove, and who I am is my own responsibility.'

'Yes—' I stammered. 'Of course. And if I might introduce myself—'

'I know who you are, sir. And your companion. What is it you want from me? Or would you rather ask my brother as I am unlikely to have an opinion of my own?'

'That girl,' I blurted. 'That dead girl. Mary Mercer. You knew her because she lived here?'

'What business is it of yours?'

'Because, like you, I believe she was murdered,' I said. How quickly she had wrong-footed me. I felt as though I were scrabbling to stop myself from falling. I looked at Will for help, but he merely folded his arms, and grinned.

'You didn't say that to the police inspector,' she said.

'No,' I replied. I realised now why the inspector had been so discourteous. Her race set her apart from other women; her life at Siren House put her still further outside his limited conception of respectability. No doubt his insolence was no less than what she was used to, for men hate what is different and unknown, what they do not understand or cannot control. 'The inspector is a fool,' I said. '*We* will find the person or persons who did this and then *I* will tell the magistrate.'

'Will you, indeed.' She sighed, and looked out of the window at the grey walls and prison-like windows of the warehouse 'Did you stay to watch Dr Graves perform his post-mortem?' she said.

'Mary Mercer appears to have drowned,' said Will. 'Drowned, but without putting up a fight.'

'She would have fought,' said Miss Proudlove, her voice low. 'Any of us would. Women *have* to. Women like us.'

'Women like you?' said Will.

Miss Proudlove glared at him. '*Any* woman.'

'She didn't drown,' I said. 'Though it was made to look as if she had.'

'How could you tell?'

'Because the water in her lungs was clear. And yet the water of Deadman's Basin is the vilest liquid it is possible to conceive of. *That* sort of water was not present. So, I ask you again, miss, what can you tell us about Mary Mercer?'

'How long was she in the water?' she said quietly.

'I would say perhaps two days. Certainly no more than four.'

'Can you be sure?'

'The water was very cold, which would have kept her submerged for longer than if it had been summertime. Her skin was waterlogged, but not unduly so. The epidermis was loosening at the hands, the nails in the nail beds – and yet it had not deteriorated further than that. Had it been longer – say four or five days – then the skin at her hands and feet would have peeled away like gloves and stockings—'

'Jem,' murmured Will. 'You are speaking to a lady.'

'And yet one who has asked more questions than she has answered,' I said. 'Your friend, madam, has been treated shamefully. Don't you want to know who did this? Will you not do what you can to help us find her murderer?'

But my description of peeling skin had troubled her, and I saw that she was crying. I offered her my hand-kerchief, but she ignored me, dashing away her tears with the back of her hand. 'Yes, I knew Mary Mercer,' she said. 'I knew her because she had been on the streets. After that she came here.'

'When did you last see her?'

'About a week ago.'

'How long did she live here?'

'Ten months.'

'Out of an indenture of twelve?'

'The girls have twelve months here, yes. After that they must emigrate, or find a situation.'

'And so she ran away?'

'No. At least – I don't know. Perhaps. She may have done. She took work on the *Blood*. Some of the girls go there.'

'The *Blood*?' I said. 'Neither Dr Cole nor Dr Antrobus mentioned that they knew her.'

'Perhaps that is because they did *not* know her,' replied Miss Proudlove. Her face was in shadow, but I sensed a change in her. Her voice was flat now, angry and controlled.

'Do the women here have possessions?' I said.

'No.'

'None at all?'

'They are given all they need when they arrive. If they run away then Dr Birdwhistle says they are stealing.'

'Even their clothes?'

'Even their clothes.'

'Do *you* say they are stealing?'

'I don't say anything,' she replied bitterly.

'It doesn't seem a very joyful place,' said Will. 'Despite the homeliness Dr and Mrs Birdwhistle insist upon.'

'No one from the streets is joyful,' she replied. 'If they are it is only thanks to the gin. And when they come here, well, sometimes they find there was something to be said for the freedoms they had before.'

'I knew Annie before she came here,' I said.

'Did you, sir?' She threw me a disdainful glance. I had not made a friend of her by sharing that information, I could see.

'I'm trying to help you,' I said.

'Help *me*?' she laughed. '*I'm* not dead, Mr Flockhart. *I* don't need your help.'

'Then what can you tell us about Mary?' said Will. 'If we know who she was, her history, her habits, the places she went and people she knew, then perhaps we can find out what happened – find justice, at least. Goodness knows, Miss Proudlove, if she found herself on the streets before she came here then she had little enough of it while she was alive. Besides, do you want to see more girls in the mortuary? What if she is only the first?'

'I knew Mary when she was here, that's all. She was a good girl. Quiet. Intelligent.'

'And because of that she became a nurse on the *Blood*?' I thought about the visit Will and I had paid to the upper ward of the floating hospital ship, the darkness and the gloom, the men hunched beneath their blankets, the sound of dice and cards, the silhouette of a tall, slim woman bending over this patient, the clink of the spoon against the bottle. 'You work on the *Blood* too, Miss Proudlove,' I said. 'Don't you?'

'I make no secret of it,' she said.

'And you knew Mary Mercer when she was there?'

'I did. She was there every day. I go only once or twice a week.'

'And you knew Mr Aberlady?'

'Of course. Why?'

'Because we are almost certain that Mr Aberlady watched Mr Quartermain and me pull Mary Mercer from the waters of Deadman's Basin.'

She said nothing.

'Now he is dead too.'

124

'Yes,' she said after a moment. 'I am sorry to hear it.'

I handed her the two sixpences I had taken from the Toads, one from Mary, one from Aberlady. Miss Proudlove turned them both over and over in her fingers. On one side, the crown and the date, on the other side, the fern and flower. Forget-me-not. A secret unspoken.

'Were they lovers?' I said.

'I don't know,' she said. Her voice sounded flat. Her eyes were downcast, the tokens now still between her fingers. I took them from her.

'And this key?' I said. 'Have you seen this before?'

She blinked. 'Why, yes,' she said. 'Yes, I have.'

'Where?'

'Here at Siren House. It is Dr Birdwhistle's key.'

We all have stories, ones we whisper to ourselves to explain the direction our lives have taken; others to distract us from the lives we lead. We tell stories that make us seem worthier or more interesting than we are; stories behind which we hide our fear and self-doubt. We learn them from birth – who we are, where we come from – the narratives of others weaving in and out of our own until we can hardly distinguish one from the next. My name is Gethsemane Proudlove, and I have a story like no other.

When you meet me, you will ask me the same question everyone asks: 'Where are you from?' You will think it is merely a polite, indifferent inquiry. An expression of interest. 'Where are you from?' In fact, you are telling me that I do not fit in. That I am a curious, exotic thing whose presence must be explained before it might be accepted. It is a judgement on my fitness to be here at all. I can see by the way people look at me that they are often surprised that I speak English, let alone that I speak it better than they, for my mother is keen that I talk like a lady – my voice low and decorous, any rough sentences or harsh vowels smoothed and rounded. That's what the gentlemen like, after all, especially from one as unexpected as I.

My mother is what might be romantically termed a courtesan. She never talks about her own history. Any stories of slave ships and whips, and cruel masters beneath blazing skies are no more a part of her story than they are of mine, for there have been Proudloves in London for hundreds of years. And yet still people stare. Do they expect me to boil them up in a cooking pot? To walk naked and barefoot, to wear a grass skirt or have a bone through my nose?

'Where are you from?'

'Lambeth,' is my answer. 'My mother's womb,' is another. Sometimes I say 'Grosvenor Square', just to see their faces. Looking at the crowds that fill the teeming streets, the people who pour in from the countryside, from Scotland, Ireland, Kent, Norfolk, Sussex, Oxfordshire, my own roots sink far deeper into the sticky London clay than any of theirs.

⚜

My mother describes the man who keeps her as two things: 'a gentleman' and 'your father'. He pays for my mother to serve his needs alone, and she rents out rooms in her house to other women in the same line of business. Our gentleman father does not wish to be reminded of his paid-for couplings with a black woman on the back streets of Kennington, and the fat, pale boys and girls, begotten with his fat, pale wife are the only progeny he is prepared to acknowledge. Whenever he comes, Erasmus and I are packed off into the kitchen, out into the yard or upstairs into our rooms, so that he might not be reminded of his weakness.

Erasmus is taken away from us when he is nine. He and I attend the dame school on Neptune Street and both of us excel, though as he is a boy his destiny is always going to be different to mine.

'Erasmus is to make something of himself,' my mother says. 'We are not to begrudge him his opportunities in life.' The money she takes from our gentleman father pays for Erasmus's education, and he is sent to school in the country, far away from the world of quims and cocks that spawned us both. I don't see him for years. He writes and says he will come to get me one day, but I never believe him.

I stay with my mother. She knows no other trade but the one she is born to. 'There will always be men,' she says, 'and they will always have their needs.' She says that their fat, colourless wives spend their days lolling on sofas, and can do nothing to relieve them. That is why they come to us, night after night, their cabs creaking and rattling in the darkness, their footsteps hasty and furtive on the path between the bushes. My mother keeps the greenery thick, so that they have to push through it to reach the front door. She says the gentlemen like it that way, that it reminds them of why they have come.

We are not a house with a great number of different visitors. The girls keep a warm and cosy sitting room each, and their gentlemen stay for hours, for my mother insists that her girls be more than just holes for men to squirt into and leave. That is something that might be got on any street corner in London, and if that is all they want then that is where they might get it. Far better to offer the gentlemen something more substantial, she says, something worth returning to again and again. Something worth paying for.

Every day at eleven o'clock my mother's girls assemble in the downstairs parlour. She has me read The Times *to them, so that*

*each might ask her gentleman, 'How was the city today, my love?'
or 'I hear the Company's shares have fallen in value this week'
and 'Do you think Mr Peel will do such and such?' They must
know what is playing at which theatre, the rules of cricket and
who has won, what the news is from the Continent, from India,
from America. They should seek opinions, she says, and then nod
and smile and pretend they have never heard anything so
fascinating and intelligent in all their lives. Then, they are to do
as their gentlemen wish, whatever it might be.*

*And my role? What my mother plans for me is unclear. She
seems hardly to know herself, though she keeps me away from the
gentlemen. For a time, at least.*

Chapter Nine

❦

'I can't put it off any longer,' said Will, as we left Siren House. 'I must go back up to Deadman's Basin. The area has to be cleared before anything else can happen and I have to finish my drawings, my measurements.' He sighed. 'It reminds me of St Saviour's,' he said bleakly. 'The buildings, the shadows, the wet stinking earth—' He pulled his tall hat down low over his forehead. 'Am I never to find a commission that doesn't involve the reeking mud of London?'

'Not while you stay in the city,' I said.

'But here is where the work is so here is where I must stay. I have some men coming tomorrow, men and carts to begin clearing the area. In the meantime, I need to look around again so as to be sure where to start. Besides, I cannot bear the idea of it standing there, that terrible muddy basin, that poor girl—' He shook his head. 'I have to destroy it. There's nothing about this commission that fills me with pride or pleasure – a warehouse is hardly a glorious achievement for any architect. But I must get on with the job, so that Deadman's Basin can be wiped off the face of the earth forever.'

I did not like the idea of him being alone there, but I could see that he would not be persuaded. 'What about you,' he said. 'You're going to the *Blood*?'

I nodded. 'It's still early, and there's plenty to do. But I will come and find you after lunch, once the ward rounds have been done and I am confident that Mrs Speedicut knows what she's doing.'

'But you're not staying there at night? You are coming home to sleep?'

'It's usual for the apothecary to live on board—'

'But these are not usual circumstances.' He took my arm, his face tense. 'Don't stay aboard, Jem,' he said. 'Not at night, for God's sake. Think what might happen.'

'Nothing will happen. And the only thing I am thinking of right now is a pot of coffee—'

'But you will not stay the night—'

I patted his hand. 'We must get through the rest of the day first.'

❦

I approached the *Blood* from the west. Looking up, I could see the grey smudge of a face at the apothecary window. Mrs Speedicut – that pebble-like visage was unmistakable. I was relieved to have her aboard, for all that she and I had our differences. She was right when she said the Asylum was no place for one such as her. She was used to sickness and disease that could be seen and managed – sputum, blood and pus were the elements of Mrs Speedicut's universe. The mad – with their curious behaviour, their unexpected laughter, or their strange doltish silences – she had been unable to comprehend. Well, I thought, she would find plenty of sputum, blood and pus on board the *Blood*.

The shutters over the gun-ports were open now, the windows too, and as I drew closer I could hear the sounds of shouting and the rasp and clatter of brooms and brushes. On board, the place was busy with nurses and orderlies – I'd had no idea there were so many of them, for they had been largely absent on my previous visit. Now, they were everywhere, a dozen cross-faced women with dirty aprons and mutinous faces, a half-dozen burly tattooed men heaving laundry and scrubbing decks. I could see that Mrs Speedicut was making her presence felt. A hospital matron for thirty years, violence, both physical and verbal, had always been her preferred means of persuasion. She threw things – scrubbing brushes, blocks of soap, mousetraps – at anyone who failed to obey. Everywhere there was evidence of industry. The door to the laundry stood open, the great copper tubs within filled with a bubbling soup of soap scum and ancient grey bedding. The air was heavy and damp, the steam that billowed out a reeking brew of urine, dirt and carbolic. From below deck came the sound of brushes chafing at wooden boards and the wet slop and flail of mops. An orderly stumped up onto the deck carrying a sack, lumpen and heaving.

'Rats,' he said to me. 'Caught twenty of 'em this morning.' He grinned, and added in a tone of deep awe, 'That new matron whacks them with a broom handle, quick as you like!' I watched him toss the squirming sack into the river.

Across the deck, I noticed that the door to Aberlady's quarters – now my quarters – was standing ajar. I pushed it open. Inside, the room was boiling hot. A man was standing over the snake's glass enclosure. He was small, no taller than five and a half feet, but bent over, as if from a lifetime of stooping beneath the timbers of the ship's low ceilings. His ancient frock coat was as black as pitch, his neckerchief grey with age and repeated washing. His face too was hoary, etiolated from years spent in the dark, close wards of the *Blood*. In his left hand he held a dead rat by the tail. At the sound of the door opening, he turned. In the bright light of Aberlady's room his tin eye looked garish, its gaze unwavering. His real eye blinked at me, moist and curious.

I had met him only once as a child, though I had thought about him for a long while afterwards. At the time, I had not realised that his eye was false, but had noticed only that he looked strange – unusual, like I did. Even then he had mostly stayed below, in the dim world of the tween decks. I had thought he was hiding. Hiding, the way I wanted to, from the scrutiny of others. Now that I was older I knew better: a man like Dr Rennie did not fret about his injured face or the stares it might elicit. I wondered now what it really was that had kept him on the *Blood* for so long.

'Dr Rennie,' I said. 'Good day, sir.' His hand beneath mine was cold and dry. In the fingers of his other hand the dead rat swung like a furry pendulum.

'Who are you?' he said.

'Jem Flockhart, sir,' I said. 'I believe you knew my father. He was apothecary at—'

'St Saviour's. Yes, yes,' he smiled and pumped my hand

up and down. 'A good man. Had a daughter with a birthmark, I seem to remember.'

I felt my blood turn to ice. 'It was a son,' I stammered.

'A son? Oh no. No, the son died. And the mother too. A very sad business. But a daughter remained to him.'

'It was a son. Me. *I* am his son. And I am the replacement apothecary here too, for a while at least, now that Mr Aberlady has gone.'

'*You?*' His tin eye, gimlet sharp, stared up at me. 'Well, well,' he said after a moment. He chuckled softly. 'It seems I owe your father three guineas. I told him he'd never pull it off. And yet here you are. Jemima Flockhart, *gentleman*-apothecary.'

'I'm *Jem* Flockhart, sir, after my father. My father was Jeremiah—'

'Oh, of course, of course,' he waved a hand. 'You must be whoever you wish to be, my dear. I'm too old to care, and your father's dead, poor fellow, and not likely to miss his three guineas now. You say Aberlady is gone?'

'Dead, sir.'

'Dead!' He stared at me with his mis-matched eyes, and his chin trembled. 'Are you sure? The poor fellow. How on earth—'

'I believe he was poisoned, sir. Can you think of anyone who might want to do such a thing? Had he many enemies?'

'Enemies? No.'

'What of his friends?'

'Aberlady had no friends. Not here. Not apart from me, of course.'

'Not even Dr Cole and Dr Antrobus?'

'Especially not Dr Cole and Dr Antrobus.'

'What about Dr Sackville?'

'Ha!'

'Or Dr Proudlove?'

He glanced over my shoulder, at the open door, the bustling deck, his expression suddenly fearful. I turned to look – had there been a movement, a shadow at the door? I stepped out, but there was only an orderly flailing a mop in a careless figure of eight against the side of the ship. I recognised him as the fellow with the clipped ear who had helped to drag Aberlady from the river.

Back inside, Dr Rennie was staring vacantly at the rat in his hand as if surprised to see it there. 'You were saying, sir? About Mr Aberlady?'

'Was I? I can't imagine why,' he said. 'But if poor Aberlady is dead then this will be your room now, will it not? You are no doubt wondering what I am doing in it.'

'And how, sir,' I said. 'For I thought I alone had the key.'

'I've been on this ship for more than fifty years,' he said sharply, his metal eye staring straight at me. 'You think I don't have a key to everywhere and anywhere?'

'Of course—'

'I know everything that goes on here and I come and go wherever I please.' His voice was brusque, commanding. 'Trust has to be *earned*, sir, by hard work, and loyalty. Knowledge of our ways, our methods, is not simply *given*.' He turned his head, the light shifted, and once again that piercing gaze was nothing more than paint on metal. His real eye looked frightened and tearful. He dabbed at it with his cuff, and then he pulled open the tank's wooden lid and flung the rat inside. 'This room is never locked,' he said, suddenly affable. He smiled up at me, toothless and benign. 'Who would feed Minimus and Maximus here and keep the fire going if it were?' We watched as the dark muscular length of Maximus started to uncoil. 'I've got rather a soft spot for this fellow. Comes all the way from India, you know – probably wishes he was back there too, on a day like this. There was another one, but he died. We're hoping to stop this one from suffering the same fate.'

'We?'

'That pestle girl – what's her name? She looks after the frogs too. And Proudlove's sister helps. Says she feels sorry for anything kept as a pet, or trapped in a cage.' He shook his head. 'Dr Cole torments them both – offering a rat then snatching it away. He has tested whether the creatures feel pain too – you see the wound upon the back of each of them? An experiment, he said. Miss Proudlove was furious. And Aberlady too, when he found out. The snakes are Aberlady's pride and joy, especially Maximus. He loves Maximus.' He frowned at me. 'I'm sorry, my dear fellow, but – who did you say you were?'

'Flockhart, sir. The new apothecary.'

'Ah.' He turned back to the snake. The rat was now lodged in its throat, Maximus's mouth stretching effort-lessly around the furry corpse. The snake's body gave a ripple, and the rat eased out of sight. 'Extraordinary,' murmured Dr Rennie. 'You know, it doesn't even *chew*. It just swallows! Its jaws expand – and its body too. Like rub-ber! I believe it could take a man, you know, if it were big enough. A big enough snake, I mean, and a small enough man – one like Sackville, perhaps, or Antrobus.'

'Let us hope we never find out, sir.'

'On the contrary,' Dr Rennie laughed, a thin hissing sound, which I thought at first might be coming from the snake. His metal eye glanced at me wickedly. 'I would be more than happy to find out!'

'Did you light the stove in here, sir?' I said, mopping my brow.

'I don't light stoves, man. I'm the ship's surgeon!'

'Of course—'

'The stove's always on in here. Got to keep the place warm for the snake and the frogs. And moist for the frogs – you see they have water? The snakes prefer a dry heat. Especially Maximus. Minimus, however.' He peered into another tank, inside which the smaller, brightly coloured snake was draped across a log. I saw its tongue flicker. 'I don't really know what *he* likes. Sometimes I drop a live pigeon in there. He's very quick and the poison works instantly.'

I noted the feathers at the bottom of Minimus's tank. 'I think it is not long since he dined,' I said. I looked at the narrow brass bed, the rumpled bedding. 'And Aberlady slept in here?'

'Slept in the apothecary mostly,' Dr Rennie replied, reaching into the tank and running his hand down the snake Maximus's smooth body. 'Or on shore. I've no idea whose bed he slept in then.' He shuffled over to a tank of tiny coloured frogs. 'And what about these beauties?' he said. 'Just look at them! What colours they are! Like fragments of the sun and the sea, or living drops of blood!' It was true, for the tiny frogs, some no bigger than my thumb nail, were luminous – daffodil yellow, lime green, cobalt blue and a glowing vivid crimson. Some were mottled with patches or stripes of black. All of them glistened moistly, shamelessly brilliant against the dark green foliage, like splashes of living oil paint. 'Poison dart frogs,' he said. 'Beautiful.'

He pulled a tobacco tin from his pocket and opened the lid. Within was a scrambling tangle of earwigs, woodlice, ants and weevils. 'Breakfast,' he said. He reached up and scattered the insects into the frogs' tank. 'This old ship is home to an army of insects. No doubt she'll be glad there's a few dozen less of them tickling her ribs.' He put the tin away. 'I have something to show you.'

In the corner of Aberlady's room, between the two snake tanks, was a small door no more than five feet high. I had assumed it was a cupboard, for it seemed to be embedded in the hull of the old ship. When Dr Rennie pulled it open, however, I saw that inside was a steep and narrow flight of stairs.

It was dark, once the light from the door was behind us, so that I almost missed my footing as we plunged down into the reeking bowels of the ship. Dr Rennie, two steps ahead, moved with easy assurance. Through the ancient hull I could hear the muffled sounds of the waterfront – the shouts of dock workers, the creak and scrape of loads being hauled, the rumble of wheels. From overhead came the sound of footsteps and voices. I felt my skin turn cold as the darkness closed in. I told myself that my growing fear was irrational and foolish, that I might go back the way I had come at any moment, should I choose to. It did not make me feel any better.

'Where are we going?' I cried. 'Sir, I must protest. I have the ward rounds to attend to—' My voice sounded absurd, high-pitched and frightened, even to my own ears. Up ahead, Dr Rennie heard it too, and gave his thin, hissing laugh.

He opened a door, and led me into a room, dark, but

dimly lit from a skylight cut into the deck above. The square of light it emitted fell directly onto an operating table, scrubbed bone-white. On the floor, the sawdust glimmered against the black shapes of the blood box and the broom, but the rest of the room was dark. Was this where Aberlady had crouched, deep in the shadows, his pen clutched in his shaking fingers? *Come quickly, Jem, but come ready to face the Devil.* The wooden walls that surrounded us, sticky with pipe smoke and long dried blood, were as dull and lustreless as knitting.

'I've seen this place full of wounded men,' said Dr Rennie, his voice suddenly loud. 'Nothing like you see it now, but packed with bodies and deafening with screams, the ship rolling and heaving beneath us, the air trembling from the roar of cannons and the crack of muskets. Chloroform? There was no such thing when I was your age. Speed, sir, that was what counted. It was the only way any of them stood a chance.' He shook his head. 'Blood? You never saw so much of it. I was red from my wig to my boots – all of us were.'

He leaned in towards me, his tin eye alive and glittering, as though he drew strength and purpose from the fabric of the old ship. His real eye was hooded, as if sleeping beneath the drooping skin of its lid. The light from overhead threw the rest of his face into a chiaroscuro of shadows, like a mask of the Devil from a medieval morality play. I saw a movement out of the corner of my eye, and saw the scaly tail of a rat slip out of sight. All at once the place felt hot, hot as hell and sticky and feverish. They had the cholera there, sometimes, and gaol fever too. Dr Rennie was speaking again now, but I could hardly hear him for the buzzing in my ears.

'Nothing for you here,' I heard him say. His real eye stared at me now, wide and fearful as he seized my lapels, his bony hands tight as tree roots. 'Leave this place. Leave it while you still have your soul.' He pointed to the wall, only dimly visible in the gloom, and upon which generations of seamen, doctors, students, patients had scrawled and gouged their names in a criss-cross of black scars. 'There,' he said. His voice was a whisper. 'D'you see? D'you see it?'

Perhaps it was the close, dark space in which we were standing, perhaps it was the image he had put into my mind of bloody bodies and ruined limbs, the stink of powder and shot and fear, but the floor seemed to heave beneath my feet. I put up a hand to steady myself and felt the warm sticky wood of the ship's ancient timbers, the carved graffiti-scabs beneath my fingers. I saw the bone-white operating table, Dr Rennie's glittering eye, his corpse-hands reaching out to me – some months earlier, up at Angel Meadow Asylum, I had been bludgeoned into unconsciousness and trapped in a coffin. I thought I had put that fearful episode from my mind, thought I had mastered the terrors that had assailed me during the nights that had followed. It seemed I had not, for they came at me now like great shadowy wraiths, pulling the walls closer, turning them as dark as the earth in which I had been buried, making my skin crawl as though worms writhed upon it. I tried to conjure up thoughts of air and light and space, of the blue skies that the *Blood* had once sailed beneath, the open seas – but my mind flew instead to the few black inches of caulked and tarred planks that lay between me and the choking waters of the Thames. I reeled, and stumbled, sinking down into the darkness.

I heard voices, as if from far away, and a roaring sound in my ears. I felt as though I was nodding my head, nodding it up and down, and saying 'Yes, yes, Dr Rennie, I saw what was chalked upon the wall at the back of the operating theatre, though I did not understand what it meant.' I felt my body move and sway, as if caught in an undertow, I sensed a brightness around me, and then came a terrible smell, so strong that it was like a physical assault at the base of my brain. My eyes flew open and I batted away the bottle of salts that a stranger's hand was wafting beneath my nose. Around me were the faces of people I didn't know. I recognised Mrs Speedicut's amongst them.

'Fainted,' she said, knowledgeably. 'Must o' been the heat of the place. And the stink.'

'Undoubtedly,' I said. I staggered to my feet, dusting myself down. I saw some of the nurses exchange smirks. I knew how absurd I must look, struggling to appear dignified after being carried up the ward steps to the weather deck like a sack of laundry. What did it matter that the *Blood* was overheated, dark and stinking, I was supposed to be used to such places. And so I was – when I was not required to descend into unlit, ill-ventilated spaces in the company of a man with a mind half lodged in the past and half befuddled by the present.

'Bet you ain't had your breakfast, neither,' said Mrs Speedicut. '*That's* enough to make anyone dizzy—'

'Where's Dr Rennie?' I said.

'He's gone downstairs,' came the reply.

I remembered the operating theatre, the darkness, the writing upon the wall. What had it said? I had thought I knew, but now I was not so sure. I seized the salts and took a few hasty sniffs. I pushed aside the nurses and orderlies who had gathered around me, and headed back down the steps to the ward below, stalking between the beds and through the doors at the stern that led to the operating theatre. Inside, a lamp was burning on the table, and a man laboured with a mop and bucket. The sawdust had been swept up and dumped into the blood box. A wet chamois leather was draped over the edge of the bucket, the walls running from where he had clumsily lathered them with soap and wiped them down. I saw his clipped ear, his tattooed forearms—

'What are you doing?' I said.

'Cleaning, sir,' he said, swirling his mop about the floor. His bald head glinted with sweat in the lamplight. 'Like we was told to.'

'But why here?'

'I done everywhere else.'

'Did you clean that writing off the wall?' I snapped, eyeing the chamois.

'I didn't see no writing,' he said. He grinned, revealing teeth that were broken and stubby, as if he had been gnawing on stones. 'Perhaps you're having another turn, sir. Like one of the ladies.'

I clicked my tongue and stalked out. I *did* remember the writing, though it made no more sense to me now than it had done then. I closed my eyes, picturing the space, the darkness, the light from overhead falling dim against the wall. It had been written low down, some two feet above the sawdust-scattered ground as if its author had been crouched and afraid. Had it been Aberlady's hand? That I could not say, for it had been written in capital letters. Seven capital letters, scrawled in haste, forming a single curious word: ICORISS.

Chapter Ten

~

The smell of carbolic on the top ward was so strong that my eyes smarted. Beside the stairs a large brass bell hung, and I rang it four times for silence, the way Aberlady used to. 'Gentlemen,' I cried, as the ward sank into a muttering silence. 'My name is Mr Flockhart and I am your apothecary. I knew Mr Aberlady, and am here to continue his work amongst you—' I was more nervous than I had expected. It had been a while since I'd been in charge of an infirmary, and I had never before stepped into a dead man's shoes. Around me the men coughed and muttered as I droned on about cleanliness and discipline. My voice sounded flat and dead to me, absorbed by the wooden walls, by the beds mounded with ragged blankets. How many other voices had roared out instructions in that confined space? Smoke hung in the air in layers of blue and grey. No one spoke. I saw Mrs Speedicut at the bow, sitting in an armchair beside a giant pot-bellied stove. She leaned upon a deck brush held upright in her hand, her legs wide beneath her damp-hemmed skirts, like a slatternly Britannia.

I went from bed to bed. I wondered whether I should ask about Aberlady, but the men were subdued, and seemed reluctant to talk about anything but their own ailments, upon which subject they were loquacious. I asked about the man with 'something like yaws' that Dr Sackville had spoken about the day before, but I was told that he had died in the night and been taken away.

A number of patients sported the yellowed skin of the malaria sufferer, and to these I gave cinchona, along with ginger, and cinnamon against the fever. Others were plagued by a profound lethargy that I understood to be a form of sleeping sickness prevalent in the Congo. I had never seen the symptoms before, though I had read of them. The outcome was almost certainly death, and there was little in my apothecary to ameliorate the condition. I administered cinchona to these too, along with tincture of Kola nut, the stimulant properties of which I hoped might offer some relief. Another man had what looked to me to be the beginnings of tetanus, though there was nothing in the apothecary on the *Blood* that would help him. I resolved to bring what I needed from my apothecary on Fishbait Lane. Overall the place seemed well ordered, with the prescriptions being the usual mixture of purgatives, sedatives and iron tonics, and I passed through the wards quickly enough. I wondered where the doctors were, for I had seen no one but Dr Rennie that day. When I asked I was informed that the others rarely arrived before eleven o'clock in the morning. 'Six bells,' said the orderly with the clipped ear. I looked at my watch. It was approaching noon.

144

Back on deck, I heard the sound of raised voices – men's voices – coming from inside the consultants' sitting room. I knocked, and opened the door, the voices within falling silent instantly. The room was warm and smelled of dried-out books, and rosemary, citrus and cedar wood from a bowl of pot pourri on the mantel. A tray of hot nuts rested on the stove top, the hearth scattered with their empty shells. The stove belched out a fierce heat, so that I longed to remove my coat. Dr Cole and Dr Antrobus were lounging in armchairs; Dr Birdwhistle was standing with his elbow resting on the mantel. His face was crimson, and moist with sweat.

'Did you run all the way, from Siren House, sir?' I said.

He smiled, and swabbed at his face with a handkerchief. 'So much to do, Mr Flockhart, so many places where I am needed.'

'Do *we* need you, Birdwhistle?' said Dr Cole languidly. 'I'm not sure that we do. You would probably be more use on board if you helped with the cleaning. There seems to be the devil of a lot of it going on today.'

Dr Birdwhistle ignored him, though his pimpled cheeks turned pink with annoyance. 'Have you met Dr Cole and Dr Antrobus, Mr Flockhart?'

I admitted that I had. 'Don't get up, gentlemen,' I said, though neither of them had made as if to rise.

He saw me looking at a small galvanic battery that stood on a table in the sunlight. Its wires were attached to the legs of a large dead frog. 'One of Dr Antrobus's little projects,' he said, by way of explanation. 'There are a number of such things about the place.' He cleared his throat, his face flushing. 'Mostly one has to approve of such attempts to further our knowledge of God's creations, though Dr Cole's attempt to graft a cock's comb to a mouse's back was, I still maintain, an abomination.'

'You weren't supposed to see that,' said Dr Antrobus. 'If you will insist on barging in—'

'Dr Cole and Dr Antrobus are our fiery young men,' said Dr Birdwhistle in a tone of forced brightness. 'Full of ideas, and questions, both of them.'

'Yes, well, I fear you find us rather *un*-fiery this morning, Flockhart,' said Dr Cole. 'And you were perhaps wondering why we were not on the ward rounds with you.' He sighed, and stretched out his long limbs. 'But you seemed to be doing a good enough job on your own. And Dr Sackville isn't in till later, so we thought we may as well leave you to it.'

'Mr Flockhart, you are the answer to our prayers,' said Dr Birdwhistle. 'A replacement for poor dear Mr Aberlady.'

'I make no prayers, Dr Birdwhistle,' said Dr Antrobus sharply. 'For "poor dear Mr Aberlady", or anyone. God is no more than a figment of a credulous imagination. Science shows us *that* well enough.'

Dr Birdwhistle coloured further. 'I will not discuss theology with you, sir.'

'Nor I with you,' the fellow retorted.

'*Replacing* Aberlady?' said Dr Cole. 'Are you sure, Birdwhistle?'

'Merely acting apothecary,' I said. 'Until a proper replacement is found.'

Dr Cole reached out to shake my hand, though he still did not stand up. 'Welcome aboard, sir. Come along, Antrobus, shake hands with the fellow. He's one of us now.'

Dr Antrobus regarded me sullenly, his hands thrust into his pockets. The pause was long enough for us all to see it was a snub, and when he took my hand his grip was as cold and disinterested as his manner.

'And don't forget it was this fellow here who brought us that corpse yesterday. *Most* lucrative.' Dr Cole jangled the coins in his pockets. 'I must thank you, sir. Had you not sent for Antrobus and me then St Saviour's Dr Graves would have won yet another prize for his insatiable anatomy students. The fellow has quite enough as it is.'

'And there's still Aberlady,' said Dr Antrobus.

'I'm afraid Mr Aberlady has already been anatomised,' I said.

'Oh.' Dr Cole looked disappointed. 'By whom?'

'I attended to the matter this morning, with Dr Graves and Dr Proudlove.'

'Proudlove?' Dr Antrobus sounded surprised. 'Didn't know *he* was back on the waterfront.' He stared at me. Then, 'Do we need an acting apothecary?' he said, to no one in particular. 'We managed well enough when Aberlady wasn't here.' He put his feet up on the chair opposite, so that I might benefit from the sight of the soles of his boots. 'Besides, Proudlove knows how to run an apothecary. Get him to do it. Or that pestle girl. What's her name?'

'Oh, come now, Antrobus,' said Dr Cole. 'You can't let a girl run an apothecary.'

I laughed. 'Quite so,' I said. I shoved Dr Antrobus's feet off the chair and dropped myself into it with an air of bored familiarity. 'The place was a complete shambles! Lord knows what Aberlady had been teaching her. I don't blame you for missing the ward rounds either. If Sackville's not around then why bother? There's no one else worth impressing, from what I can make out.'

'You met Dr Rennie, I take it?' said Dr Cole.

'Yes.' I raised my eyebrows. 'Does he know what day of the week it is?'

'Only on a Wednesday,' replied Dr Cole. We laughed.

'He's not so bad,' said Dr Antrobus, watching me, unsmiling.

'But as a *surgeon*?' I said. 'Once upon a time I have no doubt he was quite brilliant. But now? I'd not like to have him bending over *me* with a knife in his hand!'

'You'd not want Antrobus here, either,' said Dr Cole with a wink. 'Last week he severed a fellow's artery. The man bled to death before our very eyes—'

'Don't exaggerate,' said Dr Antrobus, frowning. 'I sorted it out straight away.' He shrugged. 'He still didn't make it.'

'Sackville was furious. Another death in the annual reports! It's enough to make the subscribers put their shillings and goodwill straight back into their pockets.'

'Anyone might make such a mistake,' I said. 'It's far too dark down there for surgery.' I snatched up a chestnut from the stove top, snapping off its hot crisp coat with my fingers. 'First nuts of the season?' I said. I tossed the shell into the hearth. 'Always the best.'

'And what's this Birdwhistle tells us about Siren House?' Dr Antrobus said. 'I believe you've been sniffing around there too, Mr Flockhart.'

'My dear Dr Antrobus,' said Dr Birdwhistle, clearly discomfited at being revealed to be a tittle-tattle. 'I merely said that I had seen Mr Flockhart this morning already—'

'Asking questions, you said.'

I leered. 'I knew one of the girls in her old life.'

'Is that the job of an apothecary?' said Dr Antrobus. 'To ask questions?'

'She drowned,' said Dr Cole. 'Her lungs were full of water, the post-mortem was quite clear. And as for Aberlady – a week at the Golden Swan on Spyglass Lane is enough to make anyone lose their mind.'

'I believe the girl used to work here, on the *Blood*,' I said.

'Really?' said Dr Cole. 'What was her name?'

'Mary Mercer.'

He frowned, as if trying to dredge up a memory. 'Can't say I remember. What about you, Antrobus?'

'The name means nothing to me,' said Dr Antrobus. 'But they come and go, Mr Flockhart. The job doesn't always suit them. The *Blood*'s not a place for the faint hearted, after all.' He smiled, so that I knew he had witnessed my recent ignominious revival on deck.

'Even a pretty girl like that?' I said, pretending I had not noticed. I grinned again, and adopted what I hoped was a lascivious expression. I hated playing the part, but what else might I do? If I tried to interrogate them I would learn nothing. I had met men like these two before – young, arrogant, uninspired – feigning a masculine bonhomie seemed the best way to cultivate their confidence in me. 'I think *I'd* have remembered her!'

'Perhaps Birdwhistle remembers her,' said Dr Antrobus.

'*Dr* Birdwhistle,' said Dr Birdwhistle.

'He's more likely than any of us to know these trollops. Perhaps it's in one of his confessions.'

'Confessions?' I said. 'How intriguing.' I addressed Dr Birdwhistle. 'Tell me more, sir!'

'It is quite simple,' he said stiffly. 'The girls' pasts are written down, in detail, in the Case Book at Siren House.'

'By you? You old rogue!' I seized another nut, and winked broadly at Dr Cole.

'Any one of us might take it down,' said Dr Birdwhistle. His face was crimson, his mouth a tight rosebud of disapproval. 'All of us on the *Blood* are associated with Siren House. In the main the confessions are taken down by myself, but occasionally the medical men here step in. The girls often find work here after their spell at Siren so it behoves us all to know something of their pasts.'

'And what do these confessions contain?' I said.

'The girls are encouraged to say as much as they can about the road that led them to Siren House. It is all noted down, and then they are charged never to speak of it again. When they emerge from the parlour after confession they are emerging into a new life, their histories trapped – imprisoned, if you will – in the pages of the Case Book.'

'And who has the Case Book?'

'*I* am the custodian.' He patted his waistcoat pocket, and I heard the muffled sound of keys moving against one another. 'It is kept locked away at all times.'

'You know, I think I remember the Mercer girl, now you come to mention it,' said Dr Antrobus suddenly. 'Kept herself to herself, as I recall. You remember her, Cole. Didn't mix much with the others.' He grinned. 'You quite liked her, I seem to think—'

'What, that dark haired minx? The small one? Was she from Siren House? She never said—' Dr Cole blushed. 'Yes, I—' He swallowed. '*Was* it her on the slab? I didn't recognise her at all, I'm afraid. I suppose it was rather dark in there, and there were so many students, and Dr Graves always takes the head, you know.' He smiled, though had the grace to look sheepish, and when his face settled I was of the impression he was more perturbed than he admitted, though whether that was because he had been revealed to be callous, because he had been found out to have fancied a whore, or because he had actually had feelings for the girl, I could not say.

'I thought she was pretty enough,' he said. 'Certainly a cut above the others we usually get. But I'd not have expected her to run away simply because I—'

'You what?' said Dr Birdwhistle.

'Nothing.' Dr Cole looked uncomfortable. 'Nothing at all.'

'Perhaps she ran away because of you,' said Dr Birdwhistle, his face redder than ever. '*I* would!'

'You have nothing to fear from me, Dr Birdwhistle!' He gave a bark of laugher.

'Really, Dr Cole, this is not the first time.'

'I can't help it if they take a fancy to me,' said Dr Cole. He smirked, evidently pleased, no matter what he implied to the contrary. 'The girl made her expectations quite plain. Naturally I rebuffed her.'

'In case you hadn't noticed, Dr Birdwhistle,' said Dr Antrobus, sitting back with his elbows on the arms of his chair. 'There are brothels aplenty round here. On both sides of the river. We might catch the pox for a few shillings ashore easily enough without having to associate ourselves with anyone on board.'

'And yet why not?' I said. 'If it's being given out for free.'

'For heaven's sake, sir!' cried Dr Birdwhistle. 'Are you no better? Have you no shame? This is a hospital, not a . . . a . . . a place of assignation.' He snatched up his bible. 'I feel a reading is required.'

The two medical men groaned. 'Oh! Not here, man,' cried Dr Cole, pelting Dr Birdwhistle with a chestnut shell. 'Anywhere but here.' He and Dr Antrobus grinned at one another as Dr Birdwhistle scuttled out.

'And yet,' Dr Antrobus addressed me as the door banged closed, 'as I'm sure you noticed, Flockhart, he is the only one amongst us who has the pox.'

I had indeed noticed: Dr Birdwhistle's eyes, red-rimmed and watery behind his thick spectacles, their pupils unresponsive to light, in addition to his perpetually nodding head, a symptom caused by labouring blood vessels and flaccid heart valves. To anyone acquainted with the wards set aside for venereal cases the signs were unmistakable.

'The man's losing his mind,' said Dr Cole, plucking up *The Times* morning edition that lay on the floor beside his chair.

'It's often a symptom,' said Dr Antrobus. He closed his eyes. 'Lord knows *what* goes on in his head.'

❧

I went up to the apothecary and attended to my duties there, preparing remedies and doses until after one o'clock, when Mrs Speedicut came up with two of the nurses. We took the medicine down onto the wards. By this time the students had arrived, and the place was busier and warmer than ever, though everyone noticed how much cleaner the wards looked, with their newly scrubbed floors and windows. Mrs Speedicut glowed, and nudged her fellow harpies in the ribs. And yet the place still stank, so I opened all the windows, in the hope that the breeze might ventilate the place. But the river was like a sewer that day and what blew in from outside was far worse than the smell we had to contend with inside, and so I acquiesced to Mrs Speedicut's wishes and the place was shuttered once more.

Dr Cole and Dr Antrobus walked the wards. There was still no sign of Dr Sackville who was presumably engaged in the more salubrious surroundings of his private practice. I saw Dr Rennie standing in the shadows – at least, I thought I saw him, for when I looked again he was gone.

'Where's Proudlove?' said Dr Cole, though he sounded irritated rather than urgent. I saw him look at his watch, and shake his head, and say with some satisfaction that it appeared Dr Proudlove was not coming that day, and that his students would only become medical men if they followed himself or Dr Antrobus that afternoon. The students did as they were instructed.

I went upstairs to the apothecary. Already the place had become a sanctuary to me, a blessed place of light and air after the close quarters of that dark and foetid hulk. The shelves that lined the walls beneath the windows were filled with medical books. Culpeper's *Complete Herbal*, Orfila on poisons, Mckendrick's *Pharmacopoeia*, Dent and Micklewhite's *Materia Medica* – all were old friends to me. Those dealing with poisonous beasts and insects, parasites, and the climate and geography of foreign places were unknown, but were nonetheless reassuring in their solidity; the bottles and drawers that surrounded me a comforting, familiar world. And yet how safe was I? How safe was Will? Might I too return one evening to find the place filled with the fumes of poisonous seeds? Would I go up to the Basin and find Will drowned? We were no closer to finding out what had happened to Aberlady, no closer to understanding the relations that existed between those on board. I realised how much I had taken for granted at St Saviour's, and at Angel Meadow. I had been familiar with those places, and with the people who worked there. But here? Here I was an outsider: no one knew me, no one trusted me, and no one would tell me anything. But I had already thought about that, and while my efforts to ingratiate myself with the resident doctors might take some time, help was approaching at that very moment in the form of a fat old woman in a filthy apron.

There was a knock at the door, and the handle rattled. 'Come in,' I cried, though she already had. I pulled a chair towards the stove, and handed her a cup of strong coffee. 'Do sit down.' I glugged a measure of gin into the hot, black liquid and tossed her a pouch of her favourite Virginian shag. 'And tell me everything.'

❦

I was caught between the different worlds that coexisted in any hospital. I was not a patient – thank God, for once one entered a hospital there was every chance one would not be leaving it again. Equally, I was not a consultant. The authority and glamour, such as it was, that came with the post of physician or surgeon would always elude me, and I would never be treated by any of them as an equal. But even as I was marginalised by medical men, it was me, as the apothecary, who was meant to run the hospital. Only the apothecary was there all day, every day. As a result, I was far above nurses and orderlies, and despite my dislike of hierarchy I could not, in all conscience, claim any of them as my friends. Still, time and long familiarity had resulted in an uneasy comradeship between myself and the woman who now sat before the apothecary stove. Like a truffle pig in a forest she would have unearthed more in one morning than I might have found out in a month.

'You are glad to be back in a proper hospital, madam?' I said.

'Proper?' she laughed. 'Suppose it's more of a proper one than Angel Meadow Asylum, but that's not saying much.' The smile slipped from her lips. 'How long do I have to stay here?' she said. 'There's snakes, you know!'

'The snakes are confined,' I said. 'Which is more than can be said for the people. I need you to tell me what you know.'

Mrs Speedicut filled her pipe and settled back in her chair. She told me that she knew some of the nurses on board already. 'From St Saviour's,' she said. 'They wanted new nurses when St Saviour's moved over the river, and some of them what had worked at old St Saviour's came up to the *Blood*. Betty Tompkins. Martha Fisher. Jess McGinley – Jess's bunions, sir! You should see them—!'

'Never mind Jess McGinley's bunions,' I said, anxious to avoid an inventory of her old cronies and their ailments. What she was really saying, however, was that gossip had ensued. She told me what I already knew – that Dr Rennie was losing his mind, that dementia assailed him in waves, sometimes engulfing him completely, drowning the present, so that his own name became mysterious to him and those he had known all his life were transformed into complete strangers. At the same time, old memories glittered like jewels glimpsed in the deep, so that he dived down for them, seizing them as they swam into view and holding on tight – until they were sucked from his fingers by the undertow and he was hurled back up, up into the present, disoriented and afraid. He lived at the bottom of the ship, his rooms neatly ordered and comfortingly familiar, and to which he would repair in times of stress or anxiety. He still operated, said Mrs Speedicut, though only with Dr Antrobus, Dr Cole or Dr Proudlove at his side.

'There's something between him and that Dr Sackville, though no one knows what since whatever it is it's so far back no one can remember,' she said. 'Both of 'em learned their trade with one o' them famous doctors in town.'

I knew this too – my father had told me – though what 'something' there was between Dr Sackville and Dr Rennie I had no idea. Possibly it was nothing more sinister than two old men who had known each other all their working lives. Possibly.

'And Dr Sackville?'

She told me that Dr Sackville was wealthy, successful, admired. He arrived in a coach on those days when he was on board, and had numberless women patients lolling on sofas in the elegant boudoirs and drawing rooms of the west. He had no need to come to the *Blood* at all, though he did. He and Dr Birdwhistle were forever in disagreement about the running of the ship – the former saw no need for 'religious cant', the latter insisted upon it. 'Came down bothering the patients with his Bible first thing this morning,' she said. 'Then he vanished. Off to Siren House, the girls said. Two hours later back he comes, spouting on about Matthew this and Job that and chapter this and verse that. He just gets in the way. Ain't nobody interested. He made all those who could get out o' bed, go up on deck and into the chapel. Draughty place, so it is, and most of 'em should o' stayed in their beds. I told him so, too.' She wrinkled her nose. 'Don't think much of him. Nasty little runt of a man. I seen the way he looks at them younger nurses too.'

'Like what?'

'Like he wants to eat them up. Besides.' She frowned. 'I knows the pox when I sees it.'

I asked her about the others. Did they share Dr Sackville's antipathy towards the curate? What were they like towards each other? She told me that Dr Cole and Dr Antrobus hung upon Dr Sackville's every word, Dr Proudlove did too, when he was given the chance. All three of them had no connections, no family money behind them, no reputation to draw upon. They needed patronage, as well as success, if they were ever to get on, and so they clung to the Great Man's coat tails in the hope that they might somehow be swept along into prominence. So far, none of them had seen a change in fortunes. It was no more than I had suspected. In a competitive profession, it was common for younger doctors to attach themselves to a more revered medical man, though why Dr Sackville chose to associate himself with a rotten old hulk like the *Blood* was still unclear. Dr Rennie knew the answer, I was certain, even if he did not realise it himself.

'And what of Mr Aberlady?' I said. I bent closer. 'What can you tell me about him?'

'Not much,' she said. 'Hard working. Kind. Took on that Pestle Jenny, despite what the others said.'

'What did they say?'

'That he was wastin' his time. A girl as apothecary!'

'Did he have any enemies?' I knew even as I spoke that it was not the best of questions. In a competitive profession everyone had enemies, whether they knew of them or not.

'They say he and Dr Proudlove were friends,' she said. 'And Dr Cole and Dr Antrobus too. All the younger doctors together.'

'Together?' I said. Mrs Speedicut nodded. And yet Dr Rennie had said that John Aberlady had had no friends on board the *Blood*.

'And Mary?'

'That dead girl?'

'Yes,' I said. 'That dead girl.'

'No one knew much about her,' said Mrs Speedicut. 'She were only on board for a short while. Pretty girl, they all said so. Caught Dr Cole's eye. He's a handsome enough man for those what likes them tall with yellow hair and rosy cheeks. Looks too much like dear Mr Speedicut to me—'

Dr Cole was indeed a handsome man, with the languid eyes, curly hair and full lips of a poet, and the tall straight posture of a military man. The idea that a man with similar looks might lose his heart to a fat skivvy like Mrs Speedicut was a feat of imagination that was beyond me.

'He's got something of a reputation,' she added. 'Likes a pretty face, so they tell me. That Dr Antrobus ain't quite so lucky. Takes Dr Cole's leavings, if you follow.'

I did follow. And yet both men had pretended that they had never seen the dead girl before. Of course, for a young ambitious medical man to take up with a woman like Mary Mercer in anything but the most casual of relationships would have ended his career instantly. It was no surprise that they preferred to deny ever having seen her.

'And Mr Aberlady?'

'I don't know about him,' she said. She looked at me doubtfully. Afterwards, I realised that she had known exactly what sort of a man he was, though she had chosen not to tell me. Perhaps she thought I already knew. If she had spoken up then, how differently things might have turned out. I never blamed her, for I was thinking about the love token I had found in his pocket, and Mary's, about the maidenhair fern with its message of hidden affection. The apothecary struggling for respect and recognition and the ex-prostitute: it would not have been a public affair, even if it had been a genuine one. Had it been reciprocated?

'Anything else?' I said. 'Anything about Mary?'

'Quite a secretive girl, by all accounts. Kept 'erself to 'erself. Sang while she worked, they said.' She smirked. 'Must o' been in love. Or simple! Ain't no other reason to sing when you're stuck down there.'

One day I hide behind a curtain in one of the girls' rooms. She bathes, this one, for her particular gentleman likes her clean and wet, likes to sit and watch her in the rose-scented bath water, soaping herself. He shows her what he will give her when she emerges, and I hear her coo in delight at the pale sausage of flesh that hangs from his britches. She rises from the water. The firelight glints off her wet skin, her nipples dripping, the hair between her legs dark and damp. They do not know I am there, or so I think. And yet when he mounts her he does it from behind, across a footstool, in front of the curtain where I am crouching.

I see everything. I see her face when he cannot, and she looks directly at me, her eyes meeting mine through the crack in the drapery. I see her skin pink and smooth beneath his hairy-backed hands. He grunts, periodically extracting himself, pumping extra life into the thing with his hand, flourishing it, white and sticky, in my direction. But I am not looking at him. I feel my heart

160

beating through the whole of my body. I fear I have stopped breathing.

After he is finished, she rubs him with oils and plies him with brandy, as this is what he wants. He sits, fat and unclothed, before the fire, his feet upon her bare arse as she crouches before him like a footstool, as that is what he wants too. He reads the paper. He stays for hours, though I can see she is bored and tired, the draught that blows under the door as cold as a knife where her skin presses against the rug. I am bored and tired too, and in the end I fall asleep in my hiding place. When she wakes me, he has gone and she is in her nightdress. Open at the neck, she bends over me. I see that she is naked beneath it, her breasts swinging like bells. She smells of brine and roses.

'Well,' she says without smiling. 'Is that what you want?' Behind her, the bath water is cold and still, with a lace edge of scum.

Soon after, she leaves us. I don't know where she goes. Another takes her place. There is an endless supply.

❈

The one I am caught with is young, the youngest of all of them. We share a room at the top of the house, as she is the same age as me, and too young to have her own bedroom-parlour. Those rooms are large, so that the gentlemen can feel at home, can leave their favourite pipes and tobacco, and a change of clothes if they wish. But she does not yet have any gentleman of her own, and must work out of a small chamber, servicing men as and when required, unless one of them asks for her to be reserved. My mother likes to have two girls unreserved at all times. And so, when she is not with the gentlemen, Alice sleeps with me in the attic. We giggle and whisper in the night, our arms around each other, our *legs tangled, naked and warm. Her mouth is an 'o' of pleasure in the darkness.*

My mother finds out – I never know how – and Alice is sent away. I never find out where. And I? I am to be cured.

'Well,' says my mother. 'If you are as hot as a cat on heat then perhaps you would like to earn your keep like the rest of them. I have someone who has been asking about you for a long time.'

I fight, but he is strong. He likes the way I struggle too, I can sense it in his panted breath, in the way his heart thumps and his eyes fix angrily upon me. I am a wild beast that must be tamed, and he is the man to do it. My mother holds my hands above my head so that I cannot scratch his face as he takes his pleasure.

After that, as I know of no other place that I might go, and of no other person that I might be, I become what my mother is. And with Alice gone she is in need of another girl to put out to tender.

❧❧

In time, my mother goes mad, but not before she has lost what she prizes the most – her beauty – to the pox. She wears a veil then, though I know what horror lies beneath. She spends the last year of her life in Angel Meadow Asylum thinking that she is the Queen of Sheba, and that our gentleman father – the man she set to rape me when I was sixteen years old – is John the Baptist.

Chapter Eleven

hen Mrs Speedicut left, I went to see how Will was
getting on at Deadman's Basin. I was glad to get
away from the hospital ship, even for an hour or
so, though I knew there would be nothing to gladden the
heart where I was heading. When I got there, the place
seemed curiously silent after the noise and bustle of the
waterfront, and for all that I often longed for stillness – a
commodity hard to come by in London's teeming streets
– its air of malevolent calm filled me with dread. My
footsteps sounded loud, echoing against the walls as
though I were dogged by a mocking companion who
stopped as I stopped, and moved as I moved. I'd expected
carts to be there, or men beginning the process of
clearing the area, draining the basin and removing the
ugly, decayed structures, but there was nothing, nothing
but dark walls and silence. The shadows gathered thickly
in the corners, and beneath the sagging roofs of the
tumbledown buildings.

'Will?' I shouted. My voice echoed until it was swallowed up by the silence. There was no reply.

I went into the boathouse. Will's hat was on an old workbench against the wall, beside it his notebook and pencils, the drawing he had made evidence of his recent work. I peered into the shadows – nothing but a wreckage of rubble, broken wood and sacks, animated by the scuttling of rats. The boathouse gave out onto a workshop filled with more of the same, and beyond this was a yard, paved with flagstones, slippery underfoot, that had clearly been used as a latrine.

Across the yard was the old villa. Its windows had been boarded over long ago, though here and there they hung crookedly, revealing rotten window frames fringed with broken glass. Once, perhaps, it had been a handsome riverside spot, close to the quays that lined the waterfront, with a yard at the front and stabling at the back, though there was no evidence of these now, for the warehouses of Cinnamon Street had been built full-square against it. The door to the old villa stood open. It had been locked the last time we had been there. But Will would have been given a key by his master at Prentice and Hall, I thought, of course he would want to take a look inside. I only wished he had waited for me, or for the foreman who would help with the demolition – anyone, rather than enter such a place on his own.

I went back into the boathouse. On the floor beneath the workbench was a lantern. Its glass was blackened and cracked, but when I shook it there was still a little oil inside. I wiped some of the greasy soot from the glass chimney with my handkerchief, though it made little difference to the visibility of the flame, which was as dim and yellow as a guttering candle. I hoped it would be enough for me to see where I was going.

The steps that led up to the villa's entrance were green and slippery beneath my boots. Inside, away from the open door, the place was dark as a glove. I held up my lantern.

'Will?' But the house seemed to snatch the word from my throat and his name came out as a whisper.

I crept forward. Doors on either side of me stood open. The windows of every room were shuttered and boarded, and the only light that penetrated the blackness was the glow from my lamp. I was surprised the building had not been colonised by thieves and beggars, as from the outside it appeared to be wind- and watertight, the roof slates intact and the brickwork in reasonable repair. And yet the locked front door was a sturdy one and not likely to be broken down easily, the boarded windows, at least on the ground floor, tightly nailed.

Inside, I expected to find nothing but empty, dusty rooms, the building a sad, echoing shell. Instead, it was as though the people who had once owned it had only just left; as if they had become so frustrated by the clamour of the docks that they had snatched up their coats and flounced out, locking the doors behind them, for each room was furnished, as if they had expected to return but had simply not yet done so. My father had told me that the place was built by the man who owned the nearby docks. So proud had he been of his work corralling and taming the river that he had built a house overlooking the place, but the noise and the stink had driven him away within the year. Once deserted, around about it the warehouses had mushroomed.

The place was silent. The dust lay as thick as felt upon mantels and sideboards, the tops of tables and the shoulders of chairs. On a side table I saw a tray covered in tea cups and saucers, the silver teapot at its centre as black as if it had been hewn from a lump of coal. Cobwebs festooned it, as they did everything, hanging from lamp brackets and dark, formless paintings, from candlesticks and vases, like ancient ropes, ragged with weed, glimpsed at the bottom of the sea. They swayed gently, as if someone had just passed by, though I knew it was simply the air stirring as I moved.

I climbed the stairs. Beneath my feet the floorboards creaked, the carpet moth-eaten to grey fragments. I heard a noise, a groan, I was sure of it, somewhere above me, deep in the heart of the building. I looked up to see a face, monstrous, diseased, wild-eyed, coming towards me out of the darkness. I cried out, my lantern slipping from my fingers – just as I realised that what I had seen was my own face, reflected back at me in a tarnished mirror. The lantern went out as its glass chimney smashed, the shards crunching beneath my boots in the darkness.

I waited, trying to master my fear. My heart was thumping. Should I go back down and look for another lantern? But there had been no other lantern, and I could not go back, could not leave this building without Will. At length, I became accustomed to the gloom. Here and there the boards that covered the windows of the upper storeys had slipped, and slim blades of light sliced through the dark like silver knives, illuminating fragments of what lay within – the edge of a rocking chair, the belly of an oil lamp, the moth-eaten head of a child's hobby-horse. Up ahead, at the end of the hallway, I saw a glow against the wall.

I crept forward, my eyes fixed upon that dim patch of light. Was it moving? Flickering? I blinked. I could not be sure. Should I call out? What *was* it? I held my breath once more and listened. I was sure I could hear breathing, and a curious crackling sound, at once familiar and yet I could not think what it was. And then I knew, and fear stabbed me.

'Will!' I screamed out and ran along the hall, bounding up the next flight of stairs to the very top of the house.

In the attic there were four doors, all closed but one, which stood open at the top of a flight of steep, narrow stairs. Inside, the window gaped wide, throwing a square of grey afternoon light into the dark passage. My heart felt as though it had stopped dead in my chest, for at the foot of the stairs lay Will, his head at a horrible angle against the wall. Behind him, at the top of the stairs, was a dancing wall of flames

I cried out, and leaped forward. Why had I let him come here alone? I knew the place was dangerous – had we not found a girl dead and drowned in the waters outside? We should have stayed together; we were partners, companions of the closest and dearest kind. He could easily have stayed with me on the *Blood* for a few hours then we might both have come up to Deadman's Basin. Tears stung at my eyes and I felt a wail rising in my throat. I swallowed it as best I could; this was no time for noise and fury and useless panic – not before I had established the facts. I crouched at his side and put my fingers to his wrist. His pulse was strong. I moved him gently, relieved to see that his neck was not broken, but merely twisted badly. His head was bruised at the temple, his right eye blackened and his nose bloody. I saw that,

167

like me, he had dropped his lantern. But whereas mine had gone out, Will's had stayed alight, the oil coursing out into the floor of the room he had entered at the top of the narrow, uncarpeted stairs. The flames were now streaming up the peeling distemper walls.

I rummaged in my satchel, and jammed the bottle of salts beneath his nostrils. His head snapped back as the fumes of *sal volatile* struck home, and he gave a strangled cry.

'Thank God,' I said. I rubbed the tears from my cheeks. 'Can you get up? What happened?' I eyed the flames, orange and red and now stretching up the wall of the attic room in long eager tongues. 'We must get out.'

He stared at me for a moment, as if wondering who I was, and then all at once he reared up, his face a mask of horror. 'Jem!' he sounded as though he could hardly articulate the words, as though fear had frozen his lips and tongue. 'Jem! Oh God! Oh God! Did you see them?'

'See who? Can you get up? Are you hurt? We must get out—'

'In there.' He pointed over my shoulder, to where the flames jumped and reared. 'I saw them,' he whispered, seizing hold of me with iron fingers, his face inches from my own. 'I dropped my lamp. I ran, I don't know – into the door, the wall, fell down the stairs. Stupid.' His fingers dug into my shoulder, his eyes so filled with terror that I could hardly bear to look at him. 'My God, Jem,' he said. 'What happened to them? Did you see?'

I climbed the five steps to the open attic door, and peeped inside. It was a small bedroom, once the realm of servants. Its walls were plain and ugly, the floor dusty and bare. A crude wooden washstand stood to one side, the pitcher and bowl in pieces on the floor beside it. It was the only room in the house whose window was not completely covered over. Instead, the top two boards had been torn away, their nails bent, pulled from the wood by a claw hammer and scattered about the floor. The upper sash of the window had been smashed so that the room was cold and draughty. Outside, the London sky swirled with grey-brown clouds.

On either side of a blanket box were two brass beds. Their mattresses had been removed and tossed against a wall, so that the wire frames were exposed. When I saw what lay upon them I cried out and reeled back, banging my head on the combed ceiling and stumbling against the door, just as Will had done. I had been prepared for horror – no one who had seen the look on Will's face could have expected something benign – but nothing had prepared me for this.

What lay upon the first bed was no more than a skeleton. It was laid out as if had been lifted straight from the grave, its arms by its sides, its head slightly to one side, its jaw set wide. Its empty eye sockets were fixed upon the door as if in hope of rescue. There were no clothes – no rings or hair pins. Not a shred of flesh, blood or sinew remained, only the bones, and a dusty tangle of dark hair.

There is something about a skeleton that allows us to remain detached – all skeletons look broadly the same; they possess little, or nothing, that reminds us of the person they once were, and we might view them with dispassion as much as with horror. The skeleton's companion, however, allowed no such indifference.

She had once been a woman, that much was clear, though what remained of her now was no more than a grotesque relic, a withered husk of her once living, breathing body. Her skin was intact, but desiccated, leached of every drop of moisture that had ever given her form and substance. What had once been soft flesh was now nothing but a leathery sheath, a fibrous membrane as dark and withered as tobacco leaves, cleaving to the bones beneath. As the skin had dried, it had contracted, drawing back the lips to expose the teeth in a perpetual silent scream.

Behind me, the flames crept up the dry walls and lapped at the ceiling. Smoke poured from the window, drawn by a draught that came from a ragged hole in the lath and plaster above the bed frames. But then the wind changed direction and the smoke swirled into the room. It engulfed the bodies for a moment, and then streamed over the dried-out corpse, sucked out through the hole in the wall.

I heard Will enter the room behind me and felt a hand tug my sleeve. 'We must go.'

'We must take them with us.'

'What!' Will shook me. 'Are you mad?' He coughed into his handkerchief, his eyes streaming. 'Look at the flames. Look at the smoke. Do you want there to be four corpses here instead of two?'

'But I *must* see—' I stepped forward and bent over the skeleton. It was a woman – the width of the shoulders and pelvis told me as much – not much taller than five feet in height. The hair remained, though it had come away from the head in a halo of dry black fibres. The bones of the skull were small, the face narrow, the front teeth crooked, the left front one chipped so that there was a triangular gap between them. Other than that I could discern nothing that might tell us who she was or how she came to be there. It was as though she had been boiled in an anatomist's cauldron, for every bit of soft tissue was gone.

As for her companion, decay had started, I could see that from the skin at her abdomen, but then it had stopped, and the girl had simply dried out. She too was completely naked, her hair a thin mousy brown, dry as straw, her teeth small and even between her desiccated lips. But the horror did not end there, for what was far worse, what made my stomach clench and my limbs turn cold with horror, was the fact that the chest cavity of the woman's corpse had been opened up, the ribs cut through so that the heart was exposed. It lay like a dark stone, shrivelled and black. Above the hole, at her collar bones, were two familiar incisions.

I sucked a breath in through my handkerchief and dragged my gaze away from that splintered hole, those severed ribs. Was there nothing about her that might enable us to discover who she was? I bent closer. Something, surely, must remain to mark her individuality. And then I saw it. At first I thought it was a shadow, or a smoke smut. And then I touched it, and knew that it was a part of the fabric of her skin. A birthmark, large and dark, the shape of a heart and the size of a florin, right there at the top of her arm.

'Jem!' Will pulled me back. 'Come *on*!'

The wind blew in through the open window, a cold blast of air that chilled me to the bone, and made the flames leap, the smoke filling the room once more.

'We must take them,' I gasped. 'Help me.'

'They will fall to bits,' cried Will as I bent to lift the skeleton from the bed. He seized my arm. 'Jem, stop. You cannot carry them like this. Wait here.' He vanished.

I heard his feet upon the stair, the sound of something – tearing, thumping, I did not know what – and then he was back again. In his arms was a bundle of dusty curtains. He flung one over the skeleton and rolled it over. He scooped the burden up and placed it on top of the other corpse, wrapping them both together in a second curtain.

I had helped to stretcher bodies up and down the stairs at St Saviour's many times, and our load, stripped and dried as they were, weighed very little. It was a wonder we did not both fall down and break our necks, for downstairs I could see nothing – the darkness, the gritty air, the smoke in our eyes rendered us blind. For one moment I thought someone had closed the front door, for I could not see it anywhere, and I felt panic well up inside me like bile. But then suddenly we were outside, sinking to our knees in the filth of the yard as we gasped for air.

∞

It took two hours for the men from Drake's Bonded Warehouse to put out the flames. The proximity of the river, and the urgent desire of Drake's not to see their brandy go up in flames, hastened the process, but not before the old villa, and Dick Tulip's old workshop, were both burned to the ground.

Chapter Twelve

～※～

We took the bodies to the mortuary. Young Toad was sent to fetch the police inspector, and whichever medical man might be still on the *Blood*. The police inspector raised an eyebrow at the sight of us.

'You two again.' He cast his eye over the two bodies, and his face turned pale.

Beside him, Toad licked his lips in excitement. 'We don't normally 'ave quite so many,' he said. 'Mostly we only gets them what's drowned.' He reached out a hand and gingerly touched the leathery skin of the mummified girl. 'Look at this one! *She* weren't drowned.'

'In the attic of that old house on Deadman's Basin, you say?' said the police inspector. 'Thieves, probably. Or beggars.'

'They're girls,' said Will. 'Young ones.'

'Whores, probably,' said the inspector. 'Using the place for their own purposes, I imagine. Probably died of the cold. Lots of them do. You say they was lying on beds? That the window was open? There you are, then!'

'What about this?' Will pointed to the open chest, the withered heart of the mummified girl.

'Rats,' said the inspector. 'Probably.' He looked away in distaste. 'I've seen it before, unfortunately. I've seen lots of dead people in slums, and on the streets. Dead girls. It's the way things are. There's no pity in London. Not for them what's poor. Don't know if there ever will be. I dare say the magistrate would agree with me. He usually does.'

'Rats?' I said once the man had gone. 'I hardly think so.' I bent over the body. 'The bones are clearly cut through with a sharp and precise instrument, and the skin has been slit with a scalpel. There's no gnawing or scratching here. This is a work of precision.'

We heard the sound of approaching footsteps and Dr Proudlove appeared. His face, as he entered, was aghast. 'More?' he said. 'The boy said there were two of them—' He stopped when he saw the bodies. Lying side by side on the slab they looked small and thin, pathetic in their own way, but fearful, as death often is, and all the more so when it is viewed in a damp and dingy mortuary and illuminated by a sickly yellow lantern light. 'Dear God,' he whispered. But behind him came someone I had not expected to see.

'Where are they? Let me see.' She pushed past her brother.

'Gethsemane—' He tried to pull her back, to shield her from the sight, but she shook him off, sidestepping him quickly. Her hands flew to her face, and she let out a cry.

'Come away,' he said. 'There's nothing you can do for them—'

'A surgeon's knife did that,' she said, pointing to the cavity in the chest of the mummified girl.

'Perhaps,' said her brother. 'Though there are many knives that might cut as cleanly.'

'I know this girl!' She was peering at the skeleton. 'I know her. She is – was – Susan Williams. She was with us at Siren House.'

'When?' I said.

'About eighteen months. Perhaps longer.'

'And she went to the *Blood*?'

'She did.'

'How can you tell who she is?' said Will.

Miss Proudlove pointed to the teeth. 'That smile.' She covered her face and let out a sob. 'That chipped tooth, those crooked teeth. I'd know it anywhere.'

Dr Proudlove and I conducted the post-mortem. There was little more to report. The heart was in place, though exposed, the other organs, as far as it was possible to tell in so dried a state, were all in good health. There was evidence of tubercles about the spine, but nothing that would have killed the girl. Dr Proudlove worked in silence, his face tense.

'I cannot say how she died, nor whether she died before her chest was opened.' He rubbed his face, his expression desolate. 'Or after. Let us hope it was before.'

'How might we identify her?' said Will. 'Her face is not recognisable, not without the soft flesh to give it its contours, its character. Even the girl's mother could not say for certain. It's possible I might try to draw her, to imagine the face with the full flesh of youth, but I'm not sure—'

I pointed to the birthmark on the dried skin of the upper arm. 'We have this,' I said. 'It seemed to mean nothing to Miss Proudlove, but it might mean something to someone else.'

Confession of Susan Williams on arriving at Siren House

∽

My name is Susan Williams. I hail from Kent, though I'd rather not name my village if it's all the same, sir. I don't have much of a story to tell – nothing that should be written down, at any rate. I'm twenty-seven, older than most of them here and you might say that I am old enough to know better and to behave better, too. What I do know is that life isn't always how you expect it to be, for I was once a married woman. My husband was a carter – not a lofty profession such as yourself, sir, but an honest man and a hard-working one. At least, he was when I married him, for that's another thing that can't ever be predicted – how people will turn out when times change and they find themselves hard pressed to be the person they started out being. I was young when I married him, but not so green that I didn't know that marriage is a difficult road.

176

My man lost his living – through no fault of his own – and could get no work at all. I had no one but him, my mother and father being dead of the cholera some years before I was married. I was a seamstress, like my mother, so I was not without some skill. But when my husband was out of work it wasn't enough to keep us both. He took to drinking, though it pains me to admit it, and that made matters worse. I had a child by then, sir, a boy, though I'm glad he can't see what a situation his mother has found herself in now.

We came to London in the hope we might improve our circumstances. We'd heard the town was full of opportunities for folk that were willing to work. But we had no idea how hard it would be in a place like this. We thought we might go back once we came, but how could we? There was nothing for us back there, and there was always a chance things might improve if we stayed here, though they never did. We spent all we had on lodgings – poor lodgings they were, down near the docks, but at least my husband had work. He unloaded the cargo, and they liked him for a strong man who never complained. But when the ships didn't come upriver there was no work for days – not until the wind changed. And the crowd of men at the dock gates waiting to be picked grew bigger every day. He started to be known as a drinker again, and that was an end to it, for there were a hundred men to take his place and they had no room for men with liquor on their breath.

After that it was just me and my sewing. Shirts I did, simple ones as well as fancy. But it hurt my eyes to see by the candle, though it was worse without, for I often tried to save on candles, but the days were so dark it was impossible.

It all happened very quickly after that, one thing after another, till there was nowhere to fall but into the grave. The cholera came down our street. There was nothing anyone could do to stop it, and then there was my husband dead, and my little boy, both of them gone in a day. How often I'd wished it had taken me too.

One of the girls who lived upstairs from us, she worked on shirts too and she knew what had happened. She told me how she earned some extra. At first I thought I could never do it. But I was married once and I knew it for what it was, and since my boy died I had no feeling for anyone or anything. I'd not loved my husband, not for a long time, and yet I'd been obliged to give him his due. Surely it would be no different, I thought, only this time it might pay for my bed and board, which is more than I had got from my husband.

And so, one night I went out with Nora, and we went to an ale house that was known as somewhere for girls like us. There were worse places, I knew, though I hoped to be dead before I ended up in them. The life wasn't so bad. Not much worse than before, but no squinting at shirts in the dark and no sore neck and back from crouching over the candle trying to see your work. Besides, there were other girls who'd come to it like me, though I don't know any of them now. Most of them's dead, sir.

It were partly that what made me come to Siren House, sir, for it's hard when you're alone on the streets. Nora left – I don't know where she ended up – and one of the others I used to know got killed by a man who said she'd stolen his wallet. And then when I got pinched I was almost glad, though I'd not done nothing to deserve it, except begging, which is surely better than what I *had* been doing, though the magistrate seemed hardly to care one way or the other. So I was sent to prison. I can't read, sir, but one of the others read your pamphlet out loud to me and I remembered it and so here I am.

Note on Susan Williams on leaving Siren House

Susan Williams walked the streets for upwards of three years after the death of her husband and son. She has no family or friends to help her and seems a sullen, sorrowful woman. And yet her old life holds no appeal, and as a former mother who laments the death of her child one might assume her to have a more nurturing and domesticated spirit than some of the more strong-willed girls. Her skill with the needle will not go amiss either. For these reasons I recommend that she be offered a situation in the laundry on board the *Blood*.

Chapter Thirteen

⁂

I took out my notebook and flipped open the ink pot. 'My observations are as follows,' I said. 'The windows were boarded over, but the top two boards had been torn away—'

'You think the window is important?'

'I think it is vital. I think it provides the answer to how these women came to be as they were. The window was un-boarded, and smashed, so that it was impossible to close.'

Will took a mouthful of scalding tea. We were back at the apothecary on Fishbait Lane, both of us glad to be away from the river, the basin, the *Blood*.

'Do we have to talk about it now?' he said. 'Can we have a few minutes without thinking about death and corpses? I assume the two we have just found are linked in some way to the girl we pulled out of Deadman's Basin two days ago. And all are connected to the *Blood*?'

'If I was not entirely persuaded before I am convinced of it now.'

'How so?'

'The window.'

'Go on,' said Will.

'It is fairly obvious – though not necessarily for reasons you might imagine – that the first body to be put there was the skeleton, though she was not a skeleton when she went in there.'

'But she *was* dead?'

'I think so. I also think the reason why one was a skeleton and one was mummified is because the seasons changed between the one being laid there, and the other. It is the time, and the manner of abandonment, that is most important. So – the first to be put there was the skeleton. The mattresses on both beds had been removed so that as much of the bodies as possible – both of which were completely unclothed – would be exposed to the air. The window was left open to allow the flies to enter. The city is full of flies, the basin outside the place truly pestilent. And, as any anatomist will tell you, whereas it is most usual to remove skin, muscle and connective tissue by boiling the body in a large cauldron in the manner of making a broth or soup—'

Will groaned. 'Too much, Jem. You forget sometimes that I'm not as familiar with the horrors of medical men as you are. This boiling business might sound perfectly normal to you but it is the stuff of nightmares to me.'

'Shall I stop?'

'No, no—'

'I fear there is no way of saying it nicely.'

'Do go on,' he dabbed his lips. 'Broth or soup—'

'One might normally boil the body, but an equally thorough effect – completely stripping bones of soft skin and tissue – will be achieved in a matter of weeks if the corpse is left to the flies. "Fly blown" is the phrase Hunter uses.'

'But the smell!'

'Would hardly be noticed in an abandoned house at a place like Deadman's Basin. The wire bed-frames mean that the flies could get at every part of the naked corpse. Whoever left the first body would have expected to achieve the same results a second time—'

'And presumably never returned to check. I suppose there would be no need to remove the bones. No one could identify them, and it is not easy to carry a sack of bones through the streets.'

'Far wiser to leave them where they are.'

'But why was the other body not a skeleton too?' said Will.

I sipped my tea. 'I think that the first of the bodies was put there during the summer months – last year probably. The breeze is light in the summer, the city warm, the place stinks, and the flies are at their most abundant and voracious.

'The second body shows evidence of some putrefaction – but not much, and what had taken place has been arrested. Why? I believe the second body was placed there later in the year, last year, I would say, in the winter.'

'I remember it was exceptionally cold last winter.'

'Cold and dry and windy. Did you notice how the wind today came from the north and east? It blew straight through the open window into the room and – coincidentally – through that hole in the wall straight over the body. Cold, dry air, for months over a long, cold, dry winter. The body was mummified. Dried out like a piece

182

of tobacco. The dryness prevented the usual process of decomposition from taking place. And there's something else too.'

'Pray continue.'

'Both the bodies showed evidence that they had been cut in the same way that Mary Mercer had been cut.'

'Incisions at the collar bone?

'Yes. On the skeleton the abrasions of a knife were faint – if I had not been looking I would have missed them. The other girl – the girl with no name – her dried-out skin was damaged in the same place. One might say that the skin had split as it dried and was pulled tight against the bones beneath, but I was *looking* for evidence of a cut in that place, and on the feet, and I believe I found it.'

'It must be a man who did this,' said Will. 'We must surely assume an understanding of medical matters – who else would know how to make so precise an incision, or how to strip a corpse? It's hardly a subject a lady might be familiar with.' He covered his face with his hands. 'It's horrible to think of – flies everywhere. Clouds of them, all black and shimmering. Clustered about that poor girl. Feasting. Breeding. Hatching—'

'It's nature, Will. She is very efficient.'

'She may well be efficient, but I dislike hearing about her methods.'

'How's your head?'

'It's not so bad,' he said. 'Though I'm bruised all over from that fall down the stairs.' He looked at my soot-smeared face and grinned. 'What a sight we are! Like sweeps!'

Both of us were black with smoke, our eyes smarting, our clothes flecked with cinders. We stank of the mortuary too, I was sure of it, even though we had had to walk home, for no cabman would take us looking and smelling as we did.

Will licked the corner of his handkerchief and scrubbed at his face. It made no difference. 'Are those baths ready, Gabriel?' he said. 'Hurry up, lad. I don't think I can bear the smell of myself for much longer!'

While we had been talking, Gabriel and Jenny had been filling two tin baths with hot water. It was a lengthy process, for the water had to be drawn from the pump in the apothecary sink, and then boiled on the stove top. We had only one bath at the apothecary, but I had borrowed one from the baker a few doors up as I was not prepared to share Will's water, not when he was so filthy – and I doubted very much whether he would like mine.

The copper, set on the stove top, was boiling at last, and Will shared the water between the two baths. I dragged up the screen from the back of the shop.

'What d'you need the screen for?' said Gabriel.

'Privacy,' I said.

'Why?' said Gabriel. '*I* never get the screen.'

'And the draught,' I said.

'What draught? It's boiling in here.' The two of them stood side by side in their brown apothecary aprons. Gabriel put his hands on his hips. Pestle Jenny did the same.

'Why don't you go to Sorley's with Jenny,' I said. I handed him a few coins. 'Get some food – a pheasant pie, some cheese, apples. Some beer, too. And get a cake on your way home. Bring it all straight back, mind. I don't want you eating it on the way home.'

Will watched me in silence as I pulled the screen forward, positioning it between the two baths. I locked the apothecary door, and fetched some clean clothes for myself. 'Well?' I said. 'Are you going to take a bath? Your water'll get cold if you just sit staring at it.'

While he went to fetch his clothes I added some lavender oil to the water – it was good for cuts and bruises, and would aid healing – some comfrey leaves, and a muslin bag full of oatmeal to soften the skin. Will seemed to be taking an age – he was so vain sometimes. I knew he would be deciding which shirt was the crispest, which waistcoat he might wear, which of his under things was the least darned and patched. By the time he came down I was in the water up to my neck, my shoulders pressing against the cold enamel rim, my knees two tall pale islands in the milky water. Behind the screen I heard Will undress, and climb in. He sighed, as I had, as the warm water lapped over his limbs. For a while we lay there in silence, looking up at the ceiling, its lime-washed plaster and dark wooden beams hung with bunches of herbs – feverfew, rosemary, cleavers, fennel. A basket of oranges on the table glowed as a beam of sunlight filtered through the window, lighting up the bottles on the walls like the luminous panels in a church window. Behind us, the stove crackled and glowed. I had set a bowl of water upon it, swimming with a few drops of geranium, camomile and rose oil, and the warm and steamy air was now heavy with the smell of the hothouse, of high summer and warm sunny afternoons in the physic garden. I closed my eyes.

Into my mind came Eliza, as she so often did, for not a day went by when I did not think of her. I wondered again where she was and what had become of her. But that day she was joined, in my thoughts, by someone else; someone tall and dark, her eyes black and furious, her head proud and confident on her long slender neck.

'What are you thinking?' said Will suddenly. 'Is it about Miss Proudlove?' He laughed as I tried to splutter out a reply. 'You were, weren't you? I could see you were taken with her. In awe, one might say.'

'I am not.'

'Yes you are. I think you have never met a woman who is quite so forthright. A single woman, at least, for I dare say there are a thousand old battle-scarred widow women out there who aren't afraid to speak their mind. Look at Mrs Speedicut—'

'No thank you.'

'It is unusual to meet with so outspoken a woman—'

'I was thinking I might ask Miss Proudlove about Eliza,' I said.

Will was silent. I could sense him growing cold in his bath water, measuring his words carefully before he spoke. He had never known Eliza, not really, though he said he understood my feelings. It caused him pain, I knew, for me to love someone who was so lost. 'Eliza might not wish to be found,' he said at last.

'I have to try.'

'Do you, Jem? And what will you do if you find her?'

It was my turn to be silent.

'Perhaps the way things turned out – perhaps it was for the best.'

'For whom? My father is dead. Eliza is missing—'

'I didn't mean that. You know I didn't.'

'I don't know what you meant. I wish I had never mentioned it.' I plunged my head under the water, my eyes closed, my ears deaf, so that all I heard was the sound of the water slapping against the sides of the bath, and the beating of my own heart. But the truth was that I did not know what I would say to Eliza, that I could not understand the decisions she had made. I only knew that I was suddenly afraid for her. I had been so thankful that neither of the two corpses were hers that I had almost wept with relief.

I had to find her, whether it hurt Will or not.

It was late in the afternoon for a visit to the physic garden, but there was light enough, and I had promised Gabriel and Jenny that we might have a bonfire to chase away the autumn shades. Will walked slowly. He had bruised his shoulder and his knee quite badly when he fell. I had rubbed both joints with comfrey oil and arnica to soothe the swelling and reduce bruising, and he should probably have rested in front of the apothecary stove, but I wanted him to have some air, and I was sure the weather wasn't going to last.

The summer had been long, and with my commitments at the apothecary I had been obliged to engage a gardener and a boy to keep the physic garden manageable, for it was too much for Gabriel and me, even if we had Will to help us. Over the last few months the place had become unruly, though I could see where the gardener had cut back dead twigs and swept up leaves. A basket of apples stood beside the wall, waiting to be taken up to the apothecary, along with another filled with pears and a smaller one half full of crab apples. All had grown in abundance and I had watched with pleasure as their hard fruits swelled in the sunshine against the garden's south-facing wall, the branches stretching along the warmed stones like a great network of arteries. There were many more still to be picked, and the boughs hung low, laden with dull green pears and shiny blushing apples.

Jenny stood on the threshold, staring at the garden with her mouth open and her eyes wide. She put out a hand and ran her fingers through the great bank of lavender that grew beside the path. She touched the gleaming belly of an apple that hung low and ripe before her eye. Gabriel reached up and picked it for her. She looked at Gabriel, and then at the apple, in wonder. It was a good one, I had to admit. Some of them were afflicted with the blight, for the London air did not suit them well, but this one was flawless and rosy and plump.

'Shake it,' said Gabriel. 'If the pips rattle, then it's ripe. Go on.'

Jenny shook the apple against her ear, and her face lit up.

'Eat it,' I said. 'It's yours.'

I sent the two of them off to gather blackberries, for we were troubled by brambles where they had burst through from the unkempt grounds next door. Soon afterwards she came up from the bottom of the garden with a barrow full of leaves and sticks. She put them where I instructed. Her cheeks were pink with pleasure, her lips stained with berry juice, her eyes bright beneath the brim of her hat.

I dug the earth, pulling out weeds and lifting the soil to expose the rich dark loam. A robin appeared, to beadily survey my handiwork, waiting for the glistening sight of a worm or grub in the newly turned dirt. I sent Will to gather sloes. It was an easy enough job and I thought it would relax him. He'd once told me how he'd gathered the hard black fruits from the hedgerows of Wiltshire when he was a child. I forgot the name of his village – some place in the middle of nowhere with a curious double-barrelled name. He would make sloe gin for Christmas – Mrs Speedicut loved the stuff, though as Will said she would drink any kind of gin, even if he flavoured it with his own socks. He seemed to have recovered his spirits somewhat, and he whistled as he picked.

I sighed. It had been a long day. I thought back to the post-mortem I had carried out that morning on John Aberlady, and all we had seen and done since, and it felt like the longest day I had ever lived. Could I not just lie down and go to sleep?

I closed my eyes and let my mind relax, lifting my face to what remained of the sun. It was low in the sky, blood red, and filtered by the tall trees that grew in the garden of the house on the other side of the wall. Eliza had lived there with her father and mother. She had loved the physic garden, had known almost as much about it as I. Times had changed, however, and although those I had once loved were gone, there were others I had come to love just as well. Gabriel, my friends at Angel Meadow Asylum – even Mrs Speedicut, in my own way – but especially Will. I watched him amongst the sloe bushes, bare headed, his tall hat half-full now with berries. His dark hair was rumpled, his cheeks tanned from his afternoons spent in the physic garden. His shirt sleeves were rolled up, exposing strong, lean forearms, though I had cautioned him against this for the thorns were fierce. Here and there a thin line of blood beaded his skin, or blotted his shirt in a spray of tiny red stains. I could hear him humming as he worked. He must have sensed my gaze upon his back, for he stopped what he was doing and looked back at me and grinned.

I heard laughing, and I saw Gabriel racing down the slope of the garden with Jenny in a wheelbarrow, tumbling her into a mound of leaves and grass cuttings that were piled beside the compost heap. These people were my family. Without them my life was an empty corridor echoing with my own lonely footsteps.

I felt something thwack against my head, and a sloe dropped down the neck of my shirt. 'Penny for them?' said Will.

Gabriel bounded up. 'Can we light the bonfire now?' he said. 'It's getting cold.'

Gabriel and Jenny sat beside the fire, toasting bits of cheese on sticks, and eating pie and apples. Will and I sat on the wrought iron bench some distance away – we had had our fill of smoke and fire for that day – and drank Sorley's ale. I was not hungry, and Will seemed to have little appetite.

'You'll go back to the *Blood* tonight?' he said, slicing into his apple with his pocket knife. I could tell by his voice that he wanted me to say 'no'. He hated the place, though he had not said as much.

'Yes,' I said. I did not relish the prospect either.

'You must let me come with you.'

'There's no need.'

'Of course there is.'

I turned to face him. 'Look at you, Will.' I put my hand to his cheek gently. 'Your poor face is battered, your nose is bruised, your black eye is coming up nicely. To add to that you probably have concussion, as well as damaged lungs from inhaling all that smoke. I can hear you wheezing even now! You need rest, not a night on board the *Blood and Fleas*; dry air and warmth, not the damp vapours of the river—'

'I cannot let you go there alone,' he said. 'I just – I cannot. I cannot lose you.' Suddenly, he took my hand. 'What would I do if something happened? To you, Jem? There are four people dead. One of them an apothecary, a man you expected to be clever enough to stay ahead of his adversaries – whoever they might be. I cannot let you go to that place alone. And certainly not to stay the night! You do see that?' He squeezed my hand, wrapping it between his as if it were the most precious thing he owned. His eyes were dark now, downcast. Afraid. 'You must . . . You must know how I—' He glanced up and saw the expression on my face – sorrow, pity, horror – and he flinched, as if I had struck him. 'Don't look at me,' he whispered. 'Not like that. Not you.'

I put my arms around him. 'Then let us not look at each other,' I said against his ear. 'For I am not worth any man's gaze.'

'I know you cannot love me as I love you,' he said.

'But I do love you,' I said.

'Like a brother.' His voice was muffled.

'It is the best kind of love,' I replied. 'For it never fades, never grows tired, or stale, or old. I will always be your friend, always be your companion, I can be everything to you, but I cannot be . . . I cannot be . . . '

'You cannot even bear to say it,' he muttered.

'You should be glad of it,' I cried. 'For I would make a very bad one.'

'Indeed you would,' he answered. He pushed me away, wiping his face with his hands. 'But I *am* coming tonight, and I *am* staying. I will help you in the apothecary – I can go up to Deadman's Basin tomorrow to evaluate the fire damage and to decide the best way to proceed. The men'll have less work than they expected, now that we've burned the place down.'

'But where will you sleep? There's only Aberlady's room, and you would hate to sleep surrounded by poisonous frogs and flexing serpents.'

'There are frogs and serpents?'

'There are.'

'Then I will definitely sleep amongst them, for I imagine they will be more affable companions than any of the gentlemen on board.'

❧

I sent Will and Gabriel out into the street to look for a carter, for I wanted to take some plants I had potted up to the *Blood*, and we could not carry them there ourselves. I sat with Pestle Jenny by the glowing embers of the fire while the sun vanished behind the branches of the peach tree. It was unusual to have a girl about the place – I checked myself. *I* was a girl – a woman – of course I was. And yet there was nothing that was girlish or womanly, or ladylike, about me. I had never worn stays, or petticoats; I had never sat in silence while men talked, had never modified my words or behaviour so as to guard against showing any man up as a fool or to preserve his self-worth. I walked the streets without fear of having my virtue threatened, I went wherever I wished, and I might smoke and spit as I pleased. It was my father who had first dressed me as a boy; he had passed me off as his son from the moment of my birth to all at St Saviour's, condemning me to a life of disguise. All I knew was that I was one half of a twin, that my brother had lain dead beside me as I grew in the womb, and my mother was killed by us both as we emerged into the world. Had my father been punishing me for being a poor substitute for the wife and son he had lost? Was he helping me to achieve things that most women could never even dream of? I would never know, for he had never explained his actions. He had wanted an heir to run the apothecary, and that was what he had got. It was the only life I knew, and I lived it as best I could.

I thought of what Will had said to me, how tightly he had held my hand, how my heart had seized in my chest when I had found him crumpled at the foot of the stairs inside the villa at Deadman's Basin, and my heart was torn. Was I right in what I had said to him, or was I simply too afraid to admit how I felt? I could never submit to the subservient position that women seemed obliged occupy, though I knew in my heart that he was not asking that of me. He loved me as an equal, as a man, for that was how he saw me. Did he know I was a woman? I was sure he did, and yet neither of us had ever mentioned it outright.

I sighed, and rubbed my eyes. But the thoughts still swirled in my head, and my heart. Surely if I dressed as a man and acted as a man, then I *was* a man? What was there, apart from uterus and breasts, that was woman? Why should I be defined solely by parts of my body, neither of which affected my intellect, or my reason, and neither of which I had any use for? I closed my eyes. How tired I was! I tried to think about Eliza, but instead Will's face, bruised and sorrowful, came into my mind. He would never let me down, would never run away and hide from me until I was demented with worry the way Eliza had. I thought then of Miss Proudlove – her dark eyes, her burnished skin, the dull sheen of her hair. If my father had *not* dressed me as a boy, if he had *not* schooled me in the selfish, confident ways of his own sex, would I have become the woman I was expected to be? I would not. I knew it in my heart and my soul, I would not.

Jenny was staring at me, her hat pulled low over her eyes. That day she had demonstrated her aptitude in the apothecary with greater skill and competence than Gabriel ever had. I had watched the lad to see whether he was jealous, whether he would resent her being amongst us, never mind the fact that she could set up the condenser in half the time it took him to do it. But instead he seemed impressed, proud almost. She sat at my side, small and erect, watching me. A cloud of fragrant dust hung about her wherever she went; that afternoon I recognised the sweet spiciness of nigella seeds and the warm soothing smell of cloves. A linen bag hung from her shoulder. It looked heavy, as if weighted down with a boulder, and I noticed she had not let the thing out of her sight.

'What's this?' I said.

She reached into it, and pulled out a pestle and mortar. She cradled it lovingly, her fingers caressing the cool smooth stone. She took a small bag of cloves and cinnamon bark from her coat pocket, tipped them into the heavy white bowl and began to grind.

I laid my hand on her shoulder, soothed, as she was, by the sound and motion of the tools of our trade. 'Well, Jenny,' I said. 'What are we to do with you? Your master, Mr Aberlady, is dead. Did you know that?'

She nodded as she worked, her shoulders hunched, the hand that wielded the pestle moving faster and faster.

194

'Henbane,' I said. 'Someone broke the seeds and put them on a raging stove so that they smoked like incense and turned him mad.'

I could see that her whole body had tensed, though she had not stopped her work.

'I think we've stumbled upon something that is both wicked and cruel, Jenny. Did Mr Aberlady know of it, d'you think?' All at once the girl's grinding stopped, and I sensed that she was about to fling the mortar to the ground and dash away. I knew she was from the streets – if she chose to return there then we would never find her. And one day, soon, she was sure to speak again. I squeezed her shoulder. 'You're safe now,' I said. 'No one will hurt you here.' She looked up at me. I could see from her eyes that she had heard those words before. Perhaps she had believed them then. I doubted whether she believed them now.

Chapter Fourteen

⚂

In the event Will and I did not return to the *Blood* that night but went back home to Fishbait Lane. We were exhausted, and both of us were feeling the effects of the smoke we had inhaled. A night spent asleep in the damp river air seemed unwise, and so I took my own advice and stayed away from the place. Will lit fires in our rooms to keep us warm, and I prepared a cold infusion of elm bark and mulberry leaves – a vile-tasting but highly effective respiratory demulcent. A tincture of lobelia would help to relax the respiratory tract, and I put a flagon of water containing the required dose next to Will's bed, and mine, and bade him drink it during the night.

In the morning, we both felt better, though I put a flask of cold nettle and plantain infusion in both our satchels.

'More bitter weeds, Jem?' said Will gloomily. 'I'd rather have a cup of coffee.'

'There's coffee on board the *Blood*,' I said. 'But this

infusion of "weeds" as you call them, will help the lung tissue to heal. You must sip it throughout the day.'

We walked together down to the hospital ship. Will was looking pale, but there was work to be done, he said, and he would have to go back to Deadman's Basin whether he wanted to or not.

'Will you go straight away?' I asked.

'I will stall and dawdle for as long as I can.' He grinned. 'I have sent a message to my master telling him that since the place burned down I need another day before the men come to start the demolition work. I thought I might help you a little before I go up to the place. And, of course, I must sip my nettle infusion.'

The carter had brought up the plants I had gathered at the apothecary. A group of orderlies helped Will and me to carry them up from the dockside to the *Blood*'s poop deck – a small platform atop the apothecary that was one of the few spaces on the old ship that had not been turned into a room of some kind. It had been used to store barrels filled with rainwater, and as a place for the drying of clothes. But the barrels were empty, and I had the orderlies move them to the stern where they were just as likely to be replenished, and there were plenty of other places where the bedding might be hung to catch the stinking breeze that blew off the water. Now, as a result of our efforts, the poop deck was home to a tiny physic garden made up of some two dozen or so herbs potted in large earthen planters. Most of them were well established, for I had always propagated my favourite plants and had a number of them growing in pots already. To these I had added a few new ones – goldenrod, roseroot and angelica – and brought them up to the ship. Will sat on a stool he had brought out from the apothecary. He looked out at the deck as the morning grew bright, his sketch pad and pencil in his hands.

'Imagine the place in the dark,' he said. 'Wreathed in fog, its lanterns dim orbs of light, the groans and sighs from the wards echoing across the silent water—'

I shivered. 'Well you'd better make the most of it while the sun is shining,' I said. 'For I fear it won't last.' I sipped my coffee. 'I can't help but think the old girl is looking her best at the moment, with the autumn haze blurring her crooked lines.'

'Hm,' said Will. I knew he wasn't really listening. His pencil moved rapidly across the page, his gaze sweeping the deck, sizing up its proportions. I had always admired his speed and skill as an artist. I had one of his drawings of old St Saviour's Infirmary framed and hanging on the wall of the apothecary.

'You know,' he said suddenly. 'I think there are a number of ways that this place might be improved as a hospital. The deck has been added to in a piecemeal way that does not make use of the space at all well. If the majority of the existing extraneous structures were removed we might build something far more well-considered, orderly and useful. I could make it spacious and airy too, surely something the men would love after lives spent at sea, or outside at the docks.' He added to his drawing, glancing up and down, and sketching once more. 'I wonder whether the executive committee, or the medical men, would be interested in my ideas. I would need at least one of them to support me. Naturally I would charge a small fee for my design, and the cost of the building work would have to be found.'

'Dr Rennie might be interested,' I said. I pointed to a small figure passing from the snakes' quarters to the consultants' sitting room. 'There he is.'

Will stood up amongst the greenery. 'Ahoy there, Dr Rennie, sir!' he cried, his voice echoing out. He stood like an admiral, his hands clasped behind his back, his legs akimbo. His figure, illuminated by the rising sun, must have looked commanding, for Dr Rennie sprang round and snapped to attention. 'If I might speak with you, sir,' cried Will. 'I shall join you later, Jem,' he said. 'Ward rounds at four bells?'

I nodded. 'If you mean at ten o'clock, then yes.'

'Four bells by the forenoon watch,' said Will. He gathered up his sketches and his pencils, saluted smartly, and vanished down the steps to the weather deck.

I stayed amongst the plants, tamping down their soil and watering those that needed it. I had kept one water butt for the purpose, though it contained little. I wondered how long the potted garden would survive if it was fed by the Thames. I would be sure to let the stuff stand for a while before I used it, so that the brown residue might sink to the bottom of the pail. I ran my hands through the tough fronds of the rosemary, crushing the hard needle-like leaves between my fingers so that they released their astringent aroma. It was late in the season for lavender, but the leaves of the young plants I had brought up were scented enough for me, and I bruised those too, until the air was filled with the familiar sweet and woody scent. The sun was now bright against the eastern sky, silhouetting the rigging and masts that crowded the riverside in a black web of spars and ropes. I plucked some mint leaves and went down to the apothecary.

Will reappeared at ten minutes before ten o'clock. 'He's fascinating,' he said, when I asked him about Dr Rennie. 'Told me everything about the ship. He's full of stories.'

'Such as?'

'The time she was caught in a storm in the Bay of Biscay and was almost lost. The time he met Nelson himself. The time the ship was pursued by the French for three days! As for the Battle of the Nile – I have had a blow-by-blow account. The next best thing to being there! Gabriel would love him—'

'No wonder you've been gone for so long.'

Will went to sit at Aberlady's desk, pushing aside the papers and books that littered its surface. 'I have some drawings here,' he said. 'And some new ideas from Dr Rennie. He says he would like a top ward, with more hammocks for those who are convalescing and who would value the open air.'

'And Deadman's Basin?'

'Yes, yes, I will be going there soon enough. I can amend my plans while I am here and add to them when I go down later.'

'And the prescriptions?' I said. I had enjoyed a busy few hours. 'I thought you were helping.'

'I'll help you with those,' said a voice. In the door stood Dr Proudlove. 'Is there much to do?'

'Not really,' I said. 'I'm all but ready, though some help to take them down would be appreciated.'

'I'll do that,' said Will.

Dr Proudlove seemed excited, as if something thrilled

him. 'I wanted to speak to you about the patient Rintoul,' he said.

Rintoul had arrived three days earlier, so I had been told. He had been working nearby at St Catherine's Dock when a rope snapped, and he had been catapulted from the winding gear, upon which he had been working, down into the yard below. His fall had, fortunately, been broken by a cart filled with horse manure that had been scraped from the yard and was awaiting collection. The man had broken his leg, and his collar bone, and had rope burn badly on both hands, so that his palms were red raw. He had been brought up to the *Blood* on a cart, carried up the steps and winched down into the top ward. Dr Antrobus had set his broken bones; Dr Cole had treated the rope burn on his hands. The leg I had been unable to see as it had been splinted and bound, but I understood that break had been a clean one. The hands, however, had been a mess, the skin on the palms torn away as the rope whipped though his fingers like a wire through butter. They had been bandaged, and padded with iodine. The mischief, however, lay far deeper than that.

'Rintoul?' I said now. 'The fellow downstairs with incipient tetanus?'

'You saw it?' said Dr Proudlove.

'I did.'

'I was thinking,' he sounded hesitant. 'You have heard of bhang?'

'I have,' I said. 'Though it is more commonly referred to as tincture of cannabis.'

'As a treatment for tetanus?'

I held up a bottle of brownish tincture. 'I brought some

up from my apothecary on Fishbait Lane, as I did not see any on the shelves here.'

'You would advise it?'

'I believe there is no better treatment.'

'May I?' He held out his hand.

I handed him the bottle in silence, watching him as he held it up to the lamplight. His eyes glittered.

'I think this is not a common treatment?' he said.

'No,' I replied. 'I would be surprised if it was at all well known. Especially due to its Indian origins, and the applications it commonly has in that country.'

'Indeed.' Dr Proudlove smiled, and slipped the bottle into his pocket. For a moment he looked as though he wanted to say something more, but he didn't. 'Shall I help you with the prescriptions?' he said instead.

I could see he did not really want to do this, that, in fact, he had now got what he came for and no longer wanted to be in the apothecary at all, and certainly not associated with the lowly task of carrying medicines. 'Mr Quartermain will help me, sir,' I said. 'We are just about ready.'

❦

Down in the middle ward the air was thick with the smell of stale tobacco, sweat and carbolic. There was a gangrenous tang to the atmosphere too from an amputee I had seen the previous morning. I had sedated the fellow with opiates, for there was little else that might be done for him now. At the back of the ward, the doctors were gathered – Dr Sackville, tall and thin, his grey cheeks colourless in the lamplight; Dr Antrobus, serious and pensive; Dr Cole, smiling and rosy cheeked; Dr Rennie, the stuff of nightmares, with his enamel eye and ghastly smile. Beside them, but standing a little to one side, was Dr Proudlove. The students were not present that morning, which was just as well as there was little enough space down there, especially once Will and I had arrived. Mrs Speedicut was there too, her face set in a mask of tight-lipped resentment – something had gone wrong, I could tell by her face, and she was about to be blamed for it.

'Weren't me, sirs!' she said, falling back on her standard response, which was to deny everything. 'I only just got here! This fellow's been not right since yesterday morning. Dr Cole prescribed opium last night, but I can't say as it's done much good.'

'Good day, gentlemen,' I said.

'Look at the state of the fellow, gentlemen,' cried Dr Rennie. 'Look at his face, look at how he lies, look at his hands and tell me what you see – and what we might do!'

The fellow Rintoul was lying upon his bed, bathed in sweat. His hands were balled into fists – even within his bandages – his face tight and strained. And then, as we watched a great spasm overtook him. His back arched violently, his shoulder blades and heels the only parts of his body to touch the thin, stained mattress upon which he lay. Worst of all was the expression on his face, the familiar grinning rictus of lockjaw – the sinews on his neck standing out like rigging beneath the skin. His eyes rolled in his head, white spittle gathering at the corners of his mouth. The man would die, there was little doubt, if something was not done soon.

'The fellow didn't seem too bad last night,' said Dr Cole briskly. 'He was to be discharged today, so perhaps we might send him home.'

'But look at him!' said Will.

'We cannot have another one die on board,' said Dr Cole, his voice low, but insistent. 'Not if we can avoid it.'

'You cannot send him away to die!' said Will.

'What on earth does it have to do with you?' said Dr Antrobus.

'He's helping me in the apothecary,' I said. 'Since Pestle Jenny refuses to return here.'

'Refuses?' said Dr Sackville. 'You mean you've seen her, Flockhart? She's told you what happened that night?'

It seemed to me that the ward fell silent, everyone listening to what my answer might be. 'No,' I said.

'And where is she?'

'I don't know,' I said, quite truthfully, for at that moment I had no idea where Pestle Jenny might be.

The sick man before us let out a mighty groan.

'If he dies on board that's six this month,' whispered Dr Cole. 'It does not reflect well on us.'

'It does not reflect well on you to send a man home who is in this condition,' said Will.

'We all have to die,' hissed Dr Cole. 'But would *you* like to die down here?'

'No, no, Dr Cole,' said Dr Sackville. 'Mr Quartermain is quite correct. It behoves us to do all we can. He's had opium, you say?' He sighed. 'Perhaps I should send for Dr Birdwhistle and the poor fellow can be eased by the scriptures – if he likes that sort of thing.'

Before us, the man's flesh glistened, beads of sweat standing out on his brow like globules of fat. I had seen a man's bones break with the contraction of the muscles, and even as we watched, Rintoul's damaged collar bone twisted grotesquely. He slipped out of consciousness with the pain, his cries terrible to hear, those in the beds nearby falling silent and fearful. I looked at Dr Proudlove, who was standing stiffly, leaning forward as if his insides were wound as tightly as clock-springs. Was he going to speak up or not?

'The infection comes from the hands,' said Dr Cole suddenly. 'And yet I washed them myself when he came in. I have no idea what *these* bandages are.'

'The bandages must be changed every morning,' I said. 'Mrs Speedicut will have changed them this morning as per my instructions.'

'And I misted the palms with carbolic solution,' said Mrs Speedicut, her tone defensive. 'As I were *told* to do.'

'Clean bandages,' I said. 'Every day.' My old friend Dr Bain from St Saviour's Infirmary had taught me much about the importance of cleanliness when treating open wounds. He had been murdered before his ideas became common currency – certainly I saw little evidence that they had ever reached the *Blood*. 'Dead skin trimmed away with scissors that have first been boiled and left to soak in carbolic—'

'It seems rather excessive,' muttered Dr Cole.

'We must keep the area clean,' I said.

'It *is* clean,' Dr Cole replied. 'I washed it myself.'

'With a bowl of Thames water?' said Dr Proudlove.

'I have no idea where it came from,' he replied. 'From the water tank, I presume.'

The water tank was replenished by the rain, which fell through the brown city air, gathering soot as it came. It was certainly better than the stuff in the river, but not by much. The wash cloth he used would have wiped other wounds, other sores, other hands.

'Of course,' I said, realising how angry he was getting. 'My apologies, Dr Cole. I was merely reiterating your own good practice when I suggested cleanliness was necessary.'

'And yet there is much more to dirt than meets the eye,' said Dr Proudlove. 'When viewed under the microscope what appears to be clear water is, in fact, nothing of the kind.'

'The matter settles if the water is left to stand,' said Dr Antrobus.

'The larger particles, yes,' said Dr Proudlove. 'But what of those which remain suspended? I fear there is dirt everywhere – and we often cannot see it.'

'The wounds upon the hands were quite clean,' cried Dr Cole. 'I saw to them myself—'

'It is not the hands that we should be thinking about now, gentlemen,' cried Dr Rennie. 'The hands will heal, anyone can see that, but perhaps not before the man has died.'

'What do you suggest, gentlemen?' said Dr Sackville. 'Dr Antrobus?'

'Perhaps,' Dr Antrobus stammered, quailing under the gaze of the great Sackville, 'perhaps another dose?'

'Of?'

'Of opium, sir.'

'And do you concur, Dr Cole?'

'Yes, sir.'

'What about you, Mr Flockhart?' said Dr Rennie, suddenly. 'Or you, Dr Proudlove? Do you have any ideas?'

'Opium is the standard treatment,' I said. 'Though goodness knows why, as I've never seen anyone recover by it – apart from by happenstance. On those grounds the suggestion makes perfect sense—'

'And yet I think perhaps there *is* an alternative,' Dr Proudlove's voice sounded loud in the crowded space of the top ward. 'Perhaps one that is not well known, but I think its efficacy is beyond doubt.' His face, moist and anxious, glimmered in the lamplight. Before us, Rintoul's breathing had become laboured. Saliva issued from his rigid jaws, and a damp circle at his crotch betrayed the seep of urine onto the tumbled bed sheets.

Dr Rennie nodded. His tin eye caught the light of my lantern, so that for a moment I thought it had actually winked at me. 'Pray continue,' he said.

'Last night, when only the man's jaw had been affected, Dr Cole had dosed him with laudanum. This would no doubt have been more than adequate, had he not fallen into the horse dung.'

'And yet he did, Dr Proudlove,' said Dr Sackville. 'What might have occurred had he not is immaterial.'

'I believe that the dirt he fell into has caused the problem we see here, the infection entering the blood through the damaged skin on his hands.'

'You supply no answers, sir,' replied Dr Sackville. 'You may well be correct, but the question I am asking is how might we treat the fellow?'

'Bhang,' cried Dr Proudlove, stepping forward. 'Bhang is the remedy I would suggest for tetanus.'

Beside me, Dr Rennie laughed. 'Bhang! Why, I've not heard that name these thirty year or more.'

'What is it?' said Dr Antrobus and Dr Cole together.

'A concoction beloved by fakirs and thugees,' said Dr Sackville.

'The same,' said Dr Proudlove. 'But any medicine might be used and abused. In the same way that we might

207

cloak opium in medical respectability if we call it laudanum, so bhang becomes a reputable part of any pharmacopoeia if we call it tincture of hemp oil or extract of cannabis—'

'I am well acquainted with the stuff, sir,' cried Dr Sackville. 'When I was with the Company in Calcutta it was used regularly by the natives. Not in a medical capacity, I hasten to point out.'

'No, sir, but—'

'In fact the stuff was used, as Dr Rennie says, by fakirs and other idolatrous individuals. Mixed with opium, it produced a state of grave intoxication. Might I refer you, sir, to the practice known as the Swinging by Hooks?'

'I don't know of it,' said Dr Proudlove, his expression despairing.

'A grotesque form of entertainment,' said Dr Sackville. He seized his lapels in his fists, and his voice boomed out. 'I witnessed it on several occasions, a very great honour for the participant, but something quite monstrous for a civilised man to behold. The man's chest was pierced by hooks and he would be swung around in a state of acute pain – and ecstasy, the latter expedited by the great quantity of bhang the fellow had imbibed before the event. Such activities took place as a heathen ritual designed to excite the crowds, many of whom were similarly intoxicated. Have you been to India, sir?'

'No, sir.'

'If you had, Dr Proudlove, then I doubt you would be offering such substances.'

Dr Proudlove glanced at me for help, but I looked away. I could not ally myself with him, no matter how much I might agree with his arguments. I needed the fellowship of Cole and Antrobus, and their approval, if I was ever to get to the bottom of Aberlady's death.

'But sir,' said Dr Proudlove. 'It's quite evident that opium alone does nothing at all for the patient.'

'It is the usual approach, Dr Proudlove,' said Dr Sackville.

'Then the usual approach is wrong. Can you not see that other races might have something to offer us, that we should at least *try*—?'

'I "cannot see it" because what I *can* see is that the "other races" you refer to are inferior to our own,' snapped Dr Sackville. '"Other races" think the heavens are held up on the back of an elephant, or that having their likeness taken will steal their soul.' There was a moment's silence. Before us, with his face yellow and ghastly in the lantern light, the tendons on his neck standing out like wire, his teeth clenched in a grimace, the patient Rintoul arched his back and moaned. Dr Sackville turned to me.

'And your view, Mr Flockhart?'

'Dr Cole is quite right, sir,' I said. 'Opium is the standard treatment. Just as he was right about the cleanliness of the patient's hands. Laudanum is indicated in cases such as this.'

'Quite so,' snapped Dr Sackville. 'Laudanum. That is my advice, Dr Proudlove. Pray adhere to it.'

Dr Proudlove threw me a look of disgust as everyone turned away. I saw some of the patients smirking at his disgrace, and I was sorry.

'There will be another corpse down here by morning if we prescribe nothing but laudanum,' he hissed at me. 'And well you know it, Mr Flockhart. I thought you were different to the others, but it seems you are not.'

His face was furious, and I had the feeling that I had insulted more than simply his pride. As we left the ward, out of the corner of my eye I saw him take the tincture of cannabis from his pocket and administer it to the patient via a small funnel and a metal tube forced between Rintoul's gritted teeth. I was glad to see it, for I would have given the stuff to the poor fellow myself if he had not.

Beside me, Dr Cole grinned as we walked away. 'Thank you, Flockhart,' he said in an undertone. 'You helped me out of a tight spot with old Sackville there and I'm much obliged to you. Look, why don't you and Quartermain come out for supper with us tonight?'

'Thank you,' I said. 'We will. Can't think what Proudlove is doing here anyway,' I added. 'I suppose he can't find work elsewhere, and has to stick it out as a sixpenny surgeon on the waterfront where people don't care who the sawbones is.'

'Quite so,' said Dr Cole.

'Poor fellow,' I said.

'Save your pity,' said Dr Antrobus. 'Proudlove deserves to be stuck on an old tub like this. But what about us?'

'It's almost impossible to get on,' muttered Cole. 'Without money, without connections, one simply cannot get a foot on the ladder.'

'Can't Dr Sackville help?' I said. 'He must have a considerable private practice. Can't he introduce you to some of his patients?'

'He says he *will* help us,' said Dr Cole. 'But only if we prove ourselves worthy of his patronage.'

'Of course.' I shook each of their hands. 'Well, gentlemen, let me know if I can help.'

Dr Cole and Dr Antrobus moved off.

'What are you up to?' hissed Will as the doctors walked away. 'I was under the impression that you thought Cole and Antrobus were the worst kind of medical men: arrogant, desperate, competitive, mediocre.'

'You might keep your voice down,' I said.

'And you have seen to it that Dr Proudlove is humiliated in front of them. You gave him the cannabis mixture yourself. You brought it from Fishbait Lane especially, as you knew that chap needed it.'

'Yes, and it *will* make the patient better.'

'Then what are you doing?'

I took Will's arm and turned him aside. 'It would hardly help us if we allied ourselves with a man who is so clearly an outsider. I'm afraid we must use Dr Proudlove to enter the little club that comprises Antrobus, Cole and Sackville. It is they who interest me, Will. Dr Proudlove seems to me to be an unfortunate victim of prejudice and resentment. He's by far the best doctor and most intelligent man on board this ship. But showing the others to be the narrow-minded fools they are will do nothing to bring us closer to solving this problem, nothing to show us who drove Aberlady to his death or murdered Mary Mercer and the others. It will simply serve to ostracise us. And how might *that* work to our advantage? We are here on the *Blood* for a short time, Will. We must use that time strategically.'

'Then perhaps you might at least explain yourself to Dr Proudlove. He trusted you—'

'I can't.'

'Jem!'

'No! Can't you see, Will? You were right when you said we can trust no one. *No one.* We've one chance to move forward. Our actions must seem to be real and sincere. If

I seem to be rude, Proudlove must think that I *am* rude. But he's an intelligent chap. If he is all he seems then he'll understand – in the end.'

✤

I took Mrs Speedicut to one side. She was no stranger to my methods and she would follow my instructions – keeping the man as comfortable as possible, changing the salve on his hands first thing in the morning and dosing him with cannabis tincture hourly. I told her to pay attention to what Dr Proudlove did, and to help him as he wished. Any decline in the patient's condition was to be reported to me instantly.

After that, I followed Dr Sackville, Dr Cole and Dr Antrobus upstairs. Dr Rennie disappeared into the bowels of the ship. It was only afterwards that I noticed Will had gone with him.

'Antrobus and I are off to the Brass Bell on Spyglass Lane this evening,' said Dr Cole. 'About seven o'clock? Perhaps to the supper rooms on Cable Street afterwards. Would you care to join us?'

Dr Antrobus looked cross, as though he wished Dr Cole had not made the invitation, though when he spoke his words were friendly enough. 'Why don't you meet us there, Mr Flockhart? Assuming you can prise Mr Quartermain away from Dr Rennie.'

I heard their laughter as they vanished over the side of the ship. I had no idea where they were going. For a moment, I wondered whether I should follow them, but I had too many things to do on board, and I watched them disappear into the narrow streets that lead away from the river.

After that, the deck was quiet, though around us the noise from the docks was a constant clamour. I let it wash over me – the shouting of men, the clack and clatter of carts and wagons, the roar of wheels turning, of gears grinding; the squeak and clack of block and tackle, the clang of bells. I had always felt comfortable at the waterfront; everything was brighter, louder and busier, filled with the exotic and extraordinary. Even now, as I looked out from the *Blood*, I saw a man outside a lodging house carrying a pair of lime green parrots in a cage, while beside him a monkey in a purple hat and jacket jumped up and down on a white-painted barrel. Further along were a group of men in blue sailors' jackets and red neckerchiefs. Faces were pale, or black, or brown, or yellow. Some were stained or scarred, others disfigured, blighted by disease or inked with tattoos.

From my vantage point at the side of the *Blood* I saw Miss Proudlove in the door to the Seaman's Dispensary. I thought of how I had allowed Dr Proudlove to be humiliated in front of the Great Sackville and I felt sorry. Of course, part of me wished I could have said what I really thought, that Dr Proudlove was right, that the man Rintoul would die if we did not try something new; that tincture of cannabis was a most efficacious treatment, and that Dr Cole and Dr Antrobus knew nothing. I would have loved to show all of them how clever I was, to have demonstrated my superior knowledge of plants as medicine, of the human body and the nature of disease.

At that moment, the door to the consultant's sitting room opened. Dr Sackville stood on the threshold.

'Sir,' I stepped forward. 'Might I speak with you for a few moments?' I caught a movement in the shadows beneath the gantry where the convalescents swung gently in their hammocks, and I saw Dr Proudlove standing listening. I was not sure how he had got there as I had not seen him come up the main hatch. No doubt the old ship was riddled with passages and stairs. I hoped he would eavesdrop, and hear what I had to say. I assumed he probably would.

'Dr Sackville,' I said, as the sitting room door closed behind us. 'You were wrong to condemn Dr Proudlove. I said nothing at the time as I didn't want to contradict you in front of men who look up to you, but as you know opium will do nothing to help the man downstairs. The use of cannabis as an antispasmodic has been used in India for some time. Dr Proudlove was quite right.'

He blinked. 'Was he?'

'Oh yes. It's in O'Shaughnessy's *Bengal Pharmacopoeia*,' I said. 'A most comprehensive dispensatory.'

'What? Oh ... yes, yes, of course,' said Dr Sackville gruffly. 'To be sure. The *Bengal Pharmacopoeia*, Mr Flockhart. You are quite right.'

'A recent work, but one of great significance. O'Shaughnessy writes comprehensively on the uses of Indian hemp in cases of seizure and paralysis. Especially as you yourself have spent time in India, I was in no doubt that you would know of it—'

'Quite so, Flockhart. Seizure and paralysis.' He cleared his throat. 'And yet neither Cole nor Antrobus had read the piece.'

'Indeed, sir, though they are both capable men.'

'Capable of reading the *Bengal Pharmacopoeia*, at any

214

rate,' said Dr Sackville crossly. 'Should they have the wit to look in it.' He turned to me. 'And you?'

'I merely did as you did, sir, and pretended the cannabis was not to be trusted. Under the circumstances it seemed the wisest course of action—'

'The circumstances?'

'Of having one such as Dr Proudlove shown to be right, whilst two young gentlemen under your patronage are demonstrably wrong. In front of the patients, sir. Reputation matters less for Dr Proudlove, of course. I was more than happy to follow your lead in pretending he was wrong. The confidence of the patients in their doctors is essential for morale, and for the reputation of the ship, of course. The *Blood* is lucky to have a man of your standing amongst her staff,' I added. 'Such discretion and wisdom combined is a rare commodity. I just wanted to step in, sir, and compliment you on your choice of action this evening. I'm sure Dr Proudlove understands, and I have instructed the matron to follow his – and your – lead in continuing to administer the cannabis.' I thought for a moment that I had gone too far, for even one so arrogant as Dr Sackville would surely notice such arrant flattery, but it seemed I was wrong. He waved a hand, his expression pleased.

'Thank you, Mr Flockhart,' he said, sitting back in his chair.

'You are very generous to us younger men, sir.'

'Ah,' said Dr Sackville. 'But you see I entered the profession of medicine with no connections to draw upon, no money, and no patronage. Rather like Cole and Antrobus, and indeed like Proudlove. I was lucky enough to attract the attention of John Hunter, the most famous surgeon and anatomist of the age. The association was the making of me.' He sat back, his fingers steepled beneath his chin as he reminisced. 'Dr Rennie was there too. He was also one of Hunter's demonstrators – there are only the two of us left now.' He smiled. 'Two old, old men. He and I have known each other for a long time. And when the *Blood* was chosen as the hospital ship, and I discovered Dr Rennie was still aboard, it was the obvious place for me to offer my services.'

'And you knew Hunter?' I said. We had all heard of the great Scottish anatomist who had shown us more about the workings of the human body than either Vesalius or Galen, and I ensured my voice was filled with awe.

'Hunter was an old man by the time I knew him,' he replied. 'But his desire to know more about life never diminished. Even in his final years he was adding to his collections, writing up his findings. All of us fell under his spell. All of us knew the value of dissection for understanding how the human body worked. What he also showed us was the value of trying a new approach – when fully informed by the praxis of anatomy, of course. But to pioneer an approach, a procedure that might turn orthodoxy on its head, *that* is what we all dream of. Take lithotomy—'

'Bladder stones?'

'I have had them myself, and have had cause to bless John Hunter, and Dr Rennie, for it was he who performed the operation. Before Hunter the perineum itself was cut, with surgeons often rooting for hours trying to seize the stone. Hunter demonstrated that by slicing an inch or two to the right, then the procedure took only moments. The results spoke for themselves – an operation that was ten times faster, patients ten times more likely to survive. Ten times more patients, all with their sovereigns in their hands. All thanks to the slightest of modifications. I am not John Hunter, Mr Flockhart – who of us is? But might we not strive to know more?'

'Any medical man worth his salt should think so,' I replied. 'But what of the *Blood*, sir? There are more reputable hospitals in which to work.'

Dr Sackville shook his head. 'Those places are not where the future lies,' he said. 'Your new St Saviour's over the river might be bigger and better, but its patients suffer from the same ailments as ever. No, sir, it is here, where London meets the world, that our greatest achievements are yet to be made. Mr Aberlady knew that too, which was why he chose to stay.'

He stood up, and went over to the window to peer out across the river. Outside, the masts of a thousand ships bristled. The river was thick with them, every tide bringing more and taking others away.

'From these shores a great mercantile nation has taken over the world. And yet we die wherever we go. Malaria, yellow fever, sleeping sickness, cholera, the bites of spiders and snakes, worms and ticks and parasites of the most repulsive kind ravage us. How might we make progress if we are held back by disease? How might civilisation spread if nature is not defeated? Well, sir, from this little wooden ship great things will be forthcoming. London is the gateway to the world – ships from every corner of the globe find their way here. And with them come every possible disease – we have seen them all.'

'All, sir?' I said.

He nodded. 'Oh yes, Mr Flockhart.'

I stayed silent.

'I am a materialist, sir. Does that surprise you?'

'No, sir.'

'Are you one?'

'Why, yes I am,' I said, sensing that this was the answer that was required. And yet it was not a lie, for since my father died any belief I had once entertained that there might be a just and kindly God had vanished. The world was a brutal and ugly place, and humanity crawled about its surface like ants on a dung hill. If such cruelty and inequality was God's plan for us, then I wanted nothing to do with him. If Dr Sackville wanted me to deny God's very existence, then I would do so if it might help to discover what had happened to John Aberlady, and the three dead girls of Tulip's Basin.

'Physical matter is all there is,' I said. 'There is no spiritual existence, the world is made up of nothing but matter functioning in subjection to natural laws.'

Dr Sackville nodded. 'It is not a common view. Not yet, at any rate. I fear Proudlove has yet to fully embrace it.' He regarded me for a moment, and then took out his pocket book and held out a card. 'Come to my house tomorrow, Flockhart,' he said. 'Seven o'clock sharp. There will be others there who see the world as we do. The address is there.' He waved a hand. I was dismissed. 'Oh,' he said, as I turned to go, 'and if Dr Proudlove is out there – he's invariably creeping about the place somewhere – please ask him to step inside.'

When she is dead, Erasmus comes home. He takes me away from the house near Kennington Lane, and we never talk of our mother, or our gentleman father, ever again. We do not talk of our pasts either – not mine as a courtesan, not his as the butt of ridicule and torment, a black man striving for a place in a white man's world. We are to look forward, he says, not back. He brings with him his medical degree, and his ambition. I bring my resentment, and my knowledge of the ailments of whores and the desires of men. Mr Aberlady and Dr Rennie support my brother's application to be assistant surgeon on board the floating hospital, and he and I go to live above the Seaman's Dispensary. He works hard. I know he wants to be taken seriously as a medical man, and his ambitions stretch far beyond the dingy lanes and streets of the waterfront, the stinking wards of the Blood *and the roomful of dirty seamen he sees every day at the dispensary. He is as good as any of them, he says, any of them on board the* Blood, *even Dr Sackville. In fact, he is better, why might he not get on, as much as they? There have been others with lowly origins who have done so – 'Look at John Hunter,' he says. 'Michael Faraday. Dr Simpson of Edinburgh—'*

'None of them was black,' I remark. He says he knows that. He knows it will be difficult – it always has been – and he is used to the struggle to be accepted, the need to prove himself over and over again. But times have changed, he says. People have changed. Does he not have a medical degree? Is he not as deserving of the letters that come after his name as any one of them? Why might he not find fame, reputation and riches as they have? He is good enough, clever enough, ambitious enough . . . It consumes him – as I believe it consumes all of them – and every day he talks of it.

One day I see a tattoo on his arm. I ask him about it, but he covers it up and turns away. Perhaps it is the way he shrinks from me, the look of fear in his eye, but in my heart I know that something is wrong, and that he knows it too. But I am busy and distracted, I have cares of my own and I forget what I have seen.

My life, like his, is one of hard work. I become a nurse on board the Blood, I help my brother in the dispensary, and I act as visiting superintendent at Siren House. Dr Birdwhistle agrees that I should not live in, as he has a housekeeper for the day-to-day training and supervision of the girls. Instead, I am to offer guidance, to help make the place a home, to assist in their training as domestic servants and to encourage them to remain chaste. The girls respond to their new form of bondage in different ways. Some of them are silent and surly; some of them cry; some are defiant, they laugh and joke – it was an easy job, after all, fucking men for money, far easier than lugging coal upstairs or blacking grates all day.

I am sent out to the streets with Dr Birdwhistle's pamphlet. I see girls everywhere at the waterfront. I see Mary. She is small and dark haired, her face sad and distracted. She allows herself to be pulled this way and that, like a rag doll tossed on a boiling sea.

She never objects. It is as though she thinks she deserves to be used and flung aside. I ask whether she would like to come to Siren House. She says she does not deserve it. She will not come. Not yet. I give her some of my laudanum mixture. When she tastes it, she weeps. I put my arms about her, feel her head on my shoulder, her heart beating in time with her sobs, and I wonder what I can do to save her.

Chapter Fifteen

The moon hung low in the sky. It glowed like a new penny, coppery and tarnished by the smoke that stained the skies above the city. It was rare for the night to be so clear, rarer still for it to be so silent, but with nightfall the constant clatter and movement of the docks and the waterfront had fallen still. Here and there on the river I could see the light of a vessel, a barge or lighter, drifting down towards the East India Docks, or a wherry ploughing its way towards us from the south bank, the *plash* . . . *plash* . . . *plash* . . . of its oars a soothing watery rhythm. Fore and aft the moonlight had painted the masts and rigging of our neighbouring vessels a ghostly silvery-grey.

Dr Cole and Dr Antrobus linked arms as they sauntered along the waterfront. Their voices and their footsteps were loud, ringing on the flagstones and the walls of the buildings.

'I don't want to do this,' said Will as I dragged him

along. 'I have spent the entire afternoon up at Deadman's Basin, and I'm tired – especially after yesterday.'

'We have to,' I said.

'I just want to go to bed.'

I wondered whether he had seen the boiling hot den he was supposed to sleep in that night, for he had agreed to use Aberlady's old room. The snakes writhing in their tanks, the rats awaiting their fate, the anatomical specimens glimmering in the dark, globular and pale in their glass bottles. It was just the sort of location he would hate.

'So do I,' I admitted.

Will glanced at me crossly. I knew he was about to ask why on earth we were doing it then, why on earth we were striding out on a debauch with two men we hardly knew and didn't like when we might sit in the apothecary with our feet up discussing the day's events over a pot of ale and some bread and cheese. But I must have looked worried, exhausted, determined – goodness knows I felt all three – and instead he said nothing of the kind, but simply put his arm around my shoulders.

'Never mind,' he said. 'We can sleep tomorrow. And I'm not leaving you alone with those two. Not for anything.'

'You went off with Dr Rennie,' I said. 'This morning. You were gone for ages. You left me then.'

'Were you jealous?' He laughed. 'I saw Dr Rennie's rooms.' He shook his head, a faint smile on his lips at the thought. 'They are at the very bottom of the ship. Quite extraordinary!'

Up ahead there was noise and chatter. The open door of a public house exhaled a warm breath of cheap beer and coarse spirits, tobacco and dirty bodies. Its light was a sickly yellow-brown, though it seemed inviting against the chill of the night, and our stride lengthened as we approached. We had passed other similar places, but the Brass Bell on Spyglass Lane was louder, and more garish than all the rest.

The room was low ceilinged, with little more headroom than we were afforded on board the *Blood*. It was a former coaching inn, though there were few coaches that passed down those roads these days and the Bell had decayed into a damp and wretched place, its upstairs rooms given over to whores and thieves whenever business was slow.

'Dr Antrobus is buying, gentlemen,' said Dr Cole as he pushed his way through the press of bodies. They were evidently well-known for the woman who was serving beer from two great barrels had filled a jug and sent it over before we even sat down. I didn't mind the beer – it was watery stuff, and we were sure to be bloated before we were drunk. I was relieved that Cole had not asked for spirits, for the rum sold on the waterfront was the very worst kind, rough and sticky and as brown as molasses, the gin strong enough to preserve anatomical specimens.

We sat in one of the booths, an upturned barrel for our table, rough benches as our chairs, our pots of beer before us. 'Whatever you do, don't order any food,' said Dr Antrobus. 'The stuff'll kill you.'

'Or give you worms,' said Dr Cole. 'Or the shits. We'll go up to Cable Street later. There are supper rooms there that aren't so bad.'

'Put it on the slate, Mrs Flannigan,' cried Dr Antrobus to the beldam who ran the place as she came over with another jug.

'Not likely, sir,' she said. 'You owe me more than enough already. It's time your tab was paid, gentlemen, or I'll send someone over to get it, and he won't be 'alf as pretty as me.'

'How much?' said Dr Cole.

'Ten shillings.'

'Ten shillings!' cried Dr Antrobus. 'I think you mean five, madam!'

'Make it seven, sir, and we'll say no more about it.'

'Oh, pay the woman, Antrobus. She'll not stop till you do!' Dr Cole turned to Will and me. 'You see, gentlemen? This is how we're forced to live. Rooting about for pocket change to pay for watery beer. She's salted it too, I shouldn't wonder. We should be drinking wine, fine wine. Or brandy! We're little better than tradesmen, all of us.'

'Now, Cole, it's not as bad as all that,' said Dr Antrobus.

'Yes it is. In fact, it's worse. And when one tries to find a little free relief in the shape of one of those so-called nurses they get up from Siren House, well, even *that's* denied a fellow.'

'What type of relief?' asked Will.

'Nothing much,' said Dr Cole. He smiled, his full lips red and moist with beer. 'Nothing they don't want. It ain't my fault if they think they're going to be a doctor's wife. I never tell them that.'

'Not in so many words,' said Dr Antrobus.

'Not in any words at all,' he said. 'They make that assumption themselves.' He sighed. 'It doesn't do to have affairs with women who might have expectations, no matter who they might be. And especially not those who work on the *Blood*. So what if I gave Mary Mercer a squeeze? She didn't mind.'

'I think she probably did,' said Dr Antrobus. 'Since she ran away straight after.'

'The way Proudlove's sister looks at me you'd think I was the Devil himself. Do I deserve that? No I don't.'

'Don't tell me you gave her a squeeze too!' I guffawed horribly. I saw Will shudder.

'Certainly not!' replied Dr Cole. 'I do have some self-respect.'

'Besides, Proudlove would kill you,' said Dr Antrobus.

'Well, then he would be hanged and we should all be rid of the fellow.' Dr Cole scowled. 'I don't want to talk about him. Or her.' He reached into his pocket and pulled out a handful of coins. He pushed them about with his finger, and sighed. 'This can't go on much longer, Antrobus. It's all very well having students, and such, but apart from the *Blood*, and the dispensary, you and I have very little else. A few provident patients, I admit, but most of those are charity cases. We need some of Sackville's juicy old women, rich ones – surely they're sick of him by now. Why can't he pass them along? We only need a few, one or two that just need to be bled and purged to set them right again. They're all constipated, you know. A dose of salts is the only thing they need. A dose of salts and a brisk walk in the open air. I could prescribe that easily enough. And so could an idiot like you, Antrobus. And you, Quartermain, and you're not even a medical man! One hardly needs to have spent all one's inheritance training to be a doctor just to dish out iron tonic and purgatives.'

'That's part of the problem,' I said. 'Just about anyone can set themselves up in practice, whether they're qualified or not.'

'We need a register,' said Dr Antrobus. 'A register containing the names and qualifications of all those who call themselves doctor.'

'And until then,' Dr Cole sighed, 'the quacks'll keep making more money than we do!'

'How did you find your way onto the *Blood*?' said Will.

'Me? The same as Antrobus. We trained here in London; Paris for a short while. We both thought of going to India – plenty more opportunities out there – and so we walked the wards on the *Blood* with Rennie and Sackville.'

'And you stayed on board?' Will persisted.

'I suppose either of us might have worked for the Company,' said Dr Cole. 'I thought about it. But India's not for me.'

'Nor me,' said Dr Antrobus. 'There's little fame and fortune to be had as a Company doctor, and I've no wish to be buried in some upcountry station soused in gin and surrounded by natives, prescribing bile pills to fat memsahibs all day. Not on Company pay, at any rate.' He shrugged. 'At least here we have a chance.'

'A chance of what?' said Will.

'Of making a name for ourselves, of course! One needs a patron, and we have Dr Sackville. He expects to be knighted, you know.'

Dr Cole slammed his fist on the table. 'Enough of that, gentlemen,' he cried. 'It's bad enough that we have to spend our lives on the *Blood*, we don't have to talk about her too. Tonight is for sport. Cards, perhaps? Or girls? The supper rooms on Cable Street can give us cutlets, cards, music, *and* women.'

In the event we never went to the supper rooms on Cable Street, though we might have been better off if we had. Instead we stayed at the Brass Bell for another hour. Dr Antrobus ordered more beer. I paid. Mrs Flannigan brought us a bottle of spirits – rum – at Dr Cole's request.

Will paid, for they were both extraordinarily slow to put their hands into their pockets. I saw them exchange a glance, and grin. After that we left. Cole and Antrobus were both drunk, or at least gave the appearance of being so, for they had consumed half of Mrs Flannigan's rum in no time. They lurched out into the street, Dr Antrobus still clutching the bottle.

'Pretend you're enjoying it,' I hissed to Will. 'No matter how much you hate it.' I had made sure to swig some of the vile liquor myself, gasping as it burned my throat and coursed into my empty stomach. Will seized the bottle from Dr Antrobus's hands and applied it to his lips.

'Come along, gentlemen,' he cried, holding it in the air, a dribble of rum on his chin. 'There must be more to the night than Old Mother Flannigan's.' He took each of them by the arm and began to roar out a sea shanty.

'When I was a young lad I sailed with the rest,
On a Liverpool packet bound out to the west,
We anchored one day on the harbour of Cork,
Then put out to sea for the port of New York.
And it's roll, bullies roll, Ho!
Them Liverpool judies have got us in tow.'

Dr Cole and Dr Antrobus joined in with what appeared to be the chorus, and the streets echoed with their shouts. I wondered where Will had learned it, for he was not from Liverpool. No doubt it was well known about the port cities of the west.

'For thirty-two days we was hungry and sore,
The winds were agin us, the seas they did roar,
Then off Battery Point we was anchored at last,
With our jib boom stove in but our canvas all fast.
And it's roll, bullies, roll, Ho!

Them Liverpool judies have got us in tow.'

He had a fine voice. I had never heard him sing before – I had never seen him drunk before – and I sensed that he was enjoying himself, despite his reservations at the start of the evening. With his arm still slung about the shoulders of both of them, all at once it was as though Dr Cole and Dr Antrobus were the best friends he had ever had.

'After thirty-two days at the door of the bar,
The best of intentions they never get far.
So I tossed off my liquor and what do you think?
That lousy old bastard had doctored my drink.
And it's roll, bullies, roll, Ho!
Them Liverpool judies have got us in tow.'

His voice rose up. I had never heard him swear, or use coarse language. He held the bottle high, his voice mingling with the others as they joined in the chorus. He slid me a glance, his eyes glassy, his lips wet. He was not pretending to enjoy himself at all. He really was enjoying it. I laughed, and slung my arm around Dr Cole's shoulders.

'Next I remember I woke in the morn,
On a three skysail yarder bound south round Cape
    Horn.
With an old set of oilskins and two pairs of socks,
And a bloomin' great head and a case o' the pox.
And it's roll, bullies, roll, Ho!
Them Liverpool judies have got us in tow.'

He shrugged us off and flung his arms wide, standing in the middle of the street, bawling out the words. Half a dozen sailors who were loitering about the street joined in, and when it came to the chorus there was a great bellowing from all sides. I added my voice to the cacophony. I wondered whether we should get drunk more often.

'Come all you young sailors take warning by me,
Keep your eye on the drink when the liquor is free,
Don't pay no attention to runners or whores,
Or your head'll be thick and your dick'll be sore.
And it's roll, bullies, roll, Ho!
Them Liverpool judies have got us in tow.'

Will seized the bottle and drained the dregs – not that there was anything left in it – tossing it aside so that it smashed in the gutter. He was coughing now, the singing and the rum on top of the smoke he had inhaled the previous day was not a clever combination. Perhaps I should take him home, I thought. Perhaps the evening I had so casually embarked upon was a terrible mistake after all.

Dr Cole led us into a dark doorway, from which the smells of hot fat, gravy, and fried fish wafted. We sat at a table in a cavernous supper room while a half-naked girl danced on a stage to a thumping piano accompaniment. The crowd roared and screamed. Moisture dripped from the ceiling. Dr Antrobus ordered oysters and fried whitebait; Dr Cole ordered beef and potatoes and some bottles of ale for all of us. The food was horrible, but we were hungry, and eating seemed like a good idea. At least it might absorb some of the alcohol we had consumed. When the barman came for his money Dr Cole and Dr Antrobus were talking to some women at the back of the room, and so I put my hand into my pocket once more.

'How drunk are you?' I hissed at Will while the others were otherwise occupied.

'Drunk enough,' he replied. He giggled. 'But not as much as I seem. Merry, I think is how you would describe me. Can't you tell?' He hiccoughed, and put a hand to his belly. 'Some of those oysters tasted very odd.'

Heading back out into the night, we staggered past a basement whose dim steps led down into what I knew was an opium den of the most low and horrible kind.

'Let's take a pipe,' said Dr Antrobus, noticing my interest in the place. 'Aberlady said it made him see the world in a different light. A more fruitful light.'

'Is this where he came? The Golden Swan?' I said.

'One of the places,' said Dr Antrobus. 'He said it helped him to think clearly.'

'Shall we?' Dr Cole, who seemed to be very drunk indeed, lurched to the top of the steps.

'I think not,' I said, dragging him back. 'Not tonight.' I resolved to go there alone, when my head was clear.

'Girls then?'

'Yes.' I grinned, as I was supposed to. 'That's more like it.'

'What about him?' Dr Cole looked down at Will, who was sprawled on his back on the filthy ground.

'He's too drunk to care,' said Antrobus. He bent down and seized Will's hand. 'Up you come, my lad! Let's get you ready for the ladies.' And the three of them were off again, striding down the street, back towards the *Blood*.

⌘

It was clear that Dr Cole and Dr Antrobus had been to Mrs Spendwell's on Cat's Hole on many occasions.

'It's cheap,' said Dr Cole as we made our way towards

the place. 'And very obliging. Of course, Antrobus always uses his sheath, don't you, Antrobus?'

'Unless you attend the ward rounds with your eyes closed, Cole, you'll have seen the beauties of syphilis yourself. I do not intend to catch it.' He patted his pocket. 'Yes, I have a sheath, gentlemen. Made by a seamstress who specialises in such things down on Cuttlefish Lane. Finest kid skin.'

'I have one too,' said Will, rather wildly, I thought, for I was almost certain he had no such thing.

Dr Cole slung his arm around my shoulders. 'I'm generally too drunk to care.' He patted the front of his britches in imitation of Dr Antrobus. 'Lucky so far!'

Mrs Spendwell's was at the dark end of the passage. Beyond it, the dire thoroughfare of Cat's Hole narrowed still further until it became a dripping crack between the buildings known as Bishop's Entry. After that it ran straight down, through Deadman's Basin, to the river. The place was not unlike Mrs Roseplucker's house on Wicke Street – a place I would have been glad never to enter again – though it was smaller in size, and far more decrepit. Mrs Roseplucker's Home for Young Ladies of an Energetic Disposition had been frequented by the medical men of St Saviour's. Mrs Spendwell's had no such appellation, but only the vile double entendre of her name to commend it. And while Mrs Roseplucker's establishment on Wicke Street had been festooned with crimson drapery and painted in various shades of red and purple – 'the colours of Cupid's boudoir' Mrs Roseplucker had always said – the place we now entered made no such effort to appeal. The door flew open with one kick of Dr Cole's boot – there was no doorman here to let the 'gentlemen' in and out. The place smelled strongly of sweat and privies and – rather unexpectedly – of linseed. The hall was a dingy passage illuminated by a single shaded lamp set on a spindly-legged table. Before us, a flight of stairs ascended into the darkness. I glanced at Will. He looked sober enough now, his expression appalled at what activities he might now be expected to perform.

Dr Cole flung open the door to what would once have been a parlour, but which now served as a waiting room. There were no men there, only women, three of them, two playing dominoes, the third arguing with someone, as yet invisible to us, who was stationed behind a screen in the corner. The walls were painted a brown distemper, though it was clear that someone had attempted to improve the decor by daubing the walls with crimson paint. It was this which tainted the air, though the linseed and ground cinnabar that made up the mixture did much to improve the stink of the place. A bowl and brush red-stained were set down in a corner, the stuff on the walls evidently still wet, for the woman who was not playing dominoes was complaining bitterly about getting the paint on her dress.

'I sent him out to get some gin,' she was saying. 'Gin gets rid o' paint stains, everyone knows that. And I hope he don't bother to come back unless he's got some!'

'Gin?' said a voice from behind the screen. 'You don't want to waste a good drop on a dress!'

'Oh no,' groaned Will, sinking onto a bandy-legged chair that stood beside the curtained window. A patch of grease on the wall behind told where a hundred oily heads had rested. 'It can't be—'

We heard the front door bang, and the parlour door swung open. A great hulk of a man stood on the threshold, his tombstone face wide and expressionless.

'*There* you are,' cried the girl, flouncing over to him with the hem of her dress clutched in her hands. Her bony ankles were black from sitting too close to the fire, her voice as shrill as a whistle. 'Look what you did with your paint, you fucking idiot!'

'Now then, my lady!' the voice screamed out from behind the screen. I saw a taloned, ink-stained hand seize the edge of it as the woman behind heaved herself to her feet and waddled into view. 'Don't you dare speak to poor Mr Jobber like that. Ain't you got no manners? This place might well be a spit away from the docks but you'll speak like a lady as best you can for there's standards in my house no matter where I have the misfortune to be— Sirs!' Her voice changed from hectoring harridan to wheedling madam the instant she set eyes upon us. 'Welcome, sirs! Girls, girls!' She clapped her hands to chivvy the domino players into action as if rounding up poultry. 'Here's some young gentlemen come to pay you a visit.' She glanced behind us at Mr Jobber, who seemed now to be weeping. 'There, there,' she said. 'Look, Poll, you've made Mr Jobber cry with your shouting and swearing. Such a sensitive soul!' She coaxed the man into the parlour and fussed him into a seat beside the fire. Mr Jobber took a bottle from his pocket and handed it to the girl in silence. Mrs Roseplucker snatched it away and stuffed it into her pocket. 'You gets that when you've earned it,' she said. 'An' not before. There's nothing wrong with your skirts. The gentlemen ain't here to look at your skirts, my lady. Not unless you're liftin' them over your head.'

234

'I just wanted the place nice for you, Mrs R,' said Mr Jobber. 'Like at Wicke Street.'

'It's lovely, Mr Jobber,' crooned the old woman. 'Lovely and bright.'

'It looks like an abattoir,' I said.

She peered at me closely through a pair of thickly glazed lorgnettes that hung from a chain at her sagging bosom, and which she had unfolded with her teeth like a pirate opening a cut-throat razor. 'Well, well,' she said. 'If it ain't *Mr* Flockhart. Got yourself some new friends, sir? *These* young men is quite the reg'lars here. But you two—'

'Never mind that, woman,' cried Dr Cole. 'Who've you got?'

'Amy,' snapped Mrs Roseplucker. 'Nance. Get over here.'

The two girls lifted their eyes from the dominoes and pinned smiles to their faces. Coins were exchanged, watches consulted. 'Looks like you two will have to share that bad tempered one,' said Dr Antrobus, pointing to an angry-faced Poll. The door banged closed, and we heard their boots stumbling up the stairs, accompanied by the forced giggles of the domino players.

Mr Jobber took out a bag of nuts and started cracking them between his teeth.

'What happened?' said Will, without rising from his chair. He put a hand to his forehead. 'We only saw you a few months ago. Mind you,' he added, 'the old place on Wicke Street was looking rather sorry for itself.' He eyed the penny bloods, the ink pot and paper on the desk top. Mrs Roseplucker had always been a keen reader of penny dreadfuls, and when the Home for Young Ladies of an Energetic Disposition on Wicke Street had fallen on hard times after the closure of St Saviour's Infirmary, she had taken to writing her own lurid stories. I had seen her pen name, 'Prosser McLucker' in the *Tales of Violence and Blight* that Gabriel habitually read – though in a bid to impress Pestle Jenny he had, I noticed, hidden his stash of penny papers on the top shelf beside the poisons.

'You're still writing?' I said.

'Oh yes,' she answered. 'But *that* don't make enough to keep us in kindling. There ain't no money in writing – unless you're that Mr Dickens o' course. He stole one o' my stories, you know. Oh yes! Must o' read it in *Tales of Violence.* It were called "Lord of Villainy" when I wrote it. *He* makes it fifty times longer, takes out all the interesting bits and calls it "David Copperfield"! She shook her head. '*He* ain't no gentleman!'

'And so you came here?'

'Business at Wicke Street must be bad,' muttered Will, looking around at the daubed walls and threadbare floor covering, the ragged curtains and mysterious brown stains that ringed the ceiling. He rooted in his bag and pulled out his flask of nettle and plantain infusion, drinking it down thirstily.

'Oh, it was bad, sir. We could hardly pay the rent. And when the plaster fell off the wall in one o' the rooms and a stair tread gave way with the damp, well, we couldn't get it fixed, could we? Not properly. And so we had to come here. Can't get the girls though. And the gentlemen ain't really gentlemen – 'cept you two, o' course, and those two upstairs. I've taken the place over proper. Mrs Spendwell had it before. She came to a sticky end.'

'Sticky?' said Will.

'On the end of a rope, young man, that sticky enough for you? Then Mrs Bellringer had it, but not for long.

Then Mr Jobber heard it were goin' cheap and so here we are. Sailors, mostly. Nice enough. Come from all over. I taught my girls how to say "yes please!" and "ain't that big!" in four different languages. The sailors told me how. Now *that* ain't something they'll get anywhere else, I'll be bound! Worth payin' extra for, that is!'

'We saw Annie the other day,' said Will.

'Where?'

'At the League for Female Redemption.'

'Siren House? That where she went, is it?' Mrs Roseplucker smiled, her face splitting like a rotten apple. 'She owes me money, that one. Can't think what she's doing in that place. Redeemed? Our Annie? She's too lazy to stick at bein' a domestic. Too lazy by half. She'll be back. Once she's had a holiday and a bath and got sick o' blacking grates and ironing she'll be knocking on my door, you'll see. Let's hope she'll bring a couple of her new friends too!'

'Do many of the girls come back?' I said.

'How should I know? But I'll tell you what I *do* know, and that's that some of 'em takes to whoring, and some of 'em don't. It ain't so bad if you're in a decent house. Like this one. I looks after my girls, no matter what you might think. An' Mr Jobber here sees they get treated right.' She scratched at the sores beneath her wig, shifting the fuzzy auburn curls from side to side, a look of ecstasy on her face. She sighed. 'It's when you're in no house at all that it really starts to pinch. And that's the end of the road for most.'

'Did you know a girl called Mary Mercer?'

'No.'

'Or Susan Williams?'

'Ain't nothing for nothing at Mrs Roseplucker's.'

'Dear lady,' sighed Will. 'It was ever thus.' He tossed her half a crown.

'No,' she said, swiftly stowing the coin. 'I didn't know her. But if you give me another I'll tell you something that might be worth hearin'.'

'Payment after you've delivered the goods, madam,' I said.

'Nah.' Mrs Roseplucker eased her great bulk back behind her desk. 'That's not how I do *my* business.'

Will tossed her another coin. 'Well? What can you tell us?'

'I can tell you that you might get more out of young Poll over there. She worked at Mrs Spendwell's, and Mrs Bellringer's after that.'

The girl Poll was leaning against Mr Jobber, watching greasy wraiths of black smoke trickle from between the coals in the grate, and chewing on a fingernail. With her face in repose she didn't look much older than sixteen.

'Poll!' snapped Mrs Roseplucker. 'Here's two gentlemen for you.'

'Together?'

'Yes,' I said.

'That's—' Mrs Roseplucker's lips moved as she tried some mental arithmetic. She gave up. 'How much is it, Mr Jobber? How much for two gentlemen together, with special pleasures?'

'Special pleasures?' said Will in alarm. He had sobered up somewhat, I was glad to see. Perhaps he had been pretending after all. 'I don't think we need any of those—'

'Information, costs the same as special pleasures,' said Mrs Roseplucker.

'Six shillings and nine pence ha'penny,' said Mr Jobber. I did not ask how this sum had been arrived at. The coins rattled in Mrs Roseplucker's palm. I wiped my hand on my jacket. Her fingers were sticky, her hands so covered in dirt she could have sowed them with cress.

The bedroom was a dim and miserable chamber, lit by two candle ends stuffed into stubby pewter candlesticks. No fire burned in the grate, and the room had a damp unwholesome air, heavy with the smell of sweat and hot tallow. Beneath the bed I saw a brimming chamber pot. Will spotted it too, and he sighed and went to the window. But what might be seen outside was no cheerier than what we could see inside, and if he had thought to open it he quickly changed his mind and drew the curtains instead.

Poll pulled off her dress to expose grey ragged under-things, and flopped onto the bed. 'What do you want?'

'First,' I said. 'Let me see that rash on your neck.' She scratched at her skin self-consciously, but she let me see it. 'Is it anywhere else?' I asked. She showed me her arms. I rooted in my satchel and handed her a pot of salve. 'Calendula and chickweed,' I said. 'Soothes the skin and calms the itch.' She sniffed the contents warily, but I had fragranced it with lavender, and despite its ugly appearance – chickweed and calendula salve is always rather murky in appearance – it smelled nice. Her face brightened.

'Anything else?' I asked. 'What about your monthlies?'

Her face turned pale. 'Late,' she whispered.

I plunged back into my bag. I had a packet of pennyroyal and raspberry leaf in there somewhere.

'Here,' I said, handing it over. 'Drink it like tea. Four times a day and hope for the best.'

She nodded. 'Got any gin?'

'No,' I said.

'Pity. I could've done with a nip.'

I could tell by her pinched cheeks and the bluish tinge to the tip of her nose that she was a regular at the gin bottle. She coughed, two red spots of colour appearing on her cheeks. A consumptive too. There was nothing anyone could do about that.

'Poll, did you know Mary Mercer?' I said.

'No.'

'What about Susan Williams?'

'Why do you ask? Has something happened? Something bad?'

'She was at Siren House. She used to work . . . like you do.'

'There's a lot o' girls who used to work like I do.'

'I know.' I sighed. She was right. It was an impossible task. I was assuming the mummified girl with the birthmark had worked on the waterfront, but there were more girls on the game there than anywhere else in the city. And yet there was a link between Siren House, the *Blood*, the girls – and Aberlady.

'Did you know Mr Aberlady?' I said. 'From the *Blood*?'

'Look,' said Poll. 'Everyone knowed Mr Aberlady. He worked at the *Blood* and the Dispensary. He was nice – not like those two what came in with you now. And I knows Dr Proudlove, and Miss Proudlove. But I don't know either of those girls you mentioned.'

'Did you know any girls who had once been at Siren House?' I wanted to ask her whether she had ever seen Eliza – and yet I had to stay focused, had to find out who the dead girl was. Eliza had chosen to leave; she had chosen to stay away from me. Should she need me, she would come. 'Well?' I said. 'Was there anyone?'

Poll frowned. 'There was one girl,' she said. 'Before Mrs Roseplucker came. I was here back when it was Mrs Spendwell's. It was much worse then. There was a girl here who went to Siren House when Mrs Spendwell got her neck stretched for murderin' babies. She didn't like the place one bit so she came straight back. It was Mrs Bellringer's by then. But then that curate found her.'

'A curate?' I said. 'You mean Dr Birdwhistle?'

'That his name?' she said. 'Didn't like him much.'

'Red face,' said Will. 'Glasses.'

'Has the pox,' I added.

'That's him! She went with him.'

'Went where?'

'I don't know. Back to Siren for all I know. Up to her what she does, ain't it?'

'What was her name?'

'Jane Stalker.'

'What did she look like?'

'Nothing much. Not pretty, not ugly. She had a birthmark—'

'Here,' I said. I touched the top of my arm. 'In the shape of a heart. About the size of a florin.'

'Yes. Used to say she wore her heart on her sleeve – whatever that means. How did you know?'

'She's dead.'

'Did she drown herself? That's what they mostly do. I'll do it myself, one o' these days.'

'No,' I said. 'I think it was far worse than that.'

Confession of Jane Stalker
on arriving at Siren House

❦

My name is Jane Stalker. I was born in Liverpool. I can't remember much about Liverpool, except that it was noisier and dirtier even than this place. The river there flowed fast, much faster than here, where it lies still and stinking as a great wide ditch. My father was a clerk at one of the shipping offices. I got no idea which one, for he died when I was only a child, drowned going aboard a merchant ship. She was trying to catch the tide and wouldn't wait for anyone. My father had been told that he must speak business with the captain, and so he was made to climb aboard her as she moved out. But he slipped and was swept away, lost in the blink of an eye to the river and the racing tide before anyone could save him. So my mother said, though there were others who whispered that he had climbed aboard and sailed away from us by

242

his own choosing, for they never found a body. She used to take me into the city to show me the grand offices where my father once worked. Giant buildings they were, all black with soot with men going in and out, their coats and hats black as soot too, the doors opened by other men wearing white stockings and navy britches and fancy waistcoats.

We had lived in a nice little house, my mother and father and me, and my brother, but after my father drowned we couldn't stay. We moved closer to the docks as that was all we could afford. My mother had to take in washing, though she hated it, and the rooms we had was always damp because of it, and that settled on her lungs. That and the damp and rainy weather, for it always seemed to be raining in Liverpool.

We weren't the poorest, not then, but our decline had started, sir, for once you begin to slip from grace there is no way back, and though I didn't know it the best of my life was already behind me and I was not yet six years old. My brother went to sea. He was about fourteen years old, a strong lad, and angry at my father's passing. We saw him only once or twice after he left. I don't know what happened to him on board that ship but he was greatly changed when he returned to us, hard and cruel and nothing like the boy we had known. He only stayed a week before he was off again. A year or so later we heard he had drowned. His ship was carrying slaves, so they said, though slaving was outlawed. My mother said it was the same people my father had worked for. Merchants. Sugar, tobacco, slaves, it was all the same to them and as long as they made money by it they didn't care what it was or who suffered.

Soon after that my mother took me to London. She said any place would surely be better than Liverpool, and she had been to London with my father years ago and thought it a fine place. But the room we ended up in didn't look much different to the one we had left, only now we knew no one and we had no money to go back. My mother took ill soon after. I was alone in the world then. I was of little use to anyone, so my mother used to say, though I had worked hard enough at the washing and helped her as best I could, especially when she was ill.

Our neighbour on Cuttlefish Lane was a woman called Mrs Spendwell. She took me in after my mother died. Her house was always warmer than ours. She used to send some soup in to my mother, but my mother would never take it. She said there was nothing free in this world and that there would be payment expected soon enough, one way or another, especially from one like Mrs Spendwell.

'You need a long spoon when you sup with the Devil,' she said.

I said we didn't have a spoon, long or short, and that we were lucky to have any soup to sup and that Mrs Spendwell was just being kind, for she was always nice to me. And so she was, though it turned out my mother was right after all even if it did take a while before the reckoning.

Once my mother died the past disappeared completely. Mrs Spendwell was like a mother to me, for I was no more than eleven years old when I went to live with her. She kept a lodging house, and she took me in to act as maid to the actresses who lodged there. Well, soon enough I saw what went on at Mrs Spendwell's, for there were gentlemen visiting all the time. But Mrs Spendwell said I should stick to my chores with the hot water and the bedding and laying the fires. It didn't seem like bad work, though I was up till late at night, and seemed always to be in the company of the gentlemen, whether I liked it or not.

At first I was just the maid, but I was not an ugly girl, and Mrs Spendwell flattered me and told me how pretty I was. She said the gentlemen liked me ever so much. She made it sound like it was the greatest honour that they approve of my looks and fancy me. She let the gentlemen tug my ringlets, and sometimes she would let me sit up to keep them company while they were waiting to go upstairs. She bought me a new dress for that, though I had to take it off once they were gone. Once they were away she had me washing sheets and blacking the grate, and going up and down the stairs with the coal once more, for they all needed coal and that house seemed to me to be nothing but stairs. I think now that Mrs Spendwell worked me hard so that my virtue might seem less of a prize to me once my hands were blistered and my feet sore.

'Why,' she'd say, 'the girls upstairs ain't half as pretty as you and all they do is lie on their backs and let the gentlemen have their sport.' She never asked me if I wanted to do the same, but talked about it as though it were very heaven, so that in the end it was me who asked her. She said it would hurt at first, but that if I wanted I might get one of the nicest and kindest of the gentlemen to do it. After that, she said, I wouldn't feel it at all.

There were two young men who were always asking about me. Mrs Spendwell said I might go to the highest bidder, as it was a sign of how much they valued me. But one of the men had more money than the other and it was not a fair contest. Of the two men one of them was shy and quiet – acted as if he'd never been with a girl. Mrs

245

Spendwell said he hadn't which was why he wanted me as he was a gentleman mindful of his health. The other chap was young, and handsome as they come, with curly hair and plump lips, and I liked the look of him well enough so that I was glad when that first gentleman lost the game. He looked cross at that, and said it was more than likely I wasn't a virgin anyway, and he'd expect to see some evidence of the fact if he was to accept the loss as a fair one.

Mrs Spendwell had said it was best not to look when it was taking place, but that it was no more than what everyone did, even the queen, for we were all animals really, no matter that we stood on two legs and dressed ourselves up in clothes and thought our fine chatter set us above the beasts. I didn't know what she meant. Not then anyway. Later I did, for the young man who had won me made sure he did me good and proper so there was plenty of blood to show his friend. And blood there was, sir. No one told me about that, and I was not even a woman so had not bled before in any way and when I felt the pain and saw the bed sheets and felt it all slippery on my legs I thought he had killed me.

The young man wiped himself, and me, with his hand-kerchief and then went downstairs. I followed him down, hoping Mrs Spendwell would take the stick to him for hurting me so badly, but she did nothing of the kind. He tossed his bloody handkerchief in his companion's face and laughed. Mrs Spendwell laughed too, and then she asked the gentleman's friend whether *he'd* like to take his pleasure, for the usual fee this time since I was broken in now. But he said 'no'. He gave me a cold look and said he hoped I liked the pox as well as I liked my new employment.

I didn't know what he meant, though I'd seen one of the girls crying over her sores and hiding in her room till they had gone away, though she looked well enough now.

Mrs Spendwell said I should wash my cunny with her special mixture, so I did as she said. I always did, and I never got the pox nor the clap. Not as far as I know.

Well, that was my beginnings into the profession of a whore, sir, and being known as one of Mrs Spendwell's girls. And she was right: after that first time, I never felt anything again.

But times was hard for Mrs Spendwell, as much as they were for everyone, and after a year or two we went to a place on Cat's Hole. It was only sailors then. Some of them couldn't speak English, though they didn't come to us for conversation so it hardly mattered. Mrs Spendwell didn't care whether we used her special mixture any more, but I used to go up to the Seaman's Dispensary – up near the *Blood*. It's where I met Miss Proudlove, sir. She used to help her brother who worked in the dispensary. We all knew him for there was no other doctor who came amongst us, not on those streets anyway. But Dr Proudlove did – and his sister. He attended any number of girls at Mrs Spendwell's. But he'd not get rid of a baby. We knew better than to ask him to, for we knew him to be a good man.

It was Mrs Spendwell who did that. I helped her once – only once, though she had done it more times than I could count. She used a knitting needle. I'll never forget it. The white knees of that poor girl as she lay on Mrs Spendwell's kitchen table, her thighs and her petticoat stained bright red. She'd been with us for only three months. Started like me, hardly more than a child. I'd tried to look after her but there wasn't much looking after that any of us could do. And now she was on the table, Mrs Spendwell standing between her legs with the needle in her hand. There was blood on the table and on the floor in a great red pool, pouring out of her without stopping. The baby was no more than a nub of flesh, a little curled thing, lying there in a great clot of the stuff while she bled and bled until she had no more left inside.

That's what landed me in prison. Mrs Spendwell said the girl had miscarried, that she was trying to help. Dr Proudlove spoke up for us all, said that he believed we had tried to help as best we could. I'm sure he knew what had really happened but he didn't judge us for it, and those who sat at the bench and condemned us for whores and murderers were the same men who visited girls just like us in better streets and finer houses.

I didn't see Mrs Spendwell again after that, for she was hanged, despite what Dr Proudlove said in her defence, and I wasn't sorry to see an end to her. I was sent to the Bridewell, and while I was there I got to thinking about my life. I didn't want to go back to my old life but I didn't know what else to do. I read your pamphlet, sir. I'd heard of Siren House and knew it for a place that meant well, and where girls might try again, and so here I am.

Note on Jane Stalker on leaving Siren House

Jane Stalker is twenty years old – she thinks – and has been living in various houses of bad character from the age of eleven, after the death of her mother left her in a precarious position. She is an attractive girl with a quiet unassuming manner. She shows no evidence of the pox – remarkable for one who has led such a life as she. There is evidence of pregnancy, though what happened to the child she does not say. She is hard working, and so far shows herself to be able, and helpful about the House. She has, on one notable occasion, left Siren House, but was retrieved from the place she had gone and offered suitable employment. Given her former role as assistant to an abortionist, the notorious Mrs Spendwell of Cat's Hole, and the caring ways she has shown towards the other girls, she is to be recommended for a position as nurse on board the *Blood*. There is a lack of good nurses and Stalker might find the challenge preferable to the usual domestic work, or to her former life.

Chapter Sixteen

⁂

I woke up in my own bed at Fishbait Lane. I was already due at the *Blood* for the morning ward rounds, but they were going to have to wait a little that day. My head felt thick and heavy, my brain pounding as though it were bouncing against the inside of my skull with every movement I made. I remembered vomiting lavishly the previous night, Will and I helping each other as we retched and spewed the vile mixture of beer, spirits, oysters, beef, potatoes that we had consumed over the course of the preceding six hours. We both blamed the oysters – neither of us had been *that* drunk. Of course, it would have made much more sense to have gone back to the ship the night before, but Will had refused to countenance waking up in the company of Minimus and Maximus and the tank of rats, and I had taken little persuading to spend the night at home.

I washed myself quickly, pulled on a clean shirt and bundled up my dirty clothes. Downstairs, Jenny was already up. Gabriel had made a bed for her in the herb drying room, and she slept beside sacks of hops and beneath bunches of lavender and feverfew. She was still wearing Gabriel's old clothes – two sizes too big for her, though the boots fitted well enough. I told her that her dress would be going to the washer woman's along with everything else that day; would she not be glad to wear it again? She shook her head. She had found one of my old hats, a black stovepipe, not unlike the one Will favoured, though not quite so tall, and she had taken to wearing it over her shorn head. The hat was too big, but she had stuffed the band inside with newspaper to make a better fit. She was standing at the shop window in the pose of a sea captain on the poop deck – hands clasped behind her, back straight, legs slightly akimbo. Her hat was crooked on her head, her face serious, guarded, as she looked out at the awakening bustle of Fishbait Lane.

Will was still in bed, Gabriel asleep on his truckle bed beneath the apothecary table. Usually I liked to have the place to myself for a while in the mornings, but I did not mind Jenny. She had already kindled the stove and prepared a pot of coffee. I sent her out to the bakery. When she came back, I bade her come and sit with me before the stove. The bread was warm, and we ate it with some cheese that was left over from their supper the night before.

'Well, Jenny,' I said, sitting back. I felt much better, though my head still ached abominably, and the thought of spending my morning below decks on board the *Blood* made my stomach squirm. 'Did Mr Aberlady teach you to read and write?'

She pointed to the prescription ledger on the table, and the pharmacopoeia that was on the reading stand.

251

'Only medicines?' I said.

She nodded.

'So you cannot write down what happened to Mr Aberlady that night? The night you came here? The night he—?' I stopped. Her face had grown pale, the bread and cheese she had been eating forgotten in her hand. 'You're safe here,' I said. 'No one knows where you are. No one from the *Blood*. I've told no one – not even when they asked. And when it's all over, when we know why Mr Aberlady is dead, and why those girls—' I sighed. Perhaps Jenny didn't know about the dead girls, though as she too had spent time at Siren House there was every chance that she had known at least one of them. But that was a conversation for another time. 'When it's all over you can stay here with us. Always. I mean you can live here.' I wondered what Gabriel would say. And Will. And Mrs Speedicut. 'But you must dress as a girl,' I said. 'There is no shame in it, and we can't always be hiding who we are whenever we want to achieve anything. You can sit your apothecary's examination in a few years too. I'll take you on as an apprentice. It's about time they saw what women can do.'

We looked at one another. Her silence seemed to encourage the divulging of secrets, though I knew I had spoken recklessly. I hoped she hadn't noticed.

'In the meantime,' I said, 'you can have this.' I handed her a pewter fob watch, the one my father had given me when he took me on as his apprentice. I had no use for it, for he had given me a gold one when I had passed my licentiate examinations and joined him as apothecary at St Saviour's. 'Be sure to look after it,' I said. 'It is engraved with the name of Flockhart – which can be your name, if you would like it. You are one of us now.'

She stared at me. I saw disbelief in her eyes. And wariness. But also hope. She didn't know whether to cry, or to run.

'I mean it,' I said standing up. 'And now, I would like you to do something for me.'

She looked alarmed, and shifted slightly so that she was now sitting on the edge of her chair. I sensed that she would fling down the watch and bolt into the street if I said the wrong thing, and I wondered what other types of proposition she had received, what bribes and trinkets she had been given that had led her to Siren House. No wonder she was enjoying the comparative safety of her boy's apparel.

'Jenny.' I rooted in my satchel for my notebook. 'Come and sit here.' I pulled out a stool at the apothecary table and dipped a pen into the ink pot. 'Can you draw what it was that was on Mr Aberlady's arm? You know, the picture on his skin that he asked you to burn off with the poker. That was what he asked you to do, wasn't it?'

She nodded. Her hands were balled into fists, her body tense.

'Can you draw it? You must have seen it, and I know you have a good memory.' She sat on the stool as I had asked, but still she hesitated. I saw her pulse beating rapidly in her neck, her eyes darting and feral. Beneath the table where he slept, Gabriel let out a great fart. Jenny and I looked at one another, and grinned. 'Men are the most disgusting creatures,' I said. 'And yet, we must put up with them somehow.' She looked at me strangely. And then she took the pen and bent over the paper.

It meant nothing to me, the picture Pestle Jenny drew that day, the two of us sitting side by side as the wan October morning dawned. I was glad that the apothecary was warm and golden, the lamplight bright as it glistened off the bottles, the air sweet with lavender and hyssop, with the earthy, woody scent of clary-sage and the sharp tang of citrus, so that when she drew that horrible image, when I forced her to revisit those memories, she was in a place where she might feel safe. When she had finished I took the drawing from her, folded it up and put it in my pocket, so that she might never have to look at it again.

❦

Will was still asleep when I went up to the *Blood*. I took a cup of coffee in to him for when he awoke, and a glass of water, and opened the window for his room stank like a flop-house. I left him a note telling him to meet me at the *Blood* at his convenience.

I went out into the street. The wind was sharp. All my senses felt heightened – my ears pained by the noisiness of the streets, my nose revolted by the smells, my eyes seared by the brightness of the morning. There was a dampness in the air too, so that I was sure the fog would be in eventually. I looked up at the sky, at the morning sun peeping through the buildings. It had a liverish look to it. I rubbed my eyes. The day would be a long one. I felt tired already, and I had only been up for an hour. I was now very late for the morning rounds, too. The thought of those dark close wards made my heart thump and my stomach clench within me. I felt my skin grow cold and slick with sweat and I feared I was about to vomit again.

I drew a deep breath, and hoped the walk would do me good.

On board, Dr Cole and Dr Antrobus were nowhere to be seen. Dr Sackville was absent too, though that was only to be expected as he was rarely there two days in a row. I could see Dr Proudlove on shore, walking towards the Seaman's Dispensary. Mrs Speedicut was smoking a pipe on deck. The stink of her Virginian shag made me feel sick. She saw the pale clamminess of my skin and she gave a smirk. I bade her help me with the prescriptions, and she followed me into the apothecary, moaning as she always did about the laziness of the nurses and how hard she worked, and the pains in her back and her feet. Her voice grated in my ears. Downstairs, under the low ceilings and amongst the mounded beds, she seemed louder than ever. I saw Dr Rennie skulking in the shadows in the lower ward. I was anxious to get out of that dark and stuffy space, and yet I wanted to talk to him too. I started over to him, but he vanished, slinking down the hatch into the bowels of the ship like a ghost. I could not bring myself to follow him.

Out on deck, the air rang with all the usual clamour of the riverside. Ships drifted by, high in the water now that they had unloaded their cargo, and anxious to catch the morning tide. A man was brought on board with a broken foot, crushed by a falling crate at St Catherine's Docks. An old seaman suffering from exhaustion – lack of food, rough sleeping, and gin – was carried aboard by his friends, a band of equally drunk and exhausted-looking individuals in ancient sailors' coats and caps. I made Mrs Speedicut give them all a plate of slop from the cookhouse, for it was almost lunchtime.

A sailor was brought aboard via the larboard steps – those that gave out onto the Thames itself – discharged from a passing merchantman as they came upriver to unload their cargo. His legs and feet were grotesquely swollen. I knew it was elephantiasis, though how it might be treated I had no idea. I put him in the top ward, and wished Aberlady was there, or at least Dr Sackville, who claimed he had 'seen everything' and would surely know what treatment there might be for the man. Might the fluid be drained from his legs somehow? I called for Dr Rennie but he could not be found anywhere. I saw Miss Proudlove coming out of the snakes' room, a small tin in her hand. No doubt she had been feeding weevils and earwigs to the frogs. Perhaps she had tossed Maximus and Minimus a live rat or two. I was glad I had not seen it, for I felt bilious enough already. Should I show her the image Jenny had drawn and ask her whether she knew its meaning? And yet I could not bring myself to approach her, no matter how much I wanted to. I stood there in a doltish silence, watching as she vanished down into the top ward.

From my pocket I pulled the drawing Jenny had made that morning. It was crude and childish, as one might expect. And yet I sensed that what she had drawn was exactly what she had seen, that the tattoo that Aberlady had attempted to gouge from his own arm had been similarly grotesque. An inky scrawl, ugly in its lack of symmetry, meaningless to anyone but the initiated, it was an indelible stain on the skin that spoke of secrecy, and belonging. What could it have meant – to him, and to others? I knew there were men about the waterfront who made the inking of skin an art, but what Jenny had drawn was something far less proficient. At the bottom was the same word I had seen scrawled by John Aberlady in the darkness of the operating theatre. ICORISSS. I had thought it was spelled with two 'esses', but here there were three. Perhaps I had been mistaken; Perhaps Jenny was mistaken; she could not read, after all, and there were no words that ended like that. And yet it was not the word that was so arresting, but the small pictures that were drawn above it, a macabre collection of random elements – a broken chain, a pair of keys, and the crude semblance of a skeleton, death himself, perhaps, a rope looped and coiled about his bones.

I had worked amongst the men and women of the poorer classes all my life, though few of them had sported tattoos. Down on the riverside, on the *Blood*, amongst sailors and ex-soldiers, former convicts and thieves, it was not uncommon to see the skin inked – lover's initials, ships, regiments. And yet I had never seen one like this. There were a number of men on deck that morning. Those who were convalescing often came up for air, strolling about in their nightgowns, or rocking gently in hammocks strung up beneath a wooden awning adjacent to the cookhouse. I showed them Jenny's drawing. Could they identify it? Did it mean anything to them? The men shook their heads. Some of them were keen to show me their own tattoos, and to tell me the stories that lay behind them – lost ships and shipmates, marks indicative of time spent on the prison hulks at Woolwich, wives and lovers marked in perpetuity upon their skin. Some were neat and skilful – flowers, ships, hearts, names – others were crude and misshapen, initials and dates, skulls and curious marks and runes meaningful only to the eye of their owner. None of the men could explain the image I showed them. The mystery seemed as fathomless as ever – and yet I had one last idea of who I might ask. It was someone who had nothing to gain by lying, and who was sufficiently removed from the *Blood* to tell the truth. I folded the picture away and slipped it back into my pocket, beside the love tokens, and the tiny key.

The Blood *is an ugly place, filthy and stinking, though the men aboard are grateful for it, as they will not go to St Saviour's Infirmary. They do not trust a place that is not surrounded by water, and are content to brave rats and typhus, and the ungodly stench of the river, rather than find themselves bound by bricks and mortar. When I start work there it is run by male orderlies. Men with scars and tattoos, who chew tobacco and fill the ward spittoons with brown saliva. But it is my brother's belief that having women on board will raise morale, will improve behaviour, and contribute to healthfulness.*

'As a moral influence,' he says. 'All hospitals have ladies' committees, nurses, Bible women. To have women amongst us would have a good effect on behaviour, and on the health and outlook of the men.'

'But prostitutes?' Dr Sackville is incredulous when Dr Birdwhistle suggests they employ the reformed women of Siren House. 'Hardly a moral influence, sir!'

259

'They are not prostitutes,' says Mr Aberlady. 'They are women looking for honest work.'

'The women will be chosen by the medical staff,' says Dr Birdwhistle. 'As is only right and proper.' Dr Cole and Dr Antrobus agree. Only Dr Rennie objects. At the time I do not know why. He says it is unlucky to have women on board, it always has been. But I know it is more than that.

Mary comes to Siren House. She is quiet at first, her face pensive, her eyes sorrowful. The girls are charged never to talk of their pasts, but they do. Of course they do. Mary, however, says nothing. I know she is a country girl. I hear it in her soft, rounded Oxfordshire vowels, and I see it in her love of the garden, though it is little more than a shadowy patch of green at the back of the house, for we are surrounded by the high walls of the lane and the warehouses, and overlooked by the tenements of Bishop's Entry and Herringbone Court. The other girls are appalled at the idea of grubbing about in the sticky black soil. They prefer to stay indoors – perhaps because that is what they are used to – even if it means listening to Dr Birdwhistle thumping on the piano, or sitting before Mrs Birdwhistle as she reads improving essays from Benfield's Instructional Catechism.

There is only one place in the garden where the sun falls. Every morning from half past eleven to the early afternoon it warms a patch of earth in the south-west corner. After that it moves behind the shoulder of Drake's Warehouse and the whole garden is plunged into shadow. We grow lots of different plants. I don't know what they are but Mary does. She calls them by their country names, names she has grown up with: bleeding heart, foam flower, bishop's hat and lady's mantle. In our sunny corner we plant clematis. Tall and fast growing, it manages to thrive despite the damp place where we keep it, reaching its leaves, and its pale spring flowers, up to the sun. We lean against the wall, side by side with the clematis, our faces, like the flowers', basking in the sunshine.

I remember the first time she smiled – she remembers it too, for she thought she would never smile again. We are planting seeds, nasturtiums, more in hope than in expectation, for the earth is either too wet or too dry, and they are as likely to drown as to be baked hard. But we must try all the same, she says, for life deserves a chance even in the darkest corners of the city. Our fingers touch beneath the wet earth, the spring sun warm on our backs as we crouch together and sow our garden. She promises me they will be colourful, a yellow as brilliant as a blackbird's beak, the leaves round and bright like tiny lily pads. But I have never seen a blackbird, nor a lily pad, for neither of those is found in the streets I come from. Had she said 'as oily as a starling's wing and as rank as dandelions and fireweed' I would have known exactly what she meant. I tell her so – and that's when she smiles.

'One day I'll take you to the country,' she says. 'To Oxfordshire, and we'll lie in the long grass beside the water where the lilies open in the sun, and we'll watch the blackbirds singing in the trees.'

We are opposites, she and I. She small and neat, her eyes down-cast as if she has been schooled in deference; her feet and hands dainty, her waist so narrow I could have put my hands around it. I am tall and slim, but broad shouldered, my gaze proud and imperious.

'You are full of rage, Gethsemane,' she says. 'In your heart. Can't you learn to forgive them?' She is gentle and kind. She has forgiven everyone. Everyone but herself – that is something she can never do.

The other girls are abrasive and sharp-edged – as I can be. They chatter like sparrows. But Mary, like me, keeps her own counsel. It is not that she despises them, but she sees them as she can never be – indifferent, tough, hardened to the brutality and wickedness of others. She cannot make for herself the flinty carapace the others possess, no matter how hard she tries. It protects them from the world, but she has no such armour.

I love her. I know I do, though I never touch her, and I never say a word about it to her. Not then, anyway. We are so rarely alone, so rarely away from the scrutiny of others – even in the garden there are windows, watching us blankly. Who knows what malicious eyes might be looking out, unseen? I am sure she feels the same for me as I do for her. I see it in her face, in the moistness of her lip and the darting of her eye, the beating of the pulse in the hollow of her neck.

Chapter Seventeen

Will returned to the *Blood* at teatime. We were due at Dr Sackville's later that evening, and I was anxious to make the most of it. I had been drinking nettle, feverfew and ginger infusion all day in a bid to calm my stomach and soothe my head and I was feeling much better. I gave Will a cup and sat him down before the apothecary stove. Work had started at Deadman's Basin in earnest, and he was filthy with smoke smuts. He looked tired and troubled, and I could tell something was amiss. I sipped my tea, listening to the muted sounds of the river, and waited until he was ready to talk.

At first, he sat in silence. Then, after a while, he said, 'I don't think I'm very good at this, Jem.' He did not look at me as he spoke. It was as though he was ashamed, unwilling to confess his weakness, his sense of unfitness for the job he had been given. 'I love to draw, to try to make even the most humble and utilitarian of buildings as elegant as possible.' He closed his eyes. 'But in this city, building anything new seems to require the removal of the vilest and most decayed remnants of the past.' He rubbed his hands together, and stared at his palms, at the way the dirt had gathered in the lines and fissures of his skin. 'It's as though it does not want to be forgotten; as if it does all it can to stay with us, oozing up, seeping through, sticking to everything. Oh, I know that there is nothing there but dirt – soil and water and waste and dead, meaningless matter. And yet . . . it bleeds into the very pores of my flesh. I can smell it upon me, all the time. The oily stink of those horrible waters, those blackened burned buildings. And . . . and I can't get the images of those girls from my head, Jem. The bodies. The flies. The water. D'you know, the only time I've been able to forget them is last night, when I was drunk and singing fit to wake the Devil.' He put his head in his hands.

'And now I am sober and they are before me once more. One drowned, one consumed by maggots, one dried beyond all imagining. It is a waking nightmare, and I am a haunted man.' He stared up at me. 'We have seen some things, you and I, Jem, but this is the worst. This is the worst by far.'

He drove the heels of his palms into his eyes as if he hoped to obliterate the images that burned upon them. 'I wish I had not seen them. That I might go back to not knowing, but I can't. I can't go back and I can't stop seeing their faces, rising before me in my mind's eye, white spectres screaming for help. But no one helped them Jem, not then, and not now—'

I put my arms around him. What else could I do? I should have known how badly he would be affected by what we had found. He had not seen as much death as I, he was not inured to the sight of bodies – drowned, decayed, dissected, fleshless – as I was. I held him close, and felt him shake against my shoulder as he struggled to control his emotions. Around us, the shadows lengthened.

He pushed me away and sat back, his face streaked with tears. 'Who would do such a thing?' he said. He still could not look at me. 'Do you know?'

'I think I do. But I cannot say until I'm certain.'

He said nothing. It was as though he hoped that I did *not* know, as though he hoped such wickedness might be so rare as to be beyond all understanding and explanation. But it wasn't.

The bath I prepared was all I could offer, something warm and fragrant to counter the cold and dark engulfing his spirits. I drew the blinds and lit the candles. I filled a muslin bag with oatmeal and lavender, lemon balm and heartsease and dropped it into the water, squeezing it gently so that it released its scents and oils. The water grew creamy and fragrant.

'Get in,' I commanded.

He peeled off his clothes, dropping them into a stinking pile beside the stove. I hesitated for a moment, then I opened the stove door, and stuffed them in, shirt, jacket, britches – everything. The fire roared and danced, the flames transforming into leaping tongues of vivid blue and shimmering bottle green. I slammed the door closed and dropped the tongs back onto the hearth.

How pale and slim he was, hardly more than a boy once his dark suit and tall hat were gone. He sank into the water, and closed his eyes. I scrubbed his back and washed his hair, labouring in silence as the water cooled and grew murky. I drew some of it out and replaced it with more from the kettle. The steam rose in a white cloud. I took Aberlady's razor, and drew it across his cheek, his eyes closed, my hand on his chin, tilting his head this way and that. I let him soak while I fetched a towel from the laundry, and then I made him get out. He obeyed in silence. I rubbed him briskly, then dripped some lemon and comfrey oil between my hands and smoothed it over his torso. His bruises had turned purple.

'You need to eat more,' I said mildly. 'I can count your ribs.' He did not reply, but let me smooth my hands across his chest, his back, his shoulders, arms and legs. The room was warm and scented. I handed him a clean suit of clothes, neatly folded and perfumed with lavender and cedar against the moths. 'These belonged to John Aberlady,' I said. 'He was a good friend. A good man. He had an eye for a well-cut suit. I think he would be glad to see you wearing this one.'

I put my hands on his shoulders and leaned my forehead against his. 'I can't do this without you, Will,' I whispered. 'I can't go on . . . without you.'

✖

We dined, as Aberlady had usually done, on the fare dished out by the *Blood*'s cookhouse, a large shed that had been erected towards the stern of the ship and from which the smell of boiled meat and overcooked cabbage wafted twice a day. The food was basic, and not at all wholesome. I subscribe to the unorthodox view that plenty of fruit and vegetables in the diet are to be recommended – I had a section of the physic garden given over to the cultivation of these for our personal consumption at the apothecary on Fishbait Lane. But on board the *Blood* such radical notions were eschewed. And yet I had lived and worked in medical institutions all my life, and I was no stranger to the mush we were served. It was the same as the men downstairs received, and Will and I ate the stringy meat and soggy potatoes without complaint.

'Have you been to Dr Sackville's before?' asked Will. 'What do you think will happen?'

'It will probably be the usual display of medical arrogance, and competitiveness, for they are all vying for fame and fortune,' I said. 'There is no money in treating the poor. So it is those who are rich and influential that one must help, especially if you can give them something unusual that they can talk about at dinner. Mesmerism, for example. Or electrical therapeutics. Of course, ideally one needs to be a physician – like Sackville. Surgeons and apothecaries are far inferior – we still have the whiff of the tradesman about us, though I suspect chloroform will soon change that. Have you noticed how they all defer to him, falling over themselves to please him?'

'Of course,' said Will.

'And that Proudlove is "surgeon apothecary"? He's better than any of them, but he'll never be a physician. He needs a licence from the Royal College but they'll never give him one.'

'D'you think he'll come tonight?'

'Undoubtedly – if Dr Sackville invited him, which I hope he has. I told Sackville that Proudlove was right about using bhang as a treatment for tetanus. Hopefully Sackville has asked him along tonight by way of an apology for humiliating him in front of the others – that was my intention, at least.' I pushed my plate away and wiped the grease from my lips. 'I imagine Dr Proudlove has been waiting for such a moment for a very long time.'

～～

Dr Sackville lived on Livingston Fields, a wide, gracious square to the west of the city.

'Such classical beauty,' breathed Will, leaning forward as our cab turned into the square. 'The whole area was designed by Robert Adam, I believe. I realise the vogue these days is for a far greater degree of ornamentation, but the elegance of these buildings touches my heart.' He peered out from the hansom, his face rapturous. 'Which one is it?'

'Number six,' I said. 'Here.' I banged on the roof and the cabman drew his nag to a halt. I paid the fare, and watched him rattle away over the cobbles.

Number six was a fine tall building, the soot that habitually cloaked the city eradicated by a coat of white stucco that glimmered with an eerie beauty in the light of the street lamps. The house was brightly lit, and the sound of music echoed down to us.

'Are you sure this is the right place?' said Will.

I looked again at Dr Sackville's card. 'Assuredly,' I said.

We climbed the steps. The music grew louder, now accompanied by the sound of a man singing in a tremulous tenor. I reached out to pull on the bell, but the door opened before my hand had even touched it. A butler looked down at us. Beyond him we saw a lofty ante-room lit by a shimmering chandelier of candles. The light danced off gold-framed mirrors, and large round-bellied vases. Beneath a gleaming onyx mantel a fire blazed and crackled, whilst high overhead a sumptuous frieze of flowers and cherubs garlanded the wall. I heard Will draw breath in awe and pleasure.

Beside us, in the glittering hall, a towering portrait of a chinless woman stared down with bulbous green eyes. Her dress was rumpled silk, her shoulders white and fashionably sloping. Behind her there were tropical plants and a table covered with dishes of fruit. A black servant waited in the shadows. The gold frame bore a curling golden scroll at its base. *Maria Callard*, I read.

The butler followed my gaze. 'Dr Sackville's wife's late mother,' he said. He cleared his throat, holding a white gloved fist delicately to his lips. 'I think you are expected round the back, gentlemen,' he said. 'The entrance *you* require is on Mill Lane. Number six. It adjoins this house. It is a part of this house and yet,' he smiled, 'it is *very* different to *this* house. Down the lane at the side,' and he ushered us out and shut the door.

We went back down the crystalline steps and walked down the street to the 'lane at the side'. It was dark, with a high wall to left and right, and lit by the yellow smudge of a single lamp at the far end. The shadows lurched as the wind blew and the clouds covered the moon. At the street lamp we turned left and walked down another, darker thoroughfare called Mill Lane. Number six was a dark building of yellow brick, blackened and streaked with soot. It was three storeys high, with a deep basement, and yet compared to the house we had just seen it seemed mean and crouched. The windows were all shaded. The neighbours' houses were dark and ill-lit, silent and bounded by black, slimy walls. There were two entrances to number six – a door at the head of a flight of steps, and a ramp, wide enough to admit a coach and four, which plunged into a dark space beneath the building. Above this was a sort of drawbridge, which might be lowered to allow other deliveries to be made into the building itself, and which might be raised to allow access to the sub-terranean coach house.

A lamp burned beside the front door, the only sign that the place might be occupied or expecting visitors. I rang the bell. We heard it jangle deep inside the building. There came the sound of hasty footsteps on a hard floor, and then the door swung upon.

We were greeted by a young man wearing knee britches, white stockings, a thick wool coat with a shawl collar, and a white neckerchief. He had a business-like air, a brisk manner and a darting, inquiring glance. I recognised him as one of Dr Sackville's students from the *Blood*, who also worked as an assistant in the dissecting rooms of Dr Sackville's anatomy school. 'You're the last to arrive, sir,' he said. He looked askance at Will, who he evidently recognised, but who he had not expected to be admitting. 'You're not a medical man, sir. Dr Sackville said nothing about— that is to say I'm not sure that I—'

'Indeed, sir,' I said. 'But Mr Quartermain is assisting me on board the *Blood* at the moment. Besides, where would we be if we made a policy of excluding those who are interested in our work but unqualified to undertake it?' I gestured to the painting of John Hunter that hung in the passage behind him. 'Dr Sackville worked with Hunter, did he not?'

'Oh yes, sir,' said the young man, 'he is forever telling us so.'

'And was not John Hunter what many would describe as

unqualified when he first helped his brother at the anatomy tables?'

The young man blinked. 'I believe so, sir,' he said, though he was clearly unsure.

We followed the student into the building. It was tiled, like a mortuary, and smelled unmistakably of the mortuary too. The young man carried a lamp, and the shadows reared and jumped about him.

'Does Dr Sackville live at Livingston Fields, or at this house?' said Will, perplexed by the world we had glimpsed at the front, and the one we had entered at the back.

'Both,' said our guide. 'Mrs Sackville is holding a soirée this evening. Dr Sackville will step through later on, though he says that The Society for Medical Inquiry trumps any soirée or party Mrs Sackville might hold.'

'Might you show us around a little?' said Will.

'I don't think so. Not without—'

'Of course, of course,' I said, fixing him with a condescending eye. 'You are not permitted to do so without Dr Sackville's express permission. I told Mr Quartermain here that you young fellows were probably kept on a short leash and never made your own decisions about anything. It's unlikely he trusts any of you sufficiently, and you probably don't know your way around the collections anyway—'

'In fact,' he said. 'I know all about the collections.'

'I doubt that,' I said. I gave a patronising chuckle.

'Can you show us?' said Will.

The young man hesitated. 'This way.' He pushed open a door and held the lamp high. Inside was a large basement room with the shades drawn over its windows. Within, lamps burned here and there, but the room was so cavernous that they seemed like beacons in a sea of floating objects, for it was lined from floor to ceiling with shelves, more of which ran out at angles from the walls, like ribs, and all of which were laden with ranks of anatomical specimens. I had seen anatomy museums before – we had had one at St Saviour's, and a rather unambitious one containing brains at Angel Meadow Asylum. Most of the medical men I knew had their own small collections, but this! Here was the product of over fifty years of dissecting, slicing, preserving and bottling.

'This is only one room,' said the student. 'There are three others beyond this, and more at his country house up at Islington. He has animals too. Did you see the lion and the panther in the drawing room of the Livingston Fields house? No? Stuffed, of course,' he added, seeing the looks on our faces. 'And there are some two thousand specimens in this room alone.'

'Will some of these be used this evening?' said Will. I saw him stare queasily at a nearby jar that contained a six-fingered hand, the flesh pale and greyish, with that clammy water-logged appearance all specimens get after a while. The spirits in which they were kept had to be changed periodically. It would be a full-time job making sure a collection of this magnitude did not putrefy.

The student looked at him strangely. 'No, sir,' he said. 'Specimens from the collection are rarely used during a Society meeting.' A smile tugged at the corners of his lips. 'The Society is principally for live demonstrations and experiments.'

From somewhere far off a bell rang. 'It's starting in ten minutes,' he said. He led us out into the hall, moving quickly now, opening a succession of doors to show the inside of rooms, all of them deserted, and yet with lamps burning within them as if they had only just been abandoned, their former occupants intending to come back at any moment. We saw a library filled from floor to ceiling with books. A small spiral staircase led up to a narrow walkway, bounded by a filigree iron railing and skirting the higher shelves. Another room contained stuffed animals – birds and small mammals mostly – their beady eyes glittering angrily at our intrusion. The next contained bones and fossils; a fourth was home to cases of butterflies, birds' eggs and insects, laid out in neat rank and file. The last door he opened gave out into an anatomy room – by now we had ascended a flight of stairs to the top of the building.

'The bodies are brought up from the mortuary by a hoist,' said the young man. 'The mortuary is in the basement, but we need the skylights for our work.' The northlights in the ceiling, black as polished jet against the night sky, reflected our lamplight in slivers of gold. They would provide a clear harsh light without the glare from the sun, and the room was cold, as it ought to be. With the coming of the autumn it would, I knew, have entered its busiest season. It reeked of putrescence and of the spirits of alcohol used when bottling the specimens. Beneath this I detected the waxy aroma of the resins that were pumped into the veins, lungs and other delicate vessels of the body to reveal their fine tracery and preserve it forever. A carboy of embalming fluid stood on a table beside the slab.

Downstairs, the bell rang once more. 'Quickly now, gentlemen,' said the young man, ushering us out and pulling the door closed. 'Tonight we are in the lecture theatre.' He sounded urgent, and we could hear voices, louder now, echoing up the stairs.

We joined a line of serious-faced, black-clad medical men. Their feet scuffled on the tiled floor. Indeed, the entire building was paved with tiles, as if wet substances constantly dripped and spattered upon them, and were forever being mopped up.

'Are the two houses joined?' said Will, who seemed unable to believe that the golden mansion we had seen on Livingston Fields had anything to do with the dark frontage on Mill Lane and the macabre spaces we had just been through. 'Or are they completely separate?'

Our guide nodded to an ordinary-looking door. 'That leads through into the other house. The Livingston Fields residence.' He was looking nervous, as though he hoped no one was about to ask him where he had been for the last fifteen minutes. 'Mrs Sackville never comes through here.' He gave a quick grin. 'The resurrection men swear like the Devil. It would never do for a lady to hear that.'

'Indeed,' Will murmured. 'The heavens would fall.'

By now we were in a familiar place – an operating theatre and a lecture room. There were some twenty medical men present. The room was steep, cup-shaped, and ringed with wooden terraces, so that those at the top might see what was being undertaken on the operating table below. The room echoed with murmuring voices, for medical men always have plenty to say to one another. I recognised a couple of students from the *Blood,* and in the front row sat Dr Cole, with Dr Antrobus at his side. I nodded to them both as we shuffled into our place. I saw Dr Graves and Dr Catchpole, both from St Saviour's, though they had not noticed Will and me. Further back, high above the others,

Dr Proudlove sat alone. I realised then that much of the murmuring concerned his presence there that evening, for everyone raised their eyebrows in his direction.

'They probably think the poor fellow is someone's servant,' I said.

'More likely they think he's one of the exhibits this evening,' muttered Will. 'Not a man at all, but a specimen to be vivisected, like any other animal. I admire the fellow for coming.'

At that moment Dr Sackville entered. There was a genteel ripple of applause at the sight of him, and the room fell silent.

Dr Sackville held up his hands. 'Gentlemen,' he said. 'Welcome to the five hundredth meeting of the Society for Medical Inquiry.'

I had been to meetings like this before, and I had to admit that I always felt vulnerable – perhaps like Dr Proudlove, for he, like me, was unique. No one would really suggest Dr Proudlove might be brought forward as a specimen, but what if they knew I was a woman? They would not be so sanguine then. Would I be vivisected? My skull sawn open and my brain taken out so that they might examine it for signs of madness? Would my sex be scrutinised for deformity – I must be a hermaphrodite at least, they would say, to live as I did. How was it that I was not betrayed by my menses? They would be angry too, angry that they had not noticed that I was different, that they had not only tolerated me, but had treated me as an equal when I quite evidently was not. Their ideas about a woman's inferiority, their conviction that she was biologically and temperamentally unfit to practise medicine would be proved wrong, and they would not take it easily. The setting too gave me pause, for was not the theatre the place where cross-dressings were unmasked – the universe would be thrown off-kilter if they were not. I suddenly realised I was staring at Dr Proudlove – a heathen Othello sitting opposite my disguised Viola – and I felt a wild laugh rising up inside me. I swallowed it, and set my face into what I hoped was an expression of masculine gravity.

Beside me, Will was looking tired. The heavy meal we had eaten on board the *Blood*, the terrible night we had passed was sapping his strength, and I saw his eyelids drooping. I jabbed him in the ribs as Dr Sackville finished his address.

'Gentlemen,' he cried. 'Allow me to start the proceedings.' The door at the back burst open, and the patient from the *Blood* with elephantiasis was brought in by a pair of thick-set orderlies. He was a sailor, originally from Bristol, Dr Sackville told us, and he had spent much time in West Africa.

'Slaving, no doubt,' muttered Will. 'I can think of no other reason why he might need to be there.'

'This is not the first case we have seen on board the *Blood*,' said Dr Sackville. 'The disease affects the face, the genitals, the lower limbs.'

The man was wearing a long robe of white linen, and all at once Dr Sackville whisked it off and cast it aside, so that the man stood before us quite naked. 'Note the grotesque swelling of the legs and feet, the thickening of the skin, the ulceration—' He bade the man get onto the operating table.

Beside me, Will moaned faintly. '"Live demonstrations and experiments"?' he said. His lips were bloodless.

'You have your salts?' I whispered.

'I am never without them when I am with you,' he replied. I saw him slip his hand into his pocket.

'Elephantiasis is a scourge throughout her majesty's colonies,' said Dr Sackville. 'Many thousands are prevented from working. It is a blight upon the utility of the native, his health and happiness. Worse still, gentlemen, it does not confine itself to those indigenous to the countries in which we find it, but might affect all those who live or work there.'

Dr Sackville waved a hand. Dr Antrobus sprang up, a chloroform inhaler in his hand. He affixed it over the man's nose and mouth and dripped liquid from a bottle onto the gauze pad of the apparatus. When the patient was unconscious, Dr Sackville pulled out his knives and bent over the man's groin. And all the while he talked, a jocular commentary on the blood and the lymph system, which he called the 'lacteals', describing their passage through the body, the findings of his hero, William Hunter, the arguments and rivalries that had followed the lacteals' discovery.

At length, he stood back from the body and held up a silver syringe. The thick bloody patina on his apron shone like burnished rosewood in the lamplight. 'I have exposed the lacteal nodes at the groin and extracted some fluid,' he said. 'We shall examine it together. With a little help, of course.'

The door crashed open once more and another orderly wheeled in a great gleaming microscope. I could see it was the best, German, no doubt, and a beauty in brass and ivory. Dr Sackville dripped the contents of his syringe onto a glass plate and slid it beneath the microscope's golden eye. One by one we filed past to look.

'Well, gentlemen?' cried Dr Sackville.

'Worms,' said someone. 'The fluid contains worms.'

'Quite so,' said Dr Sackville 'The system of drainage usually afforded by the lacteals is blocked by worms. Parasites. Unable to drain away, fluid gathers in the body, resulting in what we see here – an unstoppable distortion of the legs, the genitals, the face.' He waved a hand towards the body still unconscious on the operating theatre. Dr Antrobus had stitched the patient's groin up and taped a gauze pad over the wounds. The orderlies appeared once more, heaved the man onto a stretcher and hauled him away.

'What might be done to help him?' said someone else.

'Black cohosh,' said another. 'Mixed with wormwood.'

'I have tried both with another patient,' said Dr Sackville. 'Neither are effective.'

'How did the worms get in there?'

'From the food, I imagine, or some other native practices.'

'But this man is English,' said someone. 'Did he eat their food? Did he engage in native practices?'

'Have you examined the blood?' I said.

'We found nothing,' replied Dr Sackville.

'Did you look during the night time, as well as the day?' It was Dr Proudlove. The room fell silent. Someone sniggered.

'No, sir, I did not,' said Dr Sackville. He sounded incredulous. 'You think *that* would make a difference?'

'The creature's larvae may be nocturnal.'

'Would you suggest we look when there is a full moon, or a waxing gibbous?' said Dr Sackville. There was another laugh. Dr Sackville turned away.

'Is it possible,' said Dr Proudlove, evidently not discouraged, and perhaps so used to the scorn of his colleagues that he hardly noticed their hostility, 'is it possible that the worms that cause this disease have their origins in tiny eggs, too small to be detected by our microscopes, and that these might enter through the skin?'

'Undetectable by this microscope?' Dr Sackville shook his head. 'It is the most powerful one available. Besides, to get such "tiny eggs" to the lacteals would require the skin to be fully penetrated. They must enter the lacteal fluid, and this assumes that first, they must enter the bloodstream. How might *that* be possible?'

Dr Proudlove held up a bottle. I recognised it as the one he had shown us on board the *Blood,* the night that John Aberlady had leaped from the apothecary window. 'I suggest—' he licked his lips, his face excited, his voice trembling with nerves. 'I suggest that it is an insect – the mosquito, that is the vector of this disease. The vector of many diseases.'

'A fly?' Dr Sackville chuckled.

'The mosquito sucks blood. But might it not also inject a foreign substance as it does so? Some of its own matter. Saliva, say—'

'Don't be ridiculous, man. These are *worms*, Dr Proudlove, not mosquitoes, and not mosquito nymphs. Did you not see them with your own eyes?'

'But if there was something in the saliva, some *other* creature's eggs. If a man might harbour parasites might not an insect harbour them too?'

'You are all "ifs" and "buts", Dr Proudlove. You are dealing in a world of the invisible. So invisible, sir, one might even say that you have entered the realm of fantasy!' There was laughter and the shaking of heads. 'You have nothing to contribute here, sir, but absurdity. Night blood and flies? We are a serious society. Not a place of superstition and old wives' tales. Had I known you were going to contribute nothing but childishness I would have followed my own counsel more closely and *not* invited you.' Dr Sackville turned away. The others, still clustered about the microscope, did the same.

Dr Proudlove opened his mouth to speak again, but then closed it. He put the bottle back into his pocket and sat down, his face tense with rage and humiliation.

But there was more – and worse – to come, for up next was Dr Cole, who had brought with him a collection of skulls, which he proceeded to set out on the operating table. I hoped he wasn't going to talk about phrenology, for I had had enough of that dubious practice up at Angel Meadow Asylum – but he didn't. Instead, he had something much more interesting to say.

'Gentlemen,' he said, 'I would like to talk to you about the complexity of the animal skull, and what it tells us about animal generation.'

We sat in silence while he talked, holding up one skull after another, dogs and cats, reptiles and birds, comparing different species and talking about slight differences in the arrangement of the skull in those of the same species. I wondered where he had got them all from, for he was not experienced enough to have amassed so many himself.

From the box at his feet Dr Cole then produced a more familiar set of craniums. He set them out side by side in what he termed their 'order of complexity'.

'The skull of a European is the superior specimen,' he said. 'In descending order we might locate those of other races, though Europeans, Indo-Europeans, Chinese, Africans, and from thence through the monkeys – chimpanzee, orang-utan—'

A murmur of consternation had started up.

Will looked about at the frowns and shaking heads. 'I wonder whether it is the hierarchy of human skulls he has presented or the inclusion of monkeys in the schema that's bothering them?' he whispered. 'No doubt it is the latter.'

'No!' a voice screamed out from the topmost standings before I had chance to reply. We all turned to look. A man was on his feet, the lamplight glinting off his small round spectacles.

'What the devil?' Dr Sackville jumped up. 'Birdwhistle! What are you doing here?'

'I came to have my suspicious confirmed,' Dr Birdwhistle cried. '"But there were false prophets also among the people, even as there shall be false teachers among you." Two, Peter, chapter two, verse one. I suspected it, but now I see that it is true. You not only tolerate these views, Dr Sackville, but you condone them!'

'I don't condone anything,' replied Dr Sackville calmly. 'This is a place for scientific discussion. Dr Cole's ideas are his own.'

'Oh, I think they are *not* his own,' cried Dr Birdwhistle. 'For if I am not mistaken, sir, a number of those skulls belong to Mr Aberlady, and the ideas you are espousing, Dr Cole, those that claim a relationship between man and monkey and deny the existence of the Creator, are also his. It's the work of the Devil. You recall what happened to Aberlady? He was driven out of his mind, driven mad by his own idolatrous views and unnatural behaviour.'

'This is no place for such wild accusations,' cried Dr Sackville. 'You may say what you wish when you are in the pulpit, but *not* when you are in my home.' He turned angrily to the student who had shown Will and me around his house. 'How the devil did *he* get in? Were you not on the door?'

'The door was open, sir,' said Dr Birdwhistle. 'I walked straight in.'

'Then, sir, I must ask you to walk straight out again.'

'I will do no such thing. Not until I have spoken!'

'Then I will have you thrown out.' The two burly orderlies were already mounting the steep staircases to the back of the lecture theatre. Dr Birdwhistle saw them and tried to get away. He darted along the unoccupied standing, only to be met by another orderly at the other end. He dashed back again, up and down, his black clergyman's coat flapping, like a crazed puppet in a Punch and Judy show. But there was to be no escape. The orderlies seized Dr Birdwhistle, one on each side, and hauled him through another door at the back. We heard the sound of muffled shouts, of heels dragging and scuffling, the bang of a door – and then silence.

All eyes turned back to Dr Cole, who was still standing beside the operating table, a skull in his hand. At Dr Birdwhistle's accusations his cheeks had turned red. He licked his lips, his gaze flickering from the skull in his hand to the door, as if, for a single instant, he considered flight to be the best option. But Dr Sackville waved a hand. 'Pray continue, Dr Cole,' he said.

'As I was saying,' Dr Cole cleared his throat. 'The skulls show a regular and continual gradation from the most advanced,' he tapped a finger on a large pale cranium. 'The head of John Aberlady himself.'

'Good God,' I said. 'It must still be warm!'

'To this chimpanzee here,' Dr Cole rested his fingers on a smaller skull with a low brow and protuberant lower face and jaw, 'to this howler monkey here. The European skull is the most perfect, the negro the least perfect.' His gaze flickered up to Dr Proudlove, and then darted away again. 'They are part of a series, the European, the negro, the monkey—'

The murmuring had started up again, but one person could no longer contain himself. Dr Proudlove sprang to his feet. 'You say the black man is inferior to the European?' he cried.

'What other conclusion might we draw? He is inferior to the European as the howler monkey is to the chimpanzee,' said Dr Cole. His smile, his spread hands, were guileless. But his eyes glittered. 'And all are related to one another.'

'Well, sir,' cried Dr Proudlove, 'if it is the case that the European is a later development, an advancement on earlier imperfections, if you are arguing that we are seeing a gradation of change, that your most primitive skull is that of a black man, that all humans spring from the black man, then it also follows that our very first parents, Adam and Eve, were also black.'

Dr Cole coloured. 'I don't think—'

'But logic demands it,' cried Dr Proudlove. 'Does it not, sir? *Your* logic, at least. Or am I being too primitive for you? I might also add—' By now he had to raise his voice to be heard, and his words rang out above the hullabaloo. 'I might also add that as God made Adam and Even in his

283

own image then it also follows that God himself is black. As this is the case, sir, then I would imagine that the black man is superior in all ways, and that what you are seeing here is a degeneration, from a state of grace to something far less noble, the development of a devilishness that seeks to put white men above all others, to set himself as superior even to God. How else might we understand the corruption and misery of the age in which we live?' The room exploded in uproar. 'I have no doubt, that was what Aberlady would have concluded,' cried Dr Proudlove, 'when he published his paper on the comparative study of the human cranium. Were you intending to take his arguments as far, sir, when you passed off his work as your own?'

Dr Proudlove looked round at that cockpit of white faces and angry shouting mouths, and turned away.

Chapter Eighteen

We left Dr Sackville's and went back to the *Blood*. I had told Will there was no need for him to sleep aboard, but he refused to return to Fishbait Lane.

'The previous apothecary jumped out of the window,' he said. 'This place is dangerous, Jem. For both of us, I should think, but for you in particular – you with your questions and your argumentative manner.'

'I'm not argumentative,' I said.

'You are. And at this moment so am I. I am *not* going back to Fishbait Lane.'

I had to do the ward rounds before bed, and I left Will in the apothecary trying to make himself comfortable with a few blankets and a sack of hops as a pillow.

Downstairs the place was subdued, the patients quiet and still, the thick air heavy with the breath of sleeping men. There was one lantern near the foot of the stairs, where the night nurse slumbered in a chair. Her head was tipped back, her mouth open, her tongue pink as a sea anemone in a dark wet hole. I walked between the beds, on silent feet. Further down the top ward, a candle glowed. Dr Proudlove was crouched beside the sleeping patient, Rintoul. His face was furious, his teeth flashing white as he spoke to the man who stood beside him: Dr Rennie, small and crouched, like a wizened goblin.

'They led me to believe I was accepted,' he said. He rubbed his arm as if something itched beneath. 'I did everything they wanted, and then they demean me—'

'Don't take it to heart, my boy,' Dr Rennie was saying. 'It is a test, that's all. Every man must be tested, must be subjected to humiliation, to mockery, his ideas ridiculed so that he might show himself able to defend them. I assume you stood up for yourself? One must stand up for one's ideas. Once a man passes the test there is no going back. You *will* have your rewards.'

'I . . . I left,' said Dr Proudlove. He struck his forehead with the heel of his hand, his face resolving into fury. 'That was no test, sir, it was . . . it was injustice. It was men who do not want their hallowed ranks tainted by the presence of a black man, men who have not a single new or original thought in their heads refusing to listen. I have no doubt that if what I had said had come from the lips of Dr Antrobus then their reaction would have been very different.'

'Perhaps,' said Dr Rennie. 'But perhaps not.' He gave a hoarse whispering laugh. 'What are the chances of Dr Antrobus ever saying anything new or original?' Dr Rennie patted Dr Proudlove's shoulder. 'It's not for everyone,' he said with a sigh. 'It was not for me—'

'But I don't *want* to be like *you*,' said Dr Proudlove. 'I'm *not* like you. I am so much more that these vile and squalid streets, more than this ship—' He put his head in his hands. 'Forgive me, sir. I didn't mean to—'

'Oh, but you *are* so much more,' said Dr Rennie. 'And you are a pioneer of your race. It was never going to be easy.'

They fell silent then, as from overhead came the sound of voices, and clattering boots. I remained where I was, in the shadows, concealed from view by a bulkhead. Behind me, Dr Cole and Dr Antrobus came down the stairs. The patients stirred in their beds, but did not wake. The two men went to the stern, to the hutches where they slept when they were on board the *Blood*, and then they noticed the candle, and the two figures at the back.

'Dr Rennie, Dr Proudlove,' said Dr Cole. 'I didn't see you there. How fares the patient?'

'Well enough,' said Dr Proudlove. His voice was cold. 'Somewhat better than if he had been dosed with opium.'

'We're going to get some supper,' said Dr Antrobus. 'Rather late, I know. Up on Spyglass, would you care to join us, Dr Proudlove? Perhaps we might,' he cleared his throat, 'resolve our little differences?'

Dr Proudlove hesitated. 'I think not,' he said finally. He turned away. At that the two other men shrugged, and climbed the stairs back up to the weather deck.

'Was I right to refuse them, Dr Rennie?' said Dr Proudlove gloomily. 'Should I make amends? I accused him of stealing another man's ideas. He argued that I was an inferior species altogether!' He put his head in his hands. 'Shall I go? Shall I join them? I no longer know what to do for the best.'

'I can't tell you that,' said Dr Rennie. He stood in silence then, his real eye pale and watery, staring into the shadows at nothing. His painted eye was fixed upon Dr Proudlove, a glinting, unblinking stare that seemed to strike into the other man's soul.

Dr Proudlove stood up. 'Thank you, sir,' he said. He shook Dr Rennie by the hand, and then he was gone. I heard his footsteps pass overhead, in the same direction that the others had taken.

The next morning, I attended to the ward rounds. I had expected Dr Proudlove to accompany me but he was nowhere to be seen. I assumed he had had as pleasant an evening as Will and I had had with Dr Cole and Dr Antrobus. We drank some coffee sitting amongst the foliage on the poop deck. Will had to go up to Deadman's Basin again. He was loath to go back, but anxious that the job should progress.

'It holds no horror for us now,' he said. 'It is simply a job that needs to be done. I couldn't get it out of my mind last night, as you saw.' He looked at me, his expression half bashful. 'I'm grateful to you, Jem,' he said. 'For what you did. What you said.'

I nodded.

'Anyway.' He drew a deep breath. 'I went up there this morning while you were on the wards. The air of menace that seemed to hang over the place yesterday has quite disappeared. Now, it is simply ugly and dirty. Those tumbled buildings, those slumped sheds sitting out on the black water, that still, eerie silence—' He shrugged. 'It is still unutterably vile, but it seems less . . . less desolate, somehow.' He finished his coffee and stood up.

'Will you be . . . will you be equal to the task ahead?'
I said.

'I will be *more* than equal.' He smiled. 'What about you?
Will you manage alone here?'

'Ah, but I am *not* alone,' I said. 'I have Dr Rennie – somewhere about. And Mrs Speedicut. I cannot see her but I
can smell her pipe – I fear she has run out of Virginian
shag and is now smoking dried dung. And there are some
nurses. Besides, how on earth do you think I managed
before I met you?'

'You were lonely and bored,' he replied.

'No,' I said. '*You* were lonely and bored. *I* was happy,
and living an enviable life.' We exchanged a glance, and
laughed.

He made a telescope with his hands and looked through
it with his right eye, squinting his left eye like an admiral
scanning the horizon for enemy ships. 'I see Miss Proudlove opening up the Seaman's Dispensary,' he said. 'She is
alone this morning. And there's Toad, at the door to the
mortuary, out for his morning constitutional, perhaps? No,
no, I see he has just come out to relieve himself in the gutter. And there's Young Toad, walking with a swagger in his
step this morning. Barefoot, as usual. Off to join the mud
larks down near Deadman's Entry – no wonder the poor
lad is always so filthy.' He turned to look further up the
dockside. 'And here comes Dr Sackville in his fine carriage,
and Dr Birdwhistle on foot with a Bible under his arm. I
see his lips moving – whether it is in prayer or as a consequence of his venereal disease it is impossible to say—'

'You're learning fast,' I said.

'I surprise myself. Last week I diagnosed my own
headache and told myself to take a nap.'

I watched Will walk along the waterfront towards Deadman's Entry. He had been to the slop shop on Spyglass Lane and bought himself a suit of sturdy navy-blue canvas, which would withstand the dirt of Deadman's Basin better than Aberlady's suit. He was met by the foreman, and I saw them shake hands and head up to the basin together. I was glad he seemed more his old self.

I sighed, and stood up, rubbing my fingers against the hard needles of the rosemary bush and raising them to my nose as I looked up and down the waterfront. Everywhere there was evidence of wealth and luxury, warehouses filled with spices, or silks; barrels stacked as high as a building, and ropes and sails enough to rig every spire in London. Shop windows gave glimpses of gleaming brass and glass, thick coils of rope and creamy swathes of sailcloth.

The door to the Seaman's Dispensary was open, for the building was south facing, looking out at the *Blood*, and the day was bright again. It wouldn't last, I knew. The city was far too dirty. The wind had dropped too, and soon the smoke and damp would gather about the water in a brown pall. I went down onto the weather deck. Some of the men had come up from below and were standing about the deck wrapped in blankets and smoking. The convalescents' hammocks were all occupied, some of the men hunched in their blankets in silence, others chatting. The cookhouse – usually a source of unpleasant aromas – today smelled of apple. Will and I had brought up a quantity of windfalls from the physic garden the day before. I had been all for handing them out to the patients, but Will had stopped me.

'Most of them have no teeth, Jem,' he'd said. 'How will they manage?'

'Stewed apple,' said Dr Rennie, who had looked at our baskets of fruit with glee. 'With a little bit of autumn spice.' He had vanished downstairs to his lair above the bilges, and returned with a giant sack of raisins, a cluster of nutmegs and a bundle of cinnamon sticks. He grinned. 'Contraband from a grateful patient.'

I contributed a fistful of cloves from the apothecary supplies, and the smell of the stewing fruits and spices was delicious. Everyone was smiling – even Dr Birdwhistle, once he had finished arguing with Dr Sackville about his appearance at the Medical Society the previous evening. Everyone had heard them.

'I shall report you to the governors,' he had said. 'You have strayed into blasphemous waters, sir. To deny God is to court disaster. Think of the consequences. Dr Cole and Dr Antrobus follow your lead, sir, and I fear for them both as a result. If they do not answer to God, then to whom do they answer? To themselves? They are fast on the way to becoming the slaves of their own arrogance and certainty, and where is the benefit in that? Or do they answer to you? Are *you* a better arbiter of right and wrong than the word of Our Lord? You must, and shall, be stopped!'

'I shall report *you* to the governors, sir,' Dr Sackville had replied. 'What I do in my own house in my own time is no concern of yours.'

Now, Dr Birdwhistle seemed to be drifting about the deck in search of someone's soul to save. The men in the hammocks fell silent, hastily feigning sleep. Those with pipes and blankets shuffled back down to the ward. The sun went in. Dr Birdwhistle sidled over.

'You've settled in, sir?'

'More or less, Dr Birdwhistle.'

'I saw you at Dr Sackville's last night, Mr Flockhart. Would I be right to assume that you and he are like minded?'

'Perhaps we are, sir, in some ways,' I replied. 'Though not in others. I was there merely as an observer.'

'It is the start of a slippery slope, sir. Observing. I have seen it before.'

'In Mr Aberlady?'

'Mr Aberlady was a man who had forsaken the Lord in many ways. He killed himself, sir. That in itself is an act deplored by God, just as his unnatural tendencies, his *addictions* and *proclivities* were further evidence of his alienation from the Lord.' He stared at me. The hand that gripped his large black Bible had left a wet stain upon it, and I saw that the leather at the spine bore a pale dusty bloom, the dried sweat from a thousand fervid clutchings. '"The vengeance of eternal fire shall fall upon him." Jude, chapter one, verse seven. I tried to reach him, sir. More than once I tried, but he would not listen. He was a sinner, sir, and he could not stop. He *would* not.'

'And what about you, sir,' I said, pushing my face close to his so that he might stare into my devilish mask. 'Are you without sin? The sin of lust, of pride? *Those* are sins that *you* chose, sir, and they do not become you.'

I turned on my heel and walked away. I thought of Aberlady's letter, its talk of God and the Devil. Perhaps he *had* believed, in the end.

I took the medicines and prescriptions for the *Blood's* outpatients over to the Seaman's Dispensary. Outside, young Toad was lolling on the kerb. He was eating an enormous currant bun. His feet were filthy, his coat as stained and muddy as ever, his trousers grazing his skinny ankles.

'Hello,' I said.

He looked at me warily. He stuffed the last of his bun between his champing jaws as if he feared I might be about to snatch it from him.

'Mornin', sir,' he muttered. Beneath his coat was a waistcoat of embroidered silk.

'Aren't you looking fine!' I said. 'Just like a gentleman.'

Young Toad looked pleased, and pulled aside the greasy flaps of his coat to reveal the finery below. The waistcoat was second-hand, I could see that. It bore a nebula of dark stains about the pocket, and was worn from where a watch had been slipped in and out. The embroidery was frayed and tatty, but to Young Toad it was an object of beauty.

'New!' he said. He looked down at it and smiled. 'I'm a reg'lar gen'man now.'

'So you are,' I said. 'Is Dr Proudlove about?' I didn't wait for an answer, but walked straight into the dispensary.

Dr Proudlove was not there, but his sister was.

'I've not seen him today,' she said. 'Nor last night. I assume he came home late and went out again early, but I don't know where, and look at the men waiting.'

She wrung her hands and looked out at the men lined up on the hard, wooden benches of the dispensary waiting room. It acted as an outpatient department for the *Blood*, and there were many men there who had been treated on board. Others came to the dispensary and were given a ticket of admittance to the ship; still more came for medicines to treat minor ailments, or to have their dressings changed. It was busy that morning. A tall black man dressed in the uniform of a Dutch sailor watched Miss Proudlove with interest. A Chinese man spat a mouthful of tobacco juice into one of the spittoons, and wiped his mouth with the back of his hand; beside him, a Lascar sat with his eyes closed. They all wore seamen's boots, they all had faces tanned and weathered from the seas. None of them said a word to Miss Proudlove, but sat there meekly awaiting their turn. I remembered the outpatients' waiting room at St Saviour's. Men, women and children all packed in together. The place had been hot and noisy, and the moisture – condensation from the closed windows, the damp clothing and the cheap coal – had run down the walls. I had never been able to decide whether the fetor or the humidity had sickened me most. Here, with the door standing open and the men sitting or standing in orderly ranks, the place seemed a model of good order.

'I have started already,' she said, looking out at the scarred and weathered faces of the patients.

'*You?*' I could not stop myself.

'Yes, Mr Flockhart. I, a woman, have made decisions about medicines and ailments that are usually made by a man. Shall I call back those who have already left and you can check my prescriptions?'

'No,' I said. 'Not at all, I just meant—'

'But that is *exactly* what you meant, sir. You meant "Why on earth did she not wait for her brother?" and "How on earth can she know what to do!" And you possibly also meant "She's descended from savages, she has probably prescribed crocodile blood and powdered monkey's brains". Or perhaps you just meant that any moment now it will all prove too much for me, and that I should sit down before I fall down and need to be taken to Angel Meadow to have my brains removed and put into a jar!'

I let her words hang in the air for a moment. Then, 'Yes,' I said. 'I meant all of those things. How well you read minds, Miss Proudlove.' I took off my jacket and plucked an apron from the back of the apothecary door. 'Now that we understand one another so well, perhaps I might help you.'

No one else from the *Blood* came in. Through the dispensary's open door I saw Dr Cole arrive there, and Dr Antrobus soon after. Neither of them came over to the dispensary. Miss Proudlove saw me watching. 'They never come,' she said. 'Not unless they have to. The dispensary is run by Erasmus and me.'

'And what does Erasmus think of that?' I said. 'Surely his ambitions are greater than running a seaman's dispensary? He's a clever man.'

'He must accept it,' she said shortly. 'These men need help, and so help them we must. But that does not mean that it is fair, or that either of us should like it.'

She sank into a resentful silence. I watched her flick through the prescription ledger, and the pharmacopoeia, and slip some jars back onto the shelf where they belonged. I had never seen a woman working in an apothecary before, and for a moment I felt disconcerted. She spoke to the patients, and attended to their ailments with confidence, and acted as though we were equals, as if she dared me to contradict her, to challenge her decisions or her actions. And yet in the eyes of the world I was *not* her equal, for in the eyes of the world I was a man, and as such I was set above her. Wasn't I? For a moment, I understood how men must feel to have their dominion threatened by a woman. And yet, I was *not* a man. Could I not delight in the evident competence of a sister?

My jealousy and perplexity lasted only a moment. After all, did I not have the same plan in my heart for Pestle Jenny? I watched Miss Proudlove attend to a seaman with an ulcerated leg, and I felt only admiration – though I knew better than to tell her so and be called patronising. Besides, there was something else about Miss Proudlove that resonated with me. Something in her unhappy face, her determined gaze and her concentration. She was lonely, I could sense it; lonely and sad and angry. I had been like that too once, though time had dampened my sorrow. It was only when I was with Eliza that I had felt any different, and it was when I lost her that my heart had broken. I had Will, of course I did, and I loved him dearly. But it was not the same. It could never be the same.

The ailments we treated that morning were little different to those we had tended at St Saviour's, though the problems the seamen brought to us were often more advanced, or had been attended to badly, so that the results of poor care – or no care – had to be remedied before the situation could be improved. Miss Proudlove was known to many of them already, and they greeted her with a knuckle to their brow, or a nod of the head. None of them spoke to her roughly or without respect.

The dispensary closed at midday. 'You know a lot about physic, Miss Proudlove,' I said, as she locked the doors.

'I've worked alongside my brother for a while now.' She went to the window to pull the blinds.

'You hardly needed me at all.'

'No, sir, I did not. Though I admit that your assistance was of some use today.'

I grinned. It was a long time since I had been anyone's assistant in an apothecary.

She closed her eyes as the sun peeped out. 'Oh, I'm so tired of these grey streets and walls,' she said. She pressed her forehead to the cool glass of the windowpane. 'And the constant noise of the place.' A dray loaded with barrels rumbled past. 'But then where else might I go?'

'There are worse places than London,' I said. 'And you have friends here at the riverside. Purpose. Your brother.'

'At least he has a profession, even if *I* do not. He works hard, Mr Flockhart, hard to make a name for himself, to be something more than the sixpenny doctor he is forced to be. He is better than his so-called friends on board the *Blood*.'

'So-called?'

'They're not his friends, no matter what they say, or what they ask him to do.'

I waited for her to say more, but she was silent. 'What about Mr Aberlady?' I said. 'Did you know him well?'

She shrugged. 'He was a friend of Erasmus's. He seemed a good man to me, though like all of them a little too fond of experimenting. Have you noticed how few stray dogs there are near the *Blood*?'

'Did he come to Siren House?'

'Very occasionally. Usually with a prescription, or to treat the pox. It was the others who came mostly. They took it in turns, or if there was an emergency – sometimes

a confinement – whoever was on the *Blood* came along.'
She looked over to the floating hospital. 'I see you have a
little physic garden there now. It's something Mr Aberlady
never bothered with.'

'Would you like to see a real physic garden?'

'Where?' She pulled out a pocket watch, an old one of
her brother's, I presumed. 'I have to get back for some
errands before this afternoon's prescriptions.' I waited.
'But . . . yes,' she said. 'I would like that.' She still had not
smiled. I wondered how she would look if she did.

❧

We headed north, away from the river and up towards St
Saviour's Street. She seemed nervous to be leaving those
familiar cramped and dingy streets, despite her
contemptuous words earlier, but most people were too
busy to pay us any attention. We walked quickly, her stride
long, like mine, her boots beneath her skirts striking the
pavement confidently. Her bonnet prevented me from
seeing her face, though she walked with her head up,
proudly, unafraid to meet the gaze of passers-by. She had
a basket on her arm, for her 'errands later on', she said,
the contents covered with a muslin cloth. She didn't tell
me what she carried, and I didn't ask.

We did not talk, not then, and I fell to thinking about
Will, and wondering how he was getting on at Deadman's
Basin. Should I have sent young Toad to fetch him? He
would have been delighted to come – he loved the physic
garden. But he was settling into his work at the basin, and
the sooner it was done the sooner he could leave the place
forever. He would be busy, I said to myself, and so I had not

sent for him. But the truth was that I wanted Miss Proudlove to myself. There was something I wanted to ask her.

As I pulled the physic garden key from my pocket Miss Proudlove traced her fingers over the plaque at the gate. 'Flockhart and Quartermain,' she read. Beneath it, as insisted upon by Gabriel – who had been told that his surname, Locke, would only be added once he had passed his apothecary examinations – was a skull and cross-bones.

'You deal in death, Mr Flockhart?'

'Behind this gate lies the most comprehensive poison garden in all of London,' I said. 'It is not for the un-initiated. But we have other things in here too.'

I pushed open the gate and stood back. I was not generally given to making dramatic gestures, but I could not help it. I wanted her to be impressed. I knew she was familiar with the pharmacopoeia, and yet she had never seen a physic garden? I watched her face as the gate swung open, the sun – who could have predicted it – shining through a gap in the jaundiced clouds like the light of God depicted in a church window, three broad golden beams of celestial light, falling onto my garden. The colours glowed like treasure. I had not seen her smile before, but I did then, a look of real pleasure and delight. I grinned back, and bowed her in at the gate.

I have never been able to decide which season I preferred in the physic garden, for they all offered delight. The dry cold of a crisp winter's day, each twig neatly sheathed in frost; the green explosion of spring, with its luminous unfurling leaves and moist, thrusting shoots. In the summer, I loved the bright, louche blowsiness of the place, and now, in the autumn, it was perhaps at its most beautiful, as the leaves turned and the fruit ripened. We strolled through the beds, the sun warm on our faces. She allowed her bonnet to fall from her head and it hung down her back in its ribbons. I showed her as much of the garden as I could. She was knowledgeable, having worked alongside her brother for so long, and interested. The poison beds fascinated her too.

'Hemlock,' she said, pointing. 'Yew. Henbane. Bloodroot. Monkshood.' She walked to a gate in the wall. 'Where does this lead?' she said.

'To the house next door.'

'Do they come in here? Is it your house over there?'

I laughed. 'No, my home is above the apothecary on Fishbait Lane – when I am not on the *Blood*.'

'So who lives there? Why do they have a gate into your garden? Did you not say the poison beds were dangerous?'

'No one lives there now,' I said. 'But it was owned by a medical man. He used to work at St Saviour's. He liked to have access to the physic garden.'

'Where is he now?'

'He's dead,' I said.

She stood up and went to the gate. The house was not what it used to be. The gardens had once been mown and tended, but now they were ravaged by weeds. Clouds of thistledown and burst dandelion clocks were forever drifting over the wall and settling amongst my medicinal plants. The house itself was a plain cube of a building. I rarely looked over at it now, but I knew that its windows were boarded over with ugly black planks, and its once white walls were streaked by the rain and stained with smoke. We stood side by side and looked over.

'So what is it you wanted to ask me?' she said, as if she had read my mind.

'I wanted to ask whether you knew a girl called Eliza Magorian,' I said. 'She used to work in Mrs Roseplucker's on Wicke Street. I don't know where she is now. I used to know her—'

'You want me to find a prostitute for you?'

'Yes. If you can.'

She turned to me, her face furious. 'I am not a pander, Mr Flockhart. I do not "find" street girls for men, no matter what.'

'We were friends. I need to find her.'

'*Friends?*' I heard the scorn in her voice, but I persisted. I had to.

'I loved her. I still love her.' I felt my face burning, and all at once my old feelings of inadequacy returned. I was too ugly to be loved. The very idea that anyone could look at me with anything other than pity and revulsion was absurd. I saw myself as she must see me, a naive fool, fancying himself in love with a street girl whom he had paid to pretend that she loved him. But I had told her nothing of myself, nothing of what Eliza had meant to me. Gethsemane Proudlove had filled the gaps in her knowledge with her own jaundiced view of the world, a world without kindness and love, where women were exploited and treated shamefully by men until the pox killed them.

She turned to leave.

'No!' I said. I felt myself blushing, my face turning uglier still. 'It was not like that!—'

'You're no different to all the rest. I was foolish to think that you might be—'

I seized her wrist, holding it tightly in my grasp. I could not let her go, not without showing her what I meant, who I really was.

'Yes I am,' I said. 'I am completely different.' And I pushed her hand to the crotch of my britches. She screamed, twisting her hand and trying to push me away. She was strong and wiry, and for a moment I thought I had lost. But I could not let her go now. I pushed her against the wall.

'Miss Proudlove,' I said. Tears ran down my cheeks. I tightened my fingers on her wrist and held her palm against me, pressing her fingers between my legs. 'I am nothing like the rest. Nothing like them at all.'

I saw her expression change from fury to horror, and just as quickly to pity, and then finally, amazement.

'What—? What is—? You're—' She put a hand to my breast, feeling the swell of it beneath my bindings. 'You live like this?' she whispered. Her eyes were wide, her lips parted. Her breathing was shallow. Her hand, relaxed now, was still cupped against me. 'For how long?'

'Always,' I said. 'Since I was a child.'

'But why?'

I shrugged. 'My father's idea. He's dead now so I can't ask him.' I did not want to explain myself, I just wanted her to know. Was I foolish to reveal my gravest secret? Time would show me. 'I know no other way of being.'

She stepped back from me. 'And this girl was your friend?'

'Yes.'

'Your lover? She *knew*?'

I hesitated. 'Yes.'

'London is a big place, and it is full of girls. I know only a small number of them. But it seems we are more alike than I had imagined, Mr Flockhart.' She watched me, without smiling. 'I will do what I can.'

❦

We walked back to the river in silence. I asked her whether I might carry her basket and she laughed. I felt my blood grow chill at the sound of it. Would she prove a friend, or not? If she chose to reveal who I was, my world would be overturned.

'I can carry it myself,' she said.

'What's in it?'

She didn't answer, not at first. Instead she said, 'There are more girls down here on the waterfront than you can count. What can we do for them? Nothing. If they were not on the streets they would starve, as there is no work for them. Or if there is, it is work they don't want to do.'

'You have medicines from the dispensary for them?'

She hesitated. 'Yes.'

I twitched the muslin cloth from her basket. Beneath were nestled thirty or so tiny dark blue poison bottles. I snatched one up.

'You would judge me, Mr Flockhart, but what do you really know? Nothing.'

I sniffed it. 'Laudanum?'

'A weak mixture. I steal it from the *Blood* and water it down a little. They give laudanum to the patients at night, but I swap it for a sleeping draught of my own formulation when I can. Valerian and hops mostly. It's more effective if it's sleep that's wanted, and there is no likelihood of a habit forming. Unless I deem a patient requires an opiate for pain relief I don't see the value of using laudanum as a regular sedative.'

'I quite agree,' I said. 'But what are these for?'

'For the girls. If they want it. It helps to take the sting out of what they have to do.'

'But—'

'Oh, don't judge me, Mr Flockhart,' she said crossly. 'There will always be prostitutes. Men will always make whores of us, though we do not have to like it. I cannot cure them of the pox, I cannot make their lives happy and worthwhile, I cannot give them a comfortable home, or a sense of self-worth. How can anyone do that?'

'And so you offer oblivion?'

'I offer to blunt the sharp edge of life. I do not charge them for it. What would you have me do? Give them some iron tonic and a lecture about God?'

By now we were on Spyglass Lane. The door to Mrs Flannigan's pub stood open. Mrs Flannigan herself was outside, sweeping what looked like a mixture of beer and urine out of her premises and onto the street. The *Blood* was visible at the end of the passage, a great dark carcass, high in the water, sheets of washing hanging in grey pennants between her severed masts.

My mind and heart were filled with conflicting feelings. I seemed no closer to uncovering what had happened to Aberlady, the links between his death and the three dead women as invisible now as when I had first come down to the river three days ago. I had told Will I knew what had happened, who had murdered them all, but in my heart I was still unsure. I fingered the love tokens I had found in the pockets of Mary Mercer and John Aberlady. The two flowers – forget-me-not, and maidenhair fern – seemed an odd choice, even if they were lovers. Forget-me-not was common enough, but the maidenhair? I could not fathom it. And yet somehow, somewhere at the back of my mind the answers shifted in the shadows. All I needed to know was already laid out before me if I could just step back and see the connections.

'Miss Proudlove,' I said. 'Have you ever seen this before?' I took out the piece of paper on which Jenny had drawn that curious fragmented picture – the keys, the broken chain, the bound skeleton.

She stared at it. But at that moment a dray rumbled past, the driver cracking his whip so that we both started, and I glanced away. When I looked back her face was closed. Impassive between the wings of her bonnet. But I was sure I had seen a flicker of something – surprise, alarm – cross her face.

'Miss Proudlove?' I said.

'No, sir.' Her voice was disinterested, as if she were bored of me now. 'Is it a child's drawing?'

I folded the paper up and put it in my pocket. 'Yes,' I said.

She pulled the cloth over her laudanum bottles and turned away. I let her walk on alone. She was tired of me, that much was clear, but I was tired of myself. Tired of thinking and worrying and trying to work out what was going on. I thought of Will. What would he say if he knew I had given away my gravest secret to a woman I hardly knew? Or if he found out that I had asked her about Eliza? All at once the first of those seemed the stupidest and most careless thing I could have done, and the second the most callous and selfish. If Eliza wanted to be with me she could find me. Why did I still think of her? And yet Will was always there. I sighed and put my hands to my head to shut out the noise. I would have liked to walk away from myself, just for a while, but I could not. I looked up – and then I saw the sign: *Cards* it said. It was hung above a shop door, which also advertised in smaller words underneath, *Spirits. Fine Wines. Pipes.* It was the 'place up on Spyglass' where Aberlady had gone. The Golden Swan.

The woman didn't say anything to me when I walked in. She was sitting before the stove eating what looked like a bowl of vomit – a mess of stew not dissimilar to the stuff that came out of the cookhouse on board the *Blood*.

'Don't taste o' much,' she said without looking up. She chewed thoughtfully on a mouthful, and then extracted something from between her lips. She stared at it. 'Been chewin' this for ages,' she said. 'Don't know what it is.'

'Perhaps a piece of cloth,' I said. 'Or a lump of shoe leather. Sometimes they forget to take the clothes off when they render the bodies. Did you get it from Mrs Flannigan's?'

She cackled. 'Yes, sir, I did.' She plucked a lump of bone from her bowl and tossed it onto the floor. A dog, a pale English mastiff, its tiny eyes beady in its great blunt muzzle, lumbered out of the shadows beneath the table, wolfed down the titbit, and vanished back into the gloom. The woman still hadn't looked at me.

'Well,' she said. 'There ain't no one here for a game o' cards, and you looks to me like you can afford to buy your spirits elsewhere, so I'm guessin' you're here for a pipe.'

'Yes. How's business?' I added.

'Sometimes we're busy, sometimes we ain't.' She shrugged her shawl up around her skinny shoulders.

'Did you know Mr Aberlady, from the *Blood*? The hospital ship? Did he often take a pipe here?'

She turned her head to look at me, surveying my red face, my feigned nonchalance. She turned back to her stew. 'Your Mr Aberlady from the *Blood* was a reg'lar customer. They all come here.' She laughed. 'Everyone likes a pipe. In the end.' She muttered something unintelligible.

'I beg your pardon, madam?' I said.

'Madam!' she laughed. 'I like that. I said "how's your father" in Chinee.' She pointed to a door. 'Go up. Pekin' Johnny'll see to you.'

The stairs were worn smooth with the passing of boots, rough boots, not the smooth leather soles of gentlemen, for they would go elsewhere for their entertainments. Places like this one – no more reputable than Mrs Flannigan's – catered for those with shallow pockets and desperate needs.

Upstairs, the windows were shuttered. The room, some thirty feet long and twenty feet wide, was lined with narrow beds, one on top of the other like berths in an emigrant ship. The room was dark, illuminated only by the dim glow of small red lanterns, and thick with a heavy, sweetish smoke. A young man, 'Peking Johnny', I assumed, was sitting on a chair beside a small stove, a cat crouched in the gloom at his side. The lad's feet were encased in a pair of Chinese slippers, on his head was a Chinese cap – but he wore a shirt and waistcoat like anyone else. He had a round, grubby face, and he was reading the latest edition of *Tales of Violence and Blight* by the light of a Chinese lantern. He could hardly take his eyes from it, though he did so long enough to hand me a long wooden pipe, as thick as two fingers and black with the patina of repeated use. He put his penny paper aside with a sigh, and dragged himself to his feet. He rummaged about, rolling a sticky blob of opium round and round in a small bowl to form it into a pellet, before leading me over to one of the low beds against the wall.

'You're not from Peking,' I said, for some reason feeling the need to converse before I sank into a drug-induced lethargy.

'You're a sharp one,' said the lad. He pointed to his head. 'See my 'at?' and at his feet. 'See my slippers? Silk they are. Cantonese. Go on, have a good look. That's all the Chinaman you're gettin'. Shadwell,' he said. 'That's where I'm from. I'm called Pekin' Johnny on account o' my 'at.'

'I see,' I muttered. The place unsettled me. The lad himself had the pinprick pupils of the opium smoker, no doubt simply from being in attendance. The cat that crouched beside the stove had the same look, its eyes blank green discs, the pupils unnervingly invisible.

The room was low-ceilinged, a dim, murmuring cavern. The charpoy on which I lay was stained and lumpy. In the darkness I could make out other bodies lying down, the pipes to their mouths resting on the lamp before them, so that the opium vapour might be heated and sucked in. Some were clearly unconscious, sunk in the warm stupor the drug was famous for. Others were stirring, replenishing their pipes, muttering to their neighbours. One of two of them rose to their feet and disappeared, vanishing wraith-like down the stairs, their faces wasted, their eyes bewildered beneath unkempt hair. The first of these was in the garb of a clergyman, the other, who rose soon after, was a tall, ashen-faced Lascar.

They said Aberlady had come here. Had he? It seemed more than possible. And surely it would not hurt to try one pipe. I might forget all my troubles. I might make the connections I was groping for between the silver sixpences, the keys, the dead girls. I might escape from myself, and who I was, just for a while.

Everyone likes a pipe. In the end.

Peking Johnny crouched down and applied the pellet

308

of opium to my pipe, the large cup-shaped bowl resting on the conical tip of the lamp he had placed before me. I put the pipe to my lips as the vapours rose.

I felt as though I were sinking into a warm bath, the liquid rising up over my limbs, supporting me so that I was as weightless as gossamer. I closed my eyes, and yet I knew they were open, I knew that what I saw was real and that the dark and smoky den had gone, and I was lying in a garden of pure enchantment, of flowers, trees, fountains and birds. I saw Eliza, my lost love, and I felt my body dissolve in the smoke, become nothing more than a mass of petals. I had in my mind the sweetest sense of order and clarity. I saw the key, small and black, and the drawing and the letters, ICORISSS, written on two shining sixpences. I saw a poison dart frog as blue as the summer sky, and a bright unblinking enamelled eye staring at me through the laden boughs of my own apple trees. I saw Miss Proudlove lying naked on an operating table, a bottle of laudanum in her hand ... and all at once everything was clear to me. I knew I had to tell Will, had to bring him to this place and show him what I had learned. I heard voices – familiar ones from the *Blood*, and even in my cocoon of warmth and light I knew there was danger nearby. I tried to rise. The edge of the pallet was hard beneath my hand and I was surprised by it, so that the curtain in my mind shifted and I glimpsed a cold world of squalor and darkness. I turned my head, and in the next bed I saw Dr Proudlove. He was on his back, his eyes looking straight at me, his teeth showing white between his smiling lips. I tried to speak to him, to ask what he was doing here, but I could not. I was surrounded by harsh voices and ugly leering faces – an old woman with gravy on her chin, a callous-faced boy in a Chinese cap, a cat with no pupils to its acid-green eyes. Hands pushed me back down. I felt a familiar smell of carbolic and effluent in my nostrils, and I recognised it as the reek of the tween decks on the *Blood*. I heard a voice, a man's voice, and I knew whose it was – and then the pipe was against my lips once more, the smoke warm and silken in my lungs and I had not strength for anything. The dragon came then, with its rolling eyes and fiery tail. It turned a summersault and I saw that it was Maximus, and that his jaws were wide open.

Do I ever think about the years I spent in our mother's house? All the time, though I never speak of those thoughts. They remain locked inside me, like a door slammed on a basement full of rats. One day I might open the door and they will all be gone. Either that or they will come seething out in a fury, hungrier and more frightened than ever. But that day is not yet.

At my mother's house I helped the girls with the misfortunes and trials of their profession. By the time I was fifteen I knew a pox sore from a pimple, could measure the correct dose of mercury so that the patient's teeth would not fall out, and could fish out a precautionary sponge stuffed deep into a cunny with one thrust and flick of my fingers. And so I understand more about the girls that come to see us at the dispensary than anyone. The bruises they sport are bruises I had once owned – they are the shape of men's fingertips, men's teeth, men's fists. They come with black eyes, with lice, with the clap and the pox, and the babies of strangers growing inside them. Erasmus is happy to leave them to me, for he has grander ambitions, and the women are glad to be seen by one of their own sex.

Do I miss my easy life as a whore? I do not, though the memory of it lures some of the others at Siren House like a false light glimpsed in a turbulent sea.

One day at the end of June I am ill. It is nothing a dose of valerian will not sort out, but I am tired too, and my head aches. I worked late in the dispensary the night before, making up prescriptions, for Erasmus had gone out with Mr Aberlady. Now, Erasmus is busy binding the broken head of a drunken Lascar, his waiting room full to bursting. When Mary comes with some medicines from the Blood, he sends her upstairs to see how I am. She finds me in bed, my hair undone, my skin glowing and burnished against the whiteness of my open nightdress. I see her lips part, the pink tip of her tongue pass between them.

⁂

We lie in my bed with our arms around each other in the lamplit gloom of the darkling afternoon. I kiss her, and it is as though all the words I have wanted to say have passed in an instant from my lips to hers. In the darkness we tell each other of our pasts. Her first love was an alabaster angel. I am the stuff of idols and totems and I am jealous, and afraid; afraid she loves her dead mistress, the pale and sickly Marianna, more than she could ever love my dark, angry face. I have felt my difference every day of my life, for all that I am as English as anyone in this hotchpotch of a nation. But she lays her hands upon my heart and says I am not to think that way, that she loves me no matter what.

We go to my room above the dispensary whenever we can, snatching at moments as we snatch at each other, all legs and arms and hasty tongues and fingers. But she is not ready, not yet. I see it in the cast of her face when she thinks I am not looking, in the way she gazes at nothing, or lets me put my arms about her, drawing her back, stiffly, onto my pillow. She says she loves me, but I know her heart still bears the imprint of another. And so, I give her the time and the solitude that she needs. What else might I do? She will come to me when she is ready. In return she gives me a token – it is nothing much, nothing at all to anyone but me. A sixpence, the crown and the year of our meeting on one side, the other side with the Queen's head smoothed away. In its place is a picture etched onto the silver: the forget-me-not, and the maiden-hair fern. She makes one for both of us. I punch a hole in mine and wear it around my neck on the thinnest of chains, so that it lies against my heart.

But I cannot wait, and in my haste I drive her away. We are alone in the Seaman's Dispensary. She has come to help me take an inventory. Erasmus is out again, and I know he will not be back for a while. I take her into the back room of the dispensary and I tell her I cannot be without her. We must live together, just the two of us, I say. We would be safe, and happy.

She says 'yes', though there is something in her eyes that should have made me pause.

That evening, I lose the token Mary has given me. It slips from my neck when I am working on the Blood. I don't see it fall. I look everywhere, but someone must have picked it up. It is an omen.

❧

The next day she is gone.

Chapter Nineteen

I stumbled from the Golden Swan with Will's arms around me. I heard laughter, and a voice babbling about keys and forget-me-nots and skeletons wrapped in chains, and I realised it was my own. He laid me down on a soft bed, and I closed my eyes. When I opened them again and turned my head I saw that I was lying in a hard and dirty place. I put my hands to my head, my mind filled with images of smoke and cats, of keys and coins and lamps as red and glowing as the eyes of a dragon.

I sat up and breathed in deep lungfuls of the salty air. I felt a deep sense of peace wash over me, and as I looked down at the squalid street where I sat, at the fish bones in the gutter, and the horse dung in the road and the beer slops upon the pavement, I felt nothing but contentment. Before me was a door. Above it, a painted sign, dirty and peeling, that read *Spirits. Fine Wines. Pipes.* The door was open. An ugly white dog stood inside barking. An old woman in a Chinese shawl came out and kicked the beast aside. I saw Will, and a young man in Chinese cap and slippers stagger out into the street, a body wrapped in a greasy length of canvas slung between them like a sack of dirty laundry. I knew that inside it was the body of Dr Proudlove. And yet . . . surely he wasn't dead. He *couldn't* be! I had seen his eyes glittering in the darkness, and he had grinned at me as I lay there.

I pulled myself up from the pavement, and took a gasp of air. Will and the lad loaded Dr Proudlove onto a hand cart that someone had brought up from the nearby quay. The woman in the shawl and the boy, both of whom were clearly no stranger to the removal of a dead or insensible body from their premises, vanished back into their smoke-filled lair.

Will was silent, thin lipped, as he wheeled the body down the lane and along the clamorous waterfront towards the mortuary. No one stopped and stared, or even paused in their work as we passed by. Death was commonplace in those streets. Men fell from the open windows of warehouses, or from the rigging of ships; they beat each other senseless over the cost of a pint of beer or fell, drunk, into the docks. Women and children were drowned or murdered, they died of cholera, hunger or cold. The sight of a body being trundled through the streets was nothing to them. I noted their indifference, and I was sorry.

I looked at Will, but he turned away from me, his face furious. 'Someone tried to make me smoke more,' I said. 'I felt hands push me back. I smelt the ship. The *Blood.* It was . . . I don't know who it was, but I believe they tried to do the same to Aberlady. They knew I would go there to ask about him. They had that woman look out for me. They tried to make me take too much—'

'Like Dr Proudlove?' said Will. 'You have much to be thankful for then, that *I* found *you* in time.'

'They tried to kill me—'

'Who, Jem?' he said. 'Who are "they"?'

I did not answer.

We took Dr Proudlove into the mortuary, and between us we laid him down on the slab. There came the sound of footsteps scuffling on the steps and Toad and Young Toad appeared. The lad looked sulky, his dirty face streaked with tears.

'Not another one?' said Toad. 'Who is it this time?'

Young Toad pushed forward. He gasped when he saw who it was. 'The darkie!'

'That's Dr Proudlove to you,' snapped Will. 'Show a little respect for your betters.'

'Where's your waistcoat?' I said. My voice was mild, languid, but the hand with which I grasped his collar was steel.

Young Toad scowled and wiped his eyes with his fists. He writhed in my grip. 'Gone, ain't it?' he said.

'Gone, ain't it, *sir*,' cried Toad. 'Forgive the young tyke, gen'men, he's aggrieved because I took 'is fancy waist-kit—'

'You stole it,' cried Young Toad.

'I took,' said Toad.

'You stole it an' pawned it and bought gin with the money. And it were mine. I bought it from Finch's up on Spyglass from what I earned—'

'How did you earn it?' I said.

Young Toad fell silent. 'I just *earned* it,' he muttered.

I did not have time or patience to wheedle and coax, and I had no intention of beating it out of the lad, though

I was sorely tempted to do so. And so I resorted to the only currency he understood. No doubt his father would do the beating later. I pulled out a shilling. I held it up between my thumb and forefinger. 'If you tell me how you earned it, I will give you this, and perhaps another too,' I said.

The boy hesitated, torn between confessing his misdemeanours and getting his hands on another coin.

'Young Toad!' I cried. 'You said you saw Dr Proudlove cut Mr Aberlady's arm that night?'

'Yes, sir,' said Young Toad. 'I seen 'im.'

'But you didn't, did you?' The coin glittered. A mere shilling for the truth. If only it were that simple. 'You didn't see Dr Proudlove at all, but *someone* told you to say it was him, and *someone* paid you to do it.'

'No!' squeaked Young Toad.

'You bought cake and a waistcoat with the money,' I said. 'How much did he give you? Half a crown?'

'No—'

'More? It must have been a serious lie, and a wealthy man asking you to tell it. How much did he give you?'

'A thick 'un,' muttered Young Toad. 'It were a crown, sir. Said I weren't to say nothing about it or I'd end up just like Mr Aberlady.' He peered fearfully over his shoulder at the dead body of Dr Proudlove. He began weeping.

'Who was it?' cried Will, stepping forward. 'Who was it or I will finish you off myself—'

'It were Dr Sackville. Dr Sackville I saw take the skin from Mr Aberlady's arm. He said I weren't to say. He gave me the money. Said I was a good lad.'

I tossed him the shilling. He reached out a dirty hand, but his father's fist shot out, and snatched it from the air. He seized his son's collar and hauled him away.

I took out my knife and went over to the body.

'Jem,' said Will. 'What are you doing—?'

'I'm quite myself again,' I said, watching the knife blade gleam like an icicle in my hand. I knew I was not, but I was sober enough to do what had to be done. 'How did you know I was in the Golden Swan?'

'I asked Toad, who said he had seen you go out with Miss Proudlove, who said she had left you on Spyglass Lane. Mrs Flannigan – on payment of half a crown – said she had seen you go into the Golden Swan opium house. What on earth possessed you?' said Will. 'To go into that place alone? To take a pipe? You an apothecary too! If anyone knows what might happen in such places it's you!'

'That's *precisely* why I went there,' I said. 'Of course I knew what would happen. At least, I didn't expect to be held down, to have the pipe put to my lips by someone else.'

'By whom?'

'I don't know. At least, I'm not sure. I saw lots of faces in my mind's eye – including yours. I can't be certain who it was.'

Will looked at me doubtfully. 'So why did you go there?'

'I wanted to think. To escape from my own thoughts. To escape from *myself*. Just for a while! You know who I am, Will, you know how I live. Have you any idea how hard it is? Always dissembling, always hiding, always afraid someone will find out? The wonder is not that I went there, but that I have never gone before.'

Will was silent.

'Besides,' I said. 'I wanted to go to the place where they said Aberlady had been.'

'Why?'

318

'Because I thought I might find something out. He *knew*, Will. He knew what was happening – perhaps not about the second two girls we found, but he knew about the first, about Mary Mercer – though in fact she was the last to be killed. Or he suspected what was going on, at least.'

'And he went to an opium den to think about it?'

'Oh, he'd gone there many times in the past. I think he went there again before he died – he could not do without the stuff. I think they intended to give him an overdose. Perhaps he was more used to it than his assailants realised, as he was a habitual user. Unfortunately, Dr Proudlove was not.' I thought again of the hands that had pressed me back onto the charpoy, the pipe I had felt against my lips.

'Would he stay in an opium den for a week?' said Will. 'You recall a week passed between his disappearance, and his throwing himself from the apothecary window.'

'I think he was hiding somewhere.'

'Where?'

'The *Blood*, perhaps? That would be the best place.'

'*Where* on the *Blood*? The place is like a floating termite hill. Where could he possibly hide?'

'Perhaps we should ask Dr Rennie that question.'

'And why? *Why* would he hide? You're not making any sense—'

'Perhaps he was waiting.'

'For what?'

'For proof? For evidence to confirm his suspicious? Perhaps he was watching someone. But then they found him and took him away.'

'But who are "they", Jem?'

I clicked my tongue. 'Must I spell it out? Aberlady discovered something was happening to certain of the girls from Siren House – some of those who had gone to work as nurses on board the *Blood*. But he had to be sure, had to be quite certain if he was about to accuse Dr Sackville, Dr Cole, Dr Antrobus—'

'All three?'

I pointed to Dr Proudlove. 'Perhaps all four.'

'All of them? Why not accuse Dr Rennie too?'

'I think his involvement is coincidental. Marginal at best—'

Will shook his head. He was still wearing the canvas trousers and jacket from his day's work at Deadman's Basin, and he looked tired, despairing. 'I fear you're not in your right mind, Jem—'

'But I'm perfectly well,' I cried. 'In fact I'm thinking clearly. Very clearly. It's a pity I can't say the same for you, for you seem exceptionally doltish and obstructive today. Anyone would think you didn't *want* to know why five people have turned up dead in the last week.'

Will looked at me coldly. 'Were you thinking clearly when you told Miss Proudlove who and *what* you really are—'

I blanched. 'She told you?' I whispered.

He turned away. 'I don't understand you, Jem. For three days now we have walked amongst death and murder of the most unspeakable kind, and yet you share your most precious confidences with strangers. Do you not know what will happen if you are discovered?' His face was tense, angry. He turned away from me. 'Sometimes I hardly know you at all, Jem. I thought we were friends. More than friends—'

320

'Did you?' I muttered. 'I'm sorry if I've disappointed you.'

I turned to the body on the slab before me, and with my knife I cut a slit in Dr Proudlove's shirt sleeve from the elbow to the shoulder. I exposed his right arm – for it had been on Aberlady's right arm that the skin had been excised, and I knew I would find the same mark. This time, I hoped, it would be complete. And there it was. Newly inked: the keys, the chains, the bound skeleton. Like John Aberlady before him, Dr Proudlove had tried to obliterate the mark, as if they no longer wished to own whatever it signified. The crude tattooed letters were scabbed and scratched, as if he had sought to tear them off with his own fingers.

'What's that word?' said Will.

'Icorisss,' I said.

'What does it mean?'

The mortuary had grown dark, the air damper and chillier than ever. 'I don't know,' I said. 'Not yet anyway.'

❧

Outside, the clear weather had vanished. The afternoon had drawn down darkly, hastened by the thickening fog, which slunk down streets and lanes like the spectre of a huge grey dog. As we emerged from the mortuary, we could hardly even see the *Blood*, and she was but fifty yards away. I saw a figure on the deck – dimly, like a ghost. I could tell by his tall stooping silhouette that it was Dr Sackville. He lit a lantern at the stern, and for a moment his face was illuminated by the yellow phosphorous flare.

The quickest route to where I wanted to go was through Deadman's Basin. The basin itself had been drained of water when we found Mary Mercer, and what filled it now was a putrid, lumpen mud. Across the basin, we could just about make out the burnt-out remains of the old villa – partly dismantled now, and the smell of old mortar and brick dust hung on the air. At the top, Bishop's Entry vanished like a drain between the buildings.

The door was opened by Mr Jobber. 'She ain't in,' he said before we could speak.

'You mean Mrs Roseplucker?' I said. 'We don't want to speak to her.'

'Ain't no gen'men allowed in without Mrs R being here,' he said. He blocked the door. He held a paintbrush in his hand, and his shirt was stained red. He looked tearful. From behind him a voice screamed out.

'Close that door, you great fat idiot. You're letting all the heat out.'

'That Poll?' I said. 'It's her we want.'

'Can't. Can't see the girls.'

'Oh, for God's sake, man,' cried Will. 'We don't want to *pay* for the girl. We just want to talk to her. It won't take long. Now just . . . get out of the way!'

Mr Jobber's chin trembled. 'Don't shout,' he said.

Inside, the place was as wretched as ever. The walls had been painted from top to bottom in red, and some of the lurid prints depicting scenes of elaborate congress that had adorned Mrs Roseplucker's old premises on Wicke Street had been hung about. The two girls we had previously seen playing dominoes were now intent on a game of snakes and ladders. They played in dogged, unsmiling silence, the dice rattling in the cup like teeth. Poll was

sitting in Mrs Roseplucker's chair, her feet – shod in a pair
of tatty satin slippers – up on the desk. Her skirts had
slipped back, revealing a pair of bruised and dirty knees.
She grinned when she saw us. ''Ello, sirs!'

'You'll get a slap if she comes back and finds you sitting
there,' said Will.

'It'll be worth it,' said Poll. She grinned, and took a
swig from a bottle that was hidden beneath the desk.
'Well now, gen'men, what can I do for you?' She said it in
a cracked harridan's voice I recognised as an excellent
imitation of Mrs Roseplucker herself. 'Lookin' for a lovely
young girl, sir? I got three. Virgins, all of 'em!'

Mr Jobber gave a great guffaw of laughter, and clapped
his hands together like a caveman smashing rocks.

'Poll,' I said. 'Have you ever been with Dr Cole and Dr
Antrobus?'

'Course,' she said. 'Far too often.'

'And do you recognise this?' I showed her the picture
of the tattoo Jenny had drawn. 'Did either of them have
this tattoo?'

'Cost you.'

'Oh, for heaven's sake,' spluttered Will, who had been
getting more and more agitated. He hated these places –
the briny smell, the lolling girls, the vile red walls and hot
damp rooms. 'Nothing for nothing at Mrs Roseplucker's,
eh?' He tossed her a shilling. 'Now tell us, Miss Poll or I'll
tip that pot of red paint over your head.'

I glanced at Mr Jobber, who was advancing on Will like
a prizefighter.

'Now then, Mr Jobber,' said Poll hastily. 'Don't hurt the
nice gentleman. Mrs Roseplucker'll go mad if she comes
home and finds you've wrung a man's neck while she were

out visitin'.' She turned to us. 'Yes, I seen a tattoo like that. Yes, they both have one. No – before you ask – I don't know what it means. I didn't ask them 'cause I'm not interested and I don't care. That enough for you?'

⚈

It wasn't far from Cat's Hole to Siren House, and it was there that we went next. All at once the urgency of our situation was clear. Four men with the same tattoo, two of them dead, the dead men both seeking to remove the mark that bound the four together. I had to find out more about the dead girls. It was they who would provide us with the link we needed, the link that would show us who the murderer was.

Annie opened the door. When she saw it was Will and me she looked relieved.

'Thank God you've come,' she said.

'What is it?' I said. 'Is it Miss Proudlove? Is she here? I presume she's heard?'

Dr Birdwhistle had been sent to tell Miss Proudlove that her brother was dead. I wondered whether I should have offered to tell her, but after what had happened between us in the physic garden it seemed better if it came from someone she knew well. And yet in my heart I knew that was just a cowardly excuse. I had seen her not two hours before we had found him; she and I had passed the door to the opium den together – had he been inside even then? The truth was that I could not bear to witness her sorrow, or hear her rebuke.

'Miss Proudlove's not in,' said Annie. All at once her face split into a grin. 'Oh, I know it's a sad house, Mr

Flockhart, after what's happened, and all. But—' she sniggered. 'You best come in.'

The house was silent. I wondered why. But then Annie led us through into the parlour. The girls of Siren House were sitting on their chairs, the way they had been the last time we had visited the place, only on this occasion there was no ladies' committee, and no singing. The mirror above the fireplace had been swathed in black crepe, along with the clock, and a rustling length of the stuff was draped along the dado. All the girls were dressed in their most sombre of clothes. Yet the atmosphere in the parlour was far from solemn, but simmered with suppressed mirth. Dr Birdwhistle was standing beside the fireplace, his hands gripping the lapels of his waistcoat, his face set into an expression of revulsion. At the same time, he appeared to be attempting to smile. Before him, sitting on one of the easy chairs usually reserved for the more august members of the ladies' committee, was Mrs Roseplucker.

'Dear God!' cried Will. He clapped his hand to his mouth.

'My good sir,' said Dr Birdwhistle – he seemed relieved to have something more familiar to deal with – 'might I remind you not to take our Lord's name in vain? Exodus, chapter twenty, verse seven. Deuteronomy, chapter five, verse eleven. Leviticus, chapter nineteen, verse twelve. And so on—'

Will gave a wild laugh. 'I'm sorry, Dr Birdwhistle. But – oh!' He gaped at Mrs Roseplucker. '*You?*'

Mrs Roseplucker turned her gaze upon him. Her eyeballs were yellow, their rims red and drooping in her pale powdered face, her lips and cheeks smeared with scarlet. I had never seen her outside of a brothel's parlour, never seen her out from under the dim candles of her whores' ante-chamber. She was not wearing her madam's crimson off-the-shoulder finery, but had got hold of some black widow's weeds and she was buttoned up to the neck in a giant woollen coat. A great black bonnet the size of a dust-bin lid framed her face.

'Mrs Roseplucker,' I said. 'What a pleasure.'

'Ain't it.' She exposed her brown, corroded teeth. 'I were just talking to this here clergyman gentleman about my redemption. We're old friends him and me, ain't we, sir?' She winked. Dr Birdwhistle's face grew sweaty as the eyes of twelve ex-prostitutes rested knowingly upon him.

'Are you hoping to join Siren House?' I said.

'I am. Is there a law what says the more mature whore ain't allowed to seek a new life?'

'No, madam,' said Dr Birdwhistle, quailing under Mrs Roseplucker's piercing gaze. 'The Lord accepts all sinners.' He held his arms wide. '"For if ye forgive men their trespasses, your heavenly Father will also forgive *you*." Matthew, chapter six, verse fourteen—'

'I ain't forgiving no *men*,' thundered Mrs Roseplucker. 'They should be askin' *us* for forgiveness.'

There was a general murmuring and nodding of heads from the assembled ex-harlots. 'I assume you have read my pamphlet, madam?' said Dr Birdwhistle desperately.

Mrs Roseplucker beamed. 'Oh, you write too, sir? I could help you with that sort o' thing if you've a mind to write more stirring tales. I brought some o' my work along, in fact.' She plunged a claw into one of her pockets and dragged out a crumpled copy of *Tales of Violence and Blight*. '"The Curse o' Black Peg",' she said. 'Ain't half nasty! You'll like it!'

'You can't really want to come here, Mrs Roseplucker,' said Will. 'You've only just set up shop around the corner.'

'I've changed me ways.'

'You're looking for girls, aren't you?' he said.

'No.'

'Mrs Roseplucker,' said Dr Birdwhistle. 'Are you aware that entry to Siren House comes with certain requirements?'

Mrs Roseplucker blinked. 'Go on, sir.'

'Girls must promise to relinquish their past life.'

'Cross my heart,' said the old hag. She licked her forefinger with a brown fissured tongue, and drew it across her bosom with all the seriousness of a priest performing a liturgical gesture.

'This must be done formally. A confession must be taken – your life story. All you have done that has led you to the steps of Siren House. Everything you say will be taken down, in writing, by me. You will sign it, and together we will lock your confession away in this box here.'

Aware that he had a rapt audience, Dr Birdwhistle seemed to swell before us, his chest puffing out. He laid a hand on top of a large box of polished walnut that was secured to the mantelpiece by two brass brackets. A hush fell upon the room, as if each of us was thinking about the stories that lay within that box. Dr Birdwhistle's spectacles glittered, his face turning pink with excitement as the girls gazed up at him. 'The confession goes into the box, where it is locked away – not once, but twice. In the outer box, which represents that secret room in our hearts where trust and redemption lie and to which only I have the key. Within that is the inner box. It is the inner box which represents the safety of Siren House. Our superintendent Miss Proudlove possesses a key to that.

'Once girls have unburdened themselves of their past then that past is locked away and never mentioned again.' He lifted his chin, his voice now a confident boom. 'Here at Siren House we look only to the future, "For I know the thoughts that I think toward you, saith the Lord, thoughts of peace and not of evil, to give you an expected end." Jeremiah, twenty-nine, eleven. Thus unburdened, you emerge into Siren House to begin your new life.' He flung out his right arm, a finger pointed accusingly at the old woman's breast. 'Will *you*, Mrs Roseplucker, allow me to take your confession? Will *you* leave your past under lock and key, never to be alluded to again? Will *you* put your trust in me, in Siren House, in the love of the Lord?' He slipped his fingers into his waistcoat pocket and rooted about for the key.

'My confession?' Mrs Roseplucker laughed, a hollow grating sound like a gate swinging in a sepulchre. 'It'll take a week to tell it and you'll need a river of ink. And it won't fit into that there box when I'm done, neither. I'll need me own box!' Mrs Roseplucker stood up. 'I'm not telling my life story to *you*,' she said. 'Who're you to take that from me?'

'It is customary for the confession to be taken by me, or by one of the medical staff,' said Dr Birdwhistle.

'Who, exactly?' I said.

'Any of the medical men on board the *Blood*,' he said. 'Usually I take them down, but as there is a great deal of overlap between that institution and this it is sometimes taken by a medical man. They often employ the girls afterwards, of course. I deem it appropriate for them to be involved with us as much as possible because of it.'

328

'Looks to me like you got the pox!' said Mrs Roseplucker. There was a murmuring of agreement from amongst the girls. 'That's one overlap you wants to get sorted out. I see your eyes, sir, and I know what *that* means well enough. So do some of the girls. Annie?'

'Yes, Mrs R,' said Annie. 'I saw it.'

'Ask Mr Flockhart here. He'll sort you out. And until you *gets* sorted out, you don't *deserve* my confession, nor that of anyone else, neither!'

But Dr Birdwhistle was not listening. 'Where's my key?' he snapped. 'Who's taken it?' He pointed to Annie. 'It was you, wasn't it? I know you for a light-fingered besom. *You* took it!'

'No, sir,' said Annie.

'Is this it?' I said. I held up the key, less than an inch long, slim as a matchstick, with a heart-shaped head and an intricate cut-away square jutting from its base, that I had found in Aberlady's stomach. It would take a desperate man to swallow such a thing.

'Yes!' cried Dr Birdwhistle. 'Yes, it is. How on earth—' His face coloured. 'Did *you* steal it?'

'I found it,' I said.

'Where?'

'Somewhere unexpected. I was wondering what lock it might fit.'

'It fits *this* lock!'

'Perhaps you might open the box, Dr Birdwhistle—' but he had already sprung across the room and snatched the key from my fingers. White faced, he shoved Mrs Roseplucker aside as he made for the fireplace. We heard the quiet *click* of a well-oiled, finely crafted lock. Dr Birdwhistle flung open the box – and fell back with a cry.

'Gone!' he screamed. Backing away, he caught his foot in the ragged festoons of Mrs Roseplucker's skirt and lurched against her.

The girls, who had been sitting about stiffly, seemed curiously liberated by the news. They began chatting to one another in huddles. One or two were crying, others had their arms around each other; some of them were laughing together, their hands on their hips, just as they used to when they were on the streets.

'Girls, please!' cried Dr Birdwhistle. 'Silence! Girls!'

In the midst of the noise and confusion I saw Mrs Roseplucker grab Annie and one of the other girls by the wrist, and sidle from the room.

'Well,' said Will, while the uproar continued. 'At least we know what the key was for. But where's the inner box?'

'Another mystery,' I said. 'But we *will* find it.'

'And I believe I have made sense of something else too,' said Will.

'Icorisss?'

'Yes.'

'What are your thoughts?' I said.

'It is not a word, it is a biblical reference. One Corinthians, chapter fifteen, verse fifty-five. It's not an "I" it's a "1", not an "s", but a "5".'

'My thinking exactly,' I said. We grinned at one another.

'The verse is well known. I'm surprised we didn't think of it before.'

'We were stupid, Will, stupid not to see it – but we must speak to Dr Rennie. We must speak to him now. Before it's too late.'

I look for her everywhere, but no one has seen her. It's not unusual for girls to run away, to decide they have had enough of Siren House with its rules and restrictions, its tedious domestic chores and bogus respectability. The grinning lechery of Dr Birdwhistle is wearisome – does he think the girls haven't noticed the tenting of his trousers as he stands amongst them? The righteous superiority of the ladies' committee, the bustling, pinching tyranny of Mrs Birdwhistle – it is not a route everyone can bear. A number of the girls have found work on the Blood, *and some have vanished from that place too – back to the streets, no doubt. Two of them have been seen plying their trade on the waterfront. The* Blood *is not for everyone. And so, when Mary vanishes, her disappearance provokes nothing more than a shrug of the shoulders, a shake of the head, a muttered 'I told you so'.*

I cannot forgive myself. Where has she gone? On the streets? On the road? Wherever she is I have driven her there. Had I not forced myself onto her, dragging her into my bed and wrapping myself about her like some monstrous sea creature she would still be near me. She submitted to my advances, but in her heart she had loved someone else. I look for her everywhere. Up and down the streets and lanes I go, in and out of vile courts, up and down the steps of Houses. I see only Mr Aberlady – my brother's friend, and a man of principle who has his own secrets to hide. Far worse than mine, they will land him in gaol if he is caught. I see him on Spyglass and I know what he is looking for. We exchange a glance. Should I ask him about Mary? But he does not have eyes for girls, and so I say nothing, and after a while, I go home. I go home, and I wait for her to come to me – which is what I should have done all along.

✦

I would have waited forever with my heart broken rather than see her as she is that last time, dead and cold in that dank and wretched place. I wish I was there beside her, dead too, so that I might keep her company in the grave, at least. But then the medical men come, and even that dream is taken from me.

Chapter Twenty

By now the fog had closed in on us so thickly that it was impossible to tell whether it was morning or evening. We made our way, half blind, along the dockside to the *Blood*. The steps that led up to the deck were slick with moisture, the rope handrail slimy and cold beneath our hands. A shadow passed across the deck on silent footsteps. I could not see who it was and they did not declare themselves, or call out a greeting. The lamps near the severed main mast were out, the foggy darkness thick and choking, the silence unnatural. Somewhere out on the river, we heard the gentle splashing of oars, and the faint rhythmic clang of a bell.

'Six o'clock,' whispered Will. At our feet, the hole in the deck that led down to the wards yawned.

Below, the atmosphere was thick as broth. Lamps had been lit, stoves belched out heat, and the windows shuttered to keep out the fog. The men lay listlessly in their beds, smoking and playing cards, just as they had when we first arrived. At the prow, near the nurses' station, I could see Mrs Speedicut sitting beside the stove, her own pipe clamped between her few remaining teeth, shuffling a pack of cards. It had been no different at St Saviour's. Once she thought there was no likelihood of any of the medical men returning for the night, she had reverted to her old familiar ways – lazy, drunken, greedy. Deep in the gloom, a figure went from bed to bed, bottle and spoon in hand. We continued on down, through the middle ward, and then down again to the lower ward. The men turned to us as they heard our footsteps on the stairs, their faces rising up, pale as jellyfish in a dark and murky ocean. But there was another deck below this that was far worse. It was below the waterline, with the Thames, that great body of sluggish stinking water, kept at bay by only a few inches of ancient oak and tar. It was here that Dr Rennie made his home. I had not been down to it, but Will had.

'I don't know how he bears it,' he said. 'I suppose it must be what he's used to.'

Once, the orlop deck had been a wide space, beneath the gun decks and crews' quarters, where the quarter-master had his lair. It was where supplies of rum and powder were kept – at least, that was what I had assumed, for I had to admit that I knew little about the layout and operation of a ship. What I did know was gleaned from my glances through Gabriel's penny bloods – the lad had a weakness for pirate stories, and I would be the first to admit that 'Dick of the Bloody Cutlass' was probably not the most authentic text. But even to my untrained eye it was apparent that the space where we now stood had undergone modifications. A wall had been fitted from port side to starboard, so that it was no longer an open deck, but had been turned into a long windowless cabin. The dark greasy beams of the ceiling were low, little more than five feet high in places, and we could not stand upright at all – enough to deter all but the smallest visitors.

The door was ajar. Will knocked. 'Dr Rennie?' There was no reply. 'Dr Rennie?' Will pushed at the door. It swung open on well-oiled hinges.

'Welcome, gentlemen, welcome.' Dr Rennie was sitting in a wooden captain's chair in front of a small iron stove. The chimney vanished up through the ceiling, through the wards overhead to emerge, smoking darkly, above the cookhouse wall. The room was furnished with a bed, hard up against the hull, a washstand, and some apothe-cary drawers. Bookshelves lined the walls. Beside the books were familiar rows of jars and bottles, containing what appeared to be chunks of wounded flesh, ragged from where musket balls, shrapnel and wooden splinters had torn through.

'Yes,' said Dr Rennie, when he saw my interest. 'I collected them from the wars. Various military wounds. The damage inflicted by the different types of ordnance is a fascinating area. I've written two monographs on it.'

'Dr Rennie is a great authority on the subject,' said Will. 'As well as being an expert on crustaceans, and animals without backbones. His specimens are in the British Museum, and collections all over the country. He has written a book on them too.'

The place was boiling hot, though Dr Rennie seemed not to notice, for he was dressed in a heavy nautical top coat and tricorn hat, not unlike those Nelson might have worn on a cold day. He eased himself to his feet. He had taken off his eye patch and without it his face looked curiously incomplete, the right eye blinking and watery, the left eye completely absent. The cheek and the socket where his eye should have been were sunken and ruined, an area the size of the palm of a hand blighted with a tangled scar of stitched skin, white and shiny.

'Forgive me,' he said, plucking up his painted mask from the table top. He tied it in place, rendering himself at once familiar and bizarre. 'I have no chairs to offer you,' he said. 'Only that stool. No one comes down here, you see. Not since that young fellow. What's his name?' he frowned. 'Used to come here for a smoke and to get away from the others upstairs. Nice fellow. Owned a snake.'

'Aberlady?'

'Yes, yes.' He shook his head. 'Laudanum. Opium. That was his weakness – one of his weaknesses, at any rate. I've seen it before, of course.' He gestured at the rows of preserved wounds, at his own face. 'The black drop is an old friend of mine too. He used to come down here. Him and the other chap. What's his name?'

'Proudlove?' said Will.

'Proudlove, that's it.'

It was going to be a long and difficult conversation – at least it would be if we stuck to recent happenings. I sighed. The place was making me feel lightheaded. I was uncomfortable being in small, enclosed spaces. The opium I had smoked had not entirely finished with me, either, for every now and then I was assailed by thoughts and images of the most macabre and unsettling kind. The walls seemed to close in on me if I did not keep my eyes fixed upon them, and yet when I did the smoke curling up from Dr Rennie's pipe took on the shape of a woman. She turned and raised her arms and I saw she had the face of Miss Proudlove. The walls, lined with their bottled wounds, their preserved fish specimens, worms, crabs and spiders heaved towards me.

'Oh!' I gasped.

'What's wrong?' said Will.

'Nothing.' I gulped. 'I'm quite well. Do go on, Dr Rennie, sir—'

Will took Jenny's drawing from me and spread it out upon his knee. He passed it to Dr Rennie. 'Do you know this, sir?'

'He'll never remember,' I murmured.

'Of course he will,' said Will. 'It's the present he forgets. The past is as clear as a bell. And, if we're lucky, he might just remember what it is he's been trying to tell us the last two days.'

'Has he been trying to tell us something?'

'Of course he has. Didn't you notice? My grandfather was just the same. But we must be patient. It will come. It's in there somewhere, we just have to help him to reach it.'

'Ah!' said Dr Rennie, peering at the drawing with his watery eye. 'Yes, yes, why, you're not the first young men I've told about this. But it was a long time ago now. Look!' He struggled out of his voluminous coat and rolled up his shirt sleeves. On the thin white flesh of his upper arm was a tattoo. There were the keys, the broken chain, the bound skeleton, and the code. It was written clearly here, for all that it was crudely done, and faded and blurred with age: I. COR. 15. 55.

'It's one Corinthians, chapter fifteen, verse fifty-five, isn't it?' said Will.

'"O death, where is thy sting? O grave, where is thy

victory?"' said Dr Rennie. He laughed. 'Yes. We were young and ambitious – it seemed a clever thing to do, a clever motto, we thought. And you see the picture – the keys and the chain – death's mysteries unlocked, the bonds broken. And the bound skeleton is death defeated.' He chuckled. 'Sackville's idea. We tattooed each other. "Bound together by blood," he used to say.'

'How many of you were there?' said Will.

'Four of us – there's only Sackville and me left now. We were all at Hunter's Anatomy School, on Leicester Square. Such an inspiring man. Taught us to ask questions, and to find answers for ourselves. He said we should trust all our senses, should experiment, and test our ideas – we all wanted to be like him. He was an old man by then, but nevertheless, his reputation was something to be envied. And there were many who *did* envy him. Like Hunter, the four of us came from nothing. Morton and Kilbride came from farming stock in the Scottish lowlands. Both are dead now, of course. Sackville was the son of a baker, and I, well, I was the son of a sailor.

'There are few who are truly great, gentlemen; few who are true pioneers, who change our way of thinking and seeing. The rest of us can only do our best. I was always the outsider, the one who lacked the ambition, the urgency to get on, to be seen and known. It was far less important to me than it was to the others to forge a reputation, and in the end I went to sea. I was glad to get away from them, truth be told, and have no regrets about it. I hope I've helped plenty of men. I *have* saved lives, made good some of the terrible consequences of war, or disease. "What cannot be cured must be endured." *That* is sometimes the hardest task of all, finding ways to help people endure.'

He put up a hand, touching his tin eye gently, as if remembering when he had been young, and whole, with his life before him still waiting to be lived.

'Death is a release for many, and we shouldn't fear it the way we do, though the quest for ways of prolonging life, or of cheating death, have preoccupied men since the beginning of time. Dr Birdwhistle finds his everlasting life through God. But for those who don't believe in such things there is only science, and medicine, that can provide us with answers.' He pulled his coat round his tiny frame as if a cold wind chilled him to the bone. 'I'm not a brilliant doctor, gentlemen, merely a good one. But I have always tried to help those who *were* capable. Capable, but without friends, shall we say.'

'Like Dr Proudlove?' said Will.

'Proudlove.' Dr Rennie nodded. 'A man of great ability. But it will be a long time before ability is enough to allow men like him to succeed.' He sighed. 'He is impatient. Impatient and ambitious and, understandably, resentful of his lack of opportunity. Especially when he sees others getting on while he stays where he is.' He shook his head. 'It consumes him.'

It was clear that Dr Rennie had no idea that Dr Proudlove was dead. I did not enlighten him, for I wanted him to keep talking. 'And John Aberlady?' I said.

'He was a clever man too. And a kind one. But he had his weaknesses. His secrets.' He smiled. 'You don't spend forty years at sea without recognising a man in thrall to *that* particular vice.' He shrugged. 'It couldn't be helped.'

'Was there something Aberlady wanted you to tell us, sir?' said Will.

'I don't know,' said the old man. 'Was there?'

'Think, sir. When did you last see him?'

'See who?'

'John Aberlady.'

But as we coaxed Dr Rennie closer to the present, his mind fogged. He blinked a watery eye and stared up at us, confused and unhappy. Beside it, his painted eye was gimlet sharp. It was as if the eye that looked to the present was dim and clouded, the eye that looked to the past was clear and unflinching. He frowned.

'Aberlady's dead, I think? I can't recall. And there was something I had to tell someone, but I can't remember who. It was something important too. Aberlady told me—' His expression grew puzzled, and anxious. He twisted his hands together as he struggled to remember. 'Don't grow old, son,' he said, blinking up at Will tearfully. 'It's a terrible business losing who you are.'

Will squeezed the old man's hands beneath his own. 'You're Dr Rennie, sir,' he said. 'A self-made man, former assistant to John Hunter, and surgeon on board the *Golden Fleece*. A man who fought beside Nelson at Trafalgar, who has sailed the seas and saved men's lives. You are the author of two important books on military surgery, and one of the British Museum's most valued benefactors and collectors. That, Dr Rennie, is who you are. It is a life well spent, sir.'

Dr Rennie peered again at the scrap of paper. He put his hand to his arm, to his own tattoo, hidden beneath his shirt sleeve. 'We called ourselves the Resurrection Society,' he said. 'Not like those fellows who supplied the anatomy rooms with corpses, though we all did our fair share of *that*, you can be sure. But we hoped we might discover the secrets of life. The more we knew about life, and about death, then the more chance we had of defeating it. "O death, where is thy sting?" It was a society for experiments. For anatomy. For testing our ideas. Dogs mostly.'

'Only dogs?' I ventured.

'Sometimes rats,' he said. 'Nothing more.'

'Are you certain?'

'Very certain. I was our secretary. I knew everything.' He chuckled. 'We were four ambitious lads hoping to impress our master by working in secret so that we might appear cleverer and more inspired than we actually were. Sackville especially took it very seriously. Especially the idea that we were a secret society.' He smiled. 'Foolish really. Of course, we dreamed that we might find a way of understanding the very essence of life, of prolonging it indefinitely, or bringing back those who had died. Imagine if we could have uncovered the precise means by which electrical impulses are carried through the body! Or revealed ways of replacing a morbid organ with a healthy one! We tried, of course we did. But we never succeeded. *That* must be the preserve of future generations.'

'What about Dr Cole and Dr Antrobus?' said Will. 'Are they in your society too? Did they know about it?'

His face became wary. 'It was a long time ago.'

'I fear the Resurrection Society has been resurrected,' I murmured to Will.

'You think Dr Sackville knew?' Will said.

'Undoubtedly.'

'And that he was a member?'

I addressed Dr Rennie. 'Did Dr Sackville ever talk about the Resurrection Society to you recently?'

'He said he had heard that the younger men had started their own. He was pleased.' Dr Rennie lowered his voice. 'But it always had to be a secret. Who knew what they might discover! And one must be careful how one shares one's ideas. Look at Hunter himself, Dr Sackville always said. Hunter's own brother stole his ideas and passed them off as his own. He was not the only one!'

'Perhaps that's why Dr Sackville took Aberlady's tattoo,' said Will. 'If he was so wedded to the idea of this little society being a secret.'

'I think so,' I said. 'I think also that both Aberlady and Proudlove came to see their little club as more evil than good. I believe they sought to remove their tattoos as a result. Aberlady knew what was going on. Knew what the club was really about, and wrote to me for help. Unfortunately I came too late.' I turned again to Dr Rennie. 'What of Aberlady?' I said. 'You remember him, sir? I think he knew of this Resurrection Society too. And of a new one?'

'He asked me about it, certainly. Was he a friend of yours?' I was leaning forward, my face illuminated in the candlelight in what must have been a horrible, lurid mask, for all at once the old man gasped, and drew back, as if seeing me properly for the first time.

'You!' he cried, grasping my arm. The candle flickered as he seized it and held it close, the better to examine my face. '*You're* the one with the mask! The mask, Aberlady said. I was to look out for it. I was to tell *you*.'

'Tell me what?'

'That Aberlady is here! Down here. Come along. Quickly now.'

And at that the old man sprang to his feet and went to the door. 'He's here,' he repeated, this time in a whisper, for by now we were out in the main orlop deck. The stairs that led back up to the lower ward, and from there to the light and air of the top deck, were right beside us. 'He had to hide, so that everyone thought he was gone. Only then could he follow them. He would follow them and find out, he said!'

'Find out what?' said Will.

'Why, the truth, of course! Where they were and what they were doing. That's how Proudlove heard about it. He was always standing in the shadows, eavesdropping, for they tried to exclude him. And then he insisted that they let him join once he knew—'

'Join the Resurrection Society?'

'Shh.' Dr Aberlady put his finger to his lips and nodded. 'But Aberlady said it was worse than experiments. There was one of them, one of them, he said, who was not as he seemed. One who thought he was God himself. But he couldn't be certain which one. He said I was only to tell *you*.' The finger he jabbed at me was as gnarled and bent as the root of a tree. '"The one with the red mask," he said. "A mask, like you, Rennie. That's how you'll know him. And if anything happens to me, he will know what to do. But tell no one else or all is lost."'

Dr Rennie took up his candle and beckoned us to follow. All at once my mouth felt dry. 'Can't you show us here?'

He shook his head. 'It's down below.'

'Down below?' whispered Will. We exchanged a horrified glance. 'I thought we *were* down below?'

But we were not, for already Dr Rennie and his candle were vanishing down another laddered staircase, hidden in a dark corner, and steeper and narrower than all the others. Will snatched up another candle. We had little choice but to follow.

∽

At the bottom of the ship, the ceiling was so low as to force us to walk at a crouch. The air was cold, the darkness, away from the candle's feeble glow, was as thick as tar. I felt panic bubble within me. Below us, at the very bottom of the ship, lay a pool of sand and filthy water. Traversing this were thick oaken beams, upon which small shed-like structures had been erected, like giant sedan chairs. 'Stores,' said Dr Rennie. 'Ropes mainly – not much else. No one comes down here these days. At least, not usually.'

'And why do you come down here, sir?' said Will.

'Me?' He turned to look back at us. The shadows behind him reared like demons. 'Why not?'

He moved quickly now, his footsteps sure and confident, so that I was certain he could have negotiated the place in the dark. I heard a movement behind us. I turned my head but there was nothing, only my own silhouette huge and looming at my back. I saw tiny eyes glinting, red as blood in the dark, and I felt the panic coursing through me once more. I had spent my life in the city; I was no stranger to cramped spaces and rats and shadows, but this? It was all I could do to stop myself from seizing the man's candle and scuttling back out of there. I imagined the timbers, softened with neglect, giving way, a sudden ingress of filthy, choking water—

'What did you wish to show us, sir?' I said. My voice sounded strange and dead in that ancient, cramped space.

344

Dr Rennie turned and grinned at me over his shoulder. 'They say this part of the ship is haunted by the souls of the drowned,' he said.

'I can't think why they'd want to spend eternity down here,' I retorted.

I heard him laugh, a thin, dry hissing noise, like rope sliding across a polished floor.

'I'm simply wondering what you could possibly have to show us down here—'

'There!' He stood back.

Between the narrow walkway and the side of the ship was a small cubby hole, the length and width of a coffin and some two feet high. Inside it was a blanket – rumpled, as if the occupant had recently flung it aside. Beside it was a candle stick, a book, a pannier of water and a tin which, upon opening, we found contained a mouldering crust of bread, a lump of cheese covered in green fuzz, and a rotten apple.

'Stops the rats getting to it if it's in a tin,' said Dr Rennie.

I picked up the book. Bartlett's *Tropical Poisons*. What fear must Aberlady have felt to hide like this, squeezed into a crack in the corpse of the old ship? *Come quickly, Jem, but come ready to face the Devil . . .* We had come too late for John Aberlady. We had come too late for Erasmus Proudlove too, and for the girls from Siren House. And yet it was still not over. Will lifted his candle high. Beneath the tangled bedding was a shape. A box. He threw the blanket aside. A rat scuttled out and Will stumbled back in alarm. I heard a movement behind me. Dr Rennie was disappearing into the darkness, humming as he went, his candle abandoned on the floor beside Aberlady's lair.

Will looked at the blankets, his face appalled. 'Aberlady slept here? Why?'

'Evidently he was involved with this Resurrection Society. Experiments, anatomy, medical inquiry all conducted in secret by ambitious young men. Perhaps all quite innocent in its way. He and Proudlove joined. And yet *something* was not right about it. Aberlady suspected it, but he didn't know what, exactly, or who. Dr Rennie said as much.' I pointed to the wooden box that lay tumbled in the blankets. The lock had been forced, a sheaf of yellow paper visible within. 'I imagine those are the confessions from Siren House. No doubt they tell us about the dead girls, what happened to them, who they really are.'

'And who took their confession,' said Will.

The box was full of paper. Each page was tightly written, each confession on a new page, each signed by a different hand. Some by Dr Birdwhistle, some by Dr Sackville. One or two had been signed by Aberlady himself. But three confessions stood out from all the rest: Mary Mercer, Jane Stalker, Susan Williams. Their confessions had been transcribed by the same hand, their note of discharge written by the same man. I recognised it from the *Blood*'s prescription ledger even before I saw the signature.

They see me, but they do not see me. I walk amongst them, behind them, listening, with my eyes downcast. I hear everything as I drift between the beds with my teaspoon in my hand, trickling drops of oblivion between men's lips. I could kill them all, if I wished, every one of them on board that ship. I have the knowledge, and I have the means. Should I fill my bottle with arsenic? With monkshood, or henbane? What balm might there be for the pain I feel? Only love, but I can have none of that, for she is dead and I am alone again.

I watch them, all of them, and I wait for them to make a mistake. I have them in my eye, and in my mind, though I don't know yet which one of them is to blame. I must be precise. I must know who as well as why, and I must be certain. I hide my grief and rage; my face is a mask – have they not always said that it was? The mask of an idol, a savage, or a false god. But there is no God, that is one thing, at least, they and I agree upon. They see it in the evidence and logic of scientific inquiry. I see it in the *cruelty and hypocrisy of men and the wickedness and injustice of their world. I will be judge, jury and executioner, for who else will step up to stop them? In the shadows, in silence, I wait.*

Chapter Twenty-One

～～～

I had never been so relieved to take a breath of London
fog as I was that night when we emerged at last from the
depths of the *Blood*. Below deck the men were silent. It
seemed that sleeping draughts had already been administered, and everyone – including Mrs Speedicut, who I
had seen napping in her chair in front of the stove – was
unconscious. Upstairs, the weather deck was quieter than
ever, for the fog suffocated all sound. With night drawing
in, the docks had fallen silent, and I could hear the wet
suck and slap of the outgoing tide. But something was not
right on board the *Blood*. Will sensed it too. The lights on
the rail were out, so that other than the lantern we had
brought up from the top ward the deck was in darkness.
On the other side of the deck the door to Aberlady's cabin
was open. We crept over, and peered into the rustling
darkness. The stove was lit, but its embers dying. The
frogs sat motionless on their moist leaves, the rats rustled
and heaved in their crate. But the tanks that usually

349

contained Maximus and Minimus were empty. We stood there listening.

'Can you hear that?' I whispered. 'A scratching sound?'

Will nodded. 'Over there.' Together, we turned. Behind us, towards the bow, the door to the library stood closed. A thin ribbon of lamplight was visible at its foot.

I felt my skin prickle as we crept towards it in the thick choking dark. The noise, I realised then, was not so much a scratching, but more a smooth, rubbing sound. I turned the handle, but the door was locked, the key still in the keyhole. I turned it, feeling the soft *click* of the mechanism through the key's cold iron shaft.

What awaited us inside was a sight I hoped never to witness again. The room was disordered, with books and papers scattered about, one of the armchairs overturned and the tea tray smashed and spilled on the hearth. Before us, crumpled on the threshold like a broken marionette, was Dr Cole. Around him, the snake Maximus was coiled. The chafing sound we had heard was the movement of his scales against the wood of the library door as he squeezed. Dr Cole was quite dead, though I had no doubt that the scratching we had heard at first had been his final attempt to attract the attention of someone – anyone – who might help him. His skin was still warm. His face was red, as if the vessels beneath the skin had ruptured, and his eyes, staring up at us, seemed to have wept blood. Two trickles of watery crimson tears had flowed down his face. On his neck a pair of red and bloody puncture marks, both of them necrotised and blackish, though I could see that they were fresh. I put out my hand to stop Will going further into the room, and pointed to the hearth. The poker, and the broken body of the poisonous Minimus, lay side by side there.

'Someone locked Dr Cole in here with Minimus?' He sounded appalled.

'Dr Cole sits with his back to the door. It would be easy to creep up on him and slide the snake onto his collar, especially if he was dozing.' I pointed to the overturned footstool upon which the lethargic Dr Cole habitually draped himself. 'The door was locked, so once he was bitten he could go nowhere for help – not that he would have been able to do much as the poison paralyses quickly, even from a snake that size. It seems he had time to beat the thing to death and make his way to the door. The exertion of killing his executioner would have exacerbated the poison's effects, I'm afraid.'

'And Maximus?' By now, Maximus had uncoiled completely. As we watched he slithered rapidly across the library floor and disappeared behind a curtain.

'Maximus is not a biting snake,' I replied. 'He squeezes his victims to death, though in this instance I think Dr Cole was already dead.'

I stepped over the corpse and went over to the curtain, gingerly pulling it aside. I was just in time to see the last of Maximus as he vanished out of the partly open window.

'Who did this?' said Will. 'Dr Antrobus?'

'Perhaps.'

'But why?'

'I don't know. Let us hope we can find him and ask.'

'Do you think he is still on board?'

'I doubt it. At least – not now.'

'He lives with Dr Cole at Dr Sackville's anatomy school—'

'Though it is very unlikely that he has gone there. There must be some other place they go. But where?'

'It must be somewhere quiet,' said Will. 'Somewhere out of the way. Near the *Blood*, but also near Deadman's Basin.'

Will was right. Deadman's Basin had always been at the heart of this; it was on the axis between Siren House and the *Blood*. 'Your drawing,' I said. 'That first sketch you did of the basin – we looked over it together in Sorley's, d'you remember? You drew me standing by the water, and Aberlady watching us from the corner. And a face at a window.'

'Looking out from above the archway to Bishop's Entry?'

'Yes.'

'But that might have been anyone.'

'Whoever it was they were standing there long enough for you to draw them. I don't mean they were recognisable, only that they were *watching*. For a long time.'

'You don't think it was Dr Antrobus, surely?'

'What else do we have that might suggest a place to look? Whoever it was, they were clearly very interested in what we were doing. Of course, it was impossible to tell who they were, but there was *something* familiar—' *Was* it Dr Antrobus? At the time I had dismissed the idea as nothing more than a foolish fancy after a long and difficult day. But what if it was not?

'It was on the top floor,' I said. 'A south-facing room.'

'What if he poisons us? What then?'

'Then we die,' I said.

We made our way to Deadman's Entry, visible only as a damp-looking smear in the dark patchwork of the night. The last street lamp was on the wall at the corner, but from there up to the passage that led through to Bishop's Entry and Cat's Hole there was nothing. We kept close to the wall, making sure that we could touch it with our fingertips, for two steps to the left and we would stumble into the basin itself. At last we came to the buildings at the head of the basin. Overhead, a tenement loomed, tall and black as a rock face. From somewhere in the darkness I could hear the sound of trickling water. I felt the moist squish of ordure beneath my boots.

There was no door, just an opening in the wall, easy to miss unless you were looking for it. It was the sort of entry most people would hasten past, hoping that the shadows within were not for them. Will hesitated – we both did, for who amongst us would enter such a place without a sense of dread? And then we went in.

The stone steps were littered with refuse, worn smooth and sunken from the trooping up and down of boots. To our right, on each storey, a window looked out. Had the weather been clear we would have been afforded a rare view up Bishop's Entry to Cat's Hole. It would be a view of black walls and dirty windows, of lines of grey washing, suspended across the street. We could have watched drunk men pissing in the gutter, and girls whisking their skirts as they looked for customers. But it was too dark to see anything, and the window looked at nothing but a grey-black void.

We passed numerous doors – some broken down, revealing dirty rooms and shattered windows; others standing open, and we saw figures huddled in blankets sitting on the floor drinking gin by the light of a tallow candle. From deep within the building we could hear men shouting, women screaming, children crying.

On the top floor, there was only one door. It opened without a sound.

Inside, a single candle burned, reflected off a familiar array of jars, bottles, knives and saws. Skulls of all kinds lined the walls, beside resin models of bodily organs – the delicate tracery of the lungs, the veins and arteries of the arm. Above, the rafters were exposed, and amongst them I could make out the dim shapes of other organs, suspended, drying in the warmth of the stove so that they might be varnished and added to the collection. There were jars containing curious fish and pale coiled worms, lizards and blobs of matter I could not make out at all. And in the middle of all this stood an operating table. Upon it lay the body of Dr Antrobus, strapped down, stripped naked, as thin and pale as a flounder. Standing over him, tall and dark in his long black travelling cloak, was Dr Proudlove.

He held a knife in his hand. To his left was a large acid pile battery, fizzing excitedly, wires springing from it like the antennae of a giant insect. It was a larger and more magnificent version of the small galvanic battery I had seen in the consultants' sitting room that first day, its wires attached to the legs of a frog. 'One of Dr Antrobus's little experiments' Dr Birdwhistle had called it. Now, I saw that both of Dr Antrobus's collar bones were bleeding from an incision. The same incisions had been made in the skin of Mary Mercer, of Jane Stalker and Susan Williams; incisions into which the wires of the battery had been thrust, clamped onto the clavicle, and the bones of the feet, so that the electrical charge could be jolted through the body.

'Dr Proudlove?' I could not keep the amazement out of my voice. Not three hours earlier we had carried him up to the mortuary on a hand cart. Will and I had laid him on the slab ourselves. There had been no post-mortem, and we had left him there beneath his winding sheet. He was dead, there had been no doubt about it. Had there?

The face he turned to us was unsmiling, half hidden in the shadows, his cheekbones catching the light in a dark gleam. I saw his eyes glitter, his lips move as he drew them back over his teeth angrily, furious with himself for not having locked the door, for being so easily discovered. I could hardly believe my eyes. Had he arisen from the dead? How was it possible that he was standing before us? For a moment I wondered whether it was a trick of my mind, a final lingering hallucination as the last traces of opium cleared from my system, and I put my hands to my head, as if to shake myself free of it. But I knew I was not seeing things. I knew there was no mistake, that there was indeed a tall black man standing before us, before an operating table upon which he had strapped the naked body of Dr Antrobus. Was there more to the Resurrection Society than we had realised? Or had we simply been mistaken when we loaded his body onto the slab? And yet resurrection was *not* possible. And I had never once mistaken a live man for a dead one.

'Dr Proudlove?' I said again.

'Yes, Mr Flockhart?' And then I understood everything, and the whole world shifted into focus around me.

Her head was newly shorn, her clothes those of her dead brother. She had his travelling bag beside her, his gloves and tall hat, and she wore his caped travelling coat, buttoned up to the neck. It was loose at the shoulders, though she wore it as if she were born to it. Her eyes were wet with tears of sorrow and fury.

'This man has taken everything from me,' she said, pointing to the pathetic figure on the table before her. 'Everything that was dear to me, and I *will* kill him.'

'Dr Cole is dead,' I said, thinking to distract her. 'The snake—'

'Is he?' she said. She gave a shrug. 'Good.'

'You killed him!' said Will.

'*I* didn't kill him,' she replied. 'He tortured Minimus and Maximus. All I did was give them the chance to take their revenge.'

'But why?' What else might I do but keep her talking while I decided which course of action might be the best. And I could not deny that I wanted explanations. 'Dr Cole was not to blame for Mary's death. For your brother's.'

'They are all culpable,' she said. 'If Antrobus worked alone it was because he was driven to it by Cole, by Sackville, by their collective ambition and lack of humility. Besides, I hardly knew which was which – does anyone? Cole, Antrobus, Antrobus, Cole. They are indistinguishable, from each other, and from the great mass of second-rate doctors who will never do anything worthwhile.

'I knew it was *one* of them but not *which* one. I listened to them whispering on the wards and I discovered what they were up to – I learned about their secret society, their little medical club. I followed them in the dark. But one of them was worse than the others, one of them was working on something of his own. Working alone, and in secret. I *knew* it was Antrobus – surly, resentful, mediocre

– but I had to be certain. And then one of the street girls said she had seen him with . . . with . . . ' Tears filled her eyes. 'It took me a long time to find someone who had seen him, but there are no secrets on the streets, not if you ask for long enough.'

'He was with a girl? With Mary?'

'Yes. A girl. It was her. It was Mary. He brought her here, to this terrible place, and he killed her.'

Naked before us on the operating table, Dr Antrobus whimpered.

'Take that cloth from his mouth,' I said. 'I need to ask him why.'

'I know why,' she replied. 'I know why he killed Mary. And Susan, and Jane. I know why he murdered my brother and Mr Aberlady.'

'I must hear it from his own lips,' I said.

To my surprise, she did as I asked. She jabbed him with the tip off her knife. 'Go on then,' she hissed. '*You* tell them. If you can.'

His voice was faint, as if he had to force the words out, but he seemed determined to speak. 'I had to show them,' he whispered. 'I had to show them I could do it. That I was better than everyone . . . I knew it was possible to re-create life. If all the organs were healthy, it needed only the right electrical impulse. Tried with a drowned body first. But I needed to be able to . . . to control the conditions of life as well as of death. And so I made my own.' He took a gasping breath. 'Made my own experiments.'

'You experimented on women?' said Will. 'On human beings?'

'Of course,' he hissed. 'What use is a dog? A rat?

Nothing can be proved or demonstrated when the subject is a different species entirely.'

'But – people?'

'Hardly *people*, sir.' He spat out the words. 'Whores. Who would miss women like that? They are ten a penny. On the waterfront. Ten a—' He stopped, his breathing laboured, his lips bluish.

'And so you killed them,' said Miss Proudlove. 'Didn't you?'

'I chose how and when they should die, yes. And then I tried . . . I tried to bring them back to life again.' He made a terrible rattling, wheezing sound, and I realised with horror that he was laughing. 'I succeeded!' Foam flecked his lips. 'Once, I succeeded. It worked! But once is not enough. It had to be replicated. And so I tried it again. I killed her again. Suffocated her. Tried to bring her back. But this time it did not work.' His expression grew puzzled. 'Don't know why . . . Did everything just the same. But I could not . . . could not show the gentlemen of the Society an experiment I could not replicate. I had to try again. I opened her up. I could see nothing. Nothing that might explain it.' He was making no effort to escape, not struggling against his bonds, nor straining his arms, though his speech was growing more and more laboured. And yet he seemed crazed with the need to explain, as if his failure filled his mind and would not let him be.

'You were in the Resurrection Society with Cole, Aberlady and Proudlove?' said Will.

'Sackville's idea,' he said. 'He'd always been in one – discussion, philosophy, experimentation.' He sneered. 'Pathetic. Limited. Childish. There *had* to be more . . . '

'And the other men? They were not working with you?'

'I didn't want *them*. I had to succeed alone. I deserved it more than any of them. *They* were not prepared to take risks, to take a useless human life and use it to push at the boundaries of what we know.' He rolled his eyes so that they were staring straight at me. 'As for Proudlove and Aberlady with their naive notions about benefiting humanity.' A sneer curled his lip. 'They knew, or guessed, that I had higher ambitions. So I had to . . . to get rid of them. They didn't have the courage for what lay ahead. For what had to be done. For it does take courage to forge a new path, to ask questions no one else will ask so that we can understand and press ahead. That's what it has all been for, gentlemen, for knowledge. For *understanding.*' His teeth were gritted, his eyes bulging. 'Aberlady disappeared. I knew he was watching me. I knew he had discovered something about me. I was sure he suspected I had killed the girl Mercer, though what proof he had— but I knew too he wouldn't be able to keep away from the Golden Swan. Opium eaters are devious, craven creatures, and he would reappear in the end. He would not be able to help himself. I told the hag and the boy to look out for him, and when he came they were to ply him with the stuff till he was dead. Paid them well!' His brow darkened. 'They said they gave him enough opium to fell an ox but it *wasn't* enough. Back he came to the *Blood*. I saw him creeping along the waterfront. I knew he'd check on his precious snakes as soon as he came aboard, and so I put some cracked henbane onto the stove.' His mouth twisted into a smile. 'I had no idea it would work quite so well.'

'And then there was Dr Proudlove,' I said. 'He didn't have to die, surely?'

'Always creeping about and eavesdropping. He suspected something too, though he couldn't be sure. Besides, he didn't *want* to know. Not really. His ambition almost matched my own. And yet he was dogged by his conscience. It was only when you found the two girls I had left at Sackville's villa—'

'Sackville's villa?' said Will. 'At Deadman's Basin?'

'Of course, at Deadman's Basin,' snapped Dr Antrobus. Foam bubbled at his lips.

'Remember the portrait in the hall at Dr Sackville's house?' I murmured. '"Dr Sackville's wife's late mother, Maria Callard," the butler said. And the villa was owned by Callard estates.' I turned to Dr Antrobus. 'Dr Proudlove guessed that you had killed those girls too?'

'He confronted me. I said it was Cole. Then I took him to the Golden Swan. Said we should go there to find out what had happened to Aberlady, so that we could confront Cole sure in our knowledge. It was easy enough after that.'

'And Cole?'

'An idiot. A plagiarist. An insult to the profession.' Dr Antrobus's skin was bathed in sweat as he forced out his words. He gave a strangled laugh, and swung his gaze to look at Miss Proudlove. 'I congratulate you, miss. If you hadn't killed him, then I would have.'

'They were your colleagues!' cried Will. 'Your friends!'

'Useless, the three of them. I didn't need any of them. I had to succeed alone. I knew there must be a way to bring back the dead. To re-ignite the vital spark. I was almost there, too! They would be queuing from here to Oxford Street for my services if I'd managed it! If I'd succeeded!' He gnashed his teeth into a hideous grin. 'Isn't *that* worth the life of a few whores?'

All this time Miss Proudlove had been standing over him, her surgeon's knife held against his neck, so that if we had leaped forward to seize her she would have slit his throat in an instant. I believed she would do it too, and I had made no effort to try to make her step away from him. Now, as he looked up at her, the spit trembling on his lips, his words ringing in her ears, she seemed to grow in stature, to draw herself up as if all the rage and sorrow, all the resentment and grief that she had kept tightly within her breast was rising up. She drew back her hand to strike.

Suddenly Will sprang forward, reaching out and snatching the blade from her fingers. The knife sliced his hand, the blood splashing across her face, but he had it. Miss Proudlove looked startled for a moment, and then she plunged her hand into her coat pocket and drew out one of her small blue poison bottles. She tore out the cork with her teeth and spat it aside. Seizing Dr Antrobus by the hair she tipped his head back and poured the contents between his lips. She slammed her hand over his mouth and clamped his nostrils closed between her fingers. He arched his body beneath his bindings, the first movement I had seen him make, and then it was gone, swallowed down in one gulp.

'Laudanum?' I said, with some relief. I knew a dose that size would not kill anyone.

'Hemlock,' she replied. 'I think he had said quite enough, don't you?' She reached for her hat – the one her brother had worn that first night on board the *Blood*. 'You should be careful to whom you show your poison garden, Mr Flockhart.' Before her, on the operating table, Dr Antrobus lay still.

'Where will you go?' I said. 'Let me help—'

'I don't need *you*,' she said. She gestured to Will. 'But *he* does. Help him, not me.'

Beside me, Will was looking pale. He was holding his hand, his handkerchief – pressed against the palm – was soaked in blood. His face was white as whey. 'That knife was daubed with slime from the skin of the blue poison dart frog,' she said. 'I nicked Antrobus with the blade to make him biddable. It paralyses almost immediately. It was only a little, not enough to make him shut up but enough so that I could get him onto this table. I wanted him to feel what *she* felt. What all of them felt. Fear. Pain.'

I looked at the battery, its stack of metal plates fizzing with bubbles, the wires, tipped with dried blood, hanging down. She had already made the deep excisions in his skin so that she might clamp the electrode to his collar bones, and to the bones of his feet.

'You would never have done it,' I said.

'Perhaps I wouldn't.' Her face was stony. 'But he's dead, and I'm glad of it.' She glanced at Will. 'He will be too, before long. He took the entire blade of poison against his hand. There is no antidote, and nothing can survive it.'

Beside me, Will sank to the ground. I dropped to his side, pulling back the handkerchief. The cut was deep, and pouring with blood. Will stared up at me, his expression terrified. I turned to her. 'Help me,' I said. 'Miss Proudlove. Gethsemane, please—' I took Will in my arms as he slid sideways. 'You can't leave us—'

She took up her travelling bag and stepped to the door. 'I'm sorry,' she said. 'There's nothing I can do.'

Chapter Twenty-Two

❧

I can hardly recall getting Will back to the apothecary in Fishbait Lane. All I remember is those endless dark stairs, the weight of his body against me as we stumbled down and down, into the howling darkness, the shouts and calls of outcast London echoing around us like the screams of demons. The poison's effect was immediate, paralysis seizing his limbs in an iron grip, for it had entered directly into the bloodstream. And yet he would not die straight away, I knew that much, for John Aberlady and I had seen it with our own eyes.

When Aberlady first acquired the frogs we had tested the effect of the poison for ourselves. At first, we had marvelled over the frogs' minute, harlequinade perfection. Such tiny, beautiful creatures! Exquisitely formed and gleaming moistly, their colours – rose red, saffron yellow, luminous greengage – were brighter than anything I had seen on any living creature. But the ones that were cobalt blue, like fragments of sky from their native South

America, those had been the most poisonous of all. How would they fare in our dismal climate, I had wondered when I first saw them; would they turn grey, to match the dreary palette of our British clouds? They could not be touched, for their poison was secreted into the slime that coated their gleaming bodies.

Aberlady had smeared the glistening matter onto the blade of a knife, and then wiped it onto a cut on a dog's back. Whether absorbed through the skin or ingested, the effects were the same: the recipient was paralysed almost immediately. Eventually the lungs were affected, the heart cramping and seizing. Death was the only outcome. We had seen not a single survivor from even the smallest of doses, and there was no antidote. Dr Antrobus had been able to speak, to move a little, but he had not taken a tenth of the quantity of poison that Will had.

I had left my lantern beside Dr Antrobus's corpse. I could not support Will and carry it at the same time, and the darkness was almost complete. Will's face, beside me, was white and frozen, his lips turning blue as he laboured to breathe. His bloody hand hung limply at his side, a crimson trail on the stairs behind us. I shouted for help, my voice echoing up and down, ringing against those damp and crumbling bricks so that I heard it over and over again. But such places clamoured with cries for help, and no one ever listened. No one cared. Why should they?

I saw faces, ugly and cruel, watching me from the shadows as I staggered down the steps, one at a time, Will's body heavy against me as his feet scraped along on the stair. And then there was a breath of cold damp air about my face and we were out in Bishop's Entry. Shadows lurched past, their faces turned away, their shoulders hunched. We were in the most crowded part of the city, where people lived crammed one on top of the other, and yet we were as alone as if we had sunk into the depths of the ocean.

I screamed for help but the fog swallowed my words before they had hardly left my lips. I knew no one would come. No one ever came. Will crumpled to the ground. I knelt beside him, and put my arms about him. His skin against my cheek was as cold as a corpse's, his breath was barely breath at all. I cried out again, and again, my voice growing raw and choked. Was he to die here, asprawl in the gutter in the most lost and dirty corner of the city? What would I do without him? I would be alone again. How would I bear it? I opened my mouth and let out a howl.

Behind me, I heard a noise. I turned to see a great lumpen shadow looming out of the darkness and a man, tall and ugly, his arms swinging at his sides, stood over us.

'Well then, sirs,' said a familiar voice. From behind the man, a small figure stepped out. 'You goin' to scream outside our window all night, then?'

∽✕∽

The journey home was the longest journey I have ever taken. Mr Jobber and Annie helped us as far as St Saviour's Street, Mr Jobber carrying Will in his arms all the way. Once there, we were lucky enough to find a hansom. And then the cabman was helping us into the apothecary, and Gabriel and Jenny were there. The lamps were burning fiercely – just when I had begun to feel as though I would never see light again. The room was warm and golden, the herbs hanging drying from the ceiling, the bottles and jars glowing. At least Will would die in comfort, in his home, with his friends at his side. I thought how I had betrayed him by telling Miss Proudlove my secret, how I had asked her about Eliza, and I felt sick inside. I thought of how I had spoken to him too, as we stood by the body of Dr Proudlove, and I felt wretched. Tears streamed down my face as I knelt beside his chair. I might have forced a purgative between his lips, but what was the use? Like Aberlady, the poison was in his blood, and there was nothing that emetics or purgatives might do for him now. I squeezed his hand, but there was no answering response. I put my head on his chest, my arms about him, and I wept.

Gabriel and Jenny stood silently side by side next to me. 'What is it, Mr Jem?' whispered Gabriel. 'What's happened?'

I could hardly answer. My heart was too full of sorrow, the loneliness I feared more than anything already stealing up on me as I felt my friend grow cold, his breath all but gone as he slipped away. 'Poisoned,' I said as the tears ran down my cheeks. 'Poisoned by the poison dart frog.'

Beside me, Pestle Jenny clicked her tongue. 'Is *that* all?' she said. 'Don't worry, Mr Jem. The poison ain't all that strong since them frogs have been living on the *Blood*. Mr Aberlady said it was probably the ants and earwigs and woodlice I were feeding them. Seems our London creepy crawlies ain't good enough to make them proper poisonous. Not like the stuff they get at home. Mr Will'll be right as rain in the morning. You'll see!'

Chapter Twenty-Three

W̶e had six more baskets of apples that year – I could not remember ever having so many. But the spring had been wet and the summer, when it came, had been long and warm. We sent Gabriel and Jenny up into the trees with sticks and baskets. Later, we weeded, and trimmed back the dead and dying growth that the summer had left behind. Since she started talking, Pestle Jenny had not stopped.

'Mr Aberlady burst in that night,' she said. 'He slammed the door on Dr Sackville, and said he weren't to be trusted. Said he was as bad as the others. Said I weren't to trust no one. He was raving! I'd kept his room downstairs warm like he'd said to, so it so can't have been that what made him so cross. I had to keep it warm for the snakes, and the frogs, though it ain't right to have animals in cages like that, I told Mr Aberlady. Miss Proudlove told him too. She said Maximus had lived in the wild with the whole desert to himself and now here he was in a tank. Perhaps he wanted to hunt and not just have rats fed to him now and again. There ain't no fun in that. Can we have him here, Mr Jem? Can we have Maximus at the apothecary? Not Minimus though. Never liked him much.' She took out her pewter watch and looked at the time. 'It would be time for his lunch about now.'

'A snake at the apothecary would frighten away what few customers remain to us,' I said. 'Maximus cannot stay here. Besides,' I added, 'Miss Proudlove let him out. The last I saw of Maximus he was giving Dr Cole a good-bye hug, shortly before vanishing out of the window altogether.'

'Where is he?'

'I have no idea. Presumably taking his chances on the streets of London, like the rest of us.'

Her face had fallen. 'He'll die,' she said.

'Oh, I don't know,' said Will. 'There are rats aplenty. And lots of warm places to slither into.'

'Besides,' I said. 'The ship moored alongside the *Blood* left for West Africa this morning. I imagine Maximus is on his way home already.'

'But you were telling us about Dr Sackville,' said Will. 'Mr Aberlady shut him out, you say?'

Jenny's chin trembled. The tale still troubled her, she would much rather have talked about snakes, though I was sure speaking about what happened would help her. She might be able to forget about it altogether then.

'Mr Aberlady got worse then,' she said. 'He went mad, raging and shouting. He heated the poker and made me take it. He showed me his arm, that's when I saw that picture on it. He said I had to burn him, to burn the poker against his skin so that the picture was gone. I

368

couldn't do it though. I couldn't, but he grabbed me and screamed at me, his face all red and furious—

'Then Dr Sackville shouted and battered on the door. Mr Aberlady was holding me up against the shelves. What could I do? I thought he was going to strangle me. And then he takes this key from his pocket and he ups and swallows it. "I can't let *him* know I've found out," he said. "*He*'s one of them!" But he wasn't, was he? Dr Sackville, I mean?' I shook my head. 'Anyway, Mr Aberlady drank down some cold tea from the pot and then he grabbed up the poker and dashed it against his own arm. That scream, sir! And the smell!' Her face had turned white. 'I'll never forget it. And the blood, and the sight of the skin all black and bubblin'. I just about fainted. Then he seizes me by the throat – the poker still in his hands all smokin' and hot next to my face. "It's too late," he whispered. I could hardly breathe for he was squeezing so tight. "It's too late for me now. Fetch Mr Flockhart. Mr Flockhart from St Saviour's." Well I knew you weren't at St Saviour's sir, as I'd heard you talking to Dr Sackville earlier.'

'You were in the cupboard, weren't you?' I said.

'I was, sir. I don't like Dr Sackville one bit. I could see he thought my job wasn't a job for girls, so I hid whenever he came. I hid so that he wouldn't be reminded of me and send me away, though I did the prescriptions right, just like Mr Aberlady showed me. Anyway, "Fetch Mr Flockhart," he says, "he'll know what to do," and then he lets me go. And so I came.'

'What about Miss Proudlove, Jem?' said Will. He rubbed his bandaged hand. 'Where is she?'

'They'll never find her,' I said.

'Can you be sure?'

'I am quite certain.'

I filled the brazier with the twigs and deadwood we had gathered from around the garden. I had some chestnuts, and we pricked them with my pen knife while we waited for the flames to die and the embers to glow. The air was cold and still, but hazy, the smoke drifting upwards in a lazy curl of grey-blue. It smelled of wood smoke and hot sap, and all the ends of the summer dried out and kindled to light in the autumn. At my feet was a box. I took out the confessions, and fed them one by one into the flames.

Dr G. Proudlove,
Harlem,
New York City,
New York.

Mr J. Flockhart,
Flockhart and Quartermain,
Fishbait Lane,
London.

21st December

Dear Mr Flockhart,

I write to apologise for leaving you alone with Mr Quartermain in what must have seemed the most impossible of circumstances. As you will now know, the poison was not fatal, only temporarily paralysing. I trust Mr Quartermain recovered completely and is now in the best of health.

You once asked me whether I knew a girl called Eliza Magorian. I said I did not. I lied. She was known to me. But it was not for me to betray her confidence. She knows where you are, and one day she will find you – but that time is not now. If you love her, as I think you do, then you must be patient. What other choice do you have?

Sincerely,

Dr G. Proudlove

Acknowledgements

Writing a novel is a lonely business. I have some good friends who have made the process less arduous than it might have been. John Burnett, always willing to listen to me talk about writing, and always my first reader, has helped, as ever, with his wise comments and thoughtful edits. Likewise, my coven of writing friends, the amazing Olga Wojtas (grammar queen), Michelle Wards (mistress of insightful critique) and Margaret Reis (all-round editing star) have made this a far better book.

As always, my mother, Jean Thomson, and sister, Anne Briffett, have cheered me on from afar. My lovely boys, Guy and Carlo, have, once again, watched me drive away on three writing retreats this year, and have been deflected with the words 'I can't come just now, I have to do some work' more often than I like to admit. Love and thanks to you all.

Adrian Searle, Penny Cunynghame, Barbara Mortimer, Helen Wilson and Paul Lynch – my kindest and most

enthusiastic readers – have all given me the encourage-
ment needed to start, and finish, writing this novel.

Once more, my gratitude goes out to the marvellous
Jenny Brown, fantastic agent-friend, as well as Krystyna
Green, Amanda Keats, Una McGovern, Ellie Russell,
Kate Truman, John Fairweather, Amy Donegan, Jess
Gulliver and all the kind and lovely people at Constable.

Thanks also to my friend Mary Mercer, for allowing me
to use her lovely Victorian-sounding name. Of course, all
characters in this novel are entirely fictitious.

Last of all, the deepest of thanks to Trevor Griffiths, a
man of infinite patience and good humour, who made
a difficult year not so bad after all.

Author's note/Bibliography

⁂

The *Blood and Fleas* was based on the *Dreadnought*, a hospital ship moored on the Thames at Greenwich, which went on to become the birthplace of the London School of Hygiene and Tropical Medicine. On the matter of 'hospital hulks', their size, appearance and administration, the best source was G. C. Cook, *From the Greenwich Hulks to Old St Pancras: A History of Tropical Diseases in London* (Athlone, 1992). I am indebted to Ross MacFarlane of the Wellcome Library for providing me with a bibliography on the subject. Also useful was Richard Barnett and Mike Jay's box of essays and maps, *Medical London: City of Disease/City of Cures* (Wellcome, 2008), especially 'Tall ships and tropical diseases: Medicine and the British Empire in Greenwich' and its accompanying essay.

For detail about the environment, a vivid contemporary account of the London docks can be found in Henry Mayhew, *London Labour and the London Poor* (1851), which

374

includes descriptions of the docks, dock workers, prostitutes, and other riverside inhabitants. It was perfect for my purposes. For detail about the decline of religious certainty I consulted A. N. Wilson, *God's Funeral* (Abacus, 2000), whilst David Olusoga, *Black and British, A Forgotten History* (Macmillan, 2016) was a valuable resource for learning about the position of black people in Britain at this time. For insights into the development of tropical medicine, attitudes toward imperialism, and the competitive nature of the medical profession in the mid-nineteenth century, I drew upon Roy Porter's *The Greatest Benefit to Mankind: A Medical History of Humanity from Antiquity to the Present* (HarperCollins, 1997) and M. Worboys, 'Tropical Diseases', in W. Bynum and R. Porter (eds) *Companion Encyclopaedia of the History of Medicine* (Routledge, 1993). Iwan Rhys Morus, *Shocking Bodies: Life, Death and Electricity in Victorian England* (The History Press, 2011) provided a fascinating account of the use of electricity in medical science during the Victorian period. Finally, Wendy Moore's *The Knife Man* (Transworld, 2005) was invaluable when I needed information about William and John Hunter, their achievements and rivalries, as well as detail about the lymphatics, anatomy museums, the preservation of anatomical specimens, and the procedures of the post-mortem and dissecting rooms.

I was fortunate to have such a wealth of excellent histories on which to draw. Any mistakes in the interpretation of that information are mine alone.